50 9
D0207224

Forever Summer

Also by Alyson Noël

Night Star

Dark Flame

Shadowland

Blue Moon

Evermore

Saving Zoë

Kiss & Blog

Fly Me to the Moon

Art Geeks and Prom Queens

Faking 19

Forever Summer

Laguna Cove and Cruel Summer

Alyson Noël

St. Martin's Griffin New York

This is a work of fiction. All of the characters, organizations, and events portrayed in this novel are either products of the author's imagination or are used fictitiously.

FOREVER SUMMER: LAGUNA COVE © 2006 by Alyson Noël LLC, and CRUEL SUMMER © 2008 by Alyson Noël, LLC. All rights reserved. Printed in the United States of America. For information, address St. Martin's Press, 175 Fifth Avenue, New York, N.Y. 10010.

www.stmartins.com

Library of Congress Cataloging-in-Publication Data

ISBN 978-0-312-60439-4

10 9 8 7 6 5

Laguna Cove

For Ryan and Kelsey Sherman,
in memory of their father, Richard Sherman, 1957–2005

chapter one

"Excuse me. You're in my seat."

Anne brushed her long blond hair out of her blue eyes and squinted at the man standing next to her. His hair was dark, with the kind of deep side part used to disguise the early stages of baldness, and his charcoal gray suit, light blue shirt, and red tie were all slightly rumpled. Still, he looked vaguely familiar.

"I always book 2A." He gave her a condescending look.

"Oh, sorry. I guess you're right. I'm supposed to be in 2B. I'll move," she said, picking up the letter she'd been writing and grabbing her bag.

"Forget it." He sighed loudly, dropping his briefcase onto the aisle seat. "Just stay. I'll take B."

"Whatever." She rolled her eyes and focused again on her letter, making sure she hunched over it so he couldn't peek. She was in no mood to be messed with by some balding old fart. It was because of old people like him (namely her parents) that she was on this stupid plane in the first place. Did they really think that buying her a first-class ticket would lessen the pain of being dragged away from everything she knew and loved? Like the group of close friends she'd had since childhood, her hard-earned status as captain of the dive team, and Justin, the love of her life whom she'd been dating for the last year and a half? Did they really think they could buy her off with an oversized seat, hot towels, and a choice of six movies?

The plane pushed away from the gate and the flight attendants asked everyone to direct their attention to the safety demonstration on the video screens. But Anne refused to look—there was no way some stupid video could save her from a crash. Thanks to her mom's affair with the senior partner at her law firm, and the bitter divorce that immediately followed her dad's walking in on them, Anne's life as she knew it was completely crashing down around her, and there was nothing she could do to save it.

"Sir, you need to turn off your cell phone immediately."

Anne looked up to see an attendant with her hands placed firmly on her navy-clad hips. She was scowling at Mr. 2B. "Sir, don't make me say it twice."

"Excuse me," he said, putting his hand over the mouthpiece and glaring. "Do you know who I am?"

"Yes, Mr. O'Rourke, I've seen your show. And if you don't turn off your phone right this minute, we will return to the gate so you can disembark and continue your call while we fly to Los Angeles without you." She reached up and smoothed her blond French twist.

Anne watched him snap his phone shut and mumble something under his breath as the attendant walked away. *Oh my God, no wonder he looks familiar.* It was Bob O'Rourke from that news show on FOX. And she was sitting in his favorite seat, and she'd even rolled her eyes at him! But he was kind of a jerk, so she didn't feel too bad about it.

The plane began its runway roll, quickly gaining speed. This was the moment when Anne would normally reach over and hold her dad's hand until the wheels lifted off the tarmac and retreated into the belly. She looked over at Bob O'Rourke, glasses perched on the end of his nose, scowling at a stack of papers in his hand,

and she knew better than to even try. She was on her own now, in more ways than one.

She closed the window shade, fearing she might cry if she glimpsed the diminishing East Coast landscape, then reread her letter. But halfway through, her throat grew hot and tight and her eyes started to sting, so she quickly scribbled at the bottom, telling Justin how much she loved and missed him. Then she folded the letter into a perfect rectangle, stuffed it into an envelope, and shoved it deep inside her purse.

She was just drifting off to sleep when that same attendant came by and asked if they'd like anything to drink. And after listening to the very important Bob O'Rourke grill her about the available wines and their grape origins, Anne was feeling so bad for her she said, "Um, I'll just have a bottle of water. I don't need a glass or anything." Then, determined to ignore the famous jerk beside her, she put on her headphones, extended her footrest, and turned on her in-seat video unit.

On channel 3 they were showing that movie *Blue Crush,* but Anne flipped right past it. No way was she gonna watch a bunch of sun-struck surfer girls talk about the beach and "killer" waves. She'd be forced to live among people like that soon enough, and she was in no rush to get there.

She was down to just a five-hour cushion between her beloved old life and her dreaded new one, and she was determined to make the most of it. The only surfing she planned on doing was channel surfing.

She thought about her last phone call with her dad, and how he sounded so excited when he told her about the house he'd bought. "It's in a private gated community called Laguna Cove, and we're right on a cliff overlooking our very own beach."

"We have our own beach?" she'd asked.

"Well, we have to share it with the neighbors." He laughed.

"Is there a pool?" Anne remembered asking.

"No, honey, there's not. But I think you're really gonna like it here if you just give it a chance."

Easy for him to say, since he's never home much anyway, always away on location, or busy schmoozing with fellow movie execs. And how could she possibly like a place with no pool? Diving was her passion! She'd spent the last three years at her private school earning a reputation as a skilled and fearless competitor. And then, right when she finally makes captain, they yank her and send her to some stupid California beach town that's probably filled with pot-smoking hippie surfers named after flowers. She wasn't being negative, she told herself, just realistic.

The flight attendant reappeared with a bottle of water for Anne and a glass of red wine for the jerk in 2B, who was currently missing in action. "I'll just set this here for when he returns," she said.

But by the time they came by with the meals, he still wasn't back.

"Do you know what happened to the person that was sitting here?" Anne asked the male attendant with a deep tan and tightly cropped, bleached blond hair. "I think his name was Bob O'Rourke?"

"He moved to 5C. Looks like you're on your own. Do you need more wine?" he asked, motioning toward the untouched glass.

"Um, no. Maybe in a little while."

Then, the second he was gone, Anne craned her head around and peered down the aisle at 5C. Sure enough, there was Bob O'Rourke, napkin tucked into his collar, smug nose buried deep into his wineglass. Carefully picking up the wine next to her, she placed it on her own tray. Then she looked around nervously, to see if anyone noticed, but nobody seemed to care. Besides, the attendant guy thought it was hers, so it may as well be.

She lifted the glass to her nose and inhaled just like that O'Rourke guy did. Though she wasn't exactly sure what she was supposed to be sniffing for. Was it to see if it's rancid? And what did rancid wine smell like anyway?

She lowered the glass to her lips and sipped cautiously. Sometimes she and her friends drank beer and once, last New Year's, champagne, but this wasn't too bad.

So she took another sip.

And no one seemed to notice she was still four years away from her twenty-first birthday.

Maybe flying first class wasn't so bad after all.

"Miss, Miss. Excuse me, we've landed."

"What?" Anne opened her eyes to find the blond attendant with the French twist kneeling next to her. "Are you feeling all right?" she asked, eyes narrowed with concern.

"Um, yeah. How much longer?"

"We're here."

"What? Oh my God! Okay, just let me get my stuff," Anne said, running her fingers through her tangled, messed-up hair and searching the seat-back pocket for her bottle of water. The inside of her mouth felt like the Mojave Desert.

"Are you sure you're okay?" the attendant asked again.

"Yeah, really I'm fine," Anne assured her, even though she felt the exact opposite of fine with her throbbing head and stinging eyes. *And where is that damn water bottle?*

"Well, we're laying over and our van is waiting, so you really need to hurry." She stood and ran her hands over her tight blue skirt.

"Okay, okay, I'm ready. Do you know where baggage claim is?" Anne asked.

"You can follow us."

Anne stumbled behind the flight crew, listening to their laughter as they made fun of Bob O'Rourke. And even though she had no idea what their lives might really be like, at that exact moment she would have traded places with any one of them, no questions asked. Because at this point just about anyone's life looked better than what she was in for.

Okay, maybe on the surface, moving to Laguna Beach, into a big house with a private beach, didn't sound so bad, but it was all relative to what she was leaving behind.

She shifted her purse to the other shoulder and mentally scolded herself for drinking too much, passing out, and generally wasting the past five hours on the plane. And now she didn't even have time to freshen up, since she knew her dad would be waiting at baggage claim. And even though she didn't have time to look in a mirror, she was willing to bet she wasn't exactly at her best right now.

The blond attendant stopped and turned while the rest of the group continued ahead. "You can take that escalator right over there all the way down to the baggage carousels. Have fun!" she said, turning and rushing to catch up with the rest of the crew.

Anne used the thirty-second escalator ride for some quick damage control. Breath mint? Check. Stila lip gloss? Check. Designer sunglasses? Check. Red wine stains on brand-new vintage-wash two-hundred-dollar jeans? Triple check. Ridiculously expensive wrinkled-up white T-shirt with drool stain dripping down the front? You bet.

God, what she really needed was a toothbrush, a shower, and a decent meal to soak up all the alcohol. But since she hadn't seen her dad for the month he spent getting the house ready, she was banking on the fact that he'd be so excited to see her that he wouldn't notice how she'd boozed it up in first class.

And speaking of Dad, where the hell was he? At six foot three, with a lean build and a head of thick silver hair, it's not like he was hard to miss. But after scanning the crowd she didn't see him anywhere.

Oh, please, don't let him be late, she thought, heading over to the baggage carousel and retrieving her cell phone from the bottom of her purse. But when she flipped it open and tried to turn it on, nothing happened. *Oh, great.* She'd used up her entire battery on the limo ride from her house in Connecticut to the JFK Airport. About thirty seconds were spent saying good-bye to her mom. The rest was saying good-bye to her friends and, of course, Justin.

She sat there with her two oversized bags and wondered what the hell she was supposed to do now. She didn't even know where she lived.

chapter two

"Are you Anne?"

Anne looked up to see a guy with messy longish wavy brown hair wearing a surf logo T-shirt, shredded flip-flops, and dark blue board shorts. He was kind of cute. *If you like that sort of thing,* she thought.

But she was a savvy New Yorker, not some sun-drained local. So she narrowed her eyes and said, "Maybe."

"Cut me some slack, would ya? Traffic on the 405 was a bitch, and if your dad finds out I was late, he'll kill me." He smiled then, exposing a slight gap between his two front teeth. But even though it made him look even cuter, Anne was unmoved. After all, she had a boyfriend. She was no pushover.

"So how do you know my dad?" she asked, folding her arms across her chest and enjoying herself for the first time in too many hours to count.

"He's my boss. I run errands for him and stuff. My name's Jake."

"Are you my new nanny?" She laughed.

Jake shook his head and glanced at the display on his cell phone. "C'mon, dude, I'm in a time crunch."

"Okay," Anne said, standing up and grabbing her bag. "But I'm driving."

"I don't think so," he said, taking her bag and leading her out the door to the parking structure.

"I'm a good driver. I've had my license for almost six months." She narrowed her eyes at him.

"Maybe so, but have you seen your teeth recently? They're all purple. Looks like you've been hittin' it hard on the plane."

"Are you serious?" she asked, panicked.

"See for yourself." He opened the door of the silver Mercedes convertible and flipped down the mirrored visor.

"Oh, God. My dad's gonna *kill* me. Can we stop somewhere so I can brush my teeth?"

"Dude, you need a little more than that. Let's get you a coffee, some aspirin, and a bottle of water. I've got some Visine right here."

Big surprise. "I really appreciate that. But can you do me a favor?" Anne asked, more than a little annoyed with him for insinuating that she was drunk, even though she was.

"Sure, what?"

"Please stop calling me dude. My name is Anne."

"Whatever."

Despite the double-shot venti nonfat latte she practically inhaled, Anne fell right to sleep. It wasn't until Jake nudged her hard in the arm and said, "You're not gonna want to miss this," that she woke up.

"Where are we?" she asked, rubbing her eyes and straightening her T-shirt, which had risen up and twisted around.

"Laguna Beach. This is Laguna Canyon Road, and in just a few minutes you won't believe your eyes."

He was right. They drove through a narrow, twisting road cut right down the center of a canyon and then suddenly came to a halt. Right in front of her was a big gorgeous beach filled with volleyball players, basketball players, sunbathers, and body boarders.

"What beach is that?" she asked, trying to sound only curious and not at all impressed.

"Main Beach."

"It's nice." She shrugged, craning her neck to look back at it, as he turned left onto Pacific Coast Highway.

"You think that's nice, wait 'til you see your beach. That's one of the best benefits of working for your dad. Your beach has awesome waves, and I get to surf there nearly every day."

"I'm not interested in that. I'm into diving," Anne said, gawking at the beautiful coastline in spite of herself.

"That's cool." He nodded. "But you really should try it."

"No thanks," she said, crossing her arms in front of her.

Jake continued down PCH, past huge custom oceanfront homes, and a spectacular, sprawling resort called the Montage. "We're almost there," he said, waving at the uniformed guard and driving through the gate.

"This is where I live? This is Laguna Cove?" Anne asked, unable to keep the excitement out of her voice.

"This is it. See the house on the end? That's yours."

"Oh. My. God." She sat and stared at the large, sprawling home built on the edge of a cliff as Jake parked in the driveway.

"Go ahead," he said. "I'll get your bags."

Anne grabbed her purse and ran for the door, excited to see her dad and check out her new room. But when she tried to open it, the door was locked. So she knocked. But nobody answered. "Dad?" she called, knocking even louder and ringing the bell.

"He's probably not home yet. Here, use the key," Jake said, tossing her a shiny gold key.

"But he'll be home soon, right?" she asked, opening the door to an expansive foyer filled with tropical plants and freshly cut flowers.

"Doubtful. They were having problems on the set, and he said he didn't know if he'd make it home tonight. But I'm sure he'll call you later."

"You mean I'm supposed to stay here *by myself*?" she asked, feeling more than a little panicked.

"Yeah. You can totally party. But if I were you, I'd just lie down and take a nap," Jake said, setting her bags on the travertine-tiled floor.

"Well, where are you going?" she asked, suddenly dreading his leaving. The last thing she wanted was to be left alone in the big unfamiliar house.

"Hittin' the beach. There's six-foot swells out there." He smiled.

"But, don't you have more work to do? You said in the airport that you were on a time crunch." She hated herself for sounding so needy.

"I didn't want to miss the surf. You were my last chore." He shrugged.

"Thanks a lot," she said, rolling her eyes.

"You know what I mean." He turned and headed for the door. "See you around," he called over his shoulder.

"Whatever," she said, standing in the foyer, watching him leave.

When the door closed behind him, she was left with nothing but an overwhelming loneliness and complete silence. *I better get used to it,* she thought. Then she grabbed her bags and walked down a long hallway in search of her new bedroom.

chapter three

Ellie weaved her long white-blond hair into a single braid that cascaded all the way down her back, landing just short of her bikini bottoms. She wriggled into her wetsuit and looked at the clock one last time. It was already five forty-five and there was still no sign of them.

Grabbing her surfboard, she headed out, closing the glass sliding door slowly and carefully behind her. The last thing she needed was to wake up her brother, who had come in late the night before, or even worse her dad, who was on her case for just about everything these days.

She made her way down the stairs leading from her house to the beach, and scanned for her friends, hoping they were already out there, but secretly knowing better.

After a few stretches and beach sprints to warm up her tired muscles, she headed into the water, dropped her board, and began paddling out. When she got past the break, she lay resting, with her chin propped against her folded arms, enjoying the mellow sway of the water and the quiet solitude of an empty beach. She loved getting out early and watching the ocean change from a moonlit sparkly sequin to a sun-warmed velvet. But even though she liked having the waves to herself and not having to wait in a never-ending lineup, she still missed the company of her best friends, Lola and Jade.

It had started last spring. The early-morning surf ritual that had bonded them all through elementary, junior high, and well into their freshman and sophomore years of high school began to gradually taper off. First to three times a week, then two, and now, by early September, she was lucky if they surfed together on a random Saturday. And even then, by the time they showed up practically all of Laguna Cove was in the lineup and it took all day just to get a turn.

But Jade and Lola didn't seem to care. Suddenly, they were content to just lie on their towels reading fashion magazines and checking out all the guys, just like all the other beach Barbies they used to make fun of, and Ellie just didn't get it. For one thing, the guys they were looking at were the same old totally immature, unfocused bros they'd known since grade school. And Ellie knew for a fact that not one of them was worth talking about, much less missing waves for.

Well, except for Chris, who was not only amazingly cute, with his aqua-blue eyes (the same color as the Fiji waters on a cloudless day), tanned skin, and shaggy, sun-streaked hair that was constantly falling into his eyes, but also incredibly smart (he was in all the same advanced-placement classes as she) and an accomplished surfer, maybe even the best in Laguna Cove (well, after her older brother, Dean).

But nobody knew how she felt about Chris—not Jade, not Lola, and definitely *not Chris*! To him, they were just good buds who went way back, and that's the way it would have to stay. Ellie couldn't afford to waste time obsessing over some guy. She had to stay focused on the important things, like maintaining her perfect 4.0 GPA, her position as Surf Club president, and taking first at the upcoming San Onofre Surf Fest competition so she could get noticed by the sponsors she'd been dreaming of for too many years to count.

With her five-foot-nine, slim, toned frame and long blond hair pulled back into its usual braid or ponytail, exposing her perfect face, there was something so graceful and delicate about her, people often assumed she was a model or ballerina—that is, until they saw her surf. In the ocean, she was a strong and fearless competitor who could carve up the face of a wave with both elegance and aggression.

Guys also came easy to Ellie, always drawn first by her looks, then later by her brains and talent. She had a handful of good guy friends she could always count on as a last-minute prom date or emergency flat-tire fixer. But she never allowed any of these friendships to go further than a quick peck on the cheek or, even more likely, a brief hug. That she could have pretty much any guy she wanted was merely a fact that didn't mean much to her. Especially since she only wanted one.

But even Chris, awesome as he was, could not get in the way of her dreams. She had a lot to live up to, and it was like her dad always said: "Go after your goals with absolute tunnel vision!" "Allow nothing to get in your way!" "You have to name it before you can claim it!"

Okay, the last may have been Dr. Phil. But whatever. The bottom line was she couldn't allow herself to get distracted. *No matter what.*

She scanned the empty beach, looking for her friends even though she knew they wouldn't show; then, feeling the water beginning to rise and swell beneath her, she started paddling, jumping up on her board with the strength and assurance of someone more comfortable in the ocean than anywhere else. But as always, on her first wave of the day (especially when no one was watching), there were no fancy tricks, no special maneuvers to impress the judges. It was just Ellie, her board, and the ocean all blending in harmony for that one perfect moment. She allowed herself one soul surf a day, but she refused to admit it was always her favorite.

After several decent waves, she checked the tide watch her dad had bought her for Christmas last year and realized she barely had time for one more before she had to head back home, change, and meet her trainer for her two-hour gym workout.

Jumping up on her board, she sensed that this last wave would be the best of the day, as she expertly cranked it around, catching the lip and slicing through the cool, green curl. *If this was the Surf Fest, those sponsors would be double-checking my name right about now,* she thought.

But just as she was going for a really big finish, she spotted another surfer paddling out. Sun-streaked hair, tanned skin, perfect body, and even though she couldn't exactly see them from this distance, she knew the eyes were clear, like blue topaz. And just as she was thinking about those eyes, she lost focus, wiped out, and swallowed salt water right in front of him.

"You okay?" Chris called, just before duck-diving under a wave.

But by the time he resurfaced, she'd already untangled the seaweed from around her legs and retrieved her board, as though nothing had happened. Giving him a casual over-the-shoulder wave, she headed toward the cliff stairs, glad that her back was now to him so he couldn't see that her face was bright red with humiliation, embarrassment, and anger at her own lack of focus.

She opened the little gate that led to the limestone terrace and leaned her board against the low fence. Reaching back to unzip her wetsuit, she looked up and saw her father sitting on a lounge chair by the Jacuzzi, drinking an orange juice.

Oh, great. How long has he been there? she wondered.

"Hey, Dad," she said, casually squeezing salt water from her braid and hoping he hadn't seen her wipe out.

"That's quite a spill you took out there," he said, eyeing her carefully.

"It wasn't that bad, really." She grabbed a towel and headed for the sliding glass doors that led to the living room, hoping he wouldn't follow.

"Tell that to the judges," he said, right behind her now.

"Well, did you happen to see any of the waves I had before that?" she asked, trying to sound neutral so he wouldn't know how upset she was by his criticism. She wiggled out of her wetsuit and hung it on a hook by the door. "Because some of them were really good." She turned to face him briefly, taking in his towering six-foot-four frame, the hair that despite the slight thinning was still as blond as hers, the tanned face, and the deep lines that fanned away from his clear green eyes that were also just like hers.

"All of them have got to be good, Ellie, not just some of them. You think your brother won NSSA by one or two merely decent waves?"

Ellie reached for the door handle and rolled her eyes. But her back was toward him, so it's not like he could see it.

"And don't roll your eyes at me. I can see your reflection in the window, you know."

Leave it to my dad to find a maid that does windows! "Okay, so I slipped a little. Trust me, it's no big deal. I'll get it straight before the contest, so you don't have to worry," she said, hurrying up the stairs to her room, where she could finally escape his never-ending scrutiny.

"Ellie?"

Jeez, what now? she thought. She was just outside her door, *so close to freedom.*

"This is for you." He handed her his platinum credit card. "Stop by the mall later and get yourself whatever you need for school tomorrow."

Taking the card, she looked at him, immediately feeling guilty for everything she'd just been thinking. But it was always like that. He'd pile on the pressure to the point where she was just about to scream, then quickly follow it up by an act of extreme kindness or generosity. She knew he meant well, but sometimes he really got on her nerves.

chapter four

Anne woke to the sound of a persistent high-pitched ringing. Assuming it was there to accompany the incessant drumming in her head (it was beginning to sound like a really bad garage band in there), she lay in her new bed with her eyes shut tight, promising to whoever might be in charge of these things that if they would just put an end to the incessant pounding, the cotton mouth, and the nausea, then she would never, ever drink red wine (or anything else, for that matter) again.

Ever!

Well, at least not until her twenty-first birthday.

Really.

She wasn't just saying that.

When the ringing abruptly stopped, her eyes popped open. *Could it be?* But when it resumed a moment later, she realized it was the phone, not her head, that was making all that racket.

Tossing the covers aside, she stumbled out of bed, wondering where the phone was located. In her old room in Connecticut, she'd had a cordless with her own private number, a cell phone with a different number, a laptop, two e-mail addresses, and a BlackBerry that they could all be forwarded to. And it was all within easy reach of her big, comfortable canopy bed. Communication with everyone who mattered had always been right at her fingertips.

But here, in her dad's strange new digs, she didn't even know where to start. Since she had fallen asleep not long after finding her room the day before, the rest of the house had so far remained a mystery. Sprinting out of her room, she headed down the hall and toward the kitchen, partly because it seemed like the logical place to start, and partly because it was the only other room she was familiar with.

"Hello?" she said, picking up the receiver of a brand-new silver-colored phone designed to look retro, but with all the modern conveniences.

"Did I wake you?" her dad asked from God-knows-where.

"Kind of. Where are you?" She settled onto a teakwood stool at a long, narrow table, the kind design magazines always refer to as a "breakfast bar."

"Still on set. Sorry I wasn't there to greet you yesterday. Things got a little hectic around here. But I should be back by tonight," he said, not sounding very convincing.

Should be? "Oh, okay," she said, feeling completely annoyed with him, yet cringing at the high-pitched whininess in her own voice.

"See you then?" he asked, obviously in a hurry to hang up.

"Dad, wait. What exactly am I supposed to do here? I mean, I feel kind of stranded," she said, looking around the unfamiliar kitchen, feeling like she'd broken into her own house.

"Call Jake if you need anything. His number is on the pad next to the phone. Or ask Christina; she should be there by noon."

Christina? Jeez, he was freshly divorced, new to the neighborhood, and he already had a girlfriend? What was with her parents? The way they played musical partners, they were worse than the kids at school!

She shook her head and rolled her eyes, but it only intensified the throbbing. "Dad, do you think you could . . . ?" She stopped, noticing the absolute silence on the other end. *Oh my God, did he already hang up?* "Hello? *Hello?*" she said, staring at the receiver. He was gone. Just like that. No good-bye, nothing. *How's that for a warm welcome?* she thought, slamming down the phone.

Hopping off the stool, she opened the fridge and peered inside, searching for something to cure what appeared to be her very first (and definitely last) hangover. She grabbed a carton of soy milk and swigged straight from the container. But she didn't get as far as the swallowing part before running straight to the sink where she gagged and spit and rinsed her mouth with tap water until that thick, nasty soy taste was no more than a bad memory. *Gag.* Was her dad turning into some kind of California hippie health freak? Or was it Christina's fault that the fridge was full of weirdo organic stuff she wasn't used to?

Anne glanced at the clock on the stove. Another hour until Christina would be guest-starring in what would surely be her most challenging role to date: that of eager new companion to handsome, newly single dad and his hung over, sulky, resentful (but ultimately well-meaning) daughter.

Anne had a tendency to view her life in movie terms, as though all moments were taking place in front of a live studio audience, and lately there had been no shortage of big, dramatic moments. She always assumed it was just a natural side effect of having a big Hollywood exec for a dad, but lately she wondered if it wasn't just plain weird.

She grabbed a bottle of water from the fridge and wondered what the Ingenue, a.k.a. Christina, would look like. Let's see, her dad was so upset with her mom these days, it was safe to assume he'd go for the complete opposite. Like maybe a Kate Hudson meets Meg Ryan type—the kind of sexy/wholesome L.A. hybrid that can make an entire career out of lame, formulaic romantic comedies.

Though, it was kind of creepy picturing her dad with someone like that. Someone so different from her mom's own look of sharp, sleek, elegant New York City attorney who ultimately cheats on her husband and destroys her family. Yeah, her mom was definitely more the femme fatale, film noir type.

But Anne didn't like thinking about her mom any more than her dad probably did. It was because of *her* that they were both living here in this dreadful, sunny place. And even though Anne knew firsthand just how much it sucked to be constantly ignored by her work-obsessed dad, the truth was *she* was dealing with it, so why couldn't her mom? After all, *they* were the adults! *They* were the ones who took the vows!

They were also the ones who taught her all about "honoring your commitments," and all kinds of other values that they themselves apparently didn't practice. It's like, ever since the divorce it seemed they'd conveniently forgotten all the lessons they'd taught her, and the line between parent and child had become extremely blurred.

Grabbing a banana from a silver wire basket, she headed out the sliding doors and onto the flagstone terrace overlooking the beach. She walked to the railing and leaned against it, peeling the banana skin and squinting into the sun toward the ocean. There were five, maybe six surfers all lined up, floating on their boards, laughing and joking while they waited their turn.

She finished her banana and left the peel lying on the railing, then walked down the stairs and sat on the very last one so she could get a closer look. The beach was a perfect little cove, with light, clean sand dotted with beachgoers' umbrellas, two wooden lifeguard stands, and what looked to be a much-used volleyball net at the far end. And even though she was determined not to like it here, the fact was she couldn't believe this beach was actually hers. Well, not hers exactly—there were plenty of other families in the neighborhood. But still, it was hers in the way that it was right at her fingertips, right at the bottom of her stairs.

She watched the surfers catching waves, one after another, some gliding gracefully to shore, some wiping out and pounding sand. But as much as she loved the water and loved to swim, she was way more comfortable in a pool than the ocean. It was the smell of chlorine, not salt water, that got her excited. She really hoped her new school would have a diving team.

Stretching her long legs out in front of her, she wondered if it was weird to be sitting outside in the hot sun in her pajamas. But since her pj's consisted of a thick white ribbed tank top and royal-blue boxers with white flowers, she decided they didn't look so out of place. Closing her eyes, she tilted her head back, enjoying the way the sun warmed her face.

"Hey, did you sleep it off?"

Anne opened her eyes to find that annoying Jake guy standing right in front of her—hair stringy with salt water, lips cracked and chapped, beat-up surfboard held under his arm. Something about his ultra-cool, laid-back way totally got on her nerves. He was *sooo* California. It's like he came right out of central casting or something.

"I don't know what you're referring to, but I slept well, thank you," she said, looking right at him and hating the way she just sounded like the most uptight bitch on the planet.

But Jake was unfazed. "Awesome. Well, your dad wanted me to check in on you. Do you need anything?" he asked, flipping his wet hair a couple times and spraying Anne with water.

"Yeah. He just called; he wants you to leave me the keys," she said, holding his gaze without blinking.

"Oh, yeah? What keys?" he asked, smiling.

"The keys to the Mercedes. I have errands to run." She crossed her legs and pointed her toes toward the sand.

"Nice try." He laughed.

Anne shrugged and looked down at her feet. She knew better than to push it; she'd get her hands on those keys eventually.

"Hey, nice ride, dude. I saw you catch some air out there."

What the heck is he talking about now? Anne thought, looking up to find this incredibly cute guy standing right in front of her, next to Jake.

"It was okay. It's a little mushy out there," he said, looking at Jake and then smiling at her.

Gorgeous turquoise eyes, straight white teeth, tight abs. . . . Uh, hello? You have a boyfriend, she thought, scolding herself. Just because she moved three thousand miles away didn't mean it was over with Justin. Just two days ago they'd promised they'd wait for each other, and now some cute local appears and she starts drooling like one of Pavlov's dogs.

"This is Anne," Jake said, nodding in her direction.

"Hey, I'm Chris." The gorgeous guy smiled and extended his hand.

Anne shook his hand briefly, then quickly pulled away.

"Do you surf?" asked Chris, still smiling.

"No," Anne said, shaking her head and looking away. *God, what's with him? It's like someone told him he has nice teeth so now he smiles all the time.*

"That's too bad," he said.

"Whatever." She shrugged, knowing she was acting like a defensive brat, but not really willing to stop.

"What school are you going to?" he asked, seemingly unfazed by her bad attitude.

"Laguna Beach."

"Me too. What year are you?"

"Junior," she said, still looking at the water and not at him.

"Me too. So I guess I'll see you Monday then," he said, *still smiling.*

"I guess." Anne stood and turned to head back up the stairs. *God, is everyone here like this? Tanned and happy and smiley and friendly and gorgeous?* She sincerely hoped not.

And then she heard Jake say, "I'll stop by later to see if you need anything."

Anne turned, looking briefly at Chris and then at Jake. "I don't need a baby-sitter. I don't need anything," she said. Then she turned and walked back up the stairs before either one of them could respond.

chapter five

"Lola? Is that all you're having?"

"*Sí, Abuela.* I'm fine." Lola looked across the table and smiled patiently at her grandmother. This was all part of the normal breakfast routine Lola had come to expect ever since her grandmother had come to live with them. And it was so predictable she was often tempted to walk into the kitchen, slap a tape recorder right next to her cereal bowl, lift her spoon, and push play.

"Let me make you some eggs and toast," her grandmother offered, smoothing her shapeless floral cotton dress as she rose from her seat.

"*Abuela,* please. I don't want eggs. Besides, Ellie will be here any second," she said, glancing at the clock and hurriedly finishing her Cheerios.

"Nonsense. You hardly ate any breakfast. You're too thin," she said, eyeing her tiny granddaughter with disapproval. "You'll never find a husband looking like that."

"Well, considering that I'm still in high school, that's probably a good thing," Lola said, getting up from the table and placing her bowl in the dishwasher.

Abuela was her father's mother, who, after *Abuelo*'s passing just over a year ago, had reluctantly moved from Mexico City to live with them, bringing nothing more than two trunks full of cotton housedresses and all of her old-school beliefs—actively disapproving of just about everything in her new life in Laguna Beach. If it was up to her, Lola's mother would stay home all day preparing meals for her family, and Lola would be twenty pounds heavier, dressed in her first communion garb, and engaged to be married to a nice Mexican boy from a good family the day after her high-school graduation. The only thing *Abuela* seemed to approve of was her son. Lola's father could do no wrong.

"Lola, don't forget you have cotillion practice this evening," her mother said, striding into the room and bending down to briefly kiss *Abuela* on the cheek.

What a contrast they are, Lola thought, looking at *Abuela*'s short, round body clothed in one of her numerous tent dresses and her mother's tall, sleek, elegant form perfectly turned out in one of her designer suits. *I got Grandma's lack of height and major stubbornness, but thankfully my mom's slim build and straight dark hair,* Lola thought. It's her eyes that were like her dad's, shiny, dark, and deep like onyx.

"Mom, I'll try to make it but I can't promise anything. It's the first day of school and all."

"No 'and all,' Lola. Say 'It's the first day of school,' period."

"Yeah, yeah," Lola said, bending down to kiss *Abuela* just as Ellie pulled into the driveway and honked.

"Is that Ellie?" *Abuela* asked.

"*Sí, Abuela.* I'll see you later," she said, grabbing her bag and heading toward the door.

"Can you please inform her, once again, that it is impolite to honk?"

Lola shook her head, put her hands on her hips, and breathed an exasperated sigh. "No, I cannot. Because she's doing me a big favor by driving me to school. And if your son and daughter-in-law would just buy me a car, once and for all, then I could drive myself and you'd be spared the honking," she said.

"What did she say?" *Abuela* asked, looking to her daughter-in-law for help with the translation. But Lola knew better. *Abuela*'s perfect English always seemed to fail in the most convenient moments.

Lola's mom shook her head. "Get your grades up, and we'll talk."

"Yeah, yeah." Lola slung her book bag over her shoulder and walked out the door. She'd gotten only one B in an all-A lineup, but that had been enough for her overly strict parents to refuse her a car. True, the deal had been all A's gets the wheels, *but still.* Lola had done her very best, and just because she got four wrong answers on that chemistry test (*Chemistry!* It's not like she wanted to be a scientist!), she was relegated to another semester of being chauffeured to school by her friends. And it was really getting old.

Usually she didn't mind being driven everywhere, but in the last few weeks she'd found a very good reason to get her own car and a little more privacy. So now she was very motivated to get straight A's and not screw up.

"Hey, El." Lola opened the passenger door of Ellie's new jet-black Mini Cooper convertible and plopped down onto the seat next to her. "Are we picking up Jade?"

"No, she's meeting us there," Ellie said, turning onto the street as Lola released her long, dark hair from its tight ponytail and removed her high-necked sweater to reveal the tight little T-shirt underneath. Her family may call her Lola, but her friends, knowing the real Lola was only revealed when her parents weren't looking, often called her Lolita. "You missed some good waves this morning," Ellie said, taking in her friend's transformation.

"I just can't wake up that early anymore. I don't know how you do it." Lola applied shiny peach lip gloss while checking out the cute guy in the black Jeep Wrangler right next to them.

"Discipline, that's how I do it."

"Yeah, discipline and no social life," Lola said, smiling at the guy with her newly shiny lips.

"Excuse me? I have a social life. For your information, I'm planning on yet another year as your class president, yearbook committee, Surf Club president . . ."

"I mean a social life that takes place after the final bell," Lola said, interrupting her friend and laughing.

"Not all of us stay out all night, Lolita!" Ellie said, looking over at her and smiling. "Oh my God, are you flirting with that guy?" She stared in disbelief.

"Maybe."

"Oh my God, he's like, *old.*"

"No, he's not. He's probably twenty-five, twenty-six tops. And he's *sooo* cute," Lola said, rolling down her window to get a better look.

"He's probably married, with three kids, and a wife at home who's gonna come after you when she hears about this," Ellie said, half joking and half worrying it could be true.

"I never flirt if they're wearing a ring, or a girlfriend is present. I'm very old-fashioned that way," Lola said, all her attention focused on the cute driver of the black Jeep.

"Well, could you please stop? The last thing I need is to have some pervert following us to school," Ellie said, sounding more than a little uptight.

"Relax; it's over. He's turning right. Well, it was good while it lasted," Lola said, waving at the back of his Jeep. "Hey, can you drop me off at the corner up there?"

"What? Why?" Ellie looked at her.

"I'm meeting someone," she said, running her fingers through her long dark hair and double-checking her lip gloss in the mirrored visor.

"Do you want me to wait for you?" Ellie asked, slowing to a stop.

"No. I'll see you at school."

Ellie gave her a suspicious look.

"Really, I'll catch up with you later."

"If I didn't know you better, I'd swear you were either a drug dealer or a special agent."

"Who, me?" Lola asked, grabbing her books and slipping quickly out of the car.

chapter six

Jade saw Ellie the second she pulled into the parking lot. And she would have run over to greet her friend, if that hadn't happened to be the exact same moment that Ben had picked her up, thrown her over his shoulder, and headed toward the quad with her.

"Ellie!" Jade called, hanging over Ben's shoulder, laughing and waving, determined to ignore the "Ellie look" her friend had plastered across her face. Jade was all too familiar with that look, as Ellie seemed to direct it at her more and more these days. It said something like, *I'm disappointed in you, but I still love you, even though I worry about you.* But Jade forgave her. Because Jade forgave just about everyone. After all, not everyone subscribed to her "live and let live" credo, *especially* Ellie.

Still, they'd been friends forever. Long before pancreatic cancer took Ellie's mother's life. Long before Ellie's dad, angry and wracked with grief, began putting enormous pressure on her to succeed at absolutely everything. Long before Ellie, suffering from the huge emotional void left by her mother's passing, started putting even more pressure on herself than her dad did.

Jade understood just how much Ellie had changed in the past few years. And Jade worried about Ellie just as much as she knew

Ellie worried about her. But she loved Ellie enough to tolerate her constant disapproval. Well, most of the time.

"Ellie!" Jade yelled again, kicking Ben in the ribs until he finally set her down. "Great sweater," she said, her smile exposing that one slightly crooked front tooth that looked like it was determined to overlap the next one, as she pushed her long, dark, out-of-control ringlets away from her face.

"Thanks," Ellie said, rubbing her hand absently over the new kelly-green cashmere cardigan she'd bought the day before with her dad's credit card. "Who is that guy?" Ellie asked, watching Ben joke with some people a few feet away.

"Ben Parker. He just transferred from Sage Hill," Jade said, wishing her friend would lighten up just a little.

"Why would someone transfer here from there? Did he mess up?"

"No. His parents split and his mom couldn't afford the tuition anymore. Cut him some slack, okay? He's a really nice guy."

"How do you know him?" Ellie asked.

"I met him last week at that barbecue at Salt Creek Beach. The one you didn't go to."

"Is he one of the ones that got busted for drinking?"

Jade shook her head. "Listen, I'm taking the Fifth on that one, because it has nothing to do with me, *or you.*" Jade was probably the only girl in school that took those yearly anti-gossip vows seriously. "Now come on, our old friend Chris is right over there and I swear he's even yummier this year than last, if you can believe it. And I don't even go for blonds." She laughed.

"I've already seen him," Ellie said, trying to sound casual, but failing miserably.

"Oh, yeah? Do tell."

"I saw him surfing yesterday morning. When I was waiting for you, I might add." Ellie looked at her.

"About that. Listen, I know you're probably really disappointed in me, but it was the last day of summer so I slept in and I just can't apologize for that because getting up at o' dark thirty just goes against the laws of nature." She smiled. "So where's Lola?"

"I dropped Lolita off on the corner. Apparently she had a date." Ellie couldn't refrain from rolling her eyes

But Jade had the opposite opinion. "Wow, talk about good time management! Leave it to Lolita to sneak a date in right before the school day has even begun. Oh, how I do admire that girl. Now come on, El, let's go drool over Chris," Jade said, smiling and pulling Ellie in his direction.

But Ellie was having none of it. "I can't. I need to stop by the office," she said.

"What for? It's the first day! What meeting could you possibly have already lined up?" Jade stared at her friend, eyes narrowed, arms folded across her chest. She knew Ellie was lying.

"I need to drop off some papers. But I'll see you at break, okay?"

"Fine. Your loss," Jade said, watching Ellie head toward the office on some sad, made-up mission. *Anything to avoid Chris,* she thought, knowing that she was the only one who knew the truth about Ellie and Chris. Heck, she probably knew it even better than Ellie did, since Ellie was a master at self-deception.

Jade, Ellie, Lola, and Chris went way back. Jade was the first to arrive in Laguna Cove *and,* as she liked to point out, was the only *true* native, having actually been born at home, under the watchful eyes of the midwife, her dad, her two older sisters Ruby and Sapphire, her worried and disapproving grandparents (who begged their daughter to come to her senses and go to a nice, sterile hospital with real doctors and nurses), and, of course, her mother.

But it was because of those very same disapproving grandparents that Jade got to live there in the first place. Jade's mother had come from a wealthy family who did not approve of Jade's father. Their daughter was beautiful and smart and had numerous doctors and lawyers to choose from. So why would she marry an artist? What future was there in that?

But marry they did, flying off to Hawaii the day after college graduation. And by the time they returned, her parents—resigned to the situation—had presented them with their summer home as a wedding gift. It was the least they could do to ensure their future grandkids would be raised properly, and not in some artists' commune or small apartment in Costa Mesa, like they feared.

And now, after several years of moderate success, the demand for her father's paintings had slumped. And with her grandparents now deceased and their debts spiking as her mother's trust fund quickly dwindled, the "ecologically correct" home remodeling that they'd been enduring for the past year was put on indefinite hold, making certain areas of the house resemble an abandoned construction site.

But Jade wasn't bothered. It was easy enough to step around the unfinished areas, and if they all had to share the same bathroom, well, so what? She knew her dad would succeed again, it was just a matter of time. Besides, she was used to living in chaos; since she had grown up with two older sisters and very social parents who believed in an open door policy, there were always all kinds of people drifting in and out of her life. You never knew who you'd find sleeping on the couch on a Sunday morning, and Jade always assumed that's how she became so accepting. She had learned early on that if you just looked hard enough, you'd see that even the most annoying person had something good in them.

By the time she was old enough to walk she was building sand castles on the beach with Ellie, and it was the two of them that had taught Lola how to dive under waves when she first moved to Laguna Cove from Mexico City when she was eight. By the time they were in fourth grade Chris was on the scene, and sharing after-school jaunts to the beach and a love of surfing, he easily became the fourth in their tight little group.

In junior high they were able to maintain their easy, casual friendship, not caring if Chris saw them in their pajamas, or with their faces covered in zit cream. But by ninth grade things started to change. They were all still friends, but it was almost like Chris had shown up that first day of high school suddenly looking like someone who, they all agreed, was really quite gorgeous. They knew him too well to ever think of him *like that,* but just because they felt that way didn't mean anyone else did, and before they knew it flocks of girls were trying to befriend them just to get to Chris. And Jade, Ellie, and Lola were forced to watch as he slowly pulled away from them, drifting from the novelty of one new girlfriend to another (usually a blonde, sometimes smart, but not always nice), until they hardly said more than a quick "hey" to each other as they passed in the halls.

Everyone seemed to get over it and move on, except for Ellie, who one night, after having a few sips of her very first beer (Jade was positive of this; Ellie gave new meaning to the term "straight-laced"), turned to Jade and confided her feelings for Chris with an emotional intensity Jade had never seen in her, much less guessed at. Then, just as Ellie was wiping her nose with the hem of the sweatshirt Jade had spontaneously thrust at her, she clapped her hand over her mouth and bolted straight for the bushes, where she vomited half a bottle of Corona Light. And the subject was never mentioned again.

It saddened Jade to know that Ellie couldn't admit her true feelings. Because the truth was, Ellie and Chris would be perfect together. It's like they were *meant* for each other. They were both gorgeous, both focused, both academic whiz kids, both awesome surfers—not to mention that for the past year Chris hadn't really dated anyone. And it seemed like he was starting to come around a little more again

Jade loved a good project—especially when it involved helping someone. And if nothing else happened this semester, she was determined to see to it that Chris and Ellie finally got together.

chapter seven

Anne stood in front of her full-length mirror, contemplating. If this were the first day of school in Connecticut, she would be dressed in her usual school uniform of white blouse, plaid skirt, and navy blazer, and she would've been out the door by now, anxious to see her friends and catch up on everything that had happened over the summer.

But Laguna Beach was like another planet compared to Greenwich, and not only did she not have any friends to meet up with, but she had no idea what the "unofficial" school uniform was. Because even though Laguna Beach High was a public school with an open dress code policy, there was still a social dress code that everyone adhered to. All schools were the same in that way. They all had an understood rule of what was acceptable and cool versus what would immediately tag you as a total dork and a complete outsider.

Her goal was simple—don't try to make a fashion statement, just blend in. But in order to blend you had to know the code, and Anne was completely clueless. The only people she knew here were her dad, who called daily but had yet to put in an appearance (it was getting to the point where Anne wondered if her parents hadn't just divorced each other, but also her); Jake, who lived in nothing but board shorts and seemed to have a permanent surfboard leash attached to his ankle; and Christina, who turned out *not* to be her dad's girlfriend, like she'd thought, but instead his housekeeper, who had a very limited command of English and didn't seem overly interested in fashion.

But maybe that isn't fair, Anne thought, *because who gets dressed up to scrub a toilet and mop a floor?*

Anne opened her door a crack and called out, "Christina?"

"Sí?" Anne could hear her hurrying down the hall.

"Hi. I mean, um, *buenos días.*" God, she'd taken two years of Spanish and where had it gotten her? "Is this okay?" she asked, pointing at her outfit and shrugging her shoulders up and down dramatically, hoping Christina would understand that she was asking a question.

"Sí. Muy bonita." She nodded, smiling.

"*Bonita?* That's good, right?" Anne asked, straining to recall some basic vocabulary.

"*Sí,* very beautiful." Christina smiled and nodded, before heading back down the hall so she could get back to doing the dishes and watching her *novelas* on the small TV in the kitchen.

Anne looked in the mirror skeptically. Christina seemed sincere, but then again her dad was paying her. Was it possible she was just being nice? Was it possible she thought Anne was needy, spoiled, insecure, and ridiculous?

Yes, it was definitely possible.

"Hey! Aren't you ready, yet?" Jake asked, knocking on her door.

"Just a minute," Anne yelled. *Ugh, Jake again.* She was so over him. And why did he have to take her to school anyway? *He should just leave me the keys and go send faxes and run errands or whatever he does for my dad,* she thought.

"You're seriously running late. And FYI, the big dogs at Laguna

Beach High don't go for that. And I should know. I was suspended twice," he yelled through the thick wood of her bedroom door, as though he was actually proud of that.

"Fine, I'm ready," she said, throwing her door open and facing him.

"Is that what you're wearing?" he asked, eyes going wide.

"Yeah? Why? What's wrong with it?" The way he was looking at her made her feel completely paranoid.

"Nothing. You look . . . really nice," he said, his face turning slightly red as he quickly turned and headed for the front door.

"I think it's time you let *me* drive," Anne said, reaching for the keys in his hand.

"Not this again." He shook his head and switched the keys to his other hand.

"Come on, Jake. How else am I gonna learn my way around?" she whined.

"By paying attention. Now come on. Get in. We've got fifteen minutes before your bell rings."

Jake pulled up to the curb in front of the administration office. "Okay, just go into the office there, introduce yourself, and they'll tell you where to go next."

"Gee thanks, Mom," she said, smiling and shutting the door between them.

"Call if you need anything. Otherwise I'll see ya around three fifteen," he told her as he put the convertible top down.

"Aren't you gonna give me my lunch money?" she asked.

"Do you need some?" He reached into his pocket.

She shook her head and laughed. "I was joking. See ya later," she called over her shoulder and headed toward the office, trying to look confident on the outside so no one would know about all the trembling on the inside.

• • •

The office lady was pretty nice, and after getting detailed directions to her classroom Anne was walking across campus when she could have sworn she heard someone call her name. *I'm losing it,* she thought. *No one here knows me.*

"Anne! Over here."

No, that was definitely someone calling her. She turned to see some total hottie smiling and waving. And after standing and squinting at him for just a little too long, she realized it was that surfer guy, Chris, who was talking to Jake on the beach yesterday.

"Come 'ere," he called.

Anne shyly approached him, noticing he was surrounded by a bunch of people, all dressed far more casually than her in surf tees, shorts, and flip-flops (the guys), or camis with minis or low-cut jeans and flip-flops (the girls). By the time she was standing in front of them in her dark-rinse designer jeans, black stiletto boots, and form-fitting, jewel-neck black cashmere sweater, she felt completely out of place and like a major dork. She'd gotten it so wrong she looked more like a teacher than a student.

"I almost didn't recognize you without your surfboard," she said, smiling and trying to sound confident and breezy, despite the fact that everyone was staring at her.

Chris smiled and put his arm loosely around her, like they'd been friends forever. Normally Anne would be creeped out by that. She couldn't stand overly confident guys who knew they were hot and just assumed all girls wanted to be wrapped not just in their presence, but also in their arms. But it was different with Chris. She could tell he was just genuinely nice, and somehow his arm felt oddly comforting.

"You guys, this is Anne. She just moved here from New York," he said.

"Connecticut," she corrected him.

"The East Coast." He laughed. "So, this is Jade, Ben, Hunter, and that's Ellie over there." He pointed to a very pretty blond girl, who had just walked up.

"Who's this?" Ellie asked, stopping to look Anne over from head to toe.

"Anne. She's new."

Ellie smiled but Anne noticed it was only perfunctory. And there was a big difference between being polite and being real.

"How do you two know each other?" Ellie asked, still staring at Anne.

"We met on the beach. She's a friend of Jake's," he said.

Anne just stood there, wishing he hadn't said she was "friends" with Jake. She really thought of him more as a nuisance.

"Oh, Jake's so cool. How do you know him?" asked the girl Anne thought was named Jade.

"He works for my dad." She shrugged.

"Oh my God, then you live right down the street from Ellie, Chris, and our friend Lola, who's not here yet. Oh, and right down the hill from me!"

Anne looked at Jade and her huge friendly smile. She seemed to be truly happy about that. Then Anne looked over at Ellie, who seemed a lot less so.

"Do you surf?" Ellie asked, shifting her backpack to her other shoulder and giving Anne a look she couldn't quite define.

"No. Actually I'm really into diving. I'd just made captain at my old school, but then—" She stopped. Oh God, what was she doing? Nobody wanted to hear her sob story. "Anyway, I've gone boogie boarding, but no, I've never surfed." She shrugged.

"*Body* boarding. No one says 'boogie.' And it's not really the same thing, is it?" Ellie said, rolling her eyes.

Anne looked down at the ground, noticing how everyone had

gone quiet. *Great, just five minutes into the school day, and it's already a disaster.* She felt completely homesick.

"What class do you have now?" Jade asked, breaking the silence.

"Um, AP English," Anne said, looking at her schedule for confirmation, even though she'd already memorized it.

"Ellie has AP English, too. Maybe she could show you where it is?" Jade said, giving Ellie a meaningful look.

"Sorry. I would walk you, but I have to stop somewhere first and I don't want to make you late," Ellie said, looking first at Jade and then at Anne.

"I'll show you," Chris volunteered.

"That's okay; I'm sure I can find it," Anne said, turning to leave, anxious to get away from Ellie.

"No worries. It's on my way," he insisted.

And even though he didn't slip his arm around her, by the look on Ellie's face, he may as well have.

chapter eight

Ellie stood in front of the bathroom mirror, gripping the sink and staring at her reflection. What was wrong with her? She'd acted so awful toward that new girl, but even when she'd realized how evil she was being, she'd been completely unable to stop. It's like there was this little voice in her head whispering, "Lighten up!" and "What's your problem?" But somehow she managed to ignore it, forging right ahead with the dirty looks, snide comments, and just overall brattiness.

Turning on the faucet, she let the cool water fall against her upturned wrists, closing her eyes until she began to feel herself grow calmer. She remembered when her mom had taught her this trick years ago. It was right after she was diagnosed with cancer, and Ellie would often find herself getting stressed out and panicked. And now, all these years later, she still relied on it to soothe herself.

Cupping her hands under the spray, she brought them to her face, splashing the water against her eyes, cheeks, and forehead, and letting it drip down her neck until her sweater grew damp. She stared at her reflection in the mirror, face glistening and wet, and then she reached for a paper towel, patted herself dry, and smoothed her long blond hair back into its usual ponytail.

As she headed out of the bathroom and toward class, she

vowed to be nicer to Anne. After all, it was ridiculous and rude not to be. Ellie knew she was pretty, popular, and smart, so there was really no reason to feel so threatened by some new girl.

Except for maybe the way Chris had looked at her.

Sliding onto her usual front row seat, Ellie opened her backpack and retrieved her new notebook and pens. She secretly loved the first day of school, with all the newly sharpened pencils and clean notebooks full of freshly lined paper. *There's something so hopeful about the first day of anything,* she thought.

Then, looking up just as the bell rang, she saw Lola charging through the door. Then she glanced nervously at Mr. Campbell, who was already standing at his podium, ready to take roll.

"Welcome, Lola," he said. "So glad you could join us." He smiled. Mr. Campbell taught all the Honors English classes, so he, Lola, and Ellie had a history together.

"I had one foot in the door before the bell actually started ringing. So technically this is not a tardy," Lola said, smiling and catching her breath.

She slipped into the same seat she'd had for the last two years—the one in the second row, right behind Ellie. "Did I miss anything?" she whispered, poking Ellie in the shoulder.

Ellie turned and smiled, noticing her hair was back in its ponytail and her sweater was once again covering her tiny top. Lolita was gone for now. "Only the new girl," Ellie told her, turning and nodding toward Anne, who was sitting in the far corner.

"The blond one?" Lola asked, craning her neck to get a better look. "In the black sweater and jeans?"

"Yeah," Ellie said, rolling her eyes despite her recent pledge to be nice.

"She's really pretty. Have you talked to her?" Lola asked.

"A little." Ellie shrugged, suddenly wishing she hadn't mentioned her now that Lola was so curious.

"Is she nice?"

Ellie watched Lola smile and wave when Anne looked over at her. *Why the hell did she have to do that?* Ellie thought. *Why does she have to be so . . . welcoming?* They'd been a tight-knit group forever. The last thing they needed was some overdressed East Coast non-surfing snob to come along and mess things up. It was like the more Ellie found herself surfing alone, the more she worried she was losing her friends. And it wasn't like she expected them to love all the same things she loved. She respected their differences. But surfing used to be the one thing they all loved equally. And now it seemed like she was left holding the board while they all drifted off toward other, new interests.

Ellie had never feared change until the summer her mother died. Her mom had somehow managed to outlive her prognosis by six months, and even though Ellie knew she was dying, she somehow refused to believe it until it actually happened. She was just twelve years old and it felt like her own life had ended. And the only thing that had gotten her through it, the only thing that kept her from going completely mental, was her friendship with Lola and Jade, and the routine she slowly built for herself and managed to stick to, no matter what.

Every single day Ellie made herself surf, study, and achieve something. Whether it was winning a school election, running a quicker mile on the treadmill at the gym, or getting the highest grade on an exam, she was completely obsessed with winning, being perfect, and having complete control of her life. Having learned at an early age that the biggest and most important things were completely beyond her reach, she was now determined to conquer the small stuff.

Though she had one creative outlet for all that nervous ambition. One activity that she allowed herself to just merely enjoy with no competition or harsh self-judgment. But it belonged only to her, and no one else knew about it.

"Uh, *hello*? Earth to Ellie!"

Ellie shook her head and looked at Lola, realizing her friend was still waiting for a response. "Oh, the new girl? She's okay, I guess." She shrugged.

"Well, she's sure got great taste in shoes. Look at those boots! I've seriously gotta find out where she scored them," Lola said, smiling in the way that lit up rooms, made clouds disappear, and guys fall to their knees. Lola was like the Julia Roberts of Laguna Beach High. No one could be mad, angry, or depressed when she smiled.

Ellie smiled back, then turned to face the front of the room. She loved Lola for her constant optimism. But there was no way she was going to look at Anne (or her stupid boots) any more than she had to.

chapter nine

Anne was not having a very good first day. Having gone to the same private school all of her life, with pretty much the same group of people, she was not enjoying the novelty of being the new girl. Not one bit. And by the time lunch rolled around, the thought of eating anything out of the bag Christina had packed completely nauseated her. Her stomach felt tight with nerves and self-pity. And even though she'd promised herself she would wait until she got home to call Justin, the second the lunch bell rang she pulled out her cell phone and went looking for a quiet, shady spot where they could talk.

Sinking down onto a patch of grass, she waited while it rang one, two, three times.

"Hello?" he said, his voice sounding so clear that she immediately closed her eyes and imagined him sitting right next to her.

"Hey," she said softly, her throat going tight with emotion.

"How's it going?" he asked. "It's your first day, right?"

"Um, yeah. It's going okay," she said, not wanting to let on just exactly how far things were from okay. She didn't want him to worry about her. "It's lunchtime here, so I just thought I'd call and say hey." God, she sounded so forced. Why did she feel so uncomfortable talking to him now? They'd been together for a year and a half. They'd shared *everything* together, well—*almost* everything. Sometimes she wished they'd gone all the way on their very last night together. But right now she somehow felt relieved that they hadn't. Everything just felt so distant and weird.

"Listen, school just let out and I'm getting a ride home from Vanessa."

"Vanessa's there?" she asked, trying not to sound overly paranoid even though she had good reason. Vanessa was Justin's next-door neighbor and former on-and-off girlfriend from grade one through eight. On the surface, she and Vanessa always acted like they got along really well. But in reality, they both knew better. Vanessa wasn't over Justin, and Anne knew it. "What happened to your car?" she asked, trying to keep her voice even, less panicked.

"It's in the shop."

"For how long?"

"At least a few days. Hey, can I call you later? Vanessa's honking, so I gotta go before she leaves without me."

"Oh, I doubt she'll leave without you," Anne said, feeling like a pathetic, jealous wife.

"What?" he asked. "I'm losing you."

And then he was gone.

Well, he may not be losing me, she thought, flipping her phone closed and lying back on the grass. But she wondered if she was losing him.

By the time Jake picked her up from school Anne was feeling so depressed and so low that she walked right up to the silver Mercedes, plopped onto the passenger seat, and slammed the door so quick and hard she barely missed her own foot.

"So how'd it go?" he asked, waving at some people he knew as he pulled out of the parking lot.

"I-don't-want-to-talk-about-it," she said, slumping down in the seat and closing her eyes against the overbearing, totally relentless California sun. *Does every day always have to be so sunny and bright? Can't it ever be just a little damp, dark, and dreary for those of us with a happiness deficiency?*

She glanced over at Jake, practically daring him with her eyes to say something positive, because then she'd really let him have it. But he just shrugged and turned up the stereo.

When he pulled into the driveway, he turned to her. "Your dad's coming home."

"Really?" she said, sounding excited in spite of herself.

"Yeah, he called this morning, he'll be here on Thursday. Friday at the latest. But for sure by the weekend."

Anne just grabbed her books and got out of the car. So it was finally official. She'd been abandoned by *both* her parents now, and quite possibly her boyfriend, too. She was tempted to call Child Protective Services.

"Don't be so bummed," Jake said, following her inside. "Most kids would be stoked to have a house like this to themselves.

"Yeah, well it's not like I have any friends to party with," she said, throwing her bag on the kitchen counter and wishing she hadn't actually said that out loud. It made her sound so pathetic.

"Relax. It'll happen," he said, grabbing two bottles of water from the fridge and handing her one. "I can introduce you to lots of people."

Anne took a sip of water and looked at him. She knew he was just trying to be helpful and make her feel better, but it's not like she really wanted to hang with him. "Thanks," she said. "But I'll work it out."

He nodded and started to head back toward the door.

"So what are you doing now?" she called after him.

"I was just gonna grab my board and head out for a while. Why? Do you need something?"

"Actually," she said, looking down at her stupid outfit that hadn't helped her blend in anywhere except for maybe in the teacher's lounge. "I need to get a few things at the mall."

"You want me to take you to the mall?" he asked, looking completely bummed.

"No, I was wondering if you'd leave me the keys?" She smiled, realizing she hadn't done that in a while. "I can drive myself."

"Do you even know where it is?"

"Jake, *I'm a girl.* I'm sure I can find the mall," she told him, hoping his love of surf would override his work ethic.

He stood there for a moment, looking at her and weighing his options. Then his eyes wandered over to the huge windows and the ocean view. "I'll MapQuest the directions for you," he said, heading into the home office.

chapter ten

By Friday, Anne had talked to her parents on the phone for a combined total of six times. Her mom had called both Tuesday and Thursday mornings before school, with each conversation ending in a very ugly emotional argument. And her dad had phoned faithfully every evening, full of apologies, yet completely trusting in his little protégé, Jake, to look after her. But Anne rarely argued with her dad, even when he completely annoyed her, like now. Though his deadline was tonight, eight o'clock max. Okay, maybe eight thirty. But no later. She was done waiting for him.

She was also done with feeling like a victim. Because even though she hadn't made any real friends yet, she was determined to stop feeling so sorry for herself all the time and instead try to stay focused on the small victories. Like on Tuesday, when she wore some of the new clothes she'd purchased during her visit to South Coast Plaza, and how she'd blended in with all the students she was still too shy to talk to. And on Wednesday, when having helped herself to the car keys while Jake was out on the deck drinking a beer with friends, she'd cruised around in the silver Mercedes, top down, hair getting tangled in the wind, until she located a gym where she could work out and try to stay in shape on the off chance she ever found a place where she could start diving again. And on Thursday, when Chris had followed her out of AP History, loosely flung his arm around her shoulder, and tried to lead her to the lunch tables where he hung with his friends. But even though she was really tempted to join him and maybe meet some people she could actually talk to, she had a telephone appointment with Justin that she just couldn't break. She knew there was something going on with him, and she was determined to get to the bottom of it.

"I'm sorry, but I can't," she'd said, ducking out from under Chris's arm.

"What do you mean? Come on, everybody's really cool," he'd said, flashing that megawatt smile of his.

"I know, but I promised my boyfriend I'd call him," she'd told him, wondering if that was still the appropriate title for Justin.

"Oh, sorry." He looked really embarrassed. "I didn't know." He held his hands up in surrender, and backed away. "I guess I'll see ya later then," he had called, turning and jogging toward the lunch tables, leaving Anne standing there alone and wondering if she'd just made a major mistake.

In retrospect, it had been a mistake. Since after going to that pathetic patch of grass that had become her usual, lonely lunchtime hangout, she sat cross-legged in the sun and made her usual, desperate bid to communicate with Justin. She flipped open her cell, pushed the right buttons, and let it ring itself all the way into voice mail.

So then she called again.

And then one more time.

And then, finally deciding to call his house and speak to his mother, she was promptly informed that Justin was next door.

"Would you like me to run over and get him?" she'd asked.

"Um, no. That's okay," Anne had said, closing her phone and lying flat on the grass, eyes closed against the sun, refusing to cry.

Justin lived on the corner.

Which meant he only had *one* next-door neighbor.

Which meant he was at Vanessa's! Apparently he no longer cared about their scheduled telephone time!

Oh God. "Telephone time"—it even sounds pathetic! She rolled over onto her stomach, burying her face in the warm grass. What had they been thinking? Had she really believed they could make it work with all those miles between them? And when they promised they'd wait for each other, what exactly did that even mean? Because from what she knew about Vanessa, she doubted Justin would be waiting for anything.

She'd sat up, rubbed her eyes, and squinted at some guys throwing a Frisbee around the quad, some cheerleaders on a bench comparing manicures, and Chris telling a story, motioning wildly with his hands, while everyone around him laughed.

She lived here now. Not Connecticut. And her first big romance was over. Strangely, she didn't feel so bad about it.

chapter eleven

Lola was in her mom's bathroom, lounging in the awesome oversized Jacuzzi tub and enjoying the hot water, the bubbles, and the candles that were lit all around her as only a luxury-loving girl could. She lifted her leg high into the air, watching the bubbles gather, skidding into each other and slipping down to her knee. Then she stared at her feet, noting that her pedicure was definitely past its prime, but hoping she could pass it off for just one more night. She was determined to wear her new metallic stilettos on her date.

Her date. For her seventeen years, Lola had already been on many dates—far more than most girls her age. The very first one took place in sixth grade at the Ocean Ranch Cinemas when she had told her mom she was seeing *How the Grinch Stole Christmas* with Ellie and Jade, when what she really saw was *Almost Famous* with Parker Knowles, the cutest boy in her class. Lola had walked out of that theater wanting to be just like Penny Lane. Except for the drugs. And the getting traded to another band for a case of beer. Not to mention that unfortunate overdose. But still, everything else just seemed so glamorous, especially the furry-collared coat, the black sunglasses, and how all the guys in the movie fell in love with her.

Up until then, Parker Knowles had been one of her longest lasting, most serious romances. They'd been boyfriend and girlfriend for the better part of three weeks.

But things were simpler back then. Going steady meant no more than a handful of awkward phone calls, some sweaty handholding, and a few embarrassing attempts at kissing. By the time she and Parker had gotten it right, it was over. And so Lola quickly moved on to a succession of junior-high crushes, one virtually indistinguishable from the next.

Lola loved boys. She loved funny, straightforward, athletic, smart boys. She didn't like the ones that acted overly cool, or dressed overly hip, or tried too hard to get noticed. Though she did like it when they fell to her feet. But pretty as she was, it was her smile that always reeled them in. From the moment she smiled, guys turned to putty, willing to do just about anything she asked.

But as much as she loved boys in general, she had never loved one in particular. Until this past summer, when everything changed.

They'd met before. But this time was different. And the girl who all her friends went to for advice (as though all that dating had made her more worldly, when the truth was she was just as much a virgin as they were) suddenly found herself completely clueless at how to proceed. So she'd spent the entire time concentrating on acting completely normal in front of her friends, even flirting with a couple other guys just out of habit. But her eyes followed *him* constantly. And if she wasn't mistaken, she was sure he'd been watching her, too.

They'd met up again at the Ocean Ranch Golden Spoon, standing in line next to each other and both laughing when they ordered the exact same thing—a regular half pistachio–half vanilla with yogurt chips (she'd ordered first, so if anyone was copying, it was *him*). Then they'd carried their cups outside and sat at one of the small round tables, talking until her plastic spoon scraped against the bottom of the cup, and there was nothing left.

The second time was not an accident. Although it was a secret. As had been every single date that followed. Until, slowly, Lola began to realize that the strange, sometimes painful feeling in the pit of her stomach, accompanied by her newfound obsession with hours and minutes and seconds (counting them until she'd get to see him again), was the exhilarating, thrilling, and somewhat scary feeling of being in love.

Too bad she couldn't confide in her friends. Or her parents. Or anyone else, for that matter. It meant way too much to her to just put it out there for other people to judge. And she knew the only way to protect it was to keep it close, and quiet, and secret.

She feared that her friends, knowing what a big flirt she'd always been, wouldn't take her seriously. Not to mention how they'd totally freak at her choice. And there was no doubt that Ellie would be the first (and worst) to judge. And so Lola, being a total people pleaser, had even flirted with that guy in the Jeep just to keep up the appearance of her "normal" self. But all the while she'd been thinking about someone else.

And she couldn't tell her parents because they, along with *Abuela,* would have a complete and total meltdown. Because for starters, he wasn't Mexican. Or Spanish. Or Puerto Rican. Or Panamanian or Argentinean or any other form of Hispanic that her parents would have grudgingly accepted after Mexican. And he wasn't interested in having the "right kind of job." He was an athlete, an artist, an innovator—a true renaissance man—but she knew her parents would not be impressed.

Right now Lola felt so insanely, blissfully happy that she just couldn't take any chances on having someone else wreck it.

"Lola?" her mother called, walking into the bathroom and leaning against the marble sink.

"Mom, I'm trying to take a bath here, jeez," she said, sinking way down so she was covered up to her neck in bubbles.

"We're leaving in an hour," her mother said, turning toward the mirror and checking her makeup.

"Okay." Lola picked up a bottle of body scrub and poured some into her palm. As far as she was concerned, the sooner they left, the better. She had lots of prepping to do for tonight, and it would all go a lot smoother if they weren't around to supervise.

"Will you be ready by then?" Her mother turned to face her.

"Ready for what?" she asked, getting a sick feeling in the pit of her stomach. "What are you talking about?" Lola had no idea what her parents had in store for her, but there was no way they would keep her from going on her date.

"Tonight's that movie screening, and your father is insisting that you go."

"What? No!" Lola said, her heart racing as she looked at her mother and pleaded. "Mom, I can't, okay? I have plans." *God, it's like they're determined to wreck my life!* She'd had a serious boyfriend for exactly three months now, and she was thinking about doing something very major to mark the occasion. It might be too soon, but she loved him so much it would probably be worth it. And she knew her dad didn't care if she went to the stupid premiere. This was her mom's doing. She was always trying to show off her pretty daughter and get her noticed by Hollywood. Even though Lola herself had no interest in any of it.

"This is very important to your father and me. You will come with us, and that's final," she said, turning to leave as though everything was settled.

"*No!* Mom, I'm serious!" Lola begged. "It's Friday night and I have plans!"

"Well, I'm very sorry you made plans, because you've known about this for over a week now."

Was that true? Had she known about it? Because she had absolutely no recollection of having been told. Was being in love giving her amnesia? "Mom, please, I'm *so* not joking. I'll do anything to make it up to you guys. Just please don't ask me to do this, *please*!"

"What on earth is so important?" her mother asked, crossing her arms coolly and surveying her wet, soapy, panicked daughter.

"I promised Ellie," she started. *Think, Lola, think!* "Um, you know how her mom died, like five years ago this month? Well, we always get together to kind of memorialize it." Okay, it wasn't a total lie, because they really did do that, and she was stopping there first. But still, using that for an excuse is definitely a guaranteed one-way ticket to Hell. Especially since what she was *really* planning to do was something her parents had always told her *would* send her to Hell.

"Fine." Her mother shook her head and sighed. "We'll take separate cars. You can drive mine. But you must come by as soon as you're finished. The screening is at eight. Don't be late," she said, giving her a stern look.

"Okay." Lola nodded, wondering what excuse she would use for when she didn't show. Ellie was too upset and she couldn't leave her? Ran out of gas? Wardrobe malfunction?

"And Lola?" her mother said, gripping the door handle.

"Yeah?"

"Don't even think about not showing up."

Lola watched until the door was completely closed. Then she took a deep breath and plunged under the bubbles, resting on the bottom of the tub for as long as she could.

chapter twelve

Anne was lounging on the couch, remote control in one hand, chip smothered in guacamole in the other, as she and Christina drank raspberry iced teas and watched Spanish-language *novelas* together. She'd been hanging out with Christina all day after school, and even though there was at least a twenty-year age gap, and definitely somewhat of a language barrier, she had to admit it beat hanging out by herself. Or, even worse, with Jake, who was always trying to get her into the ocean and onto a board.

But Anne refused to surf. And she refused to hang with people who surfed. And just for the record, she was also absolutely *done* with celebrating the "small victories." That sunny side up frame of mind had lasted an hour at best. And now she was right back to feeling sorry for herself.

It's the inventory that was so pathetic:

Friends—0.

Boyfriends—0.

Pool—0.

Diving board—0.

Dad (still missing in action)—0.

Anything remotely resembling her former life as she knew it—0.

She rolled her eyes at her sorry existence, then grabbed another chip and pulled it through the bowl of guacamole—twice. Then, holding it up in front of her, she looked over at Christina and smiled before shoving the entire thing into her mouth.

But Christina didn't smile back. Her eyes were busy watching the action on the flat screen TV. So Anne picked up another chip, repeating the same routine and wondering if maybe she should slow down just a bit since for the past hour or so her jeans had begun to feel a little, well, *confining.*

And, to be honest, hanging with Christina wasn't all it was cracked up to be. Anne had originally hoped that by asking her to stay late, they could hang out, have some fun, maybe get to know each other a little better. Thinking that in no time they'd be giggling and sharing inside jokes—*in Spanish, even.*

But now, as she undid her top button and grabbed another chip, it was becoming very clear just how misguided her plan had been. Not to mention the sad truth that Christina had probably only stayed because she thought she *had* to, and not because she *wanted* to.

chapter thirteen

The third week of September was always hard for Ellie. Not only did the responsibilities of school and home always threaten to overwhelm her, but it also marked the week her mom had died. September eighteenth, to be exact. And even though five years had passed, and it was slowly starting to get easier, whenever that day approached she always felt like a big dimmer switch had been put on her life. Everything just seemed so much darker.

With her brother always so busy and rarely around, and her father's refusal to ever mention it, she sometimes felt like she was the only one who remembered her, the only one who missed her, and the only one who hadn't gotten on with her life.

Slipping into a pair of clean khaki shorts, a white ribbed tank top, and some flip-flops, she left her long hair loose and wavy like her mom had always liked it. Then she went down the stairs and onto the beach, looking for her friends, wondering if they'd show, or if they'd even remember since it's not like it was something they organized.

It had started sort of organically, over the past few years, with the three of them just always congregating on the beach in the early-evening hours after school, and they'd laugh and talk and reminisce about all the good times. And there were never any candles, never any music, and rarely any crying. It was much more about celebrating her life than remembering her death.

Ellie sat on the old, scarred wood bench, enjoying the warmth of the sun-baked seat against the back of her legs. Some kids were out there surfing, and she felt a pang of guilt, knowing she should be out there, too. Especially if she didn't want to totally humiliate herself at the Surf Fest. But this day wasn't about surfing. It was one of the few days when she gave herself a break.

"Hey, Ellie!" Ellie looked up to see Jade smiling and waving, with her brown curls bouncing as she jogged toward her.

Ellie waved back, feeling relieved that she wouldn't have to go it alone this year. She knew that someday she would, but she was glad it wasn't now. Right now, she just wasn't ready.

chapter fourteen

Lola stood in front of the mirror, dripping water all over the mosaic-tiled floor, wondering how her life had gotten so complicated. True, she may have been just the tiniest bit responsible for keeping secrets from those she loved, but was it really such a bad thing to want to make everyone around you happy?

Her parents had already taken off. So that left only *Abuela,* who, hating all things Hollywood (despite her son's huge success as an entertainment lawyer), was firmly planted in the den watching TV in one of her ubiquitous housedresses.

Lola knew it would be easy enough to sneak past her and avoid her usual ploy of dressing in layers (sexy covered by conservative), but she knew it'd look strange and elicit all kinds of questions if she showed up on the beach to hang with Ellie and Jade in a pair of silver stilettos. *God, I never get a break!* And tonight would require no less than *three* costume changes—one for Ellie, one for her date, and one for her parents and that stupid movie screening.

She pulled her hair back into a sleek, low ponytail and put on the diamond studs she got for her sixteenth birthday, dropping her favorite silver hoops into the little pocket in her purse for later. Then she hurriedly stepped into a white terry-cloth sundress and ran out the door and down the street. She had almost made it to the top of the beach stairs when her cell rang.

"Hello?" she answered hastily. She had no time to talk, no time to waste.

"Hey," he said. It was him!

"Oh," she giggled. "I didn't look at the display—I didn't realize it was you."

"You sound like you're in a hurry."

"Well, kind of. I mean, I have to meet Ellie right now, and then my parents are insisting that I go to this movie screening thing with them." She rolled her eyes instinctively.

"I thought we were having dinner?"

"We are! I can fit it all in, trust me. I just have to juggle a few things around, that's all."

"Lola," he started.

"Trust me. I can make it work. I just might not be able to see you 'til a little later than we planned, that's all."

"I made reservations for eight," he said, his voice sounding tight.

"Oh. Well, can you change them? Because that's when I'm supposed to be in L.A."

"Change them to what? Right now for the early-bird special?" He sounded angry.

"Listen, you don't have to feed me. I can grab some popcorn at the movie, and then we can still see each other later." She felt like she was begging, just like she had earlier with her mother. "I can't wait to see you," she whispered.

"Lola," he sighed. "I've been thinking . . ."

Oh God, don't say that. Don't think! She grabbed the handrail.

"Maybe this isn't such a great idea."

She sunk down onto the top step and rested her forehead against her knees.

"It's like, maybe this just isn't good timing for us. You're still in high school, still living with your parents . . ."

"You still live at home!" she said, feeling kind of angry. *It's not like he didn't know all that. He'd always known all that.*

"Yeah, but it's different for me."

"What are you trying to say?" she asked, but only because she had to. Not because she wanted to hear the answer.

"I just think it's better if we take it easy for a while. Let things cool down a bit . . ."

She just sat there, holding the phone but not daring to speak into it. *Breathe,* she thought. *All that's required of you is to breathe.*

"Lola?" His voice sounded small, far away.

"I have to go," she whispered, closing her phone, fixing her ponytail, and running down the rest of the stairs to meet Ellie and Jade.

chapter fifteen

Anne was just contemplating changing into something with an elastic waist and opening another bag of chips when she heard a key turning in the lock.

"Is anyone home?" her dad called, dropping his bag with an audible thump and heading down the hall.

Giving Christina a guilty look, she wiped the crumbs from her face, sucked in her belly, and buttoned her jeans again. "Um, we're in here," she yelled, hurriedly grabbing a napkin to dab at a guacamole stain on her sloppy gray T-shirt. "In the den."

When she looked up and saw him standing in the doorway, she realized how much she'd missed him. "Hey, Dad," she said, smiling and getting up to hug him. Maybe it was just her imagination, but he seemed a little surprised to find her watching Telemundo with Christina.

"How've you been?" he asked, looking from one to the other.

"*Sí,* fine," Christina said, smiling and grabbing another chip.

"Um, we were just hanging out," Anne said, seeing it from his point of view and realizing it probably did look a little strange. "Christina's been helping me with my Spanish. Well, kind of." She shrugged.

"That's very nice," he said, nodding at Christina. "That's very—*bueno.*"

"Looks like you could use a little help with yours, too," Anne said, laughing.

"So do you have any plans tonight?" he asked his daughter.

"Um, this is pretty much it." She shrugged sheepishly. "My first week at school hasn't been the social whirl you might think," she admitted.

"Feel like hanging out with your old man?"

"Yeah, sure," she said, no longer feeling angry with him for being gone all week. She just wanted to spend some time with him again. "But if you were thinking about dinner, I'm really not hungry." She ran a finger between the waist of her jeans and her skin, trying to loosen them up a little, but her finger got stuck.

"That's okay; I can grab something there. Why don't you hop in the shower and get changed while I give Christina a ride home so she can spend some time with her family," he said, smiling and nodding at Christina, so she'd at least know he was talking to her even if she didn't know what he was saying.

Christina has a family? Anne thought. *Oh God, she must hate me for keeping her here!*

"And when I get back, I'll take you to a Hollywood screening. There'll be paparazzi, so wear something nice," he said, eyeing the avocado stain on her top.

Anne looked at her dad, the truth slowly sinking in. This wasn't about spending quality time with his daughter. Oh no. This was about work. It was always about work. And now, with her mom gone, apparently she would be the one he would drag to all of his functions. Oh well, it beat watching soap operas she didn't understand, and carbo-loading. "How long have I got?" she asked.

"Is forty-five minutes enough?"

"You're pushing it, but I'll be ready," she said, waving good-bye to Christina and heading into her room.

chapter sixteen

"Have you talked to Lola?" Ellie asked, scanning the beach once again, but still not seeing her.

"No, but she'll make it, don't worry." Jade smiled and sat down next to her friend. "I can't believe it's been five years already," she said, eyeing Ellie carefully.

"I know; it went so fast. But then, in a way, it didn't, you know?" Ellie said.

Jade nodded. "So, how's your dad?" she asked. Jade always found Ellie's dad to be more than a little intimidating. It's not that he was mean or anything; it's just that ever since he'd lost his wife he'd become hardened, almost aggressive, like he was some underdog fighting to get to the top, when the truth was, he was already at the top. And Jade couldn't imagine what further career goals an oncologist and chief of staff at Hoag Hospital could possibly have. But then again, maybe that's what extreme tragedy did to people—made them coarser, less trusting, more driven.

Ellie's dad was a cancer specialist who couldn't save his own wife. Who hadn't even recognized the symptoms (even if they were practically invisible) until it was far too late. And being completely unable to forgive himself, it was like he'd descended into these awful feelings of extreme self-doubt and failure. And having always been kind of a control freak in the past, he now focused all of his attention on the one thing he thought was still in his control—Ellie.

Jade shook her head and sighed. She'd always been interested in what made people tick. But she felt lucky that in this particular case she only had to guess at the truth and not actually live it, like poor Ellie.

"He's okay." Ellie shrugged. "Still on my case all the time, but he means well. And it really does help me stay focused and on track."

Jade looked at her friend. She was always so ready to defend her dad, but that's probably because he was all she had left. "But on track for *what* exactly?" she asked carefully. She never fully understood her friend's unwavering determination. It didn't seem to make her any happier, and it always seemed to come at the expense of everything else.

"*College.* I *have* to go to a good school. I don't want to be hanging around here forever. And you know how much I've been wanting a surf sponsorship."

Ellie seemed on edge, but Jade was determined to finally have the conversation she'd been mulling over for a while now. So she proceeded cautiously. "I don't know, El. It's like, well, remember when we first started surfing? How your mom taught us because your brother and his friends were making fun of us?"

They both smiled at the memory. Ellie's brother, Dean, was two years older, gorgeous, cool, and a great surfer, so of course all three girls had idolized him. But he and his friends wanted nothing to do with them. Surfing was a "boy's" sport, and they always got a good laugh watching the girls struggling to stay on their boards. One day Ellie's mom saw what was going on and packed them up, took them over to another beach, and nearly every day for the next several weeks patiently taught the girls to surf until they were good enough, and confident enough, to hold their own. By the time they returned to Laguna Cove, the boys were no longer laughing.

"Well," Jade continued, "It seemed like you were different back then. Like you just loved being in the water, and at school it was like you just liked learning new stuff."

"What are you trying to say, Jade?" Ellie eyed her warily.

"Well, what I mean is, sometimes I worry that you're not really *loving* this stuff anymore. And if you're not really loving something, then like, what's the point?" She looked at her friend carefully, but Ellie was staring off into the horizon, and Jade wondered if she had just stopped listening.

They sat quietly for a while; then Ellie looked at Jade and said, "I know you worry about me. But I worry about you, too. Only for the exact opposite reason." She smiled.

Jade shrugged, then looked across the beach and said, "Hey, there's Lola."

They both looked over to see Lola smiling and waving, holding her flip-flops in one hand, while her bare feet carved into the sand as she made her way across the beach.

"Hey, you guys," she said, leaning in to hug first Ellie, then Jade.

"Are you okay?" Jade asked.

"Yeah, why?" Lola asked.

"I don't know. Your mascara's a little smudged, and all these years I've known you I've never seen your makeup anything less than perfect."

"Jeez. Cut me some slack, will ya?" Lola said, sitting on the bench across from her friends. "So did I miss anything?"

"We were just talking about when Ellie's mom taught us to surf," Jade said, eyeing Lola, still not convinced everything was so great. That amazing smile she always had seemed a little muted now.

"That's one of my best memories of her. Well, that and those orange chocolate-chip oatmeal cookies she used to make," Lola said.

"And don't forget how she crocheted those matching sky blue bikinis for all of us," Jade added.

"Oh God. We thought we were so hot in those," Ellie laughed.

"Yeah, until they came off in the water!" Lola laughed.

"Right in front of those boys!" Jade said. "Too bad for them we were only ten, so there wasn't much to see!"

"Speak for yourself," Lola said. "I was stunning at ten!"

"Sorry, Lola, we still had baby fat. Ellie was the stunning one." Jade smiled, looking at Ellie, who had turned bright red. She'd never been good at receiving compliments.

"So what are you guys doing later?" Ellie asked.

"I'm supposed to go to this stupid movie premiere with my parents," Lola said, rolling her eyes.

"Must be rough," Jade and Ellie said simultaneously.

"Yeah, yeah. I don't mean to sound like a brat. I kind of had other plans, but I guess they just got canceled," Lola said, suddenly looking away from her friends and toward the waves crashing in front of them.

"So, postpone," Ellie said. "You've always managed to sneak out of those in the past. So what's the big deal now?"

"Well, apparently he wasn't up for a reschedule." Lola pressed her lips together and stood up suddenly.

"Are you leaving?" Jade asked, eyeing her friend with concern.

Lola nodded.

"Well, in case you do manage to escape. There's a party tonight at Aliso Beach. You should stop by. Ellie and I will be there."

"I will?" Ellie asked, looking at Jade. It was the first she'd heard of it.

"*Yes,* you are going with me. In fact, you're driving. In fact, you're the designated driver. Anyway, try to make it, Lolita; it's gonna be fun."

Lola just looked at them and shrugged. Then she turned and made her way back up the beach.

chapter seventeen

Anne sat next to her dad in the crowded, darkened theater, watching the other audience members more than the action on screen. *Or the lack of action,* she thought. The movie was a total bore. But in the audience there were a few people she recognized from *People* magazine covers and award shows. Like, just two rows up, wasn't that Renee Richards? And who was that scruffy guy she was making out with? Anne figured he must be really important, because as her father once explained to her, the more power you had in Hollywood, the more you could dress down.

She glanced quickly at her dad, mindlessly eating popcorn and shaking his head and smirking at the screen. *Well, at least we're in agreement about the movie sucking!*

She leaned toward him and whispered, "I'll be right back; I'm gonna find the bathroom."

He looked at her briefly and nodded, then quickly focused his attention back on the screen.

She made her way up the dark aisle, at one point tripping on some supermodel's shoe. The model gave her a nasty look. *Oh yeah, like it's my fault your legs are six feet long and can't fit in a normal-sized space,* she thought, rolling her eyes right back at her.

Exiting the theater, she squinted against the brightness of the movie ads, popcorn machines, and the oversized chandelier that would surely squash anybody unlucky enough to be standing underneath during an earthquake. Not that she'd ever been in an earthquake, but now that she was living in California, she thought about them a lot.

Finding the restroom, she pushed inside and after inspecting her makeup in the mirror and washing her hands, she plopped down onto a little velvet settee and closed her eyes.

She'd been sitting like that for five, ten minutes max, when someone rushed by so fast Anne barely got a look at her. Then she heard the stall door slam and lock. Then there was some very loud crying.

Anne just sat there, wondering if she should offer to help. On the one hand, it was clearly none of her business. There was no way she knew the girl, since she didn't know anyone here except for her dad. But on the other hand, the girl sounded so seriously distressed that it made it hard to just sit there and do nothing. *But what if she just wants to be left alone?*

Okay, Anne decided, *I'll offer to help.* If she wasn't interested, Anne would just go back into the theater and leave her in peace.

Just as she was getting up to investigate, the door slammed open and this tiny girl with long, dark hair, dressed in cute jeans, a white blouse, a black shrunken blazer, and awesome silver stilettos looked at her and said, "Hey, I know you."

"You do?" Anne asked, wondering how the girl could possibly know her.

"You go to Laguna High, right? You're that new girl," she said, rubbing a hand across her eyes and smearing her makeup even more.

"Yeah, I'm Anne," she said, thinking that now that the girl was right in front of her, she did look familiar.

"I'm Lola." She plopped herself down on the chair across from Anne and smiled ruefully.

"Are you okay?" Anne asked carefully, wondering if she was supposed to say anything or just pretend like a face full of smeared makeup was all the rage in the OC.

"Actually no, I'm not. I'm dying, I'm devastated, and I've been dumped," she said, shaking her head and digging through her purse. "And now I can't even find a tissue." Her eyes welled up with tears again.

"Hang on. Here," Anne said, handing her a crumpled one she'd found at the bottom of her bag. "It's clean, too, I swear." She watched Lola blow her nose over and over and over again, wondering how one little tissue could actually withstand all that.

"Thanks," she said, wadding it up and tossing it into the trash. Then she curled her legs up under her. "Sorry about all this. My parents insisted I come to this stupid thing, and because of it I got dumped. And believe me, it's not the first time they've interfered." She shook her head. "It's just so hard when they expect so much from me. I mean, they never would have approved of him, and that's why it all had to be a big secret. But I think he got tired of sneaking around." She stopped and looked at Anne. "And you want to know the worst part?"

Anne just nodded, not entirely sure that she did. She wasn't used to people just spilling their guts like this. But then she remembered how her dad had once told her that in movie speak this was called a California Conversation. Apparently this kind of soul dumping was routine for those who lived here.

"I was actually considering doing something *really* major with him, you know? God, I'm such an idiot," she said, covering her face with her hands and starting to cry again.

"Don't say that. You should be glad that you didn't, because now you don't have anything big to regret, right?" Anne said softly.

Lola looked up, nodding slowly.

"Just be glad you found out now." Anne smiled.

"God, I can't believe I just told you all that when my best friends don't even know." Lola looked suddenly panicked. "Oh God, *please* don't mention this to Ellie and Jade. They'll freak."

"Don't worry," Anne assured her. "Jade's in my art class, but we don't sit by each other. And Ellie, well, I don't think she likes me enough to ever have a conversation with me."

Lola looked at Anne and shrugged. "Ellie's cool. Really. She's just a little leery of newcomers, that's all."

Anne didn't say anything. She wasn't sure she believed that.

"Did you have a boyfriend in—where'd you move from?"

"Connecticut, and yeah, I did. His name was Justin and he just dumped me for his old girlfriend. Didn't take him long to move on, did it?" Anne said, relieved that she could finally say it out loud without choking up. Even though it did feel kind of weird to talk about him in the past tense.

"Hey." Lola looked at her and smiled in a way that lit up her whole face despite the mascara trails running down her cheeks. "This movie *blows*. What do you say we bail? I heard there's this party tonight at Aliso Beach. It's just gonna be a bunch of people from school, but it's gotta be better than this."

"But what am I gonna tell my dad?" Anne asked, feeling torn between wanting to hang with Lola and leaving her dad, who she'd barely spent any time with. *But,* was that her fault, or his?

"Tell him you don't feel well and I'm taking you home. And I'll tell my parents the same thing. Come on; it'll be fun," she said, opening her compact and surveying the damage.

"Okay. It's not like he'll miss me, anyway. He's too busy staring at the screen and inhaling popcorn. He probably won't even notice I'm gone," Anne said, hoping that wasn't exactly true.

"My mom's not even watching the movie. She's too busy sitting next to Renee Richards, hoping someone will take a picture of the two of them." She rolled her eyes.

"Did you see that guy she's making out with?" Anne asked.

"You don't know the half of it. She's my dad's client. Come on," Lola said, standing up and grabbing her purse. "I'll fill you in on the drive to Orange County."

chapter eighteen

By the time Ellie and Jade were dressed and ready to leave, they'd worked up some major excitement about the party. Never mind that it would just be the same old people talking about the same old stuff. There was something about spending the afternoon with Jade and remembering all the good times with her mom that made Ellie feel lighter, more positive, and less willing to be so damn uptight.

They were in her Mini Cooper, just about to pull out of the driveway, when Ellie's father drove up. "Hey, Mr. Stone," Jade said, smiling and waving.

Barely acknowledging her with a brisk nod, he looked at Ellie and said, "Did you finish your homework?"

"Yes," Ellie said, still backing up slowly. She was determined to get out of there before he completely killed her buzz.

"Okay, but don't stay out too late. You need to be up early tomorrow. I've booked you a coach. She'll be here by eleven."

"A coach?" Ellie slammed on her brake. "Dad, I don't need a coach," she said.

"Of course you need her! And you should try to get in a few sessions before she shows."

"But Dad," she pleaded

"No buts, it's already booked. Have a nice night," he said, climbing out of his convertible BMW and heading toward the front door.

Ellie focused on breathing, slow and deep, as she watched him open the door. *So much for being in a good mood,* she thought, backing out of the driveway and pulling onto the street.

chapter nineteen

"So aren't we a little overdressed for a beach party?" Anne asked, glancing at Lola's stilettos, then down at her own silk skirt.

"Probably." Lola shrugged. "But who cares. We'll just tell everyone we were at a big, glamorous Hollywood movie premiere. They'll be *sooo* jealous!" she laughed.

"Yeah, as long as we don't mention how bad it sucked!" Anne said, looking at Lola and smiling. She was finally having some fun, and it was all thanks to her. It was incredible how Lola had gone from choking, sobbing tears to looking completely glamorous. Anne wished she could be more like that. And after listening to Lola's nonstop chatter on the long drive down, apparently there was a lot she could learn from her. "So like, who's gonna be there? I mean, not that I really *know* anyone, but I do have most of the big names memorized." It was funny how everyone always knew the names of all the alphas, even when they didn't hang with them.

"All the usual suspects will be present and accounted for. You know, basically everyone from the lunch table." Lola smiled.

"Please, you don't even want to know where I've been eating

lunch," Anne said, looking out the window, and wondering why she had just confided that—it was kind of embarrassing.

"Well, my friend, that's all in the past. Now you will officially meet everyone and they will love you. I promise," Lola said, parking the car and rechecking her lip gloss in the rearview mirror. "And after they get to know you and see how great you are, I guarantee they will no longer call you the East Coast Ice Queen."

"What?" Anne said, getting out of the car and staring at her.

"Oh, maybe I shouldn't have told you that," Lola said, face full of regret. "Listen, *please* don't be upset. They only said that because you're so pretty but you kind of stick to yourself. You don't talk much." She shrugged.

"I get shy sometimes," Anne said, sounding really defensive and wondering if she still wanted to go to this party now that she knew what people were saying about her.

"Oh, come on." Lola looped her arm through Anne's. "What could be more fun than proving everyone wrong?"

They walked down the beach, toward the glowing bonfire, and of course, as luck would have it, the very first person Anne saw was the one who hated her the most, Ellie. She was sitting next to Jade and Chris and some guy named Duncan, and Lola was heading straight for them. Anne had the immediate urge to run in the opposite direction. She wasn't sure she was up for Ellie's dirty looks and cutting little comments. Ellie was probably the one who came up with the Ice Queen thing. But Lola was cool, and everyone else seemed okay, so if Ellie was determined to be a bitch, well, that was her problem.

"Hey, guys!" Lola said. "You remember Anne?"

Anne noticed Chris and Jade wave, but of course Ellie only narrowed her eyes and stared.

"We were just talking about surfing," Ellie said, completely ignoring Anne.

"But of course, what else is there?" Lola laughed, settling down onto the blanket and motioning for Anne to sit next to her.

"My dad got me a coach because the Surf Fest is next month, and he thinks I'm gonna choke like last year. It's so ridiculous." She shook her head. "I mean, what am I supposed to learn from a coach? I'm either gonna surf well or I'm not. And I just don't get how some trainer's gonna change that."

"I had a coach for my diving," Anne blurted out, before she could stop herself.

Ellie shook her head and rolled her eyes. "I really don't think that's the same thing," she said quickly. Then, turning back to everyone else, "*Anyway,* it just feels so—artificial. But apparently, Chris is on my dad's side." She smiled and poked him in the ribs, a little harder than she intended. She was completely hopeless at flirting, especially with a guy she really liked.

"Everything's different now," he said. "There's major big money in all the sponsorships, endorsements, and contests. A coach will just give you an edge, and maybe some techniques to deal with stress." He smiled.

"Who, me? Stress?" Ellie laughed. "Look, all I want is a sticker on my board. That's it, I swear."

"And a trophy, prize money, free clothes four times a year, and, oh yeah, your face on the cover of *SG* magazine." Lola laughed.

"You came really close last year," Jade reminded her.

"Yeah, until I choked." Ellie shook her head at the memory.

"Hence, the coach!" Chris said, laughing and throwing his arms in the air to make his point. Then, looking at Anne, he said, "So what's it gonna take to get you in the water?"

"Me?" Anne asked, surprised at being suddenly included.

"Yeah, you. I mean diving's great and all, but there's no dive team at school, so you might want to try it. Besides, you can't be a cliff dweller and not surf; it just ain't right. Right, Ellie?"

But Ellie didn't answer. And something about her absolute determination to ignore her, acting like she wasn't even worth talking to, made Anne so angry she went into full-blown flirt mode, just to mess with her. "Doesn't ice melt when it hits the water?" she asked, briefly touching Chris on the knee and smiling.

"What?" He looked at her carefully, while everyone else looked down at the ground, including Ellie.

"I told her. She knows *everything,*" Lola said, looking at Anne and winking.

"We were just fooling around," Chris said quickly. "We didn't really mean it." He looked embarrassed and guilty.

"Hmmm." Anne looked at him. "I wonder how you could make it up to me?" She tossed her long blond hair over her shoulder and smiled.

"I'll teach you to surf," he offered.

"*You'll* teach me?" She gave him a skeptical look.

"Yeah, why not? I'm an okay surfer, wouldn't you agree?"

Lola and Duncan readily agreed, Ellie just glared, and Jade looked upset.

"I have to think about it," Anne said, feeling confused by the look on Jade's face and wondering if maybe she liked Chris too. She'd only been flirting with him to bug Ellie, but if all the girls were secretly fighting over him, then she would definitely back off. No matter how cute he was, it certainly wasn't worth upsetting everyone.

"Meet me on the beach tomorrow at noon," he said. "I won't take no for an answer. And remember, I know where you live."

Chris was looking at her and smiling, but Anne just sat there, not really sure what to do. It was her fault all the girls had gone all tense and quiet, and even though she was feeling too uncomfortable to look at her, she could feel Ellie's eyes burning right into her.

"So, who wants a beer?" Duncan asked, getting up and dusting the sand off his jeans.

Chris, Lola, Jade, and Anne all took a pass. But Ellie surprised everyone by jumping up, shaking her long shiny hair from its tight ponytail, and saying, "I'll have one."

"*You're* having a beer?" Jade and Lola said in unison, staring at their friend in disbelief.

Ellie looked annoyed. "Jeez, you guys, it's not like I've never had a drink before," she said, rolling her eyes and running to catch up with Duncan.

chapter twenty

By the time Ellie and Duncan were on their third beers the party was pretty much over. "So what do you want to do now?" he asked, leaning in 'til they were almost touching.

Ellie looked at him, his face so close to hers. And even though it was a really cute face, it definitely wasn't the right face. *It isn't Chris's face,* Ellie thought, glancing over at Chris, who was *still* flirting with Anne, as he had been all night, leaving Ellie with no choice but to flirt with someone else. But now, after all the joking, laughing, and hair tossing *(why does flirting come so easy when you aren't really all that into the person?),* she looked at Duncan, his brown eyes staring into hers, and she felt guilty, knowing she'd been leading him on and that he was way more into it than she was.

But as he looked in her eyes and leaned in even closer she suddenly thought, *Oh, what the hell? I mean, how bad could it really be?* He was cute, popular, smart, a decent surfer, and she'd known that he liked her since freshman year. She could trust him. And she knew she could trust herself not to like him too much.

The first thing she thought as his lips touched hers was, *I hope Chris is watching.*

The second thing was, *Hmmm—this isn't so bad . . .*

"Uh, you guys. Yoo-hoo! Sorry, I can see that you're very busy and all, but I just wanted to tell you I'm getting a ride home with Lola. Just so you don't worry when you come up for air. *If* you come up for air," Jade said, obviously shocked by the sight of Ellie and Duncan making out.

Ellie pulled away and wiped her mouth with the back of her hand. Her face felt warm and raw from all the kissing, and her head felt weird from all the beer. "What?" She squinted at Jade.

"I'm taking off. So, um, good night," Jade said, giving an awkward little wave.

"Do you need a ride?" Ellie asked.

"Hmm," Jade said, looking them over. "Tell you what. Why don't you give *me* the keys, and I'll give *you guys* a ride. What do you say?"

"Don't be ridiculous. I'm perfectly capable of driving," Ellie said, rolling her eyes and attempting to stand, but her legs were not cooperating and she ended up right back on the sand, falling smack onto Duncan.

Jade stood there watching them, all tangled up together and laughing like it was *so hysterical.* "Okay, hand 'em over," she said, sounding like a chaperone while she reached for Ellie's keys.

chapter twenty-one

Anne woke to the sounds and smells of breakfast. A real breakfast. Like the kind her dad always used to make on the weekends, after a movie had wrapped and he had a little free time between projects.

She slipped into her terry-cloth robe and matching slippers and padded down the long tiled hallway to the kitchen. "Hey," she said, rubbing her eyes and reaching into the cupboard for a coffee mug.

"Hey, yourself," he said, turning briefly from the stove and smiling. "Feeling better?" he asked, raising one eyebrow.

"Okay, I confess. I wasn't really sick," she said, adding half-and-half to her coffee until it was light tan in color. "I met up with a friend from school and she invited me to a beach party. Are you mad?" She looked at him cautiously.

"No." He shook his head, and reached for two plates. "But you could have told me that." He came over to the table where she was sitting and handed her a plate full of eggs, toast, fruit, bacon—the works.

"I know. I didn't want to lie, but I also didn't want to make you feel bad since we haven't spent much time together," she said, inwardly thinking, *Not like that's my fault!*

"Well, you can make it up to me today. I thought we could go downtown, stroll around the galleries, have lunch, just relax," he said, taking a bite of his whole-grain toast.

Anne just looked at him. She wasn't exactly sure how to tell him that she wouldn't actually be able to "make it up" to him. "Um, well, I kind of made plans," she said, taking a sip of her coffee. "A friend has offered to teach me to surf. I'm supposed to meet him on the beach at noon."

"Don't worry about it," her dad said. "Go and have fun with your friends. In fact, it's funny you mentioned it, because I was thinking about getting back on a board myself."

"You?" Anne wished she hadn't sounded so incredulous, but the thought of her dad surfing was insane. He was *old.* He could get *hurt*! There was no way he could be serious. "What exactly do you mean, 'back on a board'?"

"Don't look so shocked. I used to surf," he said, taking a sip of his coffee.

"Uh, *when*? I mean, I've never seen any evidence of this." She shook her head and speared a piece of cantaloupe.

"Admittedly, it's been a few years, but I think I've still got it in me." He nodded. "I had a longboard. And I was pretty good, I'll have you know."

"Whatever, Dad," Anne said, finishing up her eggs. "Just please let me have the waves to myself today. No need for both of us to be humiliated."

At exactly six minutes past noon (she didn't want to look overly anxious), Anne headed down the stairs and onto the beach, looking for Chris. But not seeing him anywhere, she casually dropped her towel onto the sand, acting as though she wasn't at all concerned that she might very well possibly be getting stood up. *He did say noon, right?*

"Hey." She looked over to see Chris coming out of the water. His hair was slicked back, his board was under his arm, and even though she was trying not to stare, his body was cut, tanned, and totally amazing. "Glad to see we're still on. It's a good day to learn; the swells are kind of small," he said, smiling.

"I didn't really know what to bring," she said nervously, trying not to gawk at his six-pack abs. "So I just brought some sunscreen and a towel."

"No worries," he said. "I've got everything you need."

And when he smiled, she thought it might very well be true.

chapter twenty-two

Ellie's coaching lesson was not going well and it probably had a little something to do with the deep pool of regret she was currently wading in. Not to mention the hangover that had her not only fatigued and nauseous, but seriously longing to climb back into bed, pull the covers over her head, and forget about surfing, Surf Fest, and just about everything else.

It was Duncan, not her dad, who'd woken her this morning. And just hearing his voice had brought it all back. Her father was already at the hospital and her brother apparently didn't answer the phone anymore, so finally on the fifth ring she reached over and croaked, "Hello?"

"Ellie, did I wake you?" he'd said.

"Um yeah. Kind of. What time is it?" she'd asked.

"Ten thirty."

"Oh my God," she'd said, throwing off the sheets and jumping out of bed way too fast for her compromised condition. "Um, I gotta go. Can we talk later?" She fell back onto the mattress, gripped the edge, and closed her eyes against the banging in her head.

"Sure. I'll call you later," he'd said, sounding disappointed.

Oh, God. If that upset him, just wait 'til I tell him the truth, that

I made a huge mistake and should never have kissed him, she'd thought, feeling bad about the prospect but glad that she could put it off for a few more hours.

And now, out there in the ocean, all she wanted to do was float on her board, with the sun beating against her skin like a warm blanket while the gentle waves rocked her to sleep. She could think of nothing better.

"Maybe we should cut this short today," her coach, Lina, said.

"I'm sorry." Ellie slowly lifted her head and squinted at her. "I had kind of a rough night. And to be honest, I wasn't really into this to begin with. This was all pretty much my dad's idea." She rolled her eyes.

"Not a problem." Lina shrugged. "Either way, I'm still getting paid. But if you ever decide to get serious, give me a call," she said, heading for shore.

"Hey! Excuse me!" Ellie yelled after her. "But for your information, I *am* serious!" She sat up on her board and glared at the back of Lina's head, but all the while she wondered if it was true.

chapter twenty-three

Lola was almost out the door when she heard her mother call, "Lola? Can you come here for a minute?"

Oh God, I was so close, she thought, dutifully turning around and heading back into the kitchen to see what she could possibly want now.

"Oh, there you are," her mother said, leaning against the kitchen counter and sipping something out of a blue ceramic mug that Lola assumed contained her usual herbal tea concoction. "Did your friend get home okay last night?"

"What?" Lola squinted at her mom. "Oh, yeah," she said, suddenly remembering how she'd lied about Anne being sick. "Thanks for understanding," she added.

Her mother nodded. "I'm sorry you had to leave so early. There was someone there I wanted you to meet. So I gave him your number."

"What?" Lola dropped her beach bag onto the floor and stared at her. *She can't be serious. Please, dear God, don't let her be serious!*

"His name is Diego. He is the son of one of your father's associates. He's just a year ahead of you and I really think you two will hit it off." She smiled excitedly.

"But," Lola began, trying to think of a really good reason for why this could *never, ever* happen.

But she hesitated too long and her mom continued, "His family lives in Palos Verdes Estates and he has plans to go to Columbia University next year," she said, taking a sip of tea and watching Lola closely.

"Okay, and what does any of this have to do with me?" Lola asked calmly, trying to hide her mounting panic. "I mean, why do *I* have to meet him?" As far as Lola was concerned, she wasn't feeling very single right now, despite the fact that she'd just been dumped.

"Because I think it's important."

Lola took a deep breath and stared at her mother. She knew what this was about. Her mother had obviously found a nice Mexican boy who came from a good (i.e., wealthy, i.e., respectable) family, and she had absolutely no regard for the fact that Lola had recently had her heart *ripped to shreds* and wasn't exactly interested in meeting *anyone* right now. Okay, maybe her mom didn't know any of that because she hadn't exactly told her, but still. How could she do this to her?

"It's a shame you had to leave early to take your friend home," her mom continued, giving Lola a look that said she hadn't bought the story for one measly second. "Anyway, you should hear from him today or tomorrow. And Lola, when he asks you out, I expect you to say yes."

Lola just stood there, staring at her mother, knowing there was no way to win this one.

chapter twenty-four

Jade sat on her beach towel observing her friends. Anne was out there with Chris, doing surprisingly well. And according to Jade's unofficial count, Anne fell off Chris's longboard only a handful of times, which was pretty amazing for her very first day. But then again, it also seemed like Chris had found like a million reasons to hold on to her—like, way more than necessary.

Then there was Ellie, not doing much of anything but bobbing in the water, trying to act like she wasn't watching Chris and Anne, even though it was totally obvious that she was completely obsessed. Even from the vantage point of her towel, Jade could see Ellie's head swiveling around, watching their every move. *She must be feeling pretty lousy right about now,* Jade thought, remembering her friend's surprising behavior the night before. If it were anybody else, it wouldn't even be worth remembering. That's what parties were for! But Ellie wasn't just anybody—she held herself to a pretty impossible standard and up until last night, she'd managed to stick to it.

But it was Duncan that Jade really felt sorry for. Especially when he'd figure out that Ellie wasn't into him, that she was just using him to get back at Chris. Jade knew that Duncan had been crushing on Ellie for about as long as Ellie had been crushing on Chris. It was just so damn obvious that she couldn't understand why nobody else could see it.

She applied more sunscreen and lip balm, then lay back on her towel, closing her eyes against the sun. *Why is it so hard for people to stop lying to themselves?* she wondered.

"Hey, Jade." Lola dropped her towel right next to hers.

"What's up?" Jade peered at her friend, knowing for sure that something was definitely not going right in her life.

Lola just shrugged and dug through her beach bag, pulling out a stack of magazines that could stock an entire newsstand—*ELLEgirl, InStyle, Latina, SG, Teen Vogue, Vanity Fair, People, Shop Etc., Lucky* . . .

"Your bag must weigh thirty pounds," Jade laughed, reaching for one. "*House & Garden*?"

"Hey, I'm an addict. Any glossy will do," Lola said, putting on a straw cowboy hat to shade her face from the sun. "Oh, and have I mentioned that my mother has expanded her parental duties?"

"Oh no," Jade said. Lola's mother gave new meaning to the word "ambitious."

"Oh yes." Lola nodded. "She's now appointed herself as my very own dating director slash life coach."

"No way." Jade stared at her friend.

"Apparently she has a wonderful young man all lined up for me. So I now have the pleasure of sitting by my cell, breathlessly awaiting a call from *Diego*—the best thing to come out of Mexico City since my dad." She rolled her eyes dramatically and lay back on her towel. "Little does she know, I put my phone on vibrate so I won't have to hear it ring. He can just leave a message for all I care."

"Oh, that does not sound promising," Jade said, looking at her friend with sympathy. "But maybe it won't be as bad as you think."

Lola opened one eye and looked at her. "Jade, you've met my mother. I think we both know how bad it will be!"

"Oh, you know I hate negative thoughts, but this time you're probably right," she agreed.

"My life is a disaster." Lola shook her head and placed her hat completely over her face. "Tell you what, I'll just lie here with my eyes closed and you tell me if you see or read anything interesting. I just need to zone out for a while, but I swear I'm listening."

"Something interesting . . . Okay, well, my across-the-street neighbor keeps walking up and down the beach. This is now her fourth or fifth lap."

"Maybe she's just exercising," Lola said from under her hat.

"No, I think it's more about showing off her new boobs—those don't come cheap, you know. Okay, and Chris and Anne have been in the water for a while now, he's teaching her to surf, and believe it or not, she's actually pretty good. So good, in fact, that he probably does not need to be holding her quite as much as he is, which indicates something else entirely."

"What?"

"That Chris is totally into Anne," Jade said, impatiently.

"Chris and Anne?" Lola asked, removing her hat and opening one eye.

"Yup. So much for my big plans." Jade sighed and looked back toward the water.

"What plans?" Lola looked at her.

"Nothing," Jade said quickly, not wanting to share with Lola how she'd failed miserably at her own lame matchmaking attempt.

"Okay, continue. This is getting good," Lola said, replacing her hat.

"Okay, and poor Ellie has been bobbing out there for what must be hours now."

"Bobbing? Not surfing?" Lola's voice sounded muffled from beneath the straw.

"Not surfing. She's through with surfing. Well, at least for today. And it appears that her coach has abandoned her."

"Should we swim out there and talk to her?"

"No." Jade shook her head. "I have a feeling she just wants to be left alone. And Lola, I hate to break it to you, but your bag is vibrating."

chapter twenty-five

Realizing her fingers and toes were completely shriveled from way too many hours spent in the water, Ellie hopped on her board and rode her last, and possibly best, wave of the day.

Dragging her board up the beach, she stopped to watch three little tow-headed kids bury their father in the sand.

"Hey, Ellie!"

She looked over to see Jade, Lola, Anne, and Chris lying on their towels, laughing and talking. Seeing Anne and Chris like that, with their towels pushed so close together, made her stomach go all weird again. But now that they'd seen her she had no choice but to go over and say a quick hello.

"Hey," she said, giving a little wave.

"How'd the coach work out?" Chris asked.

Ellie dropped her board on the sand and shrugged. "I guess I just wasn't feeling very into it today."

"Maybe Anne could help you." He laughed. "She's a natural."

Ellie narrowed her eyes at him. He was so nice and easygoing that he probably meant nothing by it, but still. *What a thing to say.* Guys could be so insensitive.

"I doubt that. I've seen you surf," Anne said, looking at Ellie and smiling. "You're pretty amazing out there."

"When did you see me?" Ellie asked, wondering if Anne was spying on her or something, even though she knew how ridiculous that seemed.

"Um, early in the morning. Before school sometimes." Anne gave an embarrassed shrug.

"You get up at five thirty?" Ellie looked at her skeptically.

"Well, sometimes, yeah. I mean, when I can't sleep. I guess I'm still on East Coast time or something."

"I think you just found your new surf partner," Lola said. Then, looking at Anne she explained, "We all used to surf before school, but then Jade and I kind of dropped out. Unlike Ellie, we need our beauty sleep." She laughed.

"Speak for yourself!" Jade said, tossing her long brown ringlets and giving Lola a fake offended look.

"Well, I'm pretty serious about surfing, so I'm not really looking for company," Ellie said, feeling completely annoyed with her friends for pushing this girl on her. Why couldn't everyone just leave things the way they were?

"We're all thinking about going down to Taco Loco in a while. You wanna come?" Chris asked, grabbing Anne's water bottle and taking a sip.

Ellie just stood there, watching them. Their knees were bumping against each other, and the way he had just grabbed her water, so casually, almost like they were boyfriend and girlfriend or something. But that was impossible. *They just met!* "Um, no thanks," she said, grabbing her board and turning to leave. "I gotta be somewhere in half an hour."

"Where you going?" Jade called after her.

"Just somewhere," Ellie said, waving over her shoulder and heading toward home.

• • •

Walking up the beach stairs, she could feel her face grow hot. She was angry with her friends for totally not getting that she had no interest in hanging with Anne, not to mention how humiliating it was to watch her so effortlessly succeed at everything Ellie had worked so hard for. It's like she'd just come out of nowhere and within one week she'd moved in on Ellie's friends and Ellie's fantasy boyfriend, and now she was even showing a certain amount of skill at Ellie's sport.

She'd been watching her the whole time, and unfortunately Chris was right. Anne *was* a pretty good surfer. Maybe not good in the way that Ellie or Chris or even Jade or Lola was, but good in the way that if she got out there a couple times a week and really focused, she could definitely compete someday, and that was something that Ellie did not need. It was bad enough losing Chris to her; she certainly didn't need to lose Surf Fest, too.

Leaning her board against the wall, she threw her damp towel over a deck chair and went into the kitchen.

"Hey." Her brother was sitting at the table drinking a juice and reading last weekend's *L.A. Times* Calendar section.

"Did you just wake up?" she asked, realizing she sounded bossy and judgmental just like her dad, *but jeez,* it was three o'clock already.

"Out last night. Got home late," Dean said in that shorthand way of talking he had. He was all about word economy.

"Where?" Ellie asked, opening the fridge and looking for something to eat. All that time in the water had left her ravenous. *Too bad I can't go to Taco Loco,* she thought, grabbing a container of yogurt, determined to make do.

"Party. Monarch Beach," he said, still not looking up.

"Oh, I was at one at Aliso," she said, grabbing a spoon.

"So I heard."

"What do you mean?" she asked, panicked that word was out about her drinking three beers and making out with Duncan. Any other girl doing that would be no big deal, but Ellie idolized her brother and she wanted him to think well of her.

"Duncan called like an hour ago." He shrugged.

"What did he say?" she asked, hoping she sounded calm and casual.

"He wants you to call him." He looked up briefly.

"Did he say anything else?"

"No."

"So who was at the party?" she asked, determined to move the conversation away from herself. She did not want to think about Duncan right now.

"Some friends, some poseurs, the usual crowd." He shrugged, folded the paper in half, and looked at her.

Dean was pretty intolerant of poseurs, the kind of people who offered nothing more than their money and their presence. He, on the other hand, had accomplished so much in such a short amount of time, having won several surf championships with several major brands clamoring to sponsor him; he'd even gotten an early acceptance into a really good school. Yet despite his good looks and undeniable talents, he somehow managed to stay really low-key, often using his free time for community service, like assisting in beach cleanups or teaching autistic kids to surf or working on his ongoing surf documentary. But Ellie knew that his most amazing accomplishment to date was when he'd convinced their dad that taking the semester off school to work on his film was a genius idea. Ellie couldn't even take a sick day without getting seriously scolded. And as much as she loved Dean, sometimes it was a total bummer having a brother like him. He was a tough act to follow.

"Do you know what time Dad's coming home?" she asked, finishing her yogurt and dumping the container in the trash.

"Not 'til late." He looked at her and smiled. He knew just how hard their dad had been on her over the last few years.

"Good," she said, heading upstairs to her room so she could shower, change, and then head out to her secret place. She was looking forward to a little peace and quiet.

chapter twenty-six

Lola was staring at her half-eaten taco, impatiently waiting for Jade to take her home, even though all the immediate evidence suggested that was not about to happen anytime soon.

Impatiently chewing on the end of the straw she'd used to drink not one, but two Diet Cokes, she watched as Jade joked around with Ben and some older guys who were apparently friends of his that Lola had never seen before. Chris and Anne had taken off an hour ago, and Lola was beginning to wish she'd gone with them.

What a waste, she thought. Five single guys less than five feet away and things had gotten so bad for her that she didn't feel like flirting with any of them. But even worse was the fact that her phone hadn't rung all day. Not that she thought *he* would call. But still, it would have been nice.

But wait. Hadn't Jade told her on the beach that her bag was vibrating? She'd assumed at the time that it was that loser guy her mom was trying to hook her up with. *But what if it wasn't? What if he really did try to call?*

Anxiously, she reached into her bag, grabbing her cell and flipping it open, only to find a little envelope on the screen.

So she *had* gotten a message!

Excitedly, she pressed the voice-mail button, holding her breath and closing her eyes, anticipating the sound of his voice.

"Hi. My name's Diego. Apparently our parents think it's a good idea for us to meet. So if you want, you can give me a call back at . . ."

She erased it before he could finish. *Of course,* she thought, shaking her head and rolling her eyes. Well, there was no way she'd be calling him back. And when her mother asked, well, she'd just tell her that he never called. Because the one thing she knew for sure was that there was absolutely no way she was going out with him. No way in hell, *because only the most terminal dweeb would need his mother to set him up on a date*!

"Hey, Lola, you awake?" Jade asked, laughing and tapping her friend on the shoulder.

"Yeah, what's up?" she said, brushing her hair away from her face, hoping Jade was finally ready to bail.

"We're gonna go over to Tom's. Are you in?"

"Who's Tom?" Lola asked, squinting at the guys, unable to remember any of their names, which was so unlike her.

"Curly blond hair in the blue T-shirt, standing next to Mike who you also probably don't remember. Anyway, his apartment is just up the street. We're just gonna hang out, listen to some music . . ."

But before Jade could list all the activities that could be had at Tom's, Lola was already shaking her head. She knew they were all just gonna go back and smoke some pot, and Lola just wasn't into all that. What she really wanted was to be by herself for a while and just try to sort out all the conflicting emotions in her head. She needed a little downtime, she needed to chill, but she didn't need to do it at Tom's. "I don't think so," she said. "I think I'm gonna head home. Do you mind?" she asked, assuming Jade would go with her and feeling bad about wrecking her good time, but really, Jade didn't need to be hanging out with a bunch of older guys, either. *Oh great, now I'm even starting to think like Ellie,* she thought.

"No worries. Just take these, and leave it in the driveway," Jade said, handing her the car keys.

And before Lola could even respond, Jade was already walking down the street with Ben and his four stoner friends.

chapter twenty-seven

"See, the main difference between diving and surfing is the control issue. Like diving is all about perfect form, being in complete control of your body, and getting the moves just exactly right. But in surfing, yeah, okay, you have to be skilled enough to control your board as well as your body, but there's not just one specific way of doing it. Everyone brings their own unique experience to it. No one can tell you how to surf a wave. It's, like, as individual as your fingerprint," Chris said.

"That's the *only* difference?" Anne laughed, leaning into him. "'Cause I can think of like a million more."

"I said it's the *main* difference, not the *only* difference." He smiled.

They were sitting on her front lawn. Chris had his hands wrapped around his knees and Anne had her long, tanned legs splayed out in front of her, and they were both enjoying each other's company so much, it was pretty obvious neither of them wanted it to end.

They'd spent the entire day together, but there were still so many things to talk about. And Anne realized she hadn't been this happy since she'd left Connecticut. Then, when she looked up and saw Chris smiling at her, she was pretty sure she hadn't been this happy then, either.

"Maybe we should get a pizza and rent a movie," he said, stretching out his legs and lying back on the grass.

"After two tacos, two Cokes, nachos, Spanish rice, and refried beans?" she said, wrapping her arms around her full belly. "I don't think so. I'll burst if I eat anything else." She laughed.

"You're right," he said, sitting up abruptly and looking embarrassed. "I should bail. You're probably getting pretty sick of me by now." He looked embarrassed.

"I said I was *full*." She smiled. "I didn't say I was *bored*."

And then, mustering every last ounce of courage (since she'd never been one to make the first move), she closed her eyes, leaned in, and kissed him.

chapter twenty-eight

Ellie had been painting for hours, and now her fingers felt stiff, her back ached from standing for so long, and the light was beginning to fade so fast she could barely see her canvas. She flexed her fingers, trying to warm them up and get them limber again, then leaned over, opened her paint box, and began loading up her supplies.

She loved going to Treasure Island Park and being surrounded by all the other artists. She didn't know any of them personally, and most days there were several she'd never seen before, but there were always a few regulars she looked forward to seeing. Like the older woman with the long gray braid who painted with such bold, abstract strokes that Ellie couldn't tell if it was supposed to be the scenery in front of her or a more complicated landscape that existed only in her head. And the big, burly guy who looked like a Hell's Angel but painted in the most fragile, delicate, precise way. And then there were the wannabe bohemians, with their designer tote bags and expensive white linen shirts, who scowled in frustration when the task turned out to be much more difficult than they'd imagined. Ellie had watched more than a few of those types pack it up after ten minutes and head back to their suite at the Montage. For some people, she guessed, it was more the romantic idea of painting than the actual reality of it that was so intriguing.

Ellie had been coming here for years, but nobody knew about it. Nobody even knew she could paint—well, except for her mother, who had encouraged her daughter's natural artistic abilities ever since she was a small child, often walking her through the many downtown Laguna Beach galleries while Dean was at school.

One of Ellie's most cherished memories was of the time she and her mother visited the Getty Museum in Los Angeles, just weeks before her death. They'd spent the entire day there, exploring the grounds, enjoying a long lunch, and staring in wonder at some of the finest works of art. Ellie's mom had been thin and bald and easily exhausted from the months of chemo she'd endured, but with a colorful silk scarf tied around her head and her vintage jeans belted tightly around her waist, she'd grabbed Ellie's hand and forged ahead, determined to ignore the curious stares of others and just enjoy her last days.

But Ellie's father knew nothing of her painting. He had so little appreciation for art that Ellie was sure he could never understand how important it was to her. And even though her friends would definitely be supportive, the truth was, it was kind of nice to have something totally private that belonged only to her.

She was pretty good, too. Or at least she suspected she might be. Every now and then one of the regulars would pass by and say, "Looks nice." Or, "You really captured those wildflowers."

Of course, it was possible that they were just being kind, but there was a small part of her, deep down inside, that was convinced there really was something there.

The funny thing was that her secret place was just a short five-minute drive from Laguna Cove, yet nobody would ever think to look for her here. Which made it all the more perfect.

It was like being able to hide in plain view.

• • •

Driving through the Laguna Cove gate, she was waving at the guard just as her cell phone rang. Not recognizing the number on the display, she contemplated letting it go to voice mail, but Ellie was nothing if not dependable, and reliable, and she just wasn't capable of not answering a ringing phone.

"Hello?" she said, cautiously.

"Ellie? It's Duncan."

"Oh, hey." She rolled her eyes, wishing she'd never picked up. Oh well, she'd have to tell him sooner or later, so it may as well be now.

"Sorry to keep calling, I guess I was just a little worried about you. You didn't sound so hot this morning," he said, laughing nervously.

"I wasn't," she admitted, turning onto her street. "But I'm better now."

"Good. Um, Ellie, I was wondering." He paused.

Oh God, here it comes, she thought, cringing as though something was about to fly through the windshield and smack her in the face.

"Would you want to go out sometime? I mean, like to dinner or something?" He sounded so nervous, it made her feel awful.

"Duncan, I . . ." She hesitated. She'd turned down plenty of guys before so what was the big deal now? *Maybe it was because you totally made out with him, and led him on,* she thought, shaking her head at her own lack of control. "I just think . . ." She slowed down as she passed by Anne's house, which was right next to hers.

Oh my God! Is that Anne and Chris? MAKING OUT ON THE FRONT LAWN? She adjusted her rearview mirror, just to make sure.

"You just think what?" Duncan asked.

"Sorry, what?" Ellie said, pulling into her driveway, completely distracted, yet still gawking at the house next door. Apparently things were moving along a lot quicker than even she had imagined possible.

"I just asked you out, and you were about to answer me," he said. He was beginning to sound annoyed.

"Oh, right. Sorry." She couldn't help it. She had to look again. It was dark, but it was definitely them. They'd even lit up the motion sensor lights. Which meant they were both moving around. *Oh, God.*

"Listen, if you're not interested, it's totally cool," he said, definitely sounding like he didn't actually think it was so cool.

"Um, Duncan? Actually I'd love to go out with you," she said, shocked to hear herself actually saying the words, but somehow it just felt right. Then, taking control, as always, she asked, "So what are you doing tonight?"

chapter twenty-nine

Lola sat at the dinner table with her mother and *Abuela. So much for time alone, lying in bed, wallowing in heartache,* she thought.

"So, did he call you yet?" *Abuela* asked, eyes shining with anticipation.

Oh, great, now all the generations are in on it. Well, that just wouldn't do. "Who?" Lola asked innocently, cutting into the grilled sea bass on her plate.

"The boy! What's his name?" She looked at her daughter-in-law.

"Diego. Diego Martinez," Lola's mom said, looking right at Lola.

"So?" *Abuela* nodded, as though ready to hear the world's greatest love story.

But Lola just shook her head. "Nope, not a peep," she told her, reaching for her glass of iced tea. She wasn't a very good liar, even though she found herself doing it more and more these days.

"I can't believe this! I've never heard of such a thing!" *Abuela* said, sounding personally affronted that the very desirable Diego had dissed her precious granddaughter. "Who does he think he is?"

Lola looked up to see *Abuela* glaring at her daughter-in-law, as though it was *her* fault he hadn't called, and she knew she had to say something. Their relationship was strained enough as it is. "I had my phone on 'vibrate' all day, so maybe I missed it." She shrugged, hoping this compromise would be good enough to hold them over until she could think of something better.

"You kids and your cell phones," *Abuela* said, shaking her head.

Add that to the list of modern conveniences that aren't to be trusted, Lola thought. *Along with microwaves, computers, iPods*—although she sure learned to love that flat-screen TV.

"I really think it would be good if you two could meet before the cotillion next month. I think he'd make the perfect escort for your debut," her mother said.

My debut? Like I'm an actress or a novelist? Lola had no interest in cotillions, high society, or just about anything else her mother held dear. Where was her father when she needed him? *Oh, that's right. Working, as always.* She shook her head. She'd had enough—enough dinner and enough of this conversation. "Well, it's really not up to me if he calls or not, now is it?" she said, looking from her mother to her grandmother. Then, getting up, she excused herself from the table and headed down the hall.

When she got to her room she stripped off her clothes, slipped into some red silk pajamas, and crawled between the sheets. It was just seven forty-five on a Saturday night and she was already in bed. That's what her pathetic life had come to.

She rolled onto her side and stared at her creamy white walls, wondering what *he* was doing, and if he felt sad, too.

Or if, maybe, he'd barely even thought about her. Maybe he'd already moved on.

chapter thirty

Jade was lying on the couch, with her bare feet propped up on a pile of overstuffed cushions while her head rested on Ben's lap as he raked his fingers through her long, curly hair. Everything about being with Ben just felt so calm, peaceful, and free, and she thought how lucky she was to have a guy friend like this. One that you could just hang with, and not have to have it get all romantic and complicated. She hated when relationships got complicated.

"My dad's driving down tomorrow," Ben said, gazing down at her and rubbing her temples with his thumbs. "He wants to have lunch, so he can explain his side, but I'm not so sure I want to hear it."

"You should go. At least listen to what he has to say," Jade said, looking up at him.

"I don't know." He shook his head. "I think he's just gonna give me a bunch of crap about how hard he's got it. Even though he's the one who chose to leave." He looked at her.

Jade just nodded. They'd talked about his parents' divorce before and it was basically the same old story. Dad has an affair, Mom finds out, Dad vacates, taking most of the money, Mom works two jobs to provide the basics, and the kids feel abandoned by everyone. *Why can't people just be nicer to each other?* she thought. *What's with all the greed?*

"It's your call," she said, unwilling to judge his decisions. "But if you give him a chance and he fails, well then, at least you took the high road, right?"

Ben shrugged. "It's just, everything is so much more complicated now. My mom's totally overworked and depressed, and I don't know, sometimes I just feel like maybe I should bail on school and get a job so I can help her. Or maybe I should just move out. You know, go somewhere and do my own thing, so she won't have to worry about supporting me anymore."

Jade sat up abruptly and looked at him. "You can't quit school! That's like, a one-way ticket to Loserville! I mean, who's that gonna help? Certainly not your mother, and definitely not you," she said, hoping he was just being dramatic and wasn't actually serious.

Ben gave her a surprised look. "Okay, so tell me how you really feel."

"I'm serious. And don't look at me like that. I'm actually very practical." She smiled.

Ben glanced around the room and then back at Jade. "Hey, you wanna bail?" he asked, standing up abruptly.

"What? Now?" she asked, wondering why he was suddenly acting so anxious and strange. Just five minutes ago everything had been so mellow and perfect.

"Listen, you can hang if you want, but I really need to get some fresh air," he said, heading straight for the door.

"Hey, wait up! I'll go with you," she said, grabbing her purse and hurrying to catch up with him.

chapter thirty-one

"I'm just not sure how much longer I can get away with this," Lola said, climbing out of Ellie's car and reaching for her book bag. "I mean, he's left two messages now and it's just a matter of time before my mom finds out I'm ignoring his calls."

"How will she know?" Ellie asked, clicking her car alarm and glancing around nervously for Duncan. Not seeing him anywhere, she relaxed and focused her attention back on her friend.

"We're talking about *my mom.* She has ways of finding out *everything.* I swear, sometimes I wonder if she has a secret life as a spy or something." Lola laughed, half joking but half serious as well.

"Have you talked to Jade?" Ellie asked. "I tried calling her a few times on Sunday, but I couldn't find her."

"Haven't seen her." Lola shook her head. "I surfed a little in the afternoon with Chris and Anne; then we all went for smoothies at the Shake Shack."

Ellie stopped, right in the middle of the student parking lot, and stared at Lola. "You hung out with Chris and Anne?" she asked, feeling her face go all red but unable to stop it.

"Yeah." Lola looked more than a little confused by Ellie's reaction.

"Are they like, *a couple now*? I mean, like boyfriend and girlfriend?" Ellie felt her throat go all tight.

"I'm not sure I want to put a label on it," Lola said, tugging on Ellie's arm. "Come on, you're gonna make us late."

Ellie reluctantly followed Lola. "I just don't get what you all see in this Anne chick. I mean, what's so special about her? She seems pretty ordinary to me, yet you guys act like she's *so great*."

"She's actually pretty nice. And I really think you should cut her some slack, give her a chance."

"I don't trust her." Ellie looked right at Lola. "And I'm not sure you should, either."

"What's that supposed to mean?" Lola asked, sounding slightly annoyed.

"I mean, what do we really know about her? *Nothing!* And if you think about it, it's like, she just came here out of nowhere and already she's dating Chris, learning to surf, and you guys are all totally falling for it! You're totally hanging out with her!"

"It's called making friends and fitting in. And you really need to relax. Just think how she feels. Having to move all the way across the country and trying to fit in somewhere new. *Especially* here! People around here can be pretty exclusive, you know," Lola said, shooting her friend a look.

"What's that supposed to mean?" Ellie asked, folding her arms in front of her and sounding really defensive.

But Lola just shrugged.

"Well, I'm only saying you shouldn't go around trusting *everyone*. And I'm more than a little hurt that you could find the time to surf with *her* and not with *me*," Ellie said.

Lola took a deep, exasperated breath. "Look, for one thing, it's not like it was o' dark hundred, like when you're ready to surf. It was a normal time, for normal people. And for another, you seriously need to lighten up."

"Normal people?" Ellie just stood there looking at her. She couldn't believe Lola had just said that.

"Look, I'm sorry. But I've got my own problems right now and

I'm not going to do this with you, okay? Just try to loosen up a little, would you?" she said, turning and heading toward her locker.

Ellie stood there and watched her walk away. She knew she was acting crazy, possessive, out of control, and ridiculously jealous, but the problem was, she didn't know how to stop.

"Hey, El," Duncan said, approaching her with this huge grin on his face.

Ellie took one look at that smile and felt her heart sink. It was her fault he was so happy today. If she hadn't asked him out Saturday night, then he wouldn't be approaching her now. Well, he might be, but not like that. Not like he expected something. "Hey," she said, giving him a tight half smile.

"You have AP English now, right?" he said, as though he was all ready to walk her to class.

"Yeah, but I have to go to the restroom first, so you really don't have to wait for me. I'll see you at lunch, okay?" she said, feeling bad about the disappointed look on his face, but happy about the four-hour cushion between first period and lunch.

She headed toward the bathroom until she was sure he was no longer watching, then turned and went to class. She felt bad about blowing him off like that, because the truth was she *did* have fun with him Saturday night. They'd gone to dinner at a cozy little Thai restaurant and then they'd walked around some of the galleries in downtown Laguna, both surprising each other with their appreciation of art. And when he'd dropped her off at her door, she'd even let him kiss her again. And this time she was completely sober. *And,* she had to admit, it was pretty nice.

But still, he wasn't Chris. And by the time she was back in her room, changing for bed, she'd come to her senses, deciding that she definitely had to cut it off as soon as possible.

chapter thirty-two

Anne had initially set out to get back at Ellie, so she was pretty surprised when she found herself liking Chris as much as she did. *But what's not to like?* He was cute, smart, funny, sweet—she really couldn't find anything wrong with him. And the fact that he'd given her a ride to school (sparing her from being chauffeured by Jake), and then even walked her to class, kissing her briefly just outside the door, made her feel so happy and dreamy, *nothing* could get her down.

Until she saw Ellie glaring at her from across the room.

Anne just didn't get it. All of Ellie's friends were great, but no matter how hard she tried, Ellie refused to give her a chance. And Anne was getting tired of trying. Yet she also couldn't stand to keep things the way they were.

Taking her seat, she glanced at Lola and Ellie and waved. Lola smiled and waved back, but Ellie turned her head abruptly and stared straight ahead at the chalkboard, even though it was completely blank. The whole thing was so ridiculous that Anne almost felt sorry for her. Almost.

After roll call, Mr. Campbell leaned on the edge of his desk and, opening his book, said, "Anne, would you read the beginning of chapter two for us?"

They were reading *The Great Gatsby,* one of Anne's very favorite books. She loved it so much, she'd even rented the movie version once. But even though Robert Redford used to be a complete and total hottie, it just didn't compare to the book. And now, even though she'd read the story many times before, she finally felt like she could totally relate to Gatsby. Because now she knew just how hard it was to try to fit in.

She just hoped things would work out a little better for *her* than they did for *him.*

She cleared her throat and began reading. When she was well into the third paragraph, Mr. Campbell said, "Okay stop right there. Can anyone tell me the significance of Dr. T. J. Eckleburg?"

"Well," Anne said, feeling excited that she knew the answer and not realizing Ellie already had her hand in the air. "He symbolizes God, and the valley of ashes is like, purgatory, because later in the book . . ."

"Excuse me, Mr. Campbell, but we haven't exactly finished the book, have we? We're only on chapter two. And maybe some of us don't want to know how it ends just yet," Ellie said, glaring at Anne and shaking her head.

Anne looked at Mr. Campbell, her face turning red.

"Well, you have a point, Ellie. Though, without giving away too much, you'll see as you continue reading that the eyes are symbolic of God, and the valley does become a place filled with violence and grief. Now Harrison, would you continue reading where Anne left off?"

And as Anne listened to Harrison read, she looked across the room at Ellie. *That was the last time you get to humiliate me,* she thought as their eyes briefly met.

chapter thirty-three

By Thursday, when Ben still hadn't shown up at school, Jade was starting to freak. "You guys, what if he really did run away?" she asked, hugging her knees against her chest and shaking her head. "I have to find him."

"Whoa, wait a second. I mean, why don't you just call his house and see if he's home?" Ellie said, squeezing salt water out of her hair and twisting it into a bun.

"Thanks, Kojak." Jade rolled her eyes. She loved Ellie, yeah, but sometimes she so didn't get it. "Believe me, I already tried that. Nobody answers."

"But you said his mom works two jobs, so she's probably never there," Lola said. "Did you go by his house?"

"Nobody home. Even Tom and those guys don't know where he is. You guys so don't get it. I'm really worried, and I feel like I've got to do something. I can't just sit around here and wait," she said, getting up from her towel.

"You're right, I don't get it. Are you guys like, dating?" Ellie asked, putting on SPF 30 even though the sun would soon be fading.

"No, we're not dating, but he is my friend and I care about him. Just like I'd care if it were one of you," Jade said, shaking her head. Okay, maybe they'd seen her try to rescue one too many strays before, but this time it wasn't some lost kitten, or lonely rabbit. This time, it was serious.

"Well, maybe he's at his dad's," Lola said cautiously.

"Doubtful." Jade stood in front of her friends, curls blowing like crazy in the breeze. "He's pretty pissed at him right now, so it's not likely they're spending any quality time together. I just don't get why he hasn't called me."

"Typical. The ones you want to call never do." Lola shook her head sadly. Then, noticing her friends were staring, she said, "What? It's totally true."

"There's a guy out there who hasn't called you?" Ellie asked, laughing.

"You'd be surprised." Lola shrugged ruefully.

"Uh, hello? Back to me and my crisis," Jade said, waving her hands around to get their attention. Did they think this was a *joke*?

"Sorry, Jade. Go on," Ellie said; Lola nodded.

"Okay, so the other night after we left Tom's we took a ride up into the canyon, and we parked the car and just talked for hours. He's really upset about his parents splitting up, and he's not entirely rational right now. He was even talking about dropping out of school and stuff. I tried to explain how crazy that would be, but he was kind of messed up and I guess I wasn't able to really communicate with him like I wanted. He left me a message Sunday night, and that's the last I heard."

"Well, what'd he say in the message?" Lola asked.

"Nothing, really. But at the end he said, 'See you Monday.'"

"I don't think you should get involved, Jade. I'm sorry, but I don't. You've done everything you can, and I'm sure his mom has a handle on it. You can't save everyone, you know," Ellie said gently.

"Maybe not, El. But the least I can do is try." Jade grabbed her towel and headed toward the beach stairs.

"Jade! Wait, where you going?" Lola called after her.

"Back to Tom's. I have to start somewhere," she said.

chapter thirty-four

Anne was loving her new life—*What's not to love,* she thought. She had a great house with a private beach, she'd made good friends, and she had the most amazing boyfriend *ever*.

At least she thought he was her boyfriend. It's not like the actual words were ever spoken or anything. But they did spend a lot of time together, and she was pretty sure he was beginning to like her just as much as she liked him.

Oh yeah, and she'd finally found a sport she was as passionate about as diving. At first, she admitted, learning to surf was all about spending time with Chris. But now she loved it so much she found herself getting up early in the morning and heading out on her own. Usually she ran into Ellie, but Anne had finally learned to ignore her. There was nothing else she could do. She'd tried being quiet, she'd tired being nice—nothing worked. And it seemed like the more she hung with Chris and the better she got at surfing, the more Ellie glared at her. But that was Ellie's problem, and she was just gonna have to get used to coexisting in the same neighborhood, the same school, and with the same group of friends. Because now that Anne had found her place, she wasn't about to budge.

In fact, Anne was getting so good at surfing that just the other day Chris had mentioned Surf Fest to her.

"I can't compete! I'm just a beginner, I'll make a total fool of myself!" she'd said, shaking her head vehemently.

"True. There's no way you'll win, since there will be people there who grew up on surfboards. But it's such a cool contest, and it's open to everyone. If nothing else, just think of it as good practice, and a chance for you to get out there and see what it's like," he told her.

"Why can't I just go as an observer?" she'd asked. "You know, sit back and watch from the comfort of my very own beach chair?"

"That's not how it works. No one learns from just watching. You have to experience it to really know it. Besides, don't you miss competing?" he'd asked, leaning over to kiss her.

They were out in the water, sitting on their boards. "I have to think about it," she'd said, leaning toward him.

But ever since he'd brought up the idea, she'd been thinking about it more and more. He was right. She did miss competing. She missed the preparation before a big event, the nervous stomach the night before, and the thrill of scoring the highest at the end of the day. Okay, so she probably wouldn't be scoring the highest at Surf Fest. She probably wouldn't even come close. But hey, she had to start *somewhere*.

She opened the door to her giant walk-in closet, staring at the racks of clothes and wondering what she should wear. The wrap party for her dad's film was tonight and she'd invited all of her friends. She had a feeling that even Ellie might show. Not that she'd invited her, but she had invited Duncan and it kind of seemed like they were dating or something. Actually, it was hard to tell exactly what their deal was. While it was obvious that Duncan was totally into it, Ellie on the other hand always seemed like she was just along for the ride. But Anne knew better than to discuss it with Jade and Lola. Those three went way back, and Anne had no doubt where their loyalties lay.

But it would be a big party, with a ton of people, so she was sure it would be just as easy to ignore Ellie there as it was at school.

Slipping into her favorite jeans, a beaded cami, and some silver flats, she grabbed her purse and was heading for the living room to wait for Chris when Jake walked in.

"Oh my God, you scared me," Anne said, not expecting to see him. "What're you doing here? Aren't you going to the party?"

"I had to pick up some stuff for your dad. I'm headed up that way in a little while if you need a lift," he offered.

"No thanks, I've got a ride. You're not wearing that, are you?" she asked, realizing she sounded like a bitch, *but still.* Even by laid-back Hollywood standards, she doubted he should be showing up in his usual old shredded flip-flops, faded board shorts, and a holey T-shirt.

"Jeez, you're brutal," he said, laughing good-naturedly. "Of course I'm not wearing this. I do have other clothes, you know." He shook his head and walked down the hall toward the spare room where he kept some of his stuff.

Anne sat on the couch, trying to focus on the TV and not on her watch. It was so unlike Chris to be late, and now nearly twenty minutes had passed since he was supposed to pick her up. She went over to the window, pulled the drapes back, and checked the driveway—nothing, *nada. Should I call him?* she wondered. *Or would that seem overbearing? If he shows up right now, should I act cool, like I hadn't even noticed he was way late? Or should I stand my ground until I get an explanation?*

She shook her head and went back to the couch. What *was* with her? She'd never acted so ridiculous over a guy before. Or had she? She tried remembering what she'd been like when she first started going out with Justin, but so much had happened since then, the memory was foggy at best. Oh God, maybe she was turning into her mother—seemingly cool and confident on the outside, but a total emotional dependent on the inside. It was too horrible to think about. And it was stupid. She should just pick up the phone and find out what was taking him so long.

The second she grabbed the receiver, it rang, startling her so much she dropped it on the floor. "Hello?" she said, frantically flipping it right side up.

"Anne?" It was Chris.

"Hey, where are you?" she asked.

"Um, I'm really sorry, but I'm running late," he said. "Is there any way I can meet you there?"

"Are you serious?" she asked, sitting on the arm of the couch. "I mean, is everything okay?"

"Yeah, everything's cool. It's just that I'm over at Ellie's and we're behind schedule, and I don't want you to miss out because of me."

"You're at *Ellie's*?" She could feel the panic rise in her throat. "What are you guys doing?"

"We're lab partners, and we started a new project today," he said, as though that explained everything.

Well, maybe it did. But like a typical guy, he was missing all the subtext! She imagined Ellie sitting next to him, listening in on the whole conversation, while a big fat evil smile spread slowly across her face . . .

"But you're still coming, right?" she said, trying to sound cool and not needy, since there was nothing cool about being needy.

"Definitely. See you in a few?"

"Um, yeah, great," she said, hanging up and feeling totally shell-shocked.

"You're still here?" Jake said, walking down the hallway. His hair was still damp from the shower and combed away from his face, and he was dressed in a pair of vintage-wash denim jeans and a shirt with blue, green, yellow, and white stripes, untucked with the sleeves rolled up. His feet were bare and he was carrying his shoes.

"Yeah," Anne said, looking at him and swallowing hard. What was wrong with her? One minute she was getting all freaked out over Chris, and the next she was practically drooling at how well Jake cleaned up. It was ridiculous. *She* was ridiculous. And it meant nothing! He'd just startled her, that's all. "Chris can't make it 'til later, so do you think you could give me a ride?" She bit down on her lower lip nervously and tried not to stare at him.

"I've got a full tank of gas and the passenger seat is empty, so follow me." He smiled and headed for the front door.

chapter thirty-five

Lola was in her room, standing in front of her mirror, completely hating her life. Wouldn't you just know it—on the one night she was finally getting over being dumped, finally looking forward to breaking loose and having a little fun with her friends, her mother had arranged for her to meet Diego. She had just gotten home from school and walked into the kitchen to grab a snack when her mother had totally ambushed her.

"I've arranged for you and Diego to meet at the party tonight," she said, smiling brightly.

Lola stuck her head in the fridge and counted to ten, but it didn't really help. "Mom, I don't want to meet him. I just wanna hang with my friends," she told her, grabbing an apple and turning to face her.

"'Want to,' Lola. Not 'wanna.' And Diego is going to be there anyway, so you may as well get to know him."

"But why?" Lola looked at her mom. She felt like stomping her feet and throwing a tantrum like a two-year-old. Because that's how they made her feel—like she was totally at their mercy, and had absolutely no control over her own life.

"I think you two are going to really hit it off. *And,* I might add,

I happen to know you've been ignoring his messages. I did not raise you to be so rude, Lola," she said, giving her a stern look. "Now, are you riding with us? Or are you going with your friends?"

"*You guys* are going, too?" *Oh, that's just great. Why don't they all just double-date? Wouldn't that be fun!*

"Of course we're going," her mother said impatiently.

"Then I'm getting a ride with my friends. I'm sure you, Dad, Diego, and I will have plenty of time to hang at the party," Lola said, taking a bite of her apple, stomping down the hall, and slamming her bedroom door, not caring for one second what the consequences of *that* might be. *It's not like it can get any worse,* she thought.

And now she had the fun task of finding something cool enough to wear to a glitzy Hollywood party that her parents would also approve of. *Talk about impossible.*

"Maybe you can, like, have a major blowout, but no one gets hurt," Lola said. She was sitting next to Duncan in his dad's brand-new Lexus convertible. Lola knew he'd scored the car to impress Ellie, so it was too bad she'd canceled on him at the very last minute.

"I don't think my dad would be too cool with that," Duncan said, glancing over at her briefly. "You probably shouldn't even wish things like that; we're just getting off the freeway, for God's sake." He shook his head.

"Easy for you to say. You have no idea what I'm in for. No idea of what my mom is even capable of."

"How bad can it be?" Duncan asked. "Is he like, a big geek or something?"

"Probably," Lola laughed. "But that's not the point. It's all about *information,* and how my parents are steadily infiltrating every single corner of my life. And if I'm not careful, then the Lolita that you know and love will quietly disappear, and all that remains will be Lola. And everyone knows what a bore she is." She rolled her eyes and looked out the window.

"I kind of like Lola," Duncan said, looking at her and smiling.

"You would," she laughed. Then, staring in disbelief as they pulled into the parking lot, she shrieked, "Oh my God, don't turn here, just keep going, keep going, oh no, it's too late, they've made us." Lola sighed and rolled her eyes. "Well, it's been nice knowing ya, Duncan." She climbed out of the car, waving reluctantly at her parents, who were standing next to the valet stand, obviously waiting for her arrival. "Oh, and Duncan, you will *never, ever* get to be my getaway driver, should I need one someday. You failed miserably at this little operation. Still, I would advise you to run fast and far from the crazy Latina in the overpriced dress over there," she said, pointing at her mother, completely oblivious to the fact that the miniskirt she'd worn in rebellion had folded up in such a way that you could almost see, well, *France*.

"Here's Lola now," her mother said, arranging her lips into a tight perfunctory smile while her disapproving eyes focused on Lola's hiked-up skirt, tiny cardigan, tinier tank top, and little ballet flats. "This is Diego," she said, as though presenting a masterpiece.

"Hey," Lola said, noticing his precisely styled and gelled dark brown hair—which he'd probably spent the last hour getting to look like he hadn't thought about it in weeks—and the perfectly groomed brows that put her own to shame. And was that? Could it be? Was he actually wearing just the tiniest hint of Smith's Rosebud Salve on his bottom lip?

"Hey." He smiled, showing off his perfect white game-show-host teeth.

He must be a model/actor, she thought. *He's too perfect to be anything else.*

"Well, I'm sure you two have lots to talk about!" her mother singsonged. "So we'll be on our way. Have fun!" She smiled tightly, while discreetly grabbing the hem of Lola's miniskirt and yanking it down as far as it would go.

chapter thirty-six

Okay, this was not at all how she imagined it would be. All day at school, when Anne had been playing the movie version of the party in her head (instead of listening to her teachers drone on and on about subjects that just couldn't compare), she had cast herself in the starring role, as the girl with all the best lines. She'd pictured herself dressed in an outfit she didn't actually own but had seen recently in *Teen Vogue*, making brilliant, outrageous comments that would make Chris laugh so hard, he would look her right in the eye and say, "I just love you, Anne." And then, stopping to catch his breath, he would reach for her hand, look deep into her eyes, and say, "Really. I think I'm falling in love with you." Then, as the camera zoomed in for a close-up of the lovely young couple embracing, the background music would swell into some really sappy love song (possibly titled "Anne's Theme"), which would make the entire audience reach for a tissue, gently dabbing at their eyes while smiling through their tears.

But not once, in her wildest fantasies, did this particular movie open with her getting ditched first by her date/almost boyfriend, who was working on a science project (she hoped it wasn't a *biology* experiment) with the Villain (every good screenplay had one). And then ditched a second time by her dad's little helper (who, for one insane and vulnerable moment in the living room, she had actually thought was quite gorgeous).

It was like the second they'd walked in the restaurant, Jake had grabbed a glass of champagne from a passing waiter, thrust it at Anne, and then hightailed it to the other side of the room, as far away as possible, leaving her standing in the corner, all alone, sipping champagne and looking like the world's biggest reject.

She pulled her cell phone out of her purse and checked to see if Chris had called and she'd somehow failed to hear it ring. But the second she glanced at the blank screen, she felt embarrassed for even looking. Because even though that very same act was probably being played out at that exact same moment by millions of girls across the globe, that didn't make it any less pathetic.

Shaking her head at her own lameness, she took another sip of champagne and looked across the room to see Jade and Ben. *Finally, someone to talk to,* she thought.

"Jade!" she yelled, waving her hands around like a desperate rescue victim, beyond caring about just how far from cool she was straying. "Hey, how long have you been here?" she asked, looking from Jade to Ben and noticing his eyes were all bloodshot as usual.

"Just arrived. Did we miss anything?" Jade asked.

"No, I've just been really busy warming up this wall." She shrugged. "I guess the big stars don't arrive until later. It's mostly just crew right now."

"Hey, where'd you get the bubbles?" Ben asked, looking at Anne's glass.

"One of the waiters. They're all over the place. And it's an open bar."

"Ben, maybe we should just hang for a while," Jade said, giving him a pleading look.

"I'm hanging." He looked at her and smiled. "I'd just rather be hanging with a drink in my hand. Anybody need anything?" he asked, heading toward the bar.

Anne shook her head. She knew she should just stick with the one glass—she didn't want to end up alone, embarrassed, and drunk.

Jade shook her head and watched him walk away. "I just don't know what else to do," she whispered, the second he was out of earshot.

"What do you mean?" Anne looked at her.

"Well, it's like, I'm totally trying to be a good friend, and I'm really trying to help, but it's like he doesn't even care what happens to him. Not to mention that he still won't tell me where he was all week, and he gets totally annoyed when I ask. I never should have brought him here. I don't think Ben and an open bar is such a good combination," she said, looking really worried.

Anne watched Ben push his way to the front of the line. "I'm sure it'll all be fine," she assured her. But deep down inside, she wondered if that was really true.

chapter thirty-seven

"So," Lola said, tapping her water bottle against Diego's. "It's *so great* to finally meet you."

But Diego just looked at her and smiled. "Is it?" he asked, raising his eyebrows.

"Well, yeah. I mean, I've heard so much about you, and stuff," Lola said, trying to come off as interested and enthusiastic even though she could feel herself losing steam. Now that he was directly in front of her she was determined to just play it out—by being nice and saying all the right things. Though he wasn't making it very easy for her. And something about the look on his face told her he wasn't buying her act for one measly second.

"Is that why you didn't return my calls? Because you'd heard *too much* about me? Or were you just playing hard to get?" he asked, giving her an amused look.

Lola focused on the white linen tablecloth, running her fingernails over it and wondering what to say next. For the first time in her entire life, she was completely clueless about how to act around a guy. Normally it was so instinctive with her, but this time it was totally different. And she wasn't sure if it was because her parents were involved in the setup or what. But it almost seemed like he was toying with her, and that he wasn't all that interested. Which was even more unusual. Had getting dumped made her unconsciously send out some kind of crazy pheromone that repelled men? Was that even *possible*? Or had she finally met the one guy who genuinely had no interest in her? And if so, then didn't that mean she was destined to fall in love with him?

But Lola was still dealing with lost love, and this guy, gorgeous as he was, just didn't seem like he could inspire those kinds of feelings in her. There was something different about him. Something she just couldn't put her finger on. "Um, well, you're right. It was really rude of me to ignore your message. And I'm sorry," she said, looking up at him briefly. "My parents don't exactly know this, but I was really into someone, and he just dumped me like the day before you called. So I guess I wasn't exactly into meeting someone new. In fact, you seem really nice and all, and you're definitely really good-looking and stuff, and your outfit is like *so hot,* but I have to be honest with you, I just can't date you right now. I mean, not just you, but *anyone.* I just need to be alone for a while. I hope you can understand," she said, focusing intently on the tablecloth and hoping he was taking it okay. She was afraid to look at him. She couldn't stand hurting anyone's feelings. "I mean, I don't want to lead you on, or anything."

When she finally did look up, Diego's dark brown eyes were all watery and his knuckles were turning white as he gripped the edge of the table. "Lola, stop. Please," he said, laughing so hard he was doubled over.

Well, it's not like she'd meant to be funny! She was just trying to let him down easy! She sat there staring at him, eyes narrowed, arms folded across her chest, waiting for an explanation.

When he finally calmed down, he looked at her and said, "Please, don't worry about it, okay? You're not exactly my type."

Not his type? What's that supposed to mean? And who the hell does he think he is, laughing at me like that? "Oh, well fine," she said, shrugging like she didn't care, like she wasn't the least bit offended. "I mean, I don't exactly get why that's *so damn funny,* but obviously you do." She stood up and adjusted her miniskirt, which had risen up again. She'd never been so humiliated. She was going to find her mother and make her pay for this.

"Lola, sit down please," he said.

"Um, no thanks. Although it's been a *real pleasure* meeting you." She rolled her eyes sarcastically.

"Lola, I'm sorry, really. Look, I didn't mean to offend you," he said, looking at her and motioning for her to sit. "There's a very good reason for what I just said."

She looked at him, hands on hips, waiting. *Oh, this ought to be good.*

"I'm gay." He looked at her and shrugged.

"You're *gay*?" she repeated, raising her eyebrows and giving him a skeptical look, wondering if he was just saying that. But as she slowly sank back down onto her chair, she once again noticed the perfect brows, the buffed nails, and the fact that he wasn't flirting with her. *Of course,* she thought. *Now it all makes sense.*

He leaned toward her and smiled, revealing a row of perfectly straight white teeth. "So tell me," he said. "Where did you get that outfit? It's genius."

chapter thirty-eight

Anne's eyes had been glued to the door for the past hour and a half, and she was really starting to hate herself for it. Here she was, at a wrap party full of some of the hottest stars (well, maybe not the *hottest*), and all she could think about was Chris and Ellie. It was totally pathetic, and she was really starting to get on her own nerves.

Jade had taken off in search of Ben, who had never quite made it back from the bar. *What on earth does a cute, optimistic, happy girl like Jade see in a big loser like Ben,* she wondered. Yeah, he had his share of problems, and Anne had firsthand knowledge of just how awful it can be when your parents decide to split. But it didn't really seem like he was even trying to make it better. If anything, it almost seemed like he was using it as an excuse to mess up.

Then there were Lola and Diego. They were sitting right across the table from her, but they were so incredibly wrapped up in each other, it was like they were having their own private party in the midst of this big one. Diego seemed nice enough, and he was certainly gorgeous, but it was still kind of weird to see Lola so worked up over someone her mom had set her up with. She'd always made it sound like her mom could introduce her to Orlando Bloom and she would find a valid reason to reject him. But now, against all odds, there they were, in their own little world, heads close together, talking a mile a minute. Go figure.

Then there was the situation with her dad. As if it wasn't weird enough to be hanging at the same party and being forced to realize that he was way more popular (and from the looks of it, having way more fun) than her, so far both times she'd run into him there'd been this mysterious pretty petite redhead permanently attached to his right arm.

Okay, maybe she wasn't all that mysterious, since her dad had introduced her as Brooke, and had also mentioned something about her working in makeup or wardrobe. *Or was it set design?* Anne couldn't specifically remember because she was way too freaked out by the fact that there even *was* a Brooke in his life. A Brooke who seemed way too comfortable hanging all over her dad and knew way too much about Anne. Were they a *couple*? And if so, why had her dad failed to mention it? It's not like Anne wanted her dad to be alone for the rest of his life or anything; she just wasn't sure she was ready for him to start dating just yet. Especially since she'd just started spending time with him again, and she really didn't feel like sharing.

Thinking about her dad always made her think about her mom. And now she wondered if she wasn't turning out to be exactly like her—and not in a good way. Her mom had obsessed over some guy to the point where she'd jeopardized her entire family, and now Anne was sitting here doing the same kind of thing.

Here she was, sitting at an overdecorated table (what was with all the big golden candelabras?) at what most people would consider to be a great party (if for no other reason than the free booze and drunken B-list celebs), and she wasn't even enjoying it because she was too busy thinking about some guy who didn't even have the decency to show up. It was truly pathetic.

"Hey, you guys," she said, trying to get Lola's and Diego's attention. She was determined to have some fun. "You wanna walk around and eavesdrop on the stars or something?"

They both turned to look at her with forced patience. Then, simultaneously shaking their heads no, they immediately went back to their private conversation. *Fine, then. I'll have fun by myself,* Anne thought, grabbing her purse and getting up from the table.

Spying Duncan across the room, she made a beeline right for him. "What are you drinking?" she asked, peering at his tall glass filled with clear, bubbly liquid with a wedge of lime suspended in the middle.

"Club soda," he said, smiling sheepishly.

"It's an open bar, you know." She laughed, shaking her head.

"Yeah, but my dad will kill me if anything happens to his car, so I'm not taking any chances." He shrugged. "So where is everybody?"

"Well, I just left the two new lovebirds," Anne said, pointing at Lola and Diego.

"Yeah, what's up with that?" Duncan asked.

"Who knows?" Anne shrugged. "Also, I'm kind of avoiding my dad because I don't really want to know that he has a new girlfriend, even though it's obvious that he does. Not to mention I thought Chris would have been here by now, but apparently he's still at Ellie's," she said, sounding bitter even though she'd aimed for nonchalance.

"Chris is at Ellie's?" Duncan asked, eyes going wide.

"Yeah," Anne said, feeling suddenly really uncomfortable. "You didn't know?"

"Not exactly." He shook his head. "I invited her tonight and she said she wasn't feeling well and had to rest up, since the Surf Fest thing is in two weeks and her dad booked her a coach again for tomorrow. She didn't say anything about Chris being with her." He looked upset.

Great, thought Anne. *It's not enough that my love life sucks. Now I had to go and wreck Duncan's as well.* "Oh, well, Chris told me they were assigned as lab partners, and they were just starting a project and got a little behind. But he'd meet me here later," she said, shrugging as she looked toward the door. "I stopped holding my breath about an hour ago." She smiled.

"I should have known," Duncan said, shaking his head. "It's always been about Chris."

"What're you talking about?" Anne asked, fearing what he was about to say, yet still needing to hear it.

"Ellie's liked Chris forever. It's so obvious, but she thinks she's the only one who knows. That night when we hooked up at the beach, I really thought she was finally getting over him. I should have known she was just trying to get back at him."

"Get back at him for what?" Anne asked, confused.

"For liking you," he said, looking right at her and taking a sip of his drink.

chapter thirty-nine

"Do you think everyone's still here?" Ellie asked as Chris pulled up to the valet.

"Who knows?" He shrugged. "I guess we'll see when we get in there."

"Will they let us in?" she asked, running her fingers through her long blond hair that she was wearing down for a change. "I mean, don't we have to be on a list or something?"

"No worries," he said, getting out of the car and handing over his keys. "Anne said she put me on it, so I'm sure I can get you in, too." He smiled.

Yeah, only she probably put me on the do-not-let-in-under-any-circumstances list, thought Ellie, following right behind him. It had been pretty awful of her to take advantage of Chris's good nature by pretending to be so overstressed about school and Surf Fest and her dad and insisting on getting a head start on the science project. And even then, she'd made sure that it took way longer than necessary by pretending to not fully understand the concept, when, if anything, she'd understood it even better than he did. She rolled her eyes just thinking about it. That was definitely an all-new low for her—*dumbing it down for a guy.*

And now, as she walked into the party and scanned the room,

she was feeling pretty ashamed. *Well, at least Duncan won't be here, since I lied to him, too,* she thought.

Relieved that she hadn't spotted any of her friends, Ellie grabbed Chris's hand and pulled him toward the bar. "I really want a drink," she said, feeling suddenly pleased with herself when she saw the expression on his face. It was nice to be able to shock someone you'd known for years.

She grabbed a glass of champagne for each of them. Then, turning to hand him one, she was disappointed when he shook his head no. "Just water for me," he said. "It's late, I'm tired, and it's a long drive home."

"Fine. More for me," she said, holding up the two flutes and smiling, but then feeling kind of stupid immediately afterward.

"Glad you could make it," she heard someone say, the voice coming from right behind her.

She turned to see Duncan standing there staring at her. "Duncan, hey. Um, I thought you weren't gonna show," she said, sipping her champagne nervously and avoiding his eyes. *Oh great, this is my karma,* she thought. *And there's no doubt I deserve this.*

"Is that why *you* showed?" he asked, noticing the two drinks she was holding and giving her an odd look.

"What? No! Of course not, don't be silly," she said, laughing outwardly while feeling totally panicked inside. "Do you want some?" She offered the extra flute, but he shook his head no. "So, who'd you come with?" She took another hefty sip, hoping it would calm her nerves, and get her through this.

"I drove up with Lola, but I've been hanging with Anne," he said, nodding toward the table where Anne was sitting.

"Oh." Ellie glanced quickly at Anne, feeling a stab of guilt at seeing her sitting alone.

"So where'd Chris go?" Duncan asked, looking around.

Ellie shrugged, hoping Duncan couldn't tell how nervous she was. "Duncan, I—" She faltered, and started again. "I know how this looks. But the truth is, we were working on a project, for school, and it was so intense that we just decided to drive up here and blow off a little steam. I was totally going to call you, but then I realized how late it was." She shrugged, fully aware of how lame she sounded. There was no way he was buying her lousy excuses.

He just stood there looking at her, not saying anything.

"Hey." Chris walked up. "I just saw Anne sitting over there by herself. Why don't we go join her?" he said, already turning and motioning for them to follow.

Of course, Ellie thought, as she watched him walk away. *It's always gonna be about Anne. And I've been a total fool to think otherwise.*

chapter forty

Diego is so amazing, Lola thought, smiling as he told yet another hilarious story. Who would have thought her mom would actually introduce her to someone she had so much in common with? They loved the same movies, the same books, the same magazines, the same music, the same television shows, the same celebrities, the same clothing designers—they even liked the same hair products! But more important, they both knew firsthand what it was like to grow up with strict, overbearing parents who had even stricter ideas on how their children should and would live their lives.

It's like we're soul mates, she thought, looking into his gorgeous, dark, and long-lashed eyes. *Soul mates who would never, ever sleep together.*

"I can't wait 'til next fall," he said, taking a sip of red wine.

"Why? What's happening next fall?" she asked.

"I'll be going to Columbia, living in my own apartment three thousand miles away from my parents' watchful eyes. Free at last in New York City! It doesn't get any better than that." He smiled.

"Sounds great," Lola agreed.

"Yeah." He nodded. "All I have to do now is lay low, stay under their radar, and just get through my last year of high school," he said.

Lola looked at him. He was gorgeous, smart, ambitious, funny, totally presentable, and he'd already won the approval of her parents. In other words, *he was perfect.*

"I have an idea," she said, smiling and leaning toward him.

chapter forty-one

Ellie looked at Duncan standing in front of her. He was sweet, nice, cute, funny, athletic—so why couldn't she like him? *There must be something wrong with me,* she thought.

"I think I'm gonna take off," he said, looking at her and shrugging. "Can you tell Lola and make sure she has a ride home?"

"Oh. Okay. Sure." Ellie felt awful about lying to him, and even worse about having been caught. *He has no idea how lucky he is that I don't like him,* she thought. *Because he definitely deserves someone much nicer than me.* "But Duncan, um, you don't have to go," she said, wondering if she really did want him to stay or if she was just trying to alleviate her own guilt. *Probably the latter.*

"No, I should hit it. I'm surfing in a contest tomorrow and I've got a seven-thirty heat." he told her.

"Oh, okay, well, good luck," she said, standing there with her two champagne glasses, one empty, the other completely full.

As she watched him fumble with his keys, she contemplated asking him for a ride. She too needed to get some sleep if she was going to be in a halfway decent form for Lina tomorrow. But it was pretty obvious he just wanted to get away from her, so she just stood there and watched him walk out the door, wondering how she was going to get home. *It's not like I can ask Chris,* she thought, glancing over to see him leaning close to Anne, talking intently, his arm around her shoulder.

"Just FYI, don't be fooled by the Colin Farrell lookalike over there," Jade said, walking up and pointing toward a table in the far corner of the room.

"Colin Farrell? Are you serious?" Ellie asked, all excited. Not that she was a big fan of his, but she'd yet to see one big name and she'd been here at least twenty minutes.

"No, I repeat, *not Colin.* He has the hair, the tats, the sexy smirk, but up close, I'm telling ya, it's just fool's gold," Jade said, crossing her arms and shaking her head. "*Extremely* disappointing. Anyway, have you had any Ben sightings? Know where he might be?"

"I thought he was with you." Ellie shrugged and set both champagne glasses on the edge of a nearby table.

"He was, but then I saw the Colin wannabe and made a mad dash across the room so I could get a closer look. You know how I love my bad boys." She laughed.

"And now you can't locate the one you came with," Ellie said, smiling.

"Jeez, I hope he hasn't had any more to drink," Jade said, scanning the room with a worried look on her face. "Last time I saw him, he wasn't looking so great."

"Does he have a problem?" Ellie asked, already assuming the answer.

"Actually, he has a lot of problems," Jade said. "But he's going through a really rough time right now, so it's totally understandable. He's a really great person though, and I know he's gonna pull through this. It's just a matter of time." She nodded.

Ellie watched Jade's eyes search the room, looking for Ben. He may be a nice guy, like Jade had said, but she doubted he'd pull out of it anytime soon. She recognized a downward spiral when she saw one. But it's not like she could tell Jade that. Jade would just get mad and accuse her of being judgmental. *Besides, with the way I've been handling my own life lately, I really don't have the right to judge anyone else,* she thought.

"Oh, maybe this is him," Jade said, grabbing her ringing cell phone and placing her free hand over her other ear. "What happened? . . . Oh, great. Just stay right there." She closed her phone and looked at Ellie. "Ben got kicked out and they won't let him back in."

"Why?" Ellie asked, wondering what he could have possibly done to get kicked out of a party like this, where all the normal rules of behavior had seemingly been abandoned.

"I have no idea, but clearly the party's over for me. I gotta drive him home," she said, shaking her head and rifling through her purse for her car keys.

Ellie looked over at Chris and Anne. It was like they were in their own little world. And while she really didn't want to ride home with Ben, she was pretty much out of options. "Do you have room for one more?" she asked.

chapter forty-two

Anne looked toward the door just in time to see Ellie leave. She was embarrassed to think how ridiculous she'd been, worrying about them studying together. Chris was acting so sweet and affectionate, holding her hand and smiling, and even though it wasn't turning out anything like the movie version she'd scripted in her head, it was still pretty nice, maybe even better. Because this was real. "I'm so glad you made it here," she said, leaning toward him and smiling.

"Sorry it wasn't sooner, but Ellie was really freaked out about the project. She gets so stressed sometimes." He shook his head.

"Hmm." Anne smiled politely. The last thing she wanted to do was talk about Ellie.

"And she just couldn't seem to grasp the concept," he continued. "Which is *so weird,* because normally she's a whiz at science. But we had to go over it again and again, until finally I just asked her if we could put it away, 'cause I had to meet you. But then she got all stressed again, so I just decided to invite her." He shrugged. "I thought she needed to blow off a little steam, you know?"

Anne just looked at Chris and nodded. She knew he was telling the truth. But she also knew he was completely clueless to the fact that he'd just been totally played. *Guys so don't get girls,* she thought. But it's not like it mattered. He was with her now, and it was obvious that Ellie's sad little game had failed miserably. "Well, now that you're here, there's something I have to ask you," she said, smiling and leaning toward him.

"Anything." He grabbed both her hands.

"Do you wanna bail soon? This party isn't really as great as I thought it would be." She shrugged.

"Candelabras, an open bar, all the gourmet food you can eat, great music, table-dancing celebrities—and this party isn't fun enough for you?" he said, in mock surprise. "Just what kind of high-maintenance parties are you used to?"

"Honestly, I'm not really a party person," she admitted. "I'm really more the quiet type."

"Wanna go someplace quiet?" He smiled.

chapter forty-three

Ben was outside, sitting on the hood of Jade's car and looking pretty messed up. His blue eyes were bloodshot and etched with dark circles, his brown hair was all matted and tangled, and the sleeve of his striped shirt was ripped. "So what happened?" Jade asked, unlocking the door and motioning for him to get in the back.

"Some asshole kicked me out," he said, shaking his head and lunging onto the backseat.

"Well, what did you do?" Ellie asked, turning to look at him.

"Nothing. I didn't do anything, okay? That party's just full of pretentious Hollywood assholes," he said, looking at her.

"Well, you must have done something," Ellie insisted, not believing his version for one second and not willing to let it go, either.

"Whatever." He glared at her from the backseat. "Think what you want. But I was just minding my own business."

"Okay, you guys. Everybody just relax, okay?" Jade pleaded, merging onto the freeway and turning up her stereo. "Let's just chill out and listen to some tunes. We'll be home before you know it."

"Whatever," Ben said from the backseat, rolling his eyes.

"Fine with me," Ellie said, folding her arms across her chest and staring out the window. She couldn't wait to get home and into her nice, warm bed. She leaned her head against the window and closed her eyes, wondering if this was her punishment for the whole Duncan mess. Because ending up spending an hour in the same car as Ben, who was not only snoring way louder than the music, but who totally reeked of alcohol and cigarettes, really did seem like bad karma. *Please, just get me home soon,* she thought, right before drifting off to sleep.

"Ellie! Hey, wake up." Jade tapped her hard on the shoulder.

"What? Are we home?" Ellie asked, rubbing her eyes and squinting at Jade.

"Almost, we're on Newport Coast, but this cop has been following us for like a mile now, and I'm starting to get a little freaked."

Ellie turned in her seat and saw the police car following closely behind them. "Were you speeding?" she asked.

"No. Speed limit the whole way, I swear. I don't know what his problem is," she said, glancing nervously at the rearview mirror.

"You know, I read recently that when a cop wants to find a drunk driver, they look for the guy who's driving *too perfect,*" Ellie told her.

"So what are you suggesting? That I start driving all erratic, so he'll move on to someone else?" She rolled her eyes. "Besides, I'm not drunk. I haven't had anything to drink all night."

"Don't worry about it, then. I'm sure it's nothing," Ellie said, just about to close her eyes again when the squad car pulled up next to them with siren wailing and lights flashing.

chapter forty-four

"Where are you taking me?" Anne asked, struggling to keep up with Chris as he pulled her through the crowd of people. "You act like you know your way around this place or something," she said.

"Never been here before in my life." He looked back at her and smiled. "But I have been in a few restaurants, and I happen to know that the one thing they all have in common, besides food, is a back door. See, I told you!" he said, opening the door and leading her through it.

They entered into a beautiful lush courtyard lit by glowing white candles and filled with tall flowering trees, colorful hanging plants, and a beautiful mosaic fountain built right in the middle of it all.

"Wow, this is beautiful. I wonder why nobody's out here?" Anne said, looking at the empty linen-covered tables and rod iron chairs.

"Maybe 'cause there's no bar," Chris said, putting his arms around her and pulling her toward him.

His face was so close to hers she could feel his soft breath on her cheek, and just as he was about to kiss her, she whispered,

"Shh! Did you hear that?" Her eyes went wide as she looked around cautiously.

"I didn't hear anything," Chris mumbled, eyes still closed while he nuzzled her neck. "You're imagining things."

"I'm serious," she insisted. "Someone's out here. Listen!"

Chris reluctantly pulled away and quickly looked around. "Relax; it's just us," he said, leaning toward her again, determined to kiss her this time.

"I know I heard something," she said, sounding completely paranoid.

"So what?" Chris shrugged, kissing the side of her neck since she wouldn't stop talking. "It's probably just Brad and Jen, avoiding the paparazzi and getting a little fresh air."

Anne looked at him and laughed. "Brad and Jen? They are *so over.*" She shook her head. "You are so out of touch!" she said, finally leaning in to kiss him.

His hands were wrapped tightly around her waist, while hers were tangled in his soft, shaggy hair when someone walked up behind them and said, "Anne? Is that you?"

Oh God, oh no, don't let it be . . . , she thought, pulling away from Chris and wiping her mouth with the back of her hand. Then, slowly looking up, she saw her dad and Brooke standing there, his lips holding traces of Brooke's frosty peach lipstick.

Oh sick, they both came out here for the same reason! Which meant she'd been making out just steps away from her dad! It didn't get any grosser than that.

"Um, Chris and I were just talking," she said, immediately realizing how totally lame it sounded. "I mean, we were just getting some air . . . because . . . you know . . . it's so *stuffy* in there." She pointed toward the restaurant. *Oh yeah, that was convincing,* she thought, glancing briefly at Chris, who looked as embarrassed as she felt.

"Well, now that you've gotten some air, what do you say we all go back inside?" her dad said, giving them a stern parental look.

Oh please, like you're any better, Anne thought. *You're the parent! You're the one who should be setting the example!*

But she didn't say that. Instead she just gave him a sheepish look and said, "Um, okay."

chapter forty-five

"Oh, great," Jade said, shaking her head as she pulled over to the side of the road and came to a complete stop.

"What do you think he wants?" Ellie asked nervously.

"Well, I think we're about to find out." Jade rolled down her window and smiled politely. "Hi, officer. Is something wrong?" she asked.

"Did you know that your left taillight is out?" he said, pointing his flashlight into the car, going from Jade to Ellie, then focusing on Ben, who was sprawled out in the back, sound asleep, and not wearing a seat belt.

"Oh, really? Um, no, I had no idea," Jade said, cautiously.

"Can I see your license and registration, please?"

Jade reached for her wallet with hands that were shaking so bad she could barely open it. "Here," she said, handing over her license while Ellie searched through the mess of papers in the glove compartment, looking for the registration.

Tomorrow I will clean out this car. Tomorrow I will fix my taillight. Tomorrow I will organize my life. I really hope I make it to tomorrow, Jade thought.

"Who's been drinking?" the cop asked, watching Jade closely as he handed the papers to his partner.

"Um, they have," Jade said, pointing at Ellie and Ben. "I was just making sure everyone got home safely."

The cop stood there, eyes narrowed, looking at all three of them. "I'd like you to step out of the car, please."

"What? But why?" Jade asked, totally panicked now. No good could come of this.

"Just step out of the car," he said. "All of you."

chapter forty-six

"Do you really have to call *all* of our parents?" Jade asked, glancing nervously at Ellie, whose face had gone completely white and who looked like she was about to pass out at any second. She was way more worried about Ellie than herself, especially if they called Ellie's dad.

They were sitting in a small room at the Newport Beach police station, where they'd been for the last half hour—ever since Ben had failed the Breathalyzer test and they found the Baggie full of pot he'd thrown on the floor of the car. At first, Jade was being held responsible for the pot—her car, her possession, they'd reasoned. But since she'd breathed clean, while Ben was obviously drunk and stoned, and since the bag was found on the floor right next to his feet, they decided to let her off with just a minor curfew violation, while Ben was in another room being processed for possession and underage drinking.

The only crime poor Ellie committed was being in the wrong place at the wrong time, Jade thought, looking at her friend and feeling really guilty for getting her into this mess.

"I mean, I was the driver, so if you have to call my parents, then fine. But Ellie just needed a ride. I swear, she didn't do anything wrong. So can you maybe just like, let her go?" Jade pleaded.

"Sorry. Your parents have already been notified. They'll be here any minute," the cop said, leaving them alone in the room to wait out their fate.

Ellie looked at Jade, her eyes welling up with tears. "Well, it's been nice knowing ya," she said, looking nervously toward the door.

"Oh God, El, I am *so sorry*. I don't know what else to say." Jade hugged her. Even though technically it was totally Ben's fault, Jade took full responsibility where Ellie was concerned. But what made it even worse was knowing how Ellie felt about Ben, and how she'd tried to warn her.

Jade also thought it was weird how Ben was always ragging on his dad, and yet he'd been the one to come bail him out. And even though Jade had only gotten a quick glimpse of him, he really didn't look so awful. He just looked really worried.

"That's it. I'm dead," Ellie whispered, seeing her dad enter the room.

"Ellie, honey, are you okay?" he asked, swooping her into his arms and hugging her so tight she could barely catch her breath.

"Yeah. I'm fine, really. It wasn't that big of a deal," she said, raising her eyebrows at Jade as her dad continued to hug her, refusing to let her go. "It was just an overinflated fix-it ticket." She laughed, obviously relieved that he wasn't reacting in the way she'd expected.

"Let's get you home." He put his arm around her protectively and walked her to the door. Then, turning to look at Jade, he said, "I just spoke to your parents. They're on their way."

Jade watched Ellie and her dad leave, feeling totally relieved that he hadn't been nearly as angry and upset as she had assumed he'd be. And if *he* was acting that cool and casual about it, then surely her own parents would be a total breeze.

"Hey!" Jade said, seeing them standing in the doorway. She

smiled and jumped up from her chair, in anticipation of a big group hug.

"Grab your belongings," her father said sternly, while her mother stood silently, with her arms folded across her chest. "We'll talk when we get home."

chapter forty-seven

With Surf Fest now just three days away, it was taking all of Ellie's concentration not to be distracted by everyone around her. First, there was Duncan's insistence on ignoring her. Not that she expected anything different, and *not* that she even really cared, but still, she'd really hoped they could just move on and go right back to their old, platonic ways. But apparently Duncan had other ideas. Because not only had he stopped calling, but now he barely spoke to her at school, despite the fact that they shared two classes and sat at the same lunch table. She was surprised that she was so bothered by it—but it was probably only because she couldn't stand to hurt anyone's feelings.

And then there were Chris and Anne. The perfect, happy couple, who seemed to be everywhere Ellie was. Seriously, there was no safe place. They shared the same neighborhood, the same school, the same lunch table, the same friends, the same gym, and, worst of all, even the same waves. There was just no avoiding them, so Ellie had simply stopped trying. She was learning to ignore them just like Duncan ignored her.

And ever since the party, Lola and Diego were rarely apart. The only time Ellie got to see her now was at school, and Ellie was certain that was only because Diego was enrolled elsewhere. But even at school it was always Diego this and Diego that. It kind of bugged Ellie when girls did things like that—got all impressed over every little thing their boyfriend did. But still, it was pretty great to see Lola so happy and in love—even if Diego was kind of a strange choice.

And then there was Jade, who was under severe house arrest and was only allowed to go to school and then straight home again. Who would have thought that Ellie's dad would be so understanding and forgiving, while Jade's parents would totally lay down the law?

Even Ellie's brother, Dean, had been acting really bizarre lately, not going out with his friends, barely surfing. He just sat in his room, staring at his computer for hours on end, almost like he was stuck in his own, self-inflicted house arrest.

But unfortunately, her dad was right back to his normal, domineering self. The emotional generosity he'd shown at the police station had lasted only until the next morning. Then it was back to the usual pep talks, lectures, and dire warnings.

Ellie zipped up the back of her wetsuit, grabbed her board, and headed down the beach stairs toward the ocean. Dropping her board in the water, she paddled out, determined to clear her mind of everything but her surfboard and the waves. The competition came first right now, and everything else would just have to wait.

chapter forty-eight

Lola was lying on her bed, with the phone to her ear, talking to Diego and laughing hysterically—until her mom barged in without knocking.

"I gotta go. I'll call you later," she told him, tossing her phone onto her nightstand and giving her mother an annoyed look. "Excuse me, but could you please knock next time? Is that too much to ask?" she said, shaking her head and rolling her eyes. She'd been getting away with all kinds of rude behavior lately—ever since Diego came into her life. It's like her mom was so elated at her obvious matchmaking success that she was letting all the usual infractions slip past without mention.

"In case you've forgotten, we need to be at the dressmaker's in fifteen minutes." Her mother gazed into Lola's mirror and adjusted her blazer.

"What for?" Lola asked, rifling through some books on her shelf, searching for the one she promised to lend Diego.

"Today is your final fitting. Cotillion is this weekend! Or have you forgotten that, too?" She turned to look at her daughter.

Oh God, the dreaded cotillion. All the etiquette classes, all the waltzing, all the sweaty-palmed geeks insisting on leading when she knew the dance better than they did—it all culminated in this one big, overblown moment that she wanted nothing to do with. She had no interest in showing off her newly acquired curtsey, her fancy manners, her slick dance moves, or her dad's hefty bank account. Not to mention that hideous poufy white dress she was supposed to wear.

"Mom, I really don't feel up to it today," she said.

"Don't say another word. You are going and that's final. *Abuela* is already in the car, waiting. She's waited her whole life for this moment and you will not disappoint her."

Poor Abuela, *that can't be true,* Lola thought, hoping her mom was exaggerating as usual.

"Now, put on some shoes and let's go," her mother said as she walked out the door.

Fine, Lola thought. *I'll play along today, but Saturday is another story.*

chapter forty-nine

If I have to spend one more second inside this house, I'm going to burst, thought Jade. She'd always liked school, though she definitely liked it most when the final bell rang. But now that her parents had put her under strict house arrest, the hours between eight and three had suddenly become a lot more meaningful. It was the only time she had for any social interaction, not to mention *freedom.* And the really sad, sick thing was that now she actually found herself *dreading* the sound of the final bell.

The only good thing (and she'd searched high and low to find one) was that she now had complete possession of the remote control between the hours of three and six, when nobody else was home. But unfortunately she'd also discovered that it was only worth having the remote when someone else wanted it.

Getting up from the couch, she walked over to the big bay window, pressing her forehead against the glass and staring with longing at the distant ocean view, wondering if this meant the end of her competing in Surf Fest. She'd competed every year since she first learned to surf, and even though she didn't take it as seriously as Ellie, she still looked forward to the event all year. But even though her parents had gone totally overboard with her punishment, she was positive that if she just kept to her best behavior, and observed all the rules, then she'd ultimately be awarded a reduced sentence and get to compete on Saturday.

She thought about Ben, wondering how he was doing. His mom had called a few days ago to apologize for everything and tell her he was living with his dad now. Jade was glad he was trying to work things out, but more than a little annoyed that he hadn't bothered to call himself. After all, she'd gone out of her way to help him, had done everything she could to be there for him. Still, lately she'd begun to realize that he hadn't exactly asked for her support. And, just maybe, he had never actually wanted it.

chapter fifty

Anne was really nervous about mentioning Surf Fest to her dad—partly because she was nervous about it in general, and partly because she was afraid he wouldn't show. Yet she was also equally worried that he *would* show. Because then he might bring Brooke. And Brooke was a subject that neither one of them seemed very willing to talk about.

Ever since they'd caught each other making out at the party, they seemed to adopt this silent agreement to never, ever mention it again. Which was fine by Anne. Just thinking about it still totally grossed her out.

The only one who knew about her surfing, other than her friends at school, was Jake. And there was no way he'd tell, as Anne had blackmailed, bribed, and basically sworn him to secrecy.

A few days ago she'd been in the home office printing all the contest info, when he walked in.

"You're competing in Surf Fest?" he'd asked, peering over her shoulder, eyes wide with surprise.

"Maybe. I haven't actually decided yet, so don't say anything to anybody. Especially my dad," she'd said, turning to look at him.

"Why not? He'll be totally stoked."

"Jake, I'm serious. If you so much as tell him, then I'll . . ." She hesitated, trying to think of something good. "I'll tell him you drink beer with your bros on our terrace." She narrowed her eyes at him.

"Dude, what's with the threats? You need to relax, okay? I'm not gonna say anything." He looked at her and shook his head. "But FYI, your dad's pretty Hollywood. I'm sure he's seen a lot worse than a couple of guys drinking a beer."

Anne just looked at him, not saying anything. Unfortunately, he was right. Her dad definitely led a way cooler life and went to way better parties than she did.

But now, with the event just days away, she really had to focus. And knowing she was nowhere near good enough to impress any of the judges, her only goals were to have some fun, learn the ropes, and hopefully not make a total fool of herself.

Going into her room, she got down on her hands and knees and slid her Indo Board out from under her bed. She was just about to hop on when her phone rang.

"Hello?" she said hurriedly. She was in no mood for conversation.

"Anne? How are you, honey?"

Oh, great. It was her mom again. She'd been leaving lots of messages in the past few days, but Anne hadn't gotten around to returning any of them. She'd been too busy with school, surfing, and Chris to even bother. Besides, the last thing she needed right now was another fight with her mom. "Oh, hey," she said, getting herself balanced on her board and positioning down into a low squat.

"I've been trying to reach you for days," her mother said.

"Yeah, I know. I'm sorry I haven't called; I've just been super busy with school and stuff," Anne said, walking slowly to the end of the board, while attempting to keep it perfectly balanced.

"Well, I was really wishing we could have talked sooner, because now you won't have much time to prepare."

"Prepare for what?" Anne asked, carefully studying her reflection in the full-length mirror.

"I've reserved you a ticket on the nonstop to New York this weekend."

"What?" Anne struggled to maintain her balance.

"Your flight leaves Friday at twelve thirty your time, and lands in New York around nine fifteen our time. I've arranged for a limo to pick you up and bring you straight to the Four Seasons. That's where we'll all be staying."

"What are you talking about?" Anne asked, standing very still, while the muscles in her legs worked overtime, trying to keep her from tipping over.

"I'm getting married. And I want you to be my maid of honor."

"Mom. Oh my God. You can't be serious." Anne gripped the phone so tightly, her knuckles were fading. "I mean, are you and Dad even divorced yet?"

"The divorce has been final for weeks," her mother said, in the clipped voice she usually reserved for the courtroom.

"Weeks? You've been divorced for just a few weeks? And you think that's a sufficient amount of time to just jump back in and do it all over again?" Anne waited for a response, but all she got was the sound of light breathing. "It's like, did it ever occur to you to run it by *me* first? I am still your daughter, right? I mean, how could you do this? I've only met him once!"

"Twice, Anne. You've met him twice."

"Whatever! Twice. Fine. Do I get *any* say in this?" she asked, starting to feel really nauseous and fighting to keep her balance.

"I'm sorry, Anne, but no. I'm the adult. It's my decision. And it's already been booked and paid for. All I request from you is your presence as my maid of honor," she said.

Maid of honor? More like maid of horror! There's no way she's guilt-

ing me into this, Anne thought. *And if she thinks she's acting like an adult, well, then she's totally delusional.* "I'm sorry, but I can't make it," Anne said, watching herself in the mirror as she broke her mother's heart.

"Why not?"

"Well, for starters Friday is a school day, in case you've forgotten. And I can't go missing a whole day of school just because you started feeling all romantic and decided to pull a Britney Spears. And second, for your information I've made a life for myself here. I have friends, I have plans for this weekend, and I just can't put everything on hold because of your whims."

"It's hardly a whim, Anne," her mother said, blowing loudly into a tissue.

"Oh, that's right; I forgot. You two have been having a relationship for *years* now."

"Anne, I don't have time for this. So just tell me, are you coming or not?"

"I just don't get what the rush is. I mean, you're not pregnant, are you?" Anne laughed. The thought of her mother being pregnant was ridiculous. She was *old.* She was like, *over forty,* for God's sake. But when she stopped laughing, she realized the line had gone silent. *Oh God. Oh no. Please don't let it be true!* "Mom?" she whispered. "Is it true?"

"Is what true?" She sounded sad and very, very tired.

"What I just asked. Are you?" Anne couldn't finish the sentence. Now that it might be true, she couldn't bear to say the word out loud.

"I wasn't going to tell you until you got here," her mother said quietly.

"Oh." Anne's eyes started to sting as she fought back the tears. "Well, I wish you all the best. But I just can't support this. I'm sorry, but I just . . ." She stopped and wiped her hand across her eyes. "I just can't. And I've already got plans this weekend. I'm doing something that means a lot to me. Something that you know nothing about. But I guess there's a lot we don't know about each other these days," she said, swallowing hard.

"If you change your mind, there will be a ticket on hold for you at the Delta ticket counter," her mother told her, suddenly sounding all businesslike and professional again.

"I'm sorry, but that's not gonna happen," Anne said, flipping her phone closed, and allowing herself to fall straight off the Indo Board and right onto her ass.

chapter fifty-one

"What about that one?" Lola asked.

"Definitely gay." Diego nodded.

"No! Don't say that! He's *so* cute! Besides, you've said that about the last four guys I've picked."

"That's because the last four *were* gay." He smiled.

"Then I dare you to find me one that isn't," she said, narrowing her eyes at him.

"Okay. How about that guy right over there." Diego pointed.

"The one in the Hooters T-shirt, with the mullet and the beer gut? *Is that the one?* Gee, thanks a lot." Lola laughed and punched him in the arm. They had somehow survived the last of the many cotillion rehearsals and now they were lounging on one of the benches on Main Beach, eating frozen yogurt and watching all the people. "I double-dare you to find me another one," she said. "And this time, make sure he's cute."

Diego removed his sunglasses and scanned the beach. In the last week they had known each other they'd become extremely close, confiding all their dreams and secrets through late-night telephone calls and early-morning IMs. They had also managed to successfully fool everyone they knew into believing that they were seriously dating. And it was going so smoothly, they figured they could carry on like this for years. Allowing them both to discreetly date the men of their choice while staying under their parents' hypersensitive radar. *It's genius,* Lola thought, *a definite no-brainer, and everybody wins.* The only thing she felt really bad about was lying to her friends. But if the plan was going to work, then no one could know the truth. Because the more people were in on it, the more potential there was for a major leak.

"Come on, Diego. There must be one gorgeous straight guy on this beach. Just one. That's all I ask. Lie to me if you have to," she pleaded.

"Hold on. Just give me a minute," he said, glancing at her briefly before getting back to the task at hand. "Oh. My. Wow. Lola, right in front of us. Twelve o'clock position. He's holding a surfboard and coming out of the ocean. And check out those abs!"

But Lola wasn't looking at his abs. Her eyes were fixated on his face. While her body felt sweaty, stiff, and solid like a block of ice.

"He's looking right at you, too! You little vixen!" He punched her playfully in the arm. "Wait. Is he? It seems like he's approaching us. Lola, do you know that guy?" he whispered, looking at her in shock.

Lola did know him. She knew him better than she'd ever known any guy. And she'd told him things she'd never told anyone else. Hell, up until a few weeks ago she even thought she loved him. But she couldn't tell Diego that. Because her mouth had suddenly grown so dry and parched, she wasn't even sure if she could speak. And now he was standing right in front of her.

"Hey," he said, running his hand through his wet, sandy hair and looking from Lola to Diego, and then back again.

"Hey," she said softly, forcing her lips into a half smile.

"So, how've you been?" he asked, looking right at her.

"Great!" she said, feigning an enthusiasm she definitely didn't feel. "How've you been?" She didn't want to be mean, but she was really hoping he hadn't been doing so great. She also hoped there were no yogurt chips stuck between her teeth.

"Okay." He shrugged.

"So how's the project coming along?" she asked.

"A little stalled, but . . ." He shrugged without finishing his sentence, but Lola was in no mood to finish it for him. Not anymore.

"Um, Lola," Diego said, giving her an impatient look while not so gently elbowing her in the ribs.

"Oh, I'm sorry. I totally forgot to introduce you guys. Diego, this is my ex-boyfriend and Ellie's brother, Dean." She pointed to the gorgeous surfer standing in front of them. "And Dean, this is my new boyfriend, Diego," she said, smiling brightly and leaning over to kiss Diego on the cheek.

chapter fifty-two

All day at school Ellie could barely concentrate. She had a major bad case of precompetition jitters. It was all she could think about. So when the final bell finally rang at exactly 3:20 PM, she already had her car keys in hand and, for the first time ever, she was actually the first person out the door.

And she'd almost made it to the parking lot when she ran smack into Chris and Anne.

"Whoa, where you going in such a hurry?" he asked, leaning down to help her pick up all the books she'd dropped.

"Oh, I'm just trying to get home. I've got some stuff to do before registration tonight," she said, brushing some dirt off her AP History textbook and looking from Chris to Anne.

"We're headed up there later," he said, wrapping his arm casually around Anne's shoulders. "Why don't you ride with us?"

Ellie and Anne looked at each other, both obviously hating that idea. *Chris still doesn't get it,* Ellie thought, shaking her head and feeling totally annoyed with him. "That's okay, but thanks anyway," she said. Then looking right at Anne, she continued, "I'm surprised you're still competing. I mean, I would've thought you'd change your mind by now."

"What's that supposed to mean?" Anne asked, her eyes narrowing to angry slits.

"Well, we're the same age, so you'll be competing against *me*. I've been surfing for years and you're just starting out. I mean, I'd hate to see you embarrass yourself out there." Ellie looked right at her.

Anne just stood there, glaring at Ellie. "From what I've heard, it's just a really fun, laid-back event that's not all about winning and killer instinct. So I should be fine. It's *you* that should be worried," she said.

They both stood there, eyes narrowed, totally glaring at each other, while Chris looked increasingly uncomfortable. "Okay, that's enough. We're out of here," he said, pulling Anne away from Ellie and toward the parking lot. "See you tonight, El."

"Whatever," she said quietly, rolling her eyes as she watched them walk away, arm in arm.

chapter fifty-three

"God, she is such a bitch!" Anne said, shaking her head and looking out the window as Chris pulled out of the student lot. "I'm *so over* trying to be nice to her. You heard her this time. So even you can't deny it anymore."

"Okay, so she was a little harsh," he said, turning to look at her briefly. "She just gets really wound up, you know? But really, she's not as bad as you think. I mean, maybe you should just cut her some slack."

"You've got to be kidding? I mean, why would I do that? You heard the same thing I just did!" Anne said, feeling totally frustrated with his refusal to see Ellie for what she really was—a conniving, nasty control freak. She shook her head and stared at him.

"Listen, you haven't known her as long as I have. She's been through a really rough time the last couple years."

"For your information, I'm going through a rough time, too. But you don't see *me* treating people like that."

"What are you talking about?" he asked, glancing at her briefly before turning left on PCH.

"Nothing, forget it," she said, crossing her arms in front of her and looking out the window. She was dying to confide in someone about her mom, but this was definitely not the right time. Not to mention that it was beginning to seem like he might not be the right person.

"All right, so she got a little bitchy with you. Why can't you just let it go? I mean, what's the big deal?"

Anne turned to face him. Was he serious? And why should she let it go? She'd put up with it long enough as it was. "I guess the big deal is that you always seem to be sticking up for *her* instead of *me*."

"That's not true," he said, shaking his head. "Look, I've known her for a really long time, and I guess I just don't see her the same way you do, that's all."

"Well, I guess it's easy for you to say that, since she'd never treat *you* like that. She's totally in love with you!" Anne said, still glaring at him.

"What? Are you serious?" He looked at her.

"You didn't know?" Anne asked, regretting having told him as soon as she saw the look on his face. Was he surprised? Was he flattered? She really couldn't tell, but whatever he felt, she knew it wasn't good. She watched him avoid her eyes now, staring straight ahead at the road in front of them, his hands gripping the wheel in the proper ten and two position, instead of his usual left hand on six, right hand on hers.

And by the time he pulled up to the Laguna Cove security gate they still hadn't said a single word to each other, and Anne wasn't sure how to break the silence.

How had things gotten so awkward so quickly? Had he really not realized how Ellie felt about him? And now that he did know, had he decided that he liked her, too?

Chris pulled up to her driveway and slowed to a stop. Normally he would park the car, get out, and come inside for a little while. But now he just sat there with the engine idling.

"So what time are you picking me up?" she asked, watching his face like a detective, searching for clues as to what could possibly be going on in his head.

"I don't know. What time's registration?" he asked, rubbing his chin and looking at her, but only briefly.

"I'm not sure, exactly. But I was thinking we could get there around seven and it should be fine. There's supposed to be live music and food and stuff," she said, her voice trailing off, noticing how distracted he seemed.

"Yeah, I know. I've been a few times," he told her.

"Okay, well, you wanna come in?" she asked, opening the car door and grabbing her purse.

He shook his head. "I can't. Listen, I don't know what time I'll be by so I'll just call you a little later, okay?"

She stared at him for a moment. Did he really want to leave it like this? Because she just wasn't capable of that. "Uh, is something wrong?" she asked, reaching down to grab her books.

"No. Why?" he asked, attempting that famous smile of his. But it wasn't really working this time.

"Never mind," she said, getting out of the car and closing the door between them. "I'll talk to you later."

Walking in the door, she saw Jake sitting at the kitchen table across from her dad and Brooke. *Oh great,* she thought, *just what I need, a nice, cozy family gathering.*

"Hey, honey, how was your day?" her dad asked, looking up from his pile of papers and smiling at her.

"Okay." She shrugged, setting down her books and grabbing a container of yogurt from the fridge and a spoon from the drawer.

"What are you doing?" she asked, going over to where they were working and leaning against the table.

"Just going over some numbers," her dad said, looking up at her briefly. "Hey, try not to spoil your appetite."

"Why?" she asked, enjoying another spoonful.

"We're all going out to dinner tonight, to celebrate."

"Celebrate what?" What could there possibly be to celebrate? Her mother and her shotgun marriage? Her boyfriend, who had just discovered he was in love with someone else? But her dad didn't know about any of those things, so it couldn't be that. Besides, he wasn't nearly as cynical and sarcastic as she was.

"We've been green-lighted for our next project. And some really big names have signed on," he said. "So I've booked us a table at Studio."

"What's that?" Anne asked, scraping the bottom of her yogurt cup with her spoon.

"Supposed to be one of the best restaurants in town," he told her.

"Well, maybe you can find someone to take my place. I kind of have plans." She looked briefly at Brooke, who, up until now, she'd been trying not to look at.

"So bring Chris. He's more than welcome." Her father smiled.

"Well, actually." She hesitated. "We're supposed to go to this party at San Onofre tonight."

"Can you skip it?" he asked.

"Not really. I'm kind of supposed to register for tomorrow," she told him.

"Are we talking in code?" her father asked, shaking his head. "Can you fill me in here? Register for what?"

"Well, I've decided to enter this surf contest." She studied his face closely, trying to determine whether or not Jake had betrayed her confidence.

"I didn't know you were that good." His eyes lit up as a proud smile spread across his face.

"Believe me, I'm not. I just really love surfing, and I kind of miss competing. And this is supposed to be really low-key and fun, so I figured it would be a good opportunity to get my feet wet. So to speak." She laughed. "I mean, I'll probably just totally embarrass myself, since I'm really not very good yet. But I gotta start somewhere, right?"

"When were you planning on telling me this?" he asked.

"Maybe never?" She shrugged. "I mean, you totally don't have to go. It'll probably be really embarrassing for you to watch me wipe out and stuff."

"Nonsense. We're definitely going," he said.

We? She looked over at Brooke, who was nodding and smiling. *Oh great, she's coming, too,* Anne thought. *So let's see, in the course of one weekend, I'm losing my boyfriend but gaining a new daddy, a new sibling, and possibly a new mommy. . . .*

It really didn't seem like a fair trade.

chapter fifty-four

Lola was sitting in the passenger seat of Ellie's Mini Cooper, singing along to the radio as they drove down the 5 freeway. The top was down, the cool wind was rushing against her cheeks, and her hair was loose and slapping lightly at the air around her head. She loved moments like this, when everything just felt so free and full of promise.

"So where's Diego tonight?" Ellie asked, glancing at her briefly as she merged into the exit lane.

Lola shrugged. "I think he's out with some friends, enjoying a boys' night out or something," she told her, laughing inside at the huge difference between what Ellie probably thought that meant and the reality.

"So are you guys, like, pretty serious, or what?" she asked, slowing as she exited the freeway

"I don't know." Lola shifted uncomfortably. She felt bad about lying to her friend, but she really had no choice, since she and Diego both agreed that absolutely no one could know the truth.

"Well, you're together all the time, and you seem really happy," Ellie pressed, refusing to let it go.

Lola sighed. "Well, he is pretty awesome. And yeah, we have been spending a lot of time together, but mostly it's because of the cotillion. It'll probably slow down a bit once we're past all that. I mean, it's better if we take it slow, you know?" she said, noticing a total hottie in the parking lot and suddenly realizing how awkward it would be to flirt with him now that everyone thought she was committed. *Hmmm, maybe we should have thought this through a little better,* she thought. *Maybe if I just tell Ellie, and swear her to secrecy . . .*

"Dean said he saw you guys at the beach," Ellie said, killing the engine and pulling her key from the ignition.

"Oh, really?" Lola flipped down the mirrored visor and checked out her lip gloss.

"Yeah, he said you guys looked really cozy together." Ellie was looking right at her.

"Hmmm," Lola muttered, casually flipping the mirror back up and opening her door. *Maybe I won't tell Ellie just yet. Maybe I'll keep it a secret just a little bit longer.*

chapter fifty-five

Just as Anne was getting out of the shower, she heard her phone beeping. Wrapping one towel around her head like a turban and another tightly around her body, she walked over to her desk, flipped open her phone, and listened to the message.

"Hey Anne, it's me, Chris. Um, sorry [static] but I'm not gonna be [static] but I'm still gonna try [static] okay [more static and then nothing]."

After replaying it three times, trying to hear through all the static, she finally just erased it and threw her phone on the bed. Bad reception or not, she knew when she was getting dumped. And that brief message had exhibited all the signs.

She finished drying off, dragged a comb through her wet, tangled hair, and then stood in front of the mirror staring at her reflection. *I have no idea what just happened,* she thought, *but there's no way I'm calling him back to find out.*

Then she threw on her robe and padded down the hall to where her father was still sitting at the kitchen table.

"Hey, Dad?" she said, standing next to him and dripping water onto the floor.

"Yeah?" He and Brooke both looked at her.

"I just have to make one quick stop before I meet you at the restaurant, okay?" she said, turning and heading back to her room before he even had a chance to answer.

chapter fifty-six

"It's so weird, not having Jade here," Ellie said. She'd already registered for tomorrow's first heat, and now they were sitting on a blanket on the sand, eating fish tacos and listening to the all-girl band.

"I know." Lola covered her mouth as she swallowed. "I talked to her today in trig, and she's so bummed. She really wanted to compete. This is like her favorite event."

"I know; it's the only one she'll ever compete in because it's not all cutthroat. Jeez, I can't even believe how her parents are reacting. It's like tough love over there for weeks now. But I guess my dad totally surprised me, too, by being so nice about it. Too bad it didn't last." She shrugged.

"Yeah." Lola nodded. Then looking up, she said, "Hey, isn't that Chris?"

"Oh no, where?" Ellie said, sounding totally panicked.

"Directly in front of us. Hey! Chris!" Lola called, waving her arms so he'd see them.

"Why'd you do that? Now he's gonna come over," Ellie whined, shaking her head at Lola.

"What's the big deal?" Lola gave her a strange look.

"I saw him after school today with Anne, and I'm not proud of it, but I was a total bitch to her. So I'm sure he's not very happy with me right now. I was really hoping I could avoid him for a while," Ellie said.

"Well, too late for that. He's headed right for us."

"Hey," Chris said, walking up and smiling. "Have you guys seen Anne?"

Lola shook her head, while Ellie just sat there, staring at the ground.

"I've been trying to reach her but I can't get ahold of her. So I thought I'd drop by and see if I could find her here," he said, shaking his head and looking around.

"Well, if nothing else, she should stop by to register. Why don't you just hang with us until she shows?" Lola said, scooting over and making room between herself and Ellie.

Ellie watched him smile and squeeze in next to her. He didn't seem upset or anything, but she was sure all that would change once Anne showed up.

chapter fifty-seven

Anne climbed out of the Mercedes and looked at Jake. "Just wait here. This should only take a second," she said, anxious to get signed up quickly so they could make it to the restaurant on time.

"Sorry, but I'm coming with," he said, pocketing the keys and following behind her. "Partly because you have no idea where you're going, and partly because this place is packed with babes."

"Fine," she said, rolling her eyes at him. "Just don't get distracted, okay? We're in a hurry."

"Just don't forget who's holding the keys," he said, jangling them for her benefit.

She shook her head and pushed through the crowd. Jake was *so* annoying, and if her dad had just let her drive, then she wouldn't be stuck with him now. *And now he is gonna make a fool of himself by gawking at a bunch of girls who want nothing to do with him,* she thought, spotting the registration table and making a beeline for it.

The second she was finished filling out all the necessary forms and paying the entry fee, she went hunting for

Jake. *Of course he's not where he said he'd be,* she thought, glancing at her watch and making her way through the crowd of people, finally spotting him in the middle of a group of girls, laughing and talking and eating a fish taco.

We're about to have dinner at one of the best restaurants in Laguna Beach and he's eating a taco, she thought, shaking her head and wondering what those girls could possibly see in him. "Jake, sorry, but we've only got fifteen minutes 'til we have to be there," she said, looking from the girls to him and then back again.

He looked at Anne, nodding impatiently. And then to the girls he said, "So I'll see you ladies tomorrow."

"Bye, Jake," they sang, as Anne grabbed his arm and pulled him toward the car.

"You have really bad timing," he told her, following reluctantly.

"And you are so *not* coming tomorrow," she said, still dragging him along.

"And why not?" he asked.

"Because I don't want you watching me." She turned and gave him an annoyed look.

"Well, I hate to break it to you, but I'm not coming for *you.* Those girls invited me."

They did? Could that possibly be true? Anne wondered, feeling her stomach go all weird at the thought. "Oh. Well. Fine," she said, feeling totally embarrassed for assuming he'd want to watch her flail about in the water.

"Hey, isn't that your boyfriend?" Jake stopped just short of the car and pointed.

Anne's eyes followed the direction of his finger. And sure enough, there was Chris, sitting smack in the middle of Lola and Ellie, laughing and looking as though he was having a great time. Maybe even too good of a time.

"Hmmm," Anne mumbled, forcing herself to look away.

"Wanna say a quick hello?" he asked, already starting to head toward them.

But no way was Anne joining *that* little party. "We don't have time," she said, racing toward the car. "We really need to get out of here."

chapter fifty-eight

The morning of Surf Fest, Jade woke up really early feeling really depressed. Well, as depressed as someone who's eternally happy and optimistic can get. Being on restriction the last couple weeks had been bad enough. But missing out on her favorite weekend of the year was an all-new low.

Last night, when she was having dinner with her parents, she was positive they would relent and finally set her free. Especially after she'd cleared her throat, and said, "Tonight's the registration party at San O, and tomorrow's the junior competition." She'd even said it casually, between bites of food, so it would look like she didn't care all that much about it, thinking for sure her parents would look up and say, "Oh, we forgot all about it. Let's clean up this mess and go get you registered!" But her father just nodded and her mom just continued eating, and Jade sat there wondering if this particular punishment would ever end. Yet she didn't dare ask. She was far too terrified of what the answer might be.

Rolling over, she looked out the window next to her bed. The day was just starting to break, which meant people were already arriving, setting up the tents, and getting the coffee and hot chocolate ready to brew. *There has to be a way I can get there with-*

out my parents knowing, she thought. Saturdays were usually pretty busy days for them, with all the beach cleanups and gallery openings they participated in, so they usually weren't around all that much. And if she timed it just right, maybe she'd be able to sneak out just long enough to see Ellie and Anne surf, cheer them on, and then get back home before her parents returned.

Climbing out of bed, she padded into the kitchen and headed straight for the coffeemaker. "You're up early," her dad said, totally startling her.

"Well, today's Surf Fest." She shrugged. "So I guess I'm used to getting up early on this particular day. Even though it's obviously not necessary this year. You know, since you're not letting me compete and all," she said, giving him a sideways glance, trying to gage his reaction.

"Come here," he said, motioning for her to join him at the kitchen table. "We need to talk."

Reluctantly, she pulled out the chair across from him and plopped herself onto it. Then she just sat there, waiting for him to begin.

"I know you're feeling really victimized by your mother and me right now. You probably think we're acting like a bunch of uptight hard-asses. Am I right?"

Jade just shrugged, squirming under his heavy gaze. *Jeez,* it was like he could read her mind or something. Because that's exactly what she had been thinking.

"Well, maybe you're right. But you have no idea what it's like to get a call in the middle of the night from the police station telling you to come pick up your daughter. It's every parent's worst nightmare."

"I know, I know, but I was *fine.* I mean, I did *nothing* wrong. If anything, I was just trying to help Ben," she said, sitting up a little straighter and feeling really virtuous.

"And that's another thing," he said, ominously.

"What?" she asked, pushing her curls out of her eyes, bracing herself for whatever came next.

"Ben." He shook his head. "He's a very troubled young man, and your mother and I prefer you don't have anything more to do with him." He looked right at her.

Jade looked down at the table, running her index finger along the wood grain. "Well, first of all, you don't have to worry about that, since he's living with his dad in Venice Beach. And second, I just don't get it. I mean, you and Mom always act so laid-back and nonjudgmental, not to mention how many of *your* friends you've taken in and helped. But now I try to help just one person who really needs it, and I get punished for my efforts. So, just try and explain *that,*" she said, crossing her arms against her chest and looking at him.

"Honey, the difference is that Ben didn't exactly want your help," her dad said, reaching across the table and grabbing her hand. "He was more interested in finding someone to drag down with him. And I'm afraid that you, with your trusting nature and good intentions, were an easy target."

"Thanks a lot," she said, shaking her head and rolling her eyes. *He has no idea what he is talking about. He so doesn't get it.*

"I know you think I don't understand your friendship, but really, I do. And as your dad, I have to tell you it was very troubling to watch. That guy had no regard for your safety, and he put you in a very bad position."

"It was just a little pot." She shrugged.

"Jade, this was not the first time Ben was arrested. A couple weeks ago, he was busted for vandalism. He's in serious trouble now." He looked at her.

Oh my God, that must be why he disappeared for that whole week, she thought, staring at the table again, feeling way too nervous now to look at her dad.

"You need to know that every time we've taken someone in, it was because they *asked* for help. There were never any drugs involved, and there was never any danger posed to you or your sisters. Do you see the difference?"

Finally she looked up at him, nodding slowly. "Okay," she said. "I get it."

"Besides, I don't think we'll be having many more couch crashers in here."

"What do you mean?" she said, eyeing her dad carefully.

"Your mother and I have been talking." He hesitated. "And we're thinking about selling."

"And leave Laguna Cove? But why?" Jade looked at her father in shock. "We love it here."

"The value of this house has more than tripled, and selling it now could allow us to get out of debt and start over."

"But start over *where*? I mean, where would we go? I can't change schools! I don't want to leave my friends!" she said, her voice sounding every bit as frantic as she was feeling.

"Honey, I didn't mean to upset you. We haven't made any final decisions yet, but I want you to know it's a real possibility. It's definitely something we're considering. My last few big pieces haven't done well, you know that, right?"

"But who's to say your next one won't?" Jade said. Then feeling her eyes wet with tears, she got up and went over to the coffeemaker, grabbing the pot and heading for the sink to fill it with water.

"What are you doing?" he asked.

Afraid she'd start crying if she tried to speak, she just held up the pot.

"Put it away, and go get dressed. I figure we can grab some lattes on our way down to San O and that contest." He smiled.

chapter fifty-nine

Ellie was surprised to see her brother knocking on her passenger window. "Hey, let me in," he said.

"What are you doing?" she asked, unlocking the door and giving him a strange look. He'd never wanted to go with her before.

"I'm coming with," he told her, gently laying his video equipment on the backseat and crawling in next to her.

"Why?" she asked, watching him get settled in.

"Car's in the shop." He shrugged.

"But you'll be stuck there all day, totally stranded. I plan on advancing through to the last heat, you know."

"Not a problem. I'll be busy filming. Is Dad gonna make it?" he asked.

Ellie shook her head as she backed out of the driveway and onto the street. "He's already at the hospital," she told him, feeling kind of relieved that her father wouldn't be there to judge her if she choked, but also kind of upset that he wouldn't be there to see her if she won.

"Are any of your friends competing?" he asked, sounding a little too casual while his eyes remained fixed on the road in front of them.

"Jade's still under house arrest. And Lola has cotillion, not to mention that she's not all that into surfing anymore." Ellie shrugged and gave her brother a strange look. *Since when does he care about my friends and their activities?*

"Yeah, I guess her new boyfriend doesn't seem like much of an athlete." He stared out the window.

"Yeah, I guess not," Ellie said, wondering what was up with him as she merged onto the freeway.

chapter sixty

"Lola, are you still asleep?" her mother asked, sticking her head into her room while *Abuela* stood right behind her.

"Not anymore," she said, opening one eye to peer at them and then rolling over to face the wall.

"We have a lot to do today, so I need you to come eat some breakfast so we can get going," her mother said impatiently.

"I made you some eggs and bacon," *Abuela* said, coming over to shake her granddaughter's shoulder.

But Lola just lay there with her eyes closed, slowly counting to ten. She promised herself she would open them the second she reached that number. But she made no promises about how long it might take to get there.

"Get up!" she heard her mother say, in the shrillest voice possible.

Lola rolled over to see *Abuela* smiling down at her, while her mother listed all the very important things that had to be accomplished before this evening's cotillion. "We have to be at the spa in an hour. I've booked us manicures, pedicures, massages, and a hair appointment."

"But I don't want a haircut," Lola said, touching her long, dark hair protectively.

"It's not for a cut. It's for an updo," she told her, while glancing impatiently at her watch. "Now come on. We've got a long day ahead of us and we need to get started right away."

"I'll be there in a minute," Lola said, watching as they left her room and then glancing at the time on her clock radio. *Great. Ellie is going to be surfing her first heat in less than an hour, and there is no way I can get out of this.* Shaking her head in surrender, she stuck her feet in her slippers and walked down the long hallway toward the smell of bacon.

chapter sixty-one

Ellie looked around nervously. She recognized a few people from last year, and everyone seemed to be having so much fun, laughing and joking, as though they had showed up merely for the camaraderie instead of the trophy. But Ellie was here to win, which made her far too nervous to sit around and chat. Last year had ended in disaster, with her getting completely worked by a wave that, if she hadn't been so nervous, she could have handled. And the worst thing was that her father had been standing right there on the shoreline, witnessing every lousy second. So this year she had a lot to prove, but she felt physically and mentally ready to do it. Too bad her dad was gonna miss it.

She kneeled over her board, rubbing it with wax. It was also too bad that Lola and Jade couldn't make it; it just didn't seem the same without them. She knew Anne was already here, having seen her briefly in the parking lot, though they seemed to have a silent agreement to just ignore each other.

Still, it was weird that Anne had shown up alone. Ellie thought for sure Chris would be right there with her. But then again, he hadn't been with her at all last night, since he'd spent the whole time hanging with her and Lola. *Maybe things aren't so great between them after all,* she thought.

"Hey, want some hot chocolate?"

Ellie looked up to see Chris standing there with two steaming cups, smiling at her.

"Oh, I'd love some," she said, reaching for the warm cup.

"What time are you up?" he asked.

"Nine fifteen," she said. And then looking at her watch, "In about ten minutes."

"Are you nervous?" he asked.

"Petrified." She smiled.

"Don't be. You're an amazing surfer, Ellie. And I have no doubt that someday soon you'll be sitting over there." He pointed to the tent where all the sponsored girls were.

Ellie looked over and shrugged. That was her dream. Those girls were the cream of the crop. Talented, gorgeous, athletic, and smart—she longed to be one of them.

"I should head out," she said, finishing her hot chocolate.

"Good luck." He smiled and leaned in to hug her.

"Thanks," Ellie said, closing her eyes and leaning into him, allowing herself to enjoy the closeness, if only for a moment.

But just as she pulled away she opened her eyes and saw Anne, not more than six feet away, standing there watching them.

chapter sixty-two

Anne was bent over her board, furiously waxing it, trying to make sense of what she just witnessed. That was the second time in less than twenty-four hours that she'd seen Chris and Ellie together, and she was absolutely positive that it was not a coincidence that both those events just happened to take place after she foolishly told him all about Ellie being in love with him.

Well, that's what you get, she thought. *You practically threw him in her path.* And why wouldn't he like Ellie? Other than being a total bitch (and what guy ever cared about that?), Ellie had it all—she was beautiful, brainy, popular, rich, a great surfer, not to mention how she and Chris went way back. And there was just no way Anne could compete with that. Hadn't she already learned that lesson when Justin dumped her for Vanessa?

Picking up her board, she headed toward the water, stopping to watch Ellie paddling around and maneuvering into the best position possible. *If Ellie is a shark, then I'm her dinner,* she thought. *And I'll surely be eaten alive.*

chapter sixty-three

Ellie had only fifteen minutes to be scored on ten waves, with the bottom seven numbers being thrown out. But Ellie was determined to surf all ten waves amazingly well. There would be no throwaways as far as she was concerned.

While the other girls around her laughed and talked, Ellie kept to herself, watching the waves and devising a strategy. She'd watched Anne paddle out, looking completely lost and unsure of what to do next, but Ellie just shrugged it off. That was Anne's problem. Ellie wasn't here to baby-sit some newbie. She had a contest to win.

When the moment felt exactly right, she started paddling, and then hopping onto her board, she rode the wave confidently and carefully all the way to the shore. *But maybe I've been just a little too careful,* she thought as she turned around to head back out. She hadn't done anything remotely impressive, but then again, at least she hadn't choked.

Lying on her board, she paddled quickly toward the break. She had nine more waves to go, and no time to spare.

chapter sixty-four

Anne was totally lost. Some of the girls who seemed so nice and helpful just a moment ago were now totally focused on their own performance, and she was left wondering just what the hell she'd been thinking to even attempt this in the first place. She'd been surfing now, for what, a month? It was totally ridiculous of her to think she could pull this off. Especially after watching Ellie's awesome performance.

Ellie had just surfed her sixth wave and she was totally carving it up out there. There was no doubt that she would be advancing to the next heat, while Anne would probably be free to go home sometime within the next ten minutes.

She tried to remember her diving days, when she had been the one to beat, just like Ellie was now. But it didn't exactly compare, since she'd been diving since she was eight, and everything was just so much easier back then, mostly because people were pretty impressed with just about anything you did at that age. But now, at almost seventeen, the pressure was much greater, especially when she knew Ellie was out there like a vulture, patiently watching and waiting for her to fail.

Oh well. It beats wearing an ugly bridesmaid's dress at your pregnant mom's shotgun wedding, she thought, popping up on her board, determined to at least make it to shore without falling off.

chapter sixty-five

Lola's nails were wet, her face was caked with makeup, and her hair was all piled up high on top of her head like a big chocolate-frosted cake. "I'm supposed to walk around like this *all day*?" she asked, shuddering at her own reflection. She looked more like a Vegas showgirl than a virginal debutante about to be introduced to society.

"Well, it's not like we're going anywhere else. After here it's just home, until it's time to put on your dress and go," her mother told her.

"Uh, wrong," Lola said, shaking her head carefully so as not to dislodge the million bobby pins and sparkly barrettes that were holding the whole mess together. "I told Diego I'd meet him." She nodded, having come up with this genius excuse sometime between the massage and the body scrub.

"You are not meeting Diego," her mom said, turning away from the increasingly frustrated makeup artist. "You will see him tonight at cotillion. You two are just gonna have to wait until then."

Lola noticed the little smile on her mom's face when she said that, like she was so proud of herself for introducing her daughter to her future husband. *If she only knew,* Lola thought, shaking her head. "Mom, it can't wait. Because he wants to give me . . . " She hesitated; she hadn't really thought it all the way through to this point. ". . . a present. He has a present for me that he wants me to have . . . for tonight," she concluded, thinking how now she'd also have to stop by the mall to pick up some little trinket and then pretend it was from Diego. She'd have to make sure she wore her sunglasses, 'cause there was no way she could be seen lurking around South Coast Plaza with hair like this.

"Fine," her mother said, frowning as Lola jumped up from her chair. "But be home as quickly as possible. Your hair and makeup have to last until tonight, you know."

"Don't worry," Lola said, slipping her flip-flops onto her feet and thinking how odd she must look with her California girl clothes and Spanish soap opera hair and makeup.

chapter sixty-six

Anne could not believe when she heard her name called. "Third place," Jake said, smiling and slapping her on the back. "That means you get to go on to the next heat!"

"It does? Are you serious?" she asked. The scoring and rules were all new to her, so she sincerely hoped he wasn't just fooling around.

"Yeah, but it doesn't start for a while, so you can just chill," he said, smiling.

"Did you hear that?" she said, as her dad and Brooke approached. "I'm advancing to the next heat. I mean, I'll probably choke on that one, but I don't even care! It just feels so awesome to get to this point!" She was so excited, she even hugged Brooke.

"I just saw Chris," her father said. "He's looking for you. I told him you were over here."

"Oh, really?" Anne bit down on her lip, wondering why Chris was looking for her. Was he going to break up with her? Right now? Well, he'd just have to wait, since there was no way she was going to let him ruin her day. The last thing she needed was for some stupid relationship drama to kill her buzz, and there was no way she was gonna let him bring her down. "Well, if he comes by, just tell him I'll catch up with him later. I'm totally starving. I'm gonna grab something to eat." And then, grabbing Jake by the arm, she said, "Wanna join me?"

chapter sixty-seven

Ellie wasn't surprised she'd advanced to the second heat. Nor was she surprised that she came in first. But what did surprise her was the sight of Lola walking across the beach with the biggest hair she'd ever seen.

"Don't even mention it," Lola said, holding up her hand defensively. "In fact, please don't even look at it."

"How can I not?" Ellie said, laughing. "It's huge!'

"Can you even believe it?" She rolled her eyes. "I swear, the things Lola will do to please her mother . . ."

"And the things Lolita will do to be a good friend," Ellie said, hugging her gently so as not to get stabbed in the eye by a pink heart-shaped rhinestone barrette. "I can't believe you showed up."

"Hey, I haven't missed one of these yet. And for your information, Jade's here, too. I just saw her with her dad; they were talking to Chris."

"Is she surfing?" Ellie asked.

"No. Apparently, she had to learn a lesson about the consequences of certain actions, or however her dad phrased it." She rolled her eyes.

"Well, how long are you staying?" Ellie asked.

"Long enough to totally embarrass myself with this updo, and see you nail a trophy and a sponsorship." She smiled.

chapter sixty-eight

"So why are you using me to hide from your boyfriend?" Jake asked, taking a sip of his coffee and looking right at Anne.

"Don't be ridiculous," she said, feeling her face go every shade of fuchsia. "I don't even know what you're talking about." She shook her head and sipped her drink, avoiding his eyes.

"The dude's been looking all over for you, but you keep hiding—mostly behind me. So, what's the deal? You guys in a fight?" he asked.

"I . . ." Anne hesitated, feeling frustrated because she really didn't know how to answer. Because she really didn't know what the answer was. "I'd really rather not talk about it, if you don't mind," she said, placing her hands on her hips and narrowing her eyes at him.

"Okay, that's cool," he said, looking at her and nodding. "You know you're gonna be a real catch someday—when you grow up." He smiled.

"What's that supposed to mean?" she asked.

But he just looked at her, tossed his empty coffee cup in the bin, and started to walk away.

"For your information, you're only two years older than me!"

she yelled after him, feeling even more annoyed when he just smiled, waved, and kept walking.

Oh, that's just great, she thought, standing there and staring after him as he weaved his way through the crowd of people. *Who does he think he is, talking to me like that? He works for my dad! And he should really learn to be more respectful.* He had no idea what was going on in her life, and he had no right to judge her.

She shook her head and looked out at the water. Thirty more minutes until her next heat, and there was no way she was gonna let Jake upset her. *He is nothing to me. He's just a minor annoyance,* she told herself as she headed back toward her surfboard.

chapter sixty-nine

Lola sat on the shoreline with Jade, trying to forget about her stupid hair and the fact that everyone who walked past her turned and did a double take. Ellie and Anne were out there surfing, and even though on the surface she was rooting for them both, deep down inside she really wanted Ellie to win, mostly because she had the most riding on it.

"I wish I was out there," Jade said. "I really blew it this time."

"There's always next year." Lola shrugged.

But Jade knew that wasn't necessarily true. Feeling her eyes start to sting with tears, she closed them until the moment passed. She wished she could confide in Lola about her conversation with her dad—about how they might have to leave Laguna Cove and move far away. But she was barely able to admit it to herself, much less her best friends. So, determined to put it out of her mind, she decided not to say anything.

"Who knows, maybe I'll even enter it with you." Lola laughed, but her smile froze into place when she spotted Dean standing just a few feet away. And he was looking right at her.

"Oh my God," Jade said. "I think Anne's going for it. Oh, I can't look. It makes me too nervous. I'm gonna go pee instead." She got up from her towel.

"Now?" Lola asked, panicked. The last thing she needed was to be left alone. Because then Dean might come over. And she had no idea what she'd say to him if that happened.

"Yeah, I'll be right back." Jade gave her a strange look.

"But can't you wait?" Lola asked, realizing how needy and ridiculous she sounded. But there's no way she could let Jade leave her.

"What's the deal?" Jade said, hopping anxiously from one foot to the other.

"Nothing." Lola shook her head with resignation. "Go ahead."

Jade ran off toward the bathrooms while Lola looked out at the ocean. Anne had just fallen off her board. *That's gotta hurt*, she thought, cringing as she watched Anne get worked by a wave.

"Hey."

Lola knew the voice, so she was reluctant to look up and actually see the person it belonged to. "Hey," she said, her eyes remaining focused on the ocean in front of her, since she didn't know how to face Dean.

"How've you been?" he asked, kneeling down next to her.

"Okay." She shrugged. Then, suddenly remembering her outrageous hair and makeup, she began to feel really self-conscious. "You're not filming me, are you?" she asked, glancing nervously at his camera.

"Um, no," he said, turning it away from her and putting the lens cap back on. "Listen, Lola, I don't really know how to say this, and you know I'm not that good with words and stuff, but I miss you." He gave her a tentative, shy look.

"You do?" She turned toward him, her eyes going wide. *Could he possibly really mean that?*

"Yeah." He blushed. "But I know you have a new boyfriend now, and you guys seem really happy, so I'm not looking for anything. I just wanted to apologize for ending everything so abruptly. I can see now that I made a big mistake."

Lola just looked at him. After all this time, after all the heartache she'd endured, he'd finally just said all the right things, using all the right words. And now she had a choice. She could either tell him the truth about Diego and end the whole stupid charade right now, or she could keep her secret and let Dean suffer just a little while longer.

She looked right into his eyes and slowly trailed a finger down his cheek. "I really appreciate you saying that." She smiled. "And I really hope that we can still be friends."

chapter seventy

Ellie had one more wave to go and plenty of time in which to do it. She was on fire today, having never surfed better in her life. But Anne had just wiped out again, and Ellie noticed that her face was all red as she paddled back in. There was no way she would make it to the final heat. She'd had a decent enough start, but now she was totally falling apart. And even if she did surf a perfect last wave, it still wouldn't be enough. It was pretty much over for her.

Ellie saw Anne glance at her warily and then position herself as far from her as possible. Which also just happened to be the absolute worst place she could have picked. And it made Ellie wonder if Anne chose it because she had no idea how bad it was, or if she chose it so she could be far away from Ellie.

Oh my God, what have I done, she thought. *I've turned into such a jealous, competitive, nasty bitch that I'm actually sabotaging this poor girl's chances! And isn't that like, the exact opposite of what surfing is supposed to be about?*

Ellie looked at her watch—she had two minutes left to catch her last wave and really shred it to impress the judges.

Or she could help someone who really needed it.

chapter seventy-one

Anne sat on her board, choking back tears and hoping that the salt water pouring from her eyes was blending in with the salt water from the ocean, so no one would know what a big, pathetic baby she was being. What had started out as a pretty good day had quickly gone to hell. She felt bad about her mom's wedding, she felt bad about Chris avoiding her (or was she avoiding Chris?), and she felt inexplicably bad about Jake's stupid little comment.

Even her surfing had fallen apart, and her body felt bruised and battered from getting worked by so many waves. And now, to just top off this miserable day, that total bitch, Ellie, was sitting on her board waving at her. God, she was like a pit bull. She just never let up.

Oh well, I may as well get the last wave out of the way, she thought. *I mean, I have to get back to shore somehow.* Anne started to paddle, but stopped when Ellie charged right in front of her. "What do you want?" Anne glared at her.

"I want to help you, if you'll let me," Ellie told her.

"Yeah, right. You probably came all the way over here just to gloat. Well fine, you're winning, *okay*? You're winning at absolutely everything. You're taking Surf Fest, you're taking Chris, and now you probably want to take me down. Am I right?" Anne looked away. There was no way she would cry in front of her.

"Listen, we don't have a lot of time," Ellie said. "And you're right, I'm ahead and you're not. But it really doesn't matter anymore. I mean, don't you want to surf one really awesome wave before you go home?"

Anne just looked at her, not sure if this was for real or not.

"I can help you do that, if you'll just follow me. Oh, and for the record," Ellie said, turning back to look at her. "Chris likes *you*, not *me*. And I'm okay with that."

chapter seventy-two

"Oh my God, look at her! I think she's really gonna take it this year!" Chris said, grabbing Anne's hand and watching Ellie surf her very last wave of the junior's final heat.

"Oh, I can't look," Jade said, covering her eyes. "Just, just give me a play-by-play but don't tell me if she falls, 'cause I don't want to know about it."

"You're just gonna have to open your eyes and see it for yourself because the girl is *rippin' it up,*" Lola said, glancing back and forth between Ellie out in the water and Dean running up and down the shoreline taping her.

"Hey, don't you have cotillion?" Anne asked.

"Yeah, but I'm not budging 'til this is all said and done," Lola said, glancing briefly at Anne, and then back at the water. "Oh my God, she made it. She did it! *Yes!*" Lola got up from her towel, and jumped up and down on the sand, while bobby pins and barrettes sprang from her hair, landing all around her.

"Uh, Lola, I think your hair just popped," Jade said, pointing at Lola's sunken updo and laughing.

"Oh, who cares?" Lola yanked out the remaining bobby pins and barrettes and threw them onto her towel. Then, quickly combing her fingers through her long, dark hair, she ran down to the water, toward Dean.

chapter seventy-three

"You did it! You were *amazing*!" Jade said hugging Ellie, while Chris and Anne nodded in agreement.

"You think so?" Ellie asked, squeezing the salt water from her hair. "I mean, you never know until the scores are read, right?"

"You totally deserve to win," Anne said, looking at her and smiling.

Ellie smiled back; then looking past Anne she noticed Duncan standing just a few feet away, with his arm around a pretty brunette who she had just competed against. Their eyes met briefly, and Duncan smiled and waved. But Ellie just nodded, surprised by the way she felt at seeing him with another girl.

"Honey, there's someone waiting to talk to you," her dad said, interrupting her train of thought.

"Dad! You made it! Did you see me?" Ellie asked, feeling like a little kid begging, *Look at me, Daddy! Look at me!*

"I didn't get here 'til your final heat, but I saw all of it. You were amazing." He smiled and hugged her tight. "I'm so proud of you," he whispered.

Ellie clung to him until the threat of tears had passed, and then she pulled away and said, "So who wants to talk to me?"

"Some surf-brand big shot," he said, looking at her and smiling. "He mentioned something about a sponsorship?"

Ellie grabbed her dad's hand and headed toward the tent. Her biggest dream was about to come true, but the thing that she felt the most proud of was something the sponsors and judges never even saw. But she knew. And Anne knew. And maybe, in some strange way, even her mom knew.

Stopping for a moment, she lifted her face toward the sun, closing her eyes and feeling the warmth against her skin. Then, looking over at her father, she smiled and squeezed his hand as they continued toward the tent.

Cruel Summer

June 13

Dear Aunt Tally,

When I asked my mom for your e-mail address, she just laughed and told me you didn't have one. But I know she's just joking—right?

I mean, it's not like you have to have a computer or anything, since I'm planning on bringing my laptop anyway, I just need to make sure you have wi-fi, high speed, broadband, or whatever they call it where you live, since it's really important for me to stay connected, ~~because, well, I just started hanging with this new group of friends and~~

Anyway, so my mom just walked in and when she saw me writing to you she said, "Don't waste the postage, Colby. You'll get there long before that letter does." But just in case she's wrong, I'm sending it anyway. And just in case she's right, well, then I guess there's nothing more to say.

See you soon.

Love,

Colby

June 15

Dear Mom and Dad,

Just in case you decide to stop arguing long enough to come look for me, you should know that I'm NOT home. I'm out with my friends, determined to enjoy my LAST NIGHT OF FREEDOM.

Attempting one last stab at having a little FUN before you succeed in TAKING IT ALL AWAY.

But don't worry. I'm not running away or anything. Mostly because your decision to send me away makes running away seem almost redundant.

Besides, I've done my best to reason with you and try to put an immediate halt to all that you've started, but since I've so clearly failed, I will soon surrender, comply with your wishes, and resign myself to the fate you have so randomly chosen for me.

Only not now, later. Because now, I'm just going to try to enjoy myself—while I still can.

Though before I go I'd like to leave you with a few thoughts for you to consider:

It's not too late!

There's plenty of time to reconsider!

Everything you've done can still be undone!

At least take the time to think about it.

~Colby

COLBY'S JOURNAL FOR DESPERATE TIMES LIKE RIGHT NOW

June 16

I can't believe I'm actually writing in this journal. I mean, ~~today,~~ (well, technically it would now be yesterday), when my mom gave it to me, I just looked at her and said, "What's this?"

And she said, "I thought you could use it to write about all of the exciting things that happen to you this summer."

So then I shook my head, rolled my eyes, and sighed as loud as I could.

Then I tossed it onto my desk and watched it skid all the way across the top until it fell off the side and tumbled to the ground, as my mom just stood there, still and silent, gazing between the upside-down journal and me.

But I just narrowed my eyes and stared right back, wondering if she was going to yell at me, cry, or both.

But in the end she just shook her head and left my room. And the second the door closed behind her, I'm the one who started to cry.

Though not for too long, since I didn't want my face to be all puffy and red for the good-bye party Amanda was supposed to throw for me. Even though in the end it really wasn't much of a party since it pretty much consisted of a six-pack of her brother's beer, a bag of chips, and us.

Well, at least until she made a few calls—

Okay, I was just about to write the rest of the story, but then I decided to stop because it feels really weird to be confessing in this thing. I mean, as much as I'd like to write about EVERYTHING that just happened (and trust me, there's PLENTY to write about), because I'm thinking it might really help me to get it all down on paper and maybe even clear my head and put it all back in perspective, the thing is, I can't help but think—*what if someone reads it?*

I mean, it's not like you can password protect a leather-bound notebook.

Not to mention how I can STILL hear my parents totally yelling and screaming downstairs, which is not only making it hard to concentrate, but also freaking me out to think what will happen when they come up here to check on me while I sleep (because that's what they always do after they've exhausted themselves from one of their arguments and are ready to call it a night and head off to their separate rooms), and maybe even end up peeking at what I've written.

And even though I know that probably sounds totally paranoid, in light of how they've managed to wreck just about every aspect of my life, I think the breakdown in trust is completely justified.

So, with that in mind, it's better to just sign off for now and continue this at another time, in another place.

Or not.

June 16
Text Message:
To: Amanda
Message: This is the last txt msg Ull get from me bcuz IM packed N ready N lvg 4 LAX v soon so I wanna say bye N also 2 say last nite was soooo fun but it also makes lvg that much harder I still cant believe my rents

R doing this 2 me O well Plz say bye 2 Levi 4 me N plz give him my email cuz I 4got 2
K, ttfn, Colby

June 16

Dear Mom and Dad,

I really hope that by the time you return from dropping me off at the airport you will find this letter and realize what a big mistake you've made.

Because this is NOT fair!

It feels like I'M the one being punished because YOU GUYS decided to get a divorce—a divorce that, as you know, not only am I completely against, but that I definitely don't agree with. And yet, here I am, being banished from everything I know and love, and it just doesn't make any sense.

It's not like I'm the one causing trouble. It's not like I'm the one yelling and screaming and fighting all the time. Because that would be YOU! And yet, somehow, the plane ticket is still in my name.

I mean, did you ever stop to consider that maybe the WRONG PERSON is being sent to Aunt Tally's? Did you ever stop and think that maybe one of YOU should go cool off on a Greek island for a couple months, so I can just stay home and enjoy my summer in peace?

Apparently not.

I hope that by the time you finish this letter you will have come to your senses, stop fighting, see the error of your ways, and bring me back home immediately.

It's as simple as calling the airport and having me paged.

I will be listening for my name.

And even though it's probably not necessary to say, I want to assure you that should you choose to reverse your decision, I hereby do solemnly swear, to never mention this little digression again. I will just tuck it away in the file of Things We'd All Rather Forget.

But if not . . . then I'm afraid I can't be held responsible for my actions.

Please take the time to reconsider. And remember, it's never too late to correct a mistake.

Love,

Your sad, lonely, and already completely homesick daughter—

Colby

Colby's Journal for Desperate Times When She's Stuck at 37,000 Feet Where There Is No Internet Access

June 16

I tried. Really, I did. I gave it my best shot, but here I am anyway. Sitting on this stupid airplane, next to some stupid, smelly old man, in seat 37G, which is the second-to-last row, just around the corner from the toilets (which, believe me, I can totally smell) and right next to the window in case I want to open the shade and gaze out at—nothing. Seriously, there's nothing out there but miles and miles of white cloud tops.

That's how high up we are.

That's how far from home I am.

And it would all be fine and worth it if I was going to end up somewhere good, but I just happened to peek at the first page of the guidebook my dad slipped me at the airport and this is what it says:

> *Tinos is the most important destination in Greece for religious pilgrims, and yet it remains one of the least commercialized islands.*

Um, excuse me? Religious pilgrims? Least commercialized? And those are the good things?

And if that wasn't bad enough, it then goes on to say:

> *Tinos is also famous for its dovecotes—which are elaborate stone towers, with ornamental perches for doves.*

And then it waxes all rhapsodic over some stupid natural spring in some stupid main square in some stupid small village where the locals apparently:

> *Wash their clothes by hand.*

So basically I guess you could say that my parents are sending me to a place where religious pilgrims, doves, and villagers all hand wash their delicates right smack in the middle of the town square.

And I don't think I need to point out how it really doesn't get any worse than that.

Not to mention how I did absolutely nothing to deserve any of this in the first place. Since it's not like I got in trouble, or did anything illegal or bad, and yet, here I am, the one being punished.

I mean, just because my parents decided to wreck their lives and get divorced shouldn't mean they get to wreck my life too. Isn't it enough that they're robbing me of a two-parent home, as well as their mutual guidance, stability, and security?

DO THEY REALLY HAVE TO WRECK MY ENTIRE FREAKING SUMMER TOO???

Apparently, they do.

Because according to my mom's shrink/life coach, I need to be "removed from all negative influences," and shielded from "any harmful issues that may arise during this turbulent time," so that my parents can "work out their issues in private," so I can return to a "peaceful household." Which may sound all fine and reasonable on paper, but here's the thing—how does she know what I'll return to? And how can she guarantee it'll be PEACEFUL?

And more importantly, WILL I EVEN BE ABLE TO RECOGNIZE MY OWN LIFE ONCE I'M ALLOWED TO RETURN TO IT?

Or will they have hacked away at it so much, that by the time I get back, there'll be nothing left that's even remotely familiar?

Because last night, when I came home from Amanda's, almost a full two hours past curfew, braced and ready for big-time trouble, my mom and dad were so involved in one of their never-ending arguments they didn't even notice I was back, much less late. Heck, they probably weren't even aware that I was even gone in the first place—that's how bad it's gotten.

And just as I was sneaking past the downstairs guest room (where my dad's been camping out for the last three months), and heading upstairs to my room, I completely froze, with my eyes bugged out and my jaw on the floor, as I distinctly heard them use the words—*sell the house*—*move*—and—*Cyber School.*

In. That. Order.

And now, because of that, pretty much all I can think about is:

1) If they fight like that when I'm gone just a few hours, how bad will it get when I'm gone for three months? Ten o'clock news bad? *Dateline* Special bad? I seriously wish I was joking, but I'm not.
2) Move? Who's moving? And more importantly—*where??*
3) What the heck is *Cyber School*? And how does it apply to *me*?
4) If they really care that much about my "peace of mind," then how can they banish me to no-man's land—just ship me off to live with an aunt, who, up until two weeks ago, they both referred to as "Crazy Aunt Tally?"

I'm totally serious. That's exactly what they called her, and they didn't even laugh when they said it. They'd say things like: "Your crazy aunt Tally sent you a birthday card," and then my dad would drop a blue airmail envelope onto my desk. Or, "Your crazy aunt Tally made you these earrings," then my mom would jiggle something dangly and beaded in her hand.

And now, just because they've decided they can no longer stand each other, can no longer communicate without screaming, crazy Aunt Tally is suddenly the perfect summer chaperone?

I mean, ARE THEY JOKING?

And just exactly HOW am I supposed to survive, for a WHOLE ENTIRE SUMMER, with no car, no cell phone, no Sidekick, no Sephora, no Abercrombie, no parties, no friends, and no Internet access???

Not to mention how this was supposed to be my best summer yet, the one I'd been working toward since practically forever. Because after years of going through the motions of a ho-hum existence, after years of being just another blank face in the crowd, I finally penetrated Amanda Harmon's inner circle. And I'm not talking clinging to the outer fringes along with all the other wannabe dorks; no I'm talking right inside the Promised Land. I'm talking the glorious, golden, inner sanctum of those who are allowed to hang at her house, ride in her car, and maintain a spot on her cell phone speed dial.

Though I'm still not sure how it happened. It's like, one moment, I'd been secretly worshipping her from afar, going all the way back to elementary school when I'd pretend to make fun of her hairstyles and mannerisms (but only because my one and only friend at the time truly did despise her, which made me feel like I had to hide the fact of how I wanted to be just like her), and the next, in a complete and total fluke which also turned out to be a moment of complete and total kismet, I'd scored the winning goal in a down and dirty game of fifth-period PE volleyball, after which she came right up to me and said, "Hey, way to score."

And then she high-fived me.

And then she complimented me on my brand-new Nikes.

And the next thing I knew, I was pretty much her new best friend.

Which kind of required me to get rid of my old best friend.

But since we were kind of in a fight anyways, I decided to go with it and never look back.

Anyway, all of this happened just in time for what was gearing up to be the most amazing summer of my, so far mostly unamazing seventeen years, which, now, because of my parents, their attorneys, and my mother's personal guidance counselor, has been tragically edited down to just one single night.

Still, as far as nights go, I have to admit it WAS pretty incredible (hence the two hours past curfew return!) and since it's most likely the only great night I'll ever get, I should probably write it all down so I'll always remember it.

Only not now, later. Because now, the flight attendants are bringing the meals and I'm starving.

June 17

Dear Mom and Dad,

You may notice that this letter is written on a Coke-stained Ellas Ferry Lines cocktail napkin. Well, that's because I'm now on the boat to Tinos. That's right, THE BOAT. Because apparently there is no airport in Tinos, which means you are sending me to a place that planes refuse to land in.

Thanks for that.

Though what you may not have realized is that planes do land in Mykonos, lots of them. Which only makes me wonder why you couldn't have sent me there instead? Because according to the superhot Italian guy I sat next to on the flight from Athens to Mykonos (and his boyfriend), NOBODY goes to Tinos.

Nobody but, oh yah, that's right—ME.

At first I was thinking I'd use this napkin to get rid of my gum, but then I realized that would only deprive you of seeing the unhappy results of your decision.

Love,

The extremely unhappy but not like you care—

Colby

Colby's Journal for Desperate Times When the Electrical Outlet Is so Weird She Can't Even Plug in Her Computer to Recharge It

June 18

I don't even know what time it is, much less what day. All I know is that I just woke up and it's dark out, but whether it's night dark or early morning dark, I can't be sure. The only thing I know is that my room looks like this:

Smooth white walls
White filmy curtains
White marble floors
White sheepskin rug on white marble floors
Single bed with white sheets and sky blue comforter
White bedside table with small silver lamp with sky blue shade

So basically, you could say it looks a lot like the view from seat 37G—nothing but white, white, white, with the occasional small pocket of blue. And oh yeah, the electrical outlet is all weird and different and absolutely refuses to cooperate with my computer plug, and it makes me wonder what the rest of the house is like too. I mean, I barely got a chance to see it, because the second my aunt Tally showed me my room, I pretty much fell face-first on my bed. Partly because I was tired from the twenty-two hours of nonstop traveling, and partly because crying always exhausts me like that.

That's right, I cried.

In public.

Like the world's most pathetic baby.

It's like, the second I'd finished writing that napkin letter to my parents I felt so angry and frustrated and sad, I just broke down in tears. And even though I knew it was stupid and embarrassing and childish, I couldn't stop. I guess it just needed to come out, so there wasn't much I could do about it.

But when I finally calmed down enough to look around, I noticed this really old lady dressed in all black, and she was totally staring at me, though not in a kind grandmotherly way like you'd think. So I grabbed my bags and went outside, where I stood on deck, gazing back at where I came from, wondering what would happen if I just turned around and took the next boat back to Mykonos, found a job, a place to live, and settled in without ever contacting anyone to tell them where I am and what I'm up to. Just start over, build a new life, and grow old. Never to return.

I mean, how would my parents feel THEN?

It's funny how just fantasizing about getting revenge can actually make you feel better. So after imagining my parents so frantic with grief, worry, and guilt they vow to halt the divorce and bring me back home, I wiped my face and gazed toward Tinos, and that's when I noticed this really cute guy standing just a few feet away.

And just as I thought—*hey, maybe things are starting to look up, maybe this won't be so bad after all,* I glanced down at my hands and saw how they were all black, and inky, and streaked with mascara, which meant that my face was probably all black, and inky, and streaked with mascara too. Which was probably the only reason he was even looking at me to begin with. So I ran back inside to search for a bathroom so I could clean myself up, but then right when I found one, the horn blew, and from the way everyone stampeded for the exit, I figured it meant we were there.

It's weird how I recognized my aunt right away even though the last time I saw her I was just two, and it's not like I can even remember that time. But still, I just took one look at her and I *knew.* Though it's not because she looked like someone's crazy aunt. It was more because she looks a lot like my mom. Well, if my mom was relaxed and happy, and had kept her original nose, and let her blond bob grow back out to its natural brown waviness, and then dressed in beachwear all the time and not just when she was actually at the beach or by the pool.

Okay, so I just looked outside again and I'm guessing it's A.M. since the sun is now rising. So I think I'll stop writing and go outside, and try to figure out just where the heck I am.

Twenty Minutes Later:

Okay, all I know is this—I can totally see part of Mykonos from here. And let me just say that even at a distance I can tell it's a helluva lot better than this place.

I'm so screwed.

I think Tally just woke up.

Twelve Hours Later:

How I Spent My First Day in ~~Prison~~ Greece

1) I woke up (duh).
2) I wrote in my journal.

3) I went exploring on my own and discovered that I am surrounded by: dirt, white houses, geraniums, more dirt, rocks, and if I crane my neck a certain way I have a pretty good view of both the sea and Mykonos—which, I can tell just from looking, is a gazillion times better than here.

4) I got through a very awkward breakfast with my aunt Tally that consisted of bread with butter and honey, along with a completely horrible cup of coffee that not only tasted like mud but actually TURNED INTO MUD when I let it sit too long. Seriously! And I did everything in my power not to vomit that first sip back up (because that would be both rude and gross). Though I think Tally could tell by my face how much I hated it, because she just started laughing and said I was under no obligation to finish it. And all I can say is if the rest of Greece is as bad as their coffee, then this summer is going to suck even more than I thought.

5) During breakfast Tally tried to get me to open up about the divorce, but luckily, when I made it clear it wasn't on my list of favorite things to talk about, she let it go. Then she just started talking about herself, and how she came here fourteen years ago and never looked back. And when I asked her why she didn't go to Mykonos instead, she just shook her head and said

that wasn't her scene. Which I took to mean that she has a very high tolerance for boredom, because from what I've seen so far, that's about all this place has to offer.

6) After breakfast, I tried to be polite and help with the dishes, but Tally just shook her head and waved me away so I went back to my room where I took a shower and unpacked.

7) After, we walked into town (um, if you can even call it a "town," I mean, it's really more like a tiny village, but whatever) so Tally could show me where her shop (where she sells her jewelry and stuff), the bank, the market, and a couple other places I might need are located—even though they're pretty much all lined up on the same small street. And when I asked her where the big stores are, you know like the department stores and stuff, she just laughed and said, "In Athens."

8) After my tour of the town, we walked back home and got in her jeep and then she drove me all around the island so I could look at more dirt, more geraniums, more rocks, and more white houses.

9) And after two hours of that, she asked me if I wanted to go to the beach, but I just shook my head and told her I was jet-lagged. And even though I'm not really sure what being jet-lagged actually feels like, I'm thinking if it resembles

anything remotely like sadness, depression, and complete and overwhelming despondency, then I totally was not lying.

10) In the evening, I emerged from my ~~prison cell~~ room just long enough to have a dinner of Greek salad (~~decent,~~ no, good actually, though by no means great) and some Greek casserole dish that I won't even try to pronounce, much less spell, but that tasted like some seriously messed-up lasagna. And then I said good night, and went back to bed.

The End.

P.S. The good news is I have about seventy-five more days ahead of me that promise to be exactly like this one. Yippee!

Colby's Journal for Desperate Times When There's No Logical Explanation for What Is Happening to Her

June 19

Okay, so apparently my mom was *not* joking. And I didn't mention this before because I was really hoping that she and Tally were in cahoots, playing some kind of messed-up mind game. But evidently, I'm completely cut off from the outside world. Because not only does my aunt Tally not have a computer or Internet access, but she also does not have a TV. Which is so completely weird, not to mention practically impossible to get used to. I mean, even though the shows are probably all in Greek, which I wouldn't be able to understand anyway, not having access to a television just doesn't seem right.

Though it does explain why my parents refer to her as *Crazy*.

But unfortunately, that's not even the half of it, because believe me, there's more. For example:

1) She talks to her plants. Seriously, she thanks them for blossoming, growing, and basically doing all of the things they're supposed to be doing anyway. And when she caught me gaping at her with my jaw hanging down to my knees, watching in complete and total disbelief as she whispered sweet nothings to her geraniums, she just turned and explained (with a totally straight face) that they're *alive and aware*. And even though I'm clearly not doubting the *alive* part, since all the leaves are green and not brown, it's the *aware* part that worries me. I mean, aware of *what* exactly? So when I asked her which language they respond in—Greek or English, she just smiled in that weird peaceful way and kept at it.
2) She only keeps what she can use. Which sounds completely reasonable until she goes on to explain that collecting and acquiring things you don't *truly* need only results in "clogged energy."

Which also means that the moment she finishes a book (and she reads like, one a day) she thanks it for the knowledge it provided (believe me, I wish I was joking but I'm not) and then she passes it on to someone else. Same with CDs, clothes, you name it, nothing gets saved, it all gets thanked, blessed, and passed on to the next recipient. Which basically means this house is so spare and empty it feels like we're living in a monastery—only without the vow of silence, since we do get to talk (especially to plants and other inanimate objects). Though the truth is, I really wouldn't mind a vow of silence since I don't have much to say anyway. Mostly because I'm too busy worrying about how I'll possibly survive the next seventy-four days (and counting!), to focus on something as trivial as small talk.

3) She's totally in cahoots with my mom's shrink and thinks it's just wonderful that I'm escaping my parents' "negative energy" as well as taking a break from my "computer addiction and obsessive focus on accumulation and mass consumerism." Whatever the heck that means.

I mean, she's nice and all, don't get me wrong, and she means well, I can tell. But the freaky thing is that she actually *believes* all of this stuff. And while that may be all fine and good for her, the fact remains that she's the one who CHOSE to live this austere, serene island life, while I myself did NOT. And even though I just got here, I don't think it's too big of a stretch to say that it's really not working for me.

Because what my aunt obviously does not understand is how imperative it is for me to stay in touch with Amanda. How it's seriously and completely crucial that Amanda does NOT forget me while I'm gone. There's just too much riding on our friendship, too much at stake. I mean, if I'm going to have any fun at all during my last year of high school, if I want to go to prom, and parties, and basically partake in anything worth partaking in, then I HAVE TO STAY TIGHT WITH AMANDA!

I CANNOT allow her to replace me with some undeserving wannabe. I just can't afford to let that happen.

And the reason I'm so worried about it in the first place, is because I happen to know for a fact that Amanda has the attention span of a housefly. Seriously, she's always flitting from one object to another, unable to stay focused on any one thing. Like she has social ADD or something. And now that I'm gone I'm afraid she'll just land on someone else, and come September, all of my hard work will be wasted.

Like on Friday, my last night in town, when we were sitting in her room, flipping through magazines and listening to music (which is pretty much all she could be bothered to arrange for my big going-away party), and right after I read our horoscopes out loud, she looked at me and squinted and went, "Wait—so where are you going again?"

And honestly, I could hardly believe it. I mean, it's not like I hadn't told her like a million times already, but it's not like I could actually say that either. So I just mentally rolled my eyes, tucked my long, brown hair behind my ears, and then gazed at her perfect face, which was perfectly framed by the perfect smoke ring she just blew, and said, "Greece." Then I watched as she shrugged, grabbed a chunk of her bleached blond hair, and bent it toward her nose, brushing the ends against its dainty, slightly upturned tip.

"I don't get it. Why Greece? Why not somewhere good? You know, like Cabo or Cancun or something?" she said, dropping her hair and switching her attention to her French-manicured nails.

But I just shrugged. I mean, it really wasn't worth explaining how I only had one crazy aunt, and she just happened to live on a Greek island nobody's ever heard of. But when I saw Amanda staring at me like that, you know, with her lips all pursed and her eyebrows raised, I knew I had to at least try to explain. "It's an island, and it's supposed to be really pretty," I said, amazed to hear myself actually defending it. But then that's how I always feel around Amanda, like I need to prove my right to exist.

But she just reached for her phone and flipped it open. And just as I thought she was looking for a way to evict me, she scrolled through her contacts and said, "Levi's going to Greece. Let's call him."

LEVI BONHAM! The uber-hot guy I've been lusting after since he moved to our town back when I was just a nerdy little sixth-grader and he was already a smoking hot twelve-year-old, who also happens to be the other major reason for why I desperately need to stay connected.

Seriously, Levi is the most gorgeous guy I've ever seen (okay, maybe not including magazines, TV, and/or movies), but still, he's so amazingly hot it's surreal. He's like the male equivalent of Amanda. And luckily for me, Amanda doesn't like him like THAT, because if she did I wouldn't have stood a chance. But for whatever reason she lusts after his less hot but still cute friend, Casey Sayers. And all she had to do was place the call, and five minutes later, just like magic, they appeared.

And it's not like I haven't hung out with Levi before, because ever since I started hanging with Amanda I've had access to a whole host of things I used to only dream about. But still, it's not like we ever really exchanged more than a few words, or in his case—mumbles.

That's right, as perfect as I think Levi Bonham is, even I have to admit, he has one minor flaw—he's not much of a talker, he's way more of a mumbler. But then again, when you're that gorgeous, conversational skills aren't really required.

But since I'm not at all gorgeous, since I'm pretty much an average girl (okay, maybe I'm just *slightly* better than average since I'm more or less thin, and my skin is more or less clear, and my hair is pretty much just brown and normal, and nothing on my face really stands out in either a super positive or super negative way—which makes me pretty much the opposite of the blond, tan, and blue-eyed Amanda), I'm kind of forced to keep my small-talk abilities honed and sharpened.

I mean, in my case, showing up and standing around just isn't enough. Which means the last few times we hung out, I was forced to work overtime just trying to get him to laugh, which was completely impossible until I inadvertently tripped and fell smack onto the coffee table, which resulted in him doubling over in laughter and gasping for air, for a full five minutes. But for the rest of the time after that, I mostly just tried to ask a lot of questions about his favorite sports, favorite cars, and all kinds of other stuff that he's obviously into, but that I really don't care about.

But even so, the most I ever got for my attempts were a couple of mumbles and a grunt or two.

Until last Friday night when:

I HOOKED UP WITH LEVI BONHAM!!!!!

It's like, one minute we were sitting awkwardly on the couch, side by side, pretending to watch TV while Amanda and Casey were doing who knows what upstairs in her room, and the next thing I know LEVI BONHAM WAS PRETTY MUCH ON TOP OF ME!

Though it's not like he just pounced or anything crude like that. It was way more romantic and actually kind of cute the way he acted like he was reaching for his glass, but then somehow ended up smack on my lips.

And even though it was a little awkward at first, I mean trying to figure out where our lips and tongues should go, it wasn't long before I was totally into the zone of how he kisses, and the next thing I knew, I'd glanced at my watch and it was two hours past my curfew!

Only that's not entirely true.

Because the truth is, I was kind of worried about my curfew pretty much the entire time. I mean, even though kissing Levi was a completely amazing, dream-come-true kind of moment, the fact is, I couldn't stop worrying about my parents—wondering if they were still fighting, wondering if they'd managed to kill each other yet (joking, but not entirely).

But now, looking back, I wish I hadn't even bothered. I mean, it's not like they even noticed I was gone, and here I'd wasted a good part of my Levi Bonham Experience worrying about two people who obviously don't care all that much about me.

But after he tried to take off my dress for like the tenth time in a row, I pointed at my watch and told him I had to leave. And when I saw the way he just rolled his amazing blue eyes as he rolled right off of me, I thought:

What the heck are you doing, Colby? I mean, hello, now's your big chance, the moment you've been waiting for! So what if you don't love him? Love never lasts anyway—just look at your parents! Not to mention how you're totally gonna regret it if you let him slip away!

So then I reached for his hand and said, "Okay, maybe just a few more minutes."

And in the end, that's pretty much all it took.

Because the second it was over, he was already opening another beer before I'd even had a chance to adjust my dress, and when I finally stood and grabbed my purse and my keys, part of me couldn't help but wonder if it really did happen.

I guess I always thought The Big Moment would be, well, bigger.

And better.

And way more special than it actually was.

And I guess that's why I've put off writing about it until now. I mean, at the beginning of the night, when we first started kissing, I would occasionally open my left eye to peek at him, just so I could confirm that, yes, hard as it was to believe, I, Colby Catherine Cavendish, was totally locking lips, swapping spit, and playing big-time tonsil hockey with the hottest guy in school. And when I saw the way his eyes were closed so tight, and felt the way his lips were pressed so hard against mine, well, I couldn't help but feel like the luckiest girl in the world.

Despite the nagging voice in my head going—*why* YOU *Colby?*

You're not hideous but you're not exactly hot. You test smart but it's not like he cares. Just because you're friends with Amanda doesn't mean you're cool. So out of all the girls he knows, out of all the superhot girls he could be making out with at this exact moment, WHY YOU?

And honestly, I just didn't have an answer.

I still don't. Though I am firmly committed to no longer thinking about it.

Because even if it's just that he was bored on a Friday night and looking for something to do, it still doesn't explain why just seconds before I left he reached into the bowl of Doritos, grabbed a handful, looked me right in the eye, and said, "Hey, maybe I'll catch you in Greece. I might be going on a cruise or something."

Though it does explain why I plan to spend my entire

summer in the Internet café, waiting for some kind of contact or news of his arrival.

Waiting for proof that I didn't waste my virginity on someone who's bound to forget me.

June 20

Dear Aunt Tally,

If you come home for ~~lunch~~ siesta and I'm not here it's because I'm at the Internet café. (Yup, I found it! Even though I know you were hoping I wouldn't!) Which means I probably won't be back in time to go to the beach with you today, and I hope you're not too upset about that.

Anyway, I just didn't want you to worry about me, because I think you'll find that I'm pretty self-sufficient, very independent, and really don't require all that much guidance. Which means you can just go about your business and act like I'm not even here, because I probably won't be around the house all that much anyway now that I know about the café.

Okay, well, have a good day—

Love,

Colby

June 20

Dear Mom and Dad,

Sorry I haven't written until now, I guess time flies when you're not having any fun.

Don't be fooled by the picture on the front of this postcard, because the truth is it's really not that pretty here and I've yet to see this beach.

Just in case you are questioning your decision, or have any lingering regrets about sending me here, then I'd like to inform you that I'm willing to return at any time with no hard feelings, and no questions asked.

Seriously, scout's honor.

But if you insist on standing by your choice, if you suffer no guilt, no remorse, no qualms, no regrets, no worries, and no self-doubt, then all I have to say is this:

I, Colby Catherine Cavendish, do hereby solemnly swear to give you (my parents) joint custody of this postcard so that you can spend alternating weekends and holidays with it, sparing you the burden of meeting in a predetermined, neutral location, with your respective lawyers in tow, who would gleefully charge you thousands of dollars just to tear it in half and hand each of you an equal-sized piece.

Love,

Your former daughter, now orphaned—

Colby

June 20

To: AmandaStar

From: ColbyCat

Re: Ya'Sou!

Hey Amanda—

In case UR 1dering Ya'Sou means both hi & bye here in Greece, kinda like Aloha in Hawaii. At least I think that's what it means!

NEway, jus wanted 2 say hey since I'm soooo far from U & I don't want U guyz 2 4get me! ☺

I'm still thinking about Fri bcuz it was sooooo fun & I totally cud've stayed even L8r since no1 even noticed I was L8. O well.

Tell Levi hi from me & tell him 2msg me & tell me if he's still maybe coming 2 Greece like he sez.

But don't tell him about the totally hot guy I sat next 2 on the plane 2 Greece! ☺

L8R

Colby

P.S. Oh yah—almost 4got 2 tell U I'm starting a blog so u guyz can c my pics & stuff! So stop by & ck it out & don't 4get 2 tell Levi!

CRUEL SUMMER

Blogger Profile:

Name—Colby Catherine (Cat)
Age—17
Gender—Just a girl
Sign—Peace
Industry—Adolescence
Occupation—Prisoner of Greece
Location—Tinos via sunny CA

About me:

I'm a seventeen-yr-old girl who's being punished by her parents. Banished from everything she knows and loves and packed off to spend the summer on a Greek island—which, trust me, is far worse than you could ever imagine.

The purpose of this blog is so that I can document the most horrible summer of my whole entire life, and share a few photos (think of it as evidence!) along the way.

Interests—Going home immediately!

Favorite Movie—Best movie ever, hands down, I don't care if it's old—*Breakfast at Tiffany's.* Even though the ending in the book version is actually way more realistic than the movie version, because it's not all sappy and sweet, and is more like real life and not how Hollywood likes to portray real life. But still, either way, Holly Golightly kicks ass!

Favorite Song—Um, this changes all the time, though my all-time favorite would probably be that song "Breathe" (don't judge me!) because it pretty much sums up my view of life, which is: bad things happen, people betray you, mistakes are made, parents divorce, and in the end there's nothing you can do to erase it, you can't rewind, can't go back, the only thing you can do is breathe. (And if you can't even do that then it really doesn't matter anyway, does it?) And no, I'm not being negative, just realistic.

Favorite Book—Other than *Breakfast at Tiffany's,* I have to say that I love to read just about anything and everything except for those BORING, wordy, never-ending novels written by old dead Russians that English teachers just love to assign and make you write papers on! But other than that, it's (mostly) all good!

CRUEL SUMMER

June 20

Um, testing, 1, 2, 3, testing . . . Okay, so this is the official kickoff to my summer blogging project where I will share all of the occasionally awesome, but probably mostly horrific and boring things I'm doing and experiencing here on the Greek island of Tinos, which is famous for its religious pilgrims and superdeluxe dove condos but not much else.

But since, so far, I really haven't done much of anything (I mean, unpacking, sleeping, and searching for a place to log on isn't really worth writing about), I've decided to share a few pictures instead, so you can get an idea of what I'm dealing with here.

Ready? Here goes:

1) That's the outside of my aunt Tally's house where I'm staying. And believe it or not, they all pretty much look exactly like that. Seriously, they're all boxy, with white walls and colored doors and shutters, and they're all really stark and simple and no-nonsense. Which is pretty much the exact opposite of what I'm used to seeing back home.
2) That's my room—again, notice all the white. They're really big on white here. Though luckily that bed is more comfortable than it looks. I mean, it's way more narrow than my bed at home, but at least the pillow is halfway decent. Also, notice the evil-eye

pendant hanging over my bed? That's so I don't get "eye sick." You know, cursed by a jealous, hateful person with bad intent (which believe it or not, is something the locals take as a serious threat to one's overall well-being). And all I can say to that is: IF YOU'RE CRAZY ENOUGH TO BE JEALOUS OF ME, THEN YOU ARE MORE THAN WELCOME TO WEAR MY SHOES AND TRADE PLACES SO I CAN GO HOME AND GET BACK TO MY REGULARLY SCHEDULED LIFE!

3) If you think you're just looking at a photo of an old lady dressed all in black, and riding a donkey, then look again. Notice the basket hanging off the side of the donkey's butt? Guess what? It's filled with eggs. That's right, ladies and gentlemen, this is how you buy your eggs in Tinos. Via donkey. Delivered fresh, right to your door.

4) See that orangey-looking, round, runny lump? That's an egg yolk. Have you ever seen such a color? I know I haven't.

5) That's a picture of the Internet café where I'll be spending most all of my free time, sending e-mails, surfing the Net, and writing this blog. Notice the white walls and green shutters, then go back and reread #1 so you'll know that everything you read in this blog is legitimate and true and I'm not making anything up.

6) That's the table where I always sit and drink my Nescafé frappe—which is kind of like a foamy,

prehistoric Starbucks-type drink, only not near as good, though I am getting used to it. Mostly because I have no choice. Just like I'm trying to get used to everything around here because trust me, everything is really weird and different and, well, FOREIGN. And even though I know that's pretty much the whole point of traveling to another country, please keep in mind that I didn't exactly beg to come here. I was perfectly fine and happy at home, and I really wasn't looking for any new experiences.

7) This is the chair I sit on while I surf the Net, send e-mails, write letters and postcards, and blog. Notice how it's made of wood, which, by the way, makes it VERY uncomfortable after more than two hours of sitting. And I should know, since I've already done some major butt-in-chair time (see above about how I spend most all my free time). To the point where I'm actually thinking about bringing my own cushion in, since Petros refuses to provide one for me.

8) That's a picture of Petros, he's the owner of this café. You'd think he'd be glad to have some regular business for a change, but every morning when I come in, he takes one look at me, shakes his head, and says, "You are too white. You must to go outside and get some color. This is not good, not healthy." And then I tell him how that's really no way to treat your best customer, and to please

bring me a frappe because I have an Internet life to get back to. Then we both laugh, and he brings me my drink, but it's pretty obvious that he really wasn't joking and he seriously does not approve.

9) That's a picture of my aunt Tally's shop. It's right here in town, just a few doors down, at the end of the street. She makes jewelry and T-shirts and sells them to tourists. She also has some of her boyfriend's (Tassos's) pottery and sculptures in there as well, but only a few pieces since the shop is kind of small as you can see. Only I haven't met him yet because he's out of town. And I don't hang in her shop all that much anyway because it's usually pretty busy and I just end up feeling like I'm in the way.

10) That's my aunt Tally sitting on her terrace watching the sunset and having a glass of wine. Most of the sunsets here are really stunning like that—like a blaze of purple, orange, and red, streaking the sky before dropping into the sea. But you get used to it pretty quick.

11) That's a picture of the Meltemi wind. Yes, the wind is so strong here that not only does it have a name, but you can actually photograph it. Just look at those swaying shrubs and giant swirls of dirt. Well, just so you know, it blows like this practically every day! Aunt Tally refers to it as "nature's air-conditioning" and says I'll be sweating big-time when it stops. All I know is that I want it to stop.

12) Oops, there is no #12. Aren't you glad? Because this blog is truly PATHETIC, believe me, I know.

But please stay tuned, because you never know, it just might get better (though I seriously doubt it!).

Comment me! (Please!)

Colby

June 21

Dear Tally,

Sorry, but no beach for me today, I'm off to the café.

Hope you have a good day—

Love,

Colby

June 21

To: AmandaStar

From: ColbyCat

Re: Hey!

OMG, those pics U sent frm ur party R HILARIOUS! They made me soooo homesick! And no, Petros from the café is so NOT my boyfriend, bcuz plz, he's like 40, & trst me there's way hotter guyz here! And also no, most of the guys here don't have mustaches like that, it's mostly just the old ones.

Spkg of—Jus Idering if UV heard NEthing from Levi? Did U give him my e-mail? And do U no if he's still maybe coming here on that cruise? If U talk to him tell him 2 msg me, k? Bcuz IM going completely crazy here with no car, no phone, no good shops, no fast food, etc. etc. etc. and I really need 2 b in touch w/all my friends cuz I feel like I'm so far away it's like I'm on another planet!

Also, who was that girl with him in that one pic? U no by the pool? Do we know her? Bcuz it looked like she wuz all over him. ☹

Okay, got 2 go—miss u!

Colby

Colby's Journal for Desperate Times Like When the Electricity Goes Out for So Long the Internet Café Closes for an Even Earlier Siesta Than Usual

June 21

Um, excuse me, but am I the only one around here who's concerned by the way the hot water just inexplicably runs out in the middle of my shower, how the electricity works only when it wants (which is hardly ever), and how just about everything in this crazy place shuts down between the hours of two and five?

Because earlier today, I was in the café, blogging my heart out and minding my own business, when all of a sudden_____.

That's right, lights out, computer dead (as was my battery), I mean, a total flatline, code-blue moment. And not only did I lose my blog in progress (which was brilliant by the way, I mean, seriously the best thing I've ever written, not that anyone will ever see it now), but when I looked at Petros and raised both hands in the air, mimicking the international sign for—*What the heck?* all he did was shrug and say, "No problem, no problem, relax, it comes back."

And after what seemed like an hour of "relaxing," it still wasn't back. But he didn't seem too upset. Actually, he almost seemed happy, because he just kicked me out—seriously, he just walked right up to me, grabbed me by the sleeve, and dragged me to the door (with a big smile on his face the whole entire time I might add!). Then he flipped the sign over from OPEN to CLOSED (well, it's in Greek, but I assume that's what it says), pushed me outside, locked the door, and I just stood in the middle of the road, in a complete state of shock, watching as he practically skipped down the street, happy to be on his way to doing whatever the heck he does between the hours of two and five.

And since I haven't really been here all that long, I really didn't know what to do with myself. I mean, usually I pretty much just spend my days going back and forth from my room at my aunt's to the café. But this time, for whatever reason, I felt like taking a walk. So I wandered along the harbor and was thinking about stopping for yet another frappe at one of those cute little outdoor cafés, but since I didn't really feel comfortable with the idea of sitting all by myself like a big, lonely, friendless loser (even though I am), I decided to stop by my aunt Tally's shop where she sells all the jewelry and stuff she makes for tourists. But even though she seemed happy enough to see me, it was obvious she was really busy, so I just waved good-bye and headed back home, staring across the harbor, gazing at

Mykonos, knowing just by looking that they had no shortage of electricity over there, while wondering, yet again, why, WHY did I have to get stuck in this awful, primitive place?

And just as I was walking along the narrow dirt road that leads to the house, these two guys rode by on this old beat-up Vespa, coming so close they practically sideswiped me. Seriously, I could actually feel one of their sleeves brush right against mine as they passed. And just as I was about to yell something, the guy who was riding on the back turned and smiled.

And I stopped in my tracks and stared, knowing I recognized him from somewhere. But from where I couldn't imagine, because it's not like I really go anywhere outside of my aunt's house and the café, which also means I don't really know anyone other than Tally and Petros.

But it wasn't until I was back in my room, lying on my bed and gazing out the window that I realized it was the cute guy I saw on the boat.

June 22

Dear Mom,

I know Dad moved out but since I don't have his address yet (probably because he still hasn't sent it) I'm hoping that you or your lawyer (yes, I got your letter about how you and Dad are only speaking via legal counsel) can pass this on when you're finished.

And just in case you're at all curious, I have been to the beach on the front of this postcard, and that's pretty much what it looks like—no shops, no bars, no restaurants, no boardwalk—nothing but sand and water. Though I guess it's still kind of pretty—if you like barren landscapes, like that.

Please don't forget to pass this on to Dad, okay?

Love,

Your daughter who is doing her best to adjust to the lot you have given her,

Colby

June 22
To: AmandaStar
From: ColbyCat
Re: HI!
Hey Amanda,

So, that Penelope chick? The one in the pic who was hanging all over Levi? Does she go 2 another school? Bcuz I don't know her and I'm jus Idering & U never really said.

Well, all my news is pretty much in my blog, so U should totally stop by and comment me!

Write back!

Ciao—

Colby

P.S. NE news from Levi???

CRUEL SUMMER

June 24

So this is a picture of me (duh!) with my aunt Tally and her boyfriend, Tassos, whom I only just met because he was out of town for the last week "on business." Though to be honest, I think he was just trying to give me and Tally some time and space to get to know each other before he came on the scene.

It's funny how they kind of look like brother and sister, huh? I mean, they're both tan, both have dark, wavy hair, both have brown eyes, and, um, strong noses (not a judgment, just a fact). But I know there's no relation since no one in my family tree is Greek, but Tassos is. He's actually from here, which makes him a Tinian. Anyway, they've been together for like, twelve years or something, though they're not married and it doesn't seem like either one of them even really notices that they're not married. I mean, they act like they're married (except they don't fight), so when I asked them why they don't just go ahead and do it already, they both just shrugged and at the exact same moment, said, "It's not necessary." And then I thought about my own mom and dad, who even though they're busy getting unmarried, still can't seem to stop yelling and screaming at each other, and I just shrugged too.

I mean, maybe they're right, since everything's so temporary anyway, since everything has a beginning, middle, and end. So it's probably better just to leave the door open, since you never know when you'll need to use it.

Anyway, I've already forgotten the name of this beach, but I guess it doesn't really matter since it's not like you'd know it, and I probably wouldn't be able to spell it anyway—in either alphabet. I mean, even though everyone says Greek is phonetic, the second I see all those bizarre-looking letters, I'm lost. But all you really need to know about this beach is that it's absolutely NOTHING like our beaches at home. Seriously.

For starters, all of the beaches here are just beaches. They don't double as food courts or minimalls or gyms like most of ours do.

And second, there are living, breathing, ocean-dwelling creatures that can be found pretty close to shore, which is also unlike our beaches.

So, like the moment we got our towels all laid out and I started to settle in, Tassos tossed me some fins, a mask, a snorkel, and a large net bag, and told me to follow behind and stay close, but not too close.

And as we headed out into the water (which, I might add, is much easier here since there are no waves to dive under; seriously, the water is completely flat), I put on my gear and did my best to keep up while he swam way out by the rocks, searching for octopus and sea urchin, which, to be honest, I really doubted we'd find because it just seemed too weird to think there were octopus lurking around out there since I guess I always think of them as living WAY, WAY OUT THERE, like more in a place you can only reach by boat or submarine, and less in a place you can access with a snorkel and a pair of fins. But believe it or not, there was plenty to choose from and I watched in amazement as he proceeded to catch three of them, with nothing more than HIS BARE HANDS (!), before tossing them into the bag I was carrying.

I'd also like to mention that the whole entire time Tassos and I were swimming, my aunt Tally was lying on the beach, reading one of her many books, COMPLETELY TOPLESS!

Seriously!

And believe me, I wish I was kidding, but from what I've seen around here so far, pretty much everyone goes topless at the beach.

Well, everyone BUT ME!

And I can't imagine I ever will. I mean, it's just too weird, and it made me really uncomfortable. I seriously couldn't even look at my aunt until it was time to leave and she put her T-shirt back on.

So then later, after we got back home and we all took showers and stuff, Tassos prepared the octopus and put together a big Greek salad, while I helped Tally peel a bunch of potatoes so we could make homemade french fries. And then they poured some wine (yup, they even let me have a glass!) and put on a Beatles CD (oh yeah, I forgot to mention that she has no problem with music, just television) and we ate our meal outside and sang that old song, "Here Comes the Sun."

Only we changed the words to "There Goes the Sun" because while we were eating we were watching it set.

And even though it probably sounds pretty dorky

and lame (I mean, it was totally and completely dorky), in some weird way, it was also kind of fun.

But that's only because it's so boring around here, that's pretty much the best you can hope for.

The only bad thing is I didn't get to the Internet café until now. And since it's pretty late, Petros has spent the last five minutes giving me the international sign to skedaddle—which basically means he is now standing by the door and waving at me to get out. Which also means he's just thirty seconds away from marching right over and grabbing my sleeve.

I swear, the customer service totally sucks around here!

Anyway, before I go I should mention that the last picture is of me eating octopus—which I know is probably pretty self-explanatory, but still, it is kind of hard to believe. I mean, I never thought I'd see the day, because—gag!

And trust me, the only reason I'm smiling is because Tassos was holding the camera and I didn't want to make him feel bad.

Besides, you know what they say—"When in Greece . . ."

Okay, Petros is now yanking on my sleeve, muttering something in Greek. And even though I have no idea what he's saying, trust me, the subtext is not good.

So . . . Good night!

Please, please, comment me!

Colby

June 25

Dear Dad,

Thanks for finally sending me your new address, though I have to say it seems really weird to imagine you living in an apartment. I mean, can you hear the neighbors upstairs? And how big is it? Is there a separate room for me, for when I come visit?

Also, I've been thinking—now that you are officially out of the house and no longer arguing with Mom except through your lawyers, I thought maybe it would be okay if I come home. And it's not just because I'm feeling homesick (though I won't lie to you, Dad, I am), but I think Mom might really need me to help her through this difficult time. I mean, since you refuse to talk to each other you probably aren't aware of this, but from her last letter I could really sense her loneliness, and I think she might really need me.

Though I want to make it clear that I'm telling you this in the strictest confidence, because I'm sure she wouldn't want you to know. So let's just keep this between us and please don't make any mention of it to either her or your attorney.

If you'd like, you can either overnight the ticket, or arrange for me to pick it up at the ticket counter.

Either way, I'm sure Aunt Tally will understand.

See you soon—

Love,

Colby

June 25

Dear Mom,

Just wanted to wish you a good time on your yoga retreat!

Also, I've been thinking—now that Dad is officially out of the house and you two are no longer arguing except through your lawyers, I thought maybe it would be okay if I come home. And it's not just because I'm feeling homesick (though I won't lie to you, Mom, I am), but I think Dad might really need me to help him through this difficult time. I mean, since you refuse to talk to each other you probably aren't aware of this, but from his last letter I could really sense his loneliness, and I think he might really need me.

Though I want to make it clear that I'm telling you this in the strictest confidence, because I'm sure he wouldn't want you to know. So let's just keep this between us and please don't make any mention of it to either him or your attorney.

If you'd like, you can either overnight the ticket, or arrange for me to pick it up at the ticket counter.

Either way, I'm sure Aunt Tally will understand.

See you soon—

Love,

Colby

June 26

To: AmandaStar

From: ColbyCat

Re: Um, remember me?

Hey Amanda,

Jus ckg in 2 say hey B cuz I haven't heard from U in ages!

U haven't 4gotten me, right? ☺

Hope UR good—

I'm Gr8!

K, not really cuz IM actually completely homesick!

Write back!
Colby
P.S. Say hi 2 Levi! PLZ!!

CRUEL SUMMER

June 26

I was going to post a bunch of pictures of this name-day festival that Tally and Tassos dragged me to, but since apparently no one is even commenting on this blog, much less reading it, I'm not going to bother. I mean, what's the point?

But just so you know what you're missing, a name-day festival is actually a really big party that's held in honor of the Greeks who are named after saints (which, believe me, is practically all of them). And since just about every day of the year has been dedicated to the memory of a saint, they all celebrate their saint's day or "name-day" like they do a b-day, with roasted pigs and music and baklava (which is like a really bizarre dessert, super crusty and drenched in honey), along with other assorted delicacies.

And just in case you're wondering (though I know you probably aren't), for those unfortunate few who are not named after a saint, well, they still get to party on All Saints' Day, which is sometime after Greek Easter (yes, they even have their own separate Easter here).

Okay, well, I wish you all a warm, wonderful, and terribly exciting summer.

Because mine's turning out to be pretty much the opposite.

Colby

COLBY'S JOURNAL FOR DESPERATE TIMES WHEN SHE'S SO DEPRESSED SHE REFUSES TO LEAVE HER ROOM

June 27

Here is a list of PEOPLE WHO SUCK and the VERY VALID reasons why:

1) Amanda—Not only has she yet to respond to my last two e-mails, but she's also yet to leave a comment on my blog, which makes me think she hasn't even read it after that one time, and even then all she did was bug me about that picture of Petros, and make fun of his mustache, and ask me if I hooked up with him, and a whole lot of other rude nonsense like that. Which pretty much leads me to believe that she's not at all the friend I ~~thought~~ hoped she was.
2) Levi Bonham—No e-mail. No contact. No comment.
3) Penelope—I don't have to actually KNOW her to know how bad she sucks. That picture of her hanging all over Levi at that party I didn't get to go to (because I'm stuck HERE!) was worth a trillion, gazillion words.

4) My mom—Um, excuse me, but where to even begin?
5) My dad—Ditto.
6) Tinos—Yes I know Tinos is an island and not a person, but it's also not Mykonos, which means it sucks. Totally and completely sucks. Leave it to me to end up on the world's most boring island ever.
~~7) Tally~~
~~8) Tassos~~

Okay, the reason I crossed Tally and Tassos off the list is because I just realized that they don't actually suck. I mean, granted, they are a little weird, what with all their plant-whispering, meditating, hippie-music-loving stuff. But still, it's not like they really bug me all that bad or anything. Because the truth is, they pretty much leave me alone.

Like right now for instance, I've basically been holed up in my room for the last two days, and all Tally has done so far is stick her head in each morning and go, "Hey, no Internet café today?"

And I just shrug, sigh, roll my eyes, and stare at the ceiling some more.

And then she goes, "Okay, well, just so you know Tassos is heading out to his studio." (He's an artist, does marble sculptures and also makes ceramics and stuff. He's pretty good too, and kind of famous, at least in the world of marble sculpture and ceramics.) "And I'm heading to the shop, but we'll both be back around two in case you want to go to the beach. But if not, that's cool too."

And the funny thing is, she said all of that as though I haven't already memorized their schedules by now. I mean, every day it's pretty much the same thing—work in the morning, break at two for the beach, come home and eat a lunch made of whatever Tassos happened to catch and whatever's ripe in Tally's garden, then a quick shower before heading back to work for a few more hours, and then home for a late dinner where they usually invite a bunch of friends.

And even though it might sound like an okay life (I mean, if you really like to keep it simple, and back to basics, and enjoy a high tolerance for quiet moments with lots of boredom thrown in), and even though I sometimes relent and go to the beach with them, for the last two days, I've chosen not to.

I mean, what's the point?

What's the point of anything?

Because the fact is:

1) Amanda has moved on. Which means my senior year is destined to suck. Which means all my hard work was for nothing. Which means my shot at popularity is now null and void. Which means I'm back to being just another pathetic wannabe who fades into high school oblivion. Which means when I show up at my ten-year reunion everyone will go, "Colby? Colby WHO? Did you even go here?"

2) Levi forgot I exist. Because even though I stayed past my curfew, and even though I slept with him, I still refused to take off my dress. And because of that he's now moved on to some skinny strawberry-blond chick named Penelope who probably has no curfew and no problem with casual nudity. But the truth is, even if it wasn't Penelope it would still be someone else, because the cold hard fact is he never really liked me in the first place. He was just bored and restless and trying to pass the time. And even though I was never dumb enough to fool myself into thinking we were in love, or a couple, or anything remotely like that (mostly because I don't believe in any of that nonsense to begin with), still, you'd think he could at least take twenty seconds out of his extremely busy day to send me an e-mail, or something, since it's not like he didn't know I was a virgin.
3) My parents, who even though they cannot communicate about anything without yelling and screaming to the point where they've decided to communicate only through their attorneys, are apparently able to overcome their anger obstacles when it comes to all matters concerning me. Which means I was totally busted for my little letter-writing scam during the course of a very awkward, highly uncomfort-

> able (um, that would be ME not THEM, as they were totally cool, calm, collected, and completely in the zone) ten-minute conference call where they informed me, in no uncertain terms, that I was to remain in Tinos, until my mandatory sentence has been completed, on the day otherwise known as August 31. And that there will be no time off for good behavior, bad behavior, or consideration of time served. And to stop trying to play them against each other because they're totally on to me.

So, in a nutshell, that is why I'm giving up.

I mean, I tried to make the best of it, I tried to keep in touch by creating a cute blog, sending e-mails, and writing letters and postcards so no one would forget me, but in the end, it just didn't work.

Because everyone did forget me.

Because they never really cared about me in the first place.

So rather than continue to beat my head against the wall, I've decided to spend the rest of my summer sitting right here in my little white room, emerging only for the occasional meal and bathroom break. I mean, if they want to put me in jail, then fine, I'll do the time.

But come August 31, I WILL be on that plane.

And I WILL return to Orange County.

Where my completely crummy life WILL still be waiting for me.

CRUEL SUMMER

July 1

Okay, I know I said this blog was history since no one is reading it anyway, but the thing is, keeping this blog alive almost feels like it's keeping ME alive.

Seriously.

It's like, not only does it give me somewhere to go every day, but it also makes me feel like I have some kind of purpose.

Even if that purpose is just wasting my time, cribbing a blog that no one cares enough to read.

But since I'm actually kind of sick of just sitting in my room, I figured—*What the hey?* I'll just keep going.

Even if I am the only one who knows it exists.

Even if I am the only who cares.

So anyway, back to business:

1) This is a picture of my cat!

That's right, I adopted a kitten and he (or she, I haven't, um, really checked things out that thoroughly yet) is even more adorable in person. Seriously! Though I am really hoping it turns out to be a she because I named her/him/it Holly after Holly Golightly in *Breakfast at Tiffany's.* Partly because I totally love that movie/book, and partly because she's all black with a little white streak across her forehead—um, do cats have foreheads?

Whatever.

Anyway, she totally reminds me of Audrey Hepburn in the movie, because Audrey always dressed in those cute little black dresses, not to mention how she had a white streak too.

She was also really, really skinny, and when I found Holly she was really, really skinny too. And seemed like she needed protecting—just like Holly in both the book and movie versions!

The only thing is, I haven't actually told Tally and Tassos yet. Mostly because I know it probably wasn't the smartest thing to do since I'm leaving by the end of the summer anyway (YIPEE!!). But still, Holly was all alone when I found her (him?), just sitting in the middle of the dirt road, looking lost, and lonely and completely afraid. But the moment I knelt down, she ran right up and gazed at me with those big, sad, hungry blue eyes, and when she started rubbing against my leg and purring, well, obviously adoption was my only choice.

I mean, had I just left her there to fend for herself, there's a very good chance she never would've made it to the end of the day. But even if the best I can give her is a nice, happy, safe, and comfortable three months, then that may just be three more months than she otherwise would've gotten.

Besides, everything has a beginning, middle, and end. So when it's time to say good-bye, I'll be ready.

But for now, I totally plan to tell Tally and Tassos tonight—so wish me luck!

Even though I know I'm the only one reading this!

Colby

CRUEL SUMMER

Blog Comments:

Anonymous said:

Good to see you are back to blogging again.

From someone who has read all of your posts.

ColbyCat said:

Mom, is this you???

I mean, I know it's you so just quit with the mysterious act. It's so dumb.

Anonymous said:

I'm definitely not your mom.

Though I'm sorry you think that I'm dumb.

ColbyCat said:

Um, okay. It's not that I think you're actually dumb—whoever you are—it's just that I think the whole ANONYMOUS thing is kind of—well—dumb.

Anonymous said:

Thank you for clearing that up. Though for now, I still choose to remain ANONYMOUS, even though I know you think that it's dumb.

P.S. I like your cat.

Colby's Journal for Desperate Times for Things She Can't Possibly Post in Her Blog Now That She Knows Mysterious Someone Is Reading It

July 2

Okay, I know it was only recently that I was whining and going on and on about how no one was reading my blog. Well now, apparently somebody is. Only I don't know who, since they signed in under ANONYMOUS. And even though I seriously considered restricting all anonymous comments, in the end I just couldn't do it. Mostly because it'd be like booting out your best (and only!) customer—not unlike what Petros often does to me.

And it's weird how I originally thought I wanted lots of readers and comments, but now I'm not so sure. I mean, now that I know someone is reading it, I'm no longer sure what to write. I guess if I knew WHO was reading it, then it might make it easier. Like, if it's my mom or dad, then I could use my blog for maximum effect, and make my life sound so lonely and pathetic they'd have to be completely inhuman (which I'm beginning to think they are) not to feel awful and guilty enough to let me come home.

But if it's Levi, then obviously the pathetic angle would be all wrong. I mean, I don't want to come off as ecstatic or anything (because then he might think that things are too good here, and that I actually don't need him to visit me—which would be so completely false!). But I don't want to sound quite so bored and depressed either.

I guess the perfect balance is to sound a little bored, but only because I'm just way too cool to even be here in the first place. (Thus making my blog an experiment in fiction!)

And if it's Amanda, then I definitely need to make it sound like I'm totally partying and hanging with the cool group, so she won't start regretting that she ever started talking to me in the first place (even though she probably/obviously does).

See how complicated this has become now that I have a subscriber?

I swear, it was a whole lot easier when I was the only reader.

On another note, Tally and Tassos are totally cool with Holly. In fact, not only do they think she's totally adorable, but Tally has kind of taken over the care and maintenance of her, buying her a collar and a litter box and feeding her some organic stuff that's supposed to build a better kitty. And even though I'm really happy and relieved that they love her, at the same time all of that kindness and support makes me feel pretty bad about not telling them sooner. I mean, coming home from the café only to find Tally down on her hands and knees, wiping a puddle of cat pee from the floor definitely was not the best way to introduce our latest addition.

But still, I guess it all worked out in the end, and they're totally on board with keeping the name Holly, even though we recently discovered that she is actually a HE.

So because of all that, I've decided to make more of an effort to go to the beach, pitch in, and hang out with them. I mean, they were so cool about Holly, and just about everything else I've dumped on them, like my endless moping, silent treatment, and mood swings, that I kind of feel obligated to at least pretend like I'm having some fun (even though I'm not).

I guess I'm also starting to realize just how much I'm actually intruding on them, what a huge imposition I am. I mean, here my aunt moved all the way across the ocean to some tiny, obscure Greek island, probably for the sole purpose of getting away from everything, including my mom, my dad, my grandma, and me, only to get stuck with me for almost three months.

I mean, even though their life may be a little too ORGANIC for my tastes, a little too SLOW, LOW ON EXCITEMENT, and definitely NOTHING I'd ever choose for myself, obviously it works for them.

And just as they have it all worked out, and are firmly entrenched in their happy place, I show up, and pretty much pout, slam doors, barely talk for weeks on end, and then top it all off by dragging home a stray cat that likes to pee on the floor.

And while I'm on the subject (of Tally, not cat pee), let me just say that I'm also kind of annoyed by how my parents always used to make fun of her. I mean, okay, so she's a little quirky, and granted she's definitely more than a little weird in some ways, but really, what's the big deal?

Because she's also really nice, and generous, and understanding, and kind, not to mention how she opened her door to me when my parents closed theirs. And from the first day on she made it clear that she's there for me if I need her, but that she'll stay out of my way if I don't. And the only rule of the house is that we respect each other as well as ourselves.

That's it!

No curfew.

No chores.

No rules for the sake of having rules.

So yeah, maybe she is the opposite of my parents, but I'm beginning to think that's not such a bad thing . . .

Anyway, tomorrow, Tassos is supposed to show me how to catch an octopus with my bare hands! Apparently this is quite difficult to master, even though he makes it look easy. But I'm thinking I might just stick with swimming behind and holding the bag, because I've gotten pretty good at that. And I'm not so sure I need to add Experienced Octopus Catcher to my resume.

CRUEL SUMMER

July 4

So apparently the Greeks don't celebrate the Fourth of July. And even though you're probably thinking—duh!—let me just explain how it's always been my favorite holiday, which means BBQs and fireworks have been such a big, important part of every single one of my summers, for as far back as I can remember, that it feels really weird (and sad) not to be celebrating it in the same way today.

Though before you go thinking I'm a completely clueless dork, let me just explain that I really do get why the Greeks don't exactly care about our independence from the Brits. Though understanding their reasons doesn't do much to lessen my current case of extreme homesickness. Because I can only imagine all of the awesome beach and backyard BBQs that my friends are all going to, and that I'm totally missing out on. Not to mention how I always used to buy a new bikini, flip-flops, and cover-up to wear to those parties, but after checking out the shops here, and seeing how they're stocked with totally lame merchandise, that's so NOT going to happen!

But still, Tally and Tassos are planning to leave work early so they can throw a big party. And, I admit, when they first told me about it, I thought they were doing it for my benefit, so of course I was all—*oh, you don't have to, blah, blah, blah.* But they just laughed and explained how they do it every year as my aunt is not the only American living here (yup, there are a few other crazies as well!) so they're going to invite a bunch of friends over to BBQ and celebrate, though they did warn me there won't be any fireworks.

Anyway, I should probably get back and help them set up, but to anyone back home who might actually be reading this—Happy Fourth!

Colby

July 4
To: AmandaStar
From: ColbyCat
Re: 4th!

I haven't heard from U 4ever, so I hope UR good. Also, Happy 4th. I no UR prbly going 2 the beach or a party or somethun so have fun!

E-mail me! (When U can)

~Colby

P.S. Any news on Levi? Lemme no!

Colby's Journal for Desperate Times When Things Take an Astonishing, Surprising, Unexpected Turn for the Better

July 5

After one and a half glasses of homemade Greek wine and several test sips of ouzo on the rocks (each sip was just to make sure it was really as bad as I thought), I admit, this is probably not the best time to be writing about this, or anything else for that matter, but I'm afraid if I wait until morning then I won't remember a thing, so here goes:

I HAD FUN.

Shocking but serious. And it's not like I was expecting it, or even thought it was in any way remotely possible, but still, there you have it.

I mean, it's not like I thought it would be awful or

anything, and I guess there was a small part of me that was actually kind of looking forward to it, but still, it's not like I have any friends of my own here, so I pretty much thought I'd be stuck with a bunch of adults, listening to old music and stuff.

And even though it did kind of turn out like that, I somehow managed to have fun in spite of it. And only twice (okay, maybe thrice) did I compare it unfavorably to the Fourth of July parties back home. Though that's only because there were no fireworks—or at least not the kind you shoot into the sky!

Though there was another kind of fireworks.

The kind that explode in your chest.

And here's why:

I MET SOMEONE.

Not so earth shattering, I know, since the only people I knew to begin with were Tally and Tassos and a few of their friends, which still left quite a few other people to meet. But in this case what I mean is, I met someone ~~special~~.

Okay, I just reread that and it looks totally dorky and lame. So let me just rephrase it and say I met this really cute guy, who smiled at me from across the backyard for like two full hours before he finally came over to talk to me.

And when he did, this is what he said: "Ya'Sou, I'm Yannis." Followed by a big smile.

So I went: "Hey, I'm Colby. Your friend almost ran me over with his Vespa." And then I started laughing. And then, luckily, he started laughing too.

And then he said, "I saw you crying on the boat."

Which, to be honest, was actually really embarrassing. But still, I just laughed, partly because I WAS crying on the boat so it's not like I could go back and erase it, but mostly because he's so unbelievably cute, and has such a nice smile, I didn't really know what else to do.

Anyway, did I mention he was cute? Well, this is what he looks like:

1) Dark, wavy hair—almost, but not quite black, that on anyone else I would say he needs a haircut, but on him, that longish, messy look is totally smokin'.
2) Really nice tan.
3) Piercing green eyes (seriously, like, see-straight-through-to-your-soul kind of eyes).
4) Very thick eyelashes—the kind that are usually only provided courtesy of Maybelline.
5) Nice eyebrows, with the ability to raise only one (I've tried, but I've never been able to do that), which, by the way, is extremely sexy.
6) Amazingly hot bod—lean, muscled, and neither too tall nor too short, but just exactly right.
7) Nice, friendly smile with slightly crooked front teeth, which doesn't bother me as much as I would've thought, since it just makes him kind of quirky and even that much cuter.
8) Decent English language skills, with a supercute,

definitely sexy accent. (And even though I realize that doesn't exactly qualify as part of his appearance, I still think it's worth mentioning.)

9) Um, did I mention his amazingly hot body? I did? Oh, well, I guess it's just so amazing it's worth mentioning twice!

Okay, so anyway, after we laughed (at my expense) we both just kind of stood there looking at each other in the most uncomfortable, awkward way. And it seemed like it dragged on forever, to the point where I actually thought I heard the small hand on my watch timing me to see just how long I could sustain an embarrassing pause—but then I was even more embarrassed when I realized it was actually the sound of my own rapidly beating heart crashing against my chest!

Seriously!

Well, kind of.

Anyway, so then these two girls who looked to be somewhere around my age, walked right up, looked at me briefly, and then turned to Yannis and said something that I totally could not understand (but that made me realize I should probably stop being so resistant to change and start trying to learn Greek, *pronto*).

And then he looked at me and said, "It was nice meeting you."

And then they pulled him away. And I mean LITERALLY pulled him away, like, with one on each arm, all the way to the opposite side of the yard, which was pretty much as far from me as you could possibly get.

And even though the pulling him away part could definitely be considered the low point of the night, luckily, it didn't end there. Because later, much later, when it was dark, and a lot of the adults were pretty tipsy from all that organic homemade wine they were drinking, Tassos put on a Greek CD and everyone started dancing. Only not the kind of dancing like I'm used to, but instead they were all holding hands and kind of like running in a circle. So I just sat there, with Holly on my lap, sipping from the small glass of ouzo Tassos gave me to try, fighting the overwhelming urge to gag and vomit (I mean, it's seriously AWFUL), when everyone was like, "Hey Colby, come join us!"

But I just shook my head, determined to stay put since I don't exactly know any of those dance moves, and no way was I going to risk looking like a big, clumsy dork in front of SUPERHOT YANNIS. Not to mention how those two Greek girls were totally staring at me in a way that made it pretty obvious just how much they'd LOVE to watch me do a face plant right in front of them.

But then Yannis broke away from the circle, grabbed my hand, and pulled me into the group. And even though I probably looked like a fool, it wasn't all that long before I was too busy laughing and enjoying myself (especially the way my hand felt in his!) to even think about how dumb I appeared.

And then we pretty much danced for the rest of the

night, or at least until Tassos cut the music and made everyone go home.

And even though all we did was hold hands, and even though it was only because the dance required it, the way he looked at me when he said good-bye, was (almost) as good as any kiss I've ever had.

Okay, well, it's almost three now and I can barely keep my eyes open so—

Kalinichta!

(That means good night in Greek!)

CRUEL SUMMER

July 5

Who said the Greeks don't know how to celebrate the Fourth of July?

Certainly not me!

Granted, there were no fireworks, but that doesn't mean it wasn't fun—and if you don't believe me, then see for yourself:

1) That's me eating a mongo huge piece of watermelon. I swear, the fruit here is so much sweeter than the fruit you get at home. Seriously, it tastes like a million times better, and I just can't get enough. Oh yeah, notice the deep, dark tan I'm sporting, and the blond streaks in my hair? Believe it or not, that's after JUST A FEW DAYS at the beach. It's like, even the sun's rays are sweeter here too!

2) That's Mr. Holly Golightly, sitting on a chair, observing all the action. He can be a little aloof at times, and would rather watch than join in.
3) That's Tassos roasting a lamb. And yes, believe it or not, they roast the whole dang thing. They eat the whole dang thing too. I'm not kidding. They eat the brains, the liver, the tongue—EVERYTHING! Nothing goes to waste. And yes, I'm well aware of how sad, not to mention how completely creepy it looks, seeing it all skinned like that, but trust me, after awhile you get pretty desensitized to that stuff. I mean, that very same morning when I opened the fridge in the shed and saw that same exact lamb all hairless, bent in half, and awkwardly shoved in there, I didn't even scream! Though I did the first time I saw something like that. As well as the second.
4) That's everybody dancing—Greek dancing, which is pretty much a group activity as you can see.
5) That's me dancing!
6) That's all!

July 6
To: NatalieZee
From: ColbyCat
Re: You're moving?
Hey Nat,

In answer to your e-mail regarding the FOR SALE sign you

saw in my yard—let me just say that it's all a big misunderstanding. Though I thank you for your concern.

You're probably surprised to see me answering you back. Especially after that whole thing with Amanda and how you accused me of "selling out" so I could be "popular, shallow, and a big conforming retard."

That IS how you put it, right Nat?

And yet, here I am, not only answering you back, but also using proper English and spelling, as I know how much you hate all of those e-mail/text message shortcuts.

Still think I'm shallow?

Anyway, you're probably not even aware of this since we haven't talked for months, but I'm currently in Greece, where I'm spending the summer on the island of Tinos with my aunt Tally (and no, she's not really crazy, my parents were just joking), so I probably won't be writing you back anytime soon, since I'm super busy going to the beach and hanging in clubs with all of the really good friends I've made here.

Also, you'll never believe this but LEVI BONHAM is totally coming to visit! Seriously, I forget exactly when, but the point is that he'll be here soon! That's because we pretty much spent my whole last night together, so now he's planning to get on a cruise ship so he can come see me! I guess he misses me, or something.

Anyway, thanks for the heads-up, but it's not at all what you think. I'm DEFINITELY not moving.

Well, take care—

Colby

July 7

Dear Mom,

THE HOUSE IS FOR SALE???

Exactly how long did you think you could keep this from me? Because for your information I still have plenty of friends back home who report to me on a regular basis, one of whom informed me that THE HOUSE IS FOR SALE!

And since I know this CANNOT be happening, I'd really appreciate it if you could write me back immediately, or better yet—I'm going to call you, since we obviously have a lot to discuss.

Love,

Your soon to be homeless daughter who is SHOCKED and DISMAYED by the way her parents are gambling with her future,

Colby

July 7

Dear Dad,

It has come to my attention that my childhood home is now featuring a FOR SALE sign on the front lawn, and I'm hoping you can shed some light on the subject.

I've spoken to Mom on the phone, and according to her, this is mostly your doing. She said it's all part of the divorce settlement, because you wanted to cash in and divide the money evenly.

But here's something you may not have considered:

WHAT'S IN IT FOR ME?

I mean, while it's all fine and good for you to split the proceeds and move to opposite ends of the earth, did you ever STOP, take a deep breath, and ask yourself—

HEY, WHAT ABOUT COLBY?

You remember, YOUR DAUGHTER, Colby?

The one you BANISHED to Greece?

Just how might she feel about this? How might this affect HER?

Because I'm starting to think that neither you nor Mom even thought to consider me, at any time, during your hectic, illogical, decision-making process.

Though maybe you should have.

I mean, just because you guys decided to move on, doesn't mean I'm in on it too. Did it ever occur to you that maybe I don't want to move on? Did you ever STOP and consider THAT?

Because, truth be told, Dad, I actually LIKE living in my comfortable home, in my nice neighborhood, that's within walking distance to my school and all of my friends' houses. I used to feel good, SAFE EVEN, just knowing I had two parents to come home to. Not to mention a roof over my head.

Because now, according to Mom, once the house is sold, we will no longer be able to afford to live in Orange County, and may even have to move OUT OF STATE! She even mentioned something about going to ARIZONA! And maybe you're not aware of this, but I don't know ANYONE in Arizona! All I know about Arizona is that it's one hundred and twenty degrees IN THE SHADE! Which, you've got to admit, is not exactly a selling point.

So I strongly urge you both to reconsider, before it's too late to reverse all the damage you've set in motion.

As for me, all I can do now is sit back and helplessly watch while the two of you do your very best to destroy my life as I once knew it.

Love,

Your completely depressed, but not like you care, daughter—
Colby

July 8
To: AmandaStar
From: ColbyCat
Re: I need a favor
Hey Amanda,

Um, I no U must B really busy & all since U haven't written me back in a really long time, but I'm Idering if U could do me a favor? Next time UR driving by my house, maybe U could stop long enuff 2 remove the 4 Sale sign on my front lawn? Bcuz I'd really appreciate it.

U can just stick it in UR trunk, or a nearby trash can, or whatever.

Thanks,

Colby

P.S. Um, any news on Levi & if he's still going on that cruise? Lemme know, bcuz I still haven't heard from him & IV been Idering!?

Write back, plz!

Colby's Journal for Desperate Times When Life Becomes a Roller Coaster That Will Not Stop or Slow Down

July 8

I don't get it. I seriously do not get it. I mean, first I'm totally hating my life, and am more than happy to focus on the bad things—which admittedly, is pretty much everything here. But then one day, I wake up, take a look around, and decide to stop fighting it, decide to stop acting like such a big whiny loser, and start participating around the house (mostly because time goes by faster when you're busy) and try to show a little gratitude toward Tally and Tassos so they won't think I'm a complete and total burden.

And then, shortly after that, I meet a completely dreamy local named Yannis, who almost makes me forget about Levi, and who also, at least from what I could tell, seemed to like me too.

And I'm thinking yipee!

Things are finally looking up!

Maybe it's true what Tally and Tassos always say—that happy attracts happy—or however they put it.

But then, just as I'm starting to smile again, I get an e-mail from Natalie Zippenhoffer, my former best friend since second grade turned girl I no longer talk to much less acknowledge. And she's all too happy to inform me that my HOUSE IS FOR SALE!

Okay, to be fair, I don't really know that she was happy. Because there's a part of me that thinks she might've just been concerned, which, if that's the case, then I feel even worse for way too many reasons to mention.

But what I do know is this:

One moment I was riding high!

And the next I'm completely homeless.

And trust me, that is not an exaggeration, because the

fact is not only has my mom recently exhibited some very bad decision-making skills, but when I asked her just what she had in mind for us after the sale, just where she envisioned the two of us living—she answered with a verbal shrug. Which basically amounted to a couple of *ums,* followed by some throat clearing and *we'll sees,* along with a bunch of statistical nonsense about median home prices in Orange County, mortgage rates, and *blah, blah, blah.* All of which pretty much translates to—*Gee, Colby, I don't really know what will become of you. I hadn't really thought about it until you just now brought it up!*

And then just as I thought it couldn't get any worse, she tosses something in there about moving to ARIZONA! Just dropped it right in there, as though I wouldn't even notice.

And just for the record, I AM NOT MOVING TO ARIZONA!

There's just no way.

I WON'T do it.

She CANNOT make me.

And as for Yannis? Well, I haven't seen or heard from him since the Fourth of July party, which means I am an even worse judge of these things than I thought, because I really was convinced that he just might kinda like me. But then again, when I think back on the colossal mistake I made with Levi (which is pretty much all the time since I really can't stop thinking about it, even though I truly wish I could), I guess I shouldn't be all that surprised.

All I really know for sure is that this "happy gets happy" nonsense is a total crock of crap.

CRUEL SUMMER

Blog Comments:

Anonymous said:

Why do you call it Cruel Summer?

Do you really hate Tinos that much?

From someone who cares.

ColbyCat said:

It's after a song from the eighties, by some all-girl band called Bananarama. But you already knew that since your mom used to play it when she cleaned the house.

Yes, I know this is YOU, Natalie. So why don't you just come clean and show yourself already! This is so freaking lame.

Anonymous said:

I'm definitely not Natalie, though her mom sounds cool!

Maybe you should stop blogging so much and get out more. You might have more fun.

Just a thought.

Sorry you think I am both dumb and lame.

ColbyCat Said:

"GET OUT MORE"?

I should've known it was YOU, Petros.

So allow me to remind you that I am your VERY BEST customer, and without me, where would you be?

Maybe you should spend your next siesta trying to sharpen your customer service skills.

Seriously. Please think about it. It really couldn't hurt.

Anonymous said:

No, I'm definitely not Petros either.

Who's Petros?

Should I be jealous?

COLBY'S JOURNAL FOR DESPERATE TIMES WHEN LIFE BECOMES SO UNBELIEVABLY GOOD AGAIN SHE CAN'T POSSIBLY PUT IT IN HER BLOG

July 9

OMG—I now know who ANONYMOUS is!

It's Levi Bonham!

!!!!!!!!!!!!!!!!!!!!!!!!!!!!!!

I mean, who else could it be?

Obviously he hasn't written or e-mailed because he's too busy playing blog comment games, trying to figure out if I've met someone he should be jealous of! Which means he didn't forget me! Which also means I can stop torturing myself for making a huge error in judgment, because obviously, I didn't!

And even though I know it sounds crazy and delusional, here's the proof:

1) It's not Natalie because she's too honest, too straightforward, too in-your-face to play games like that.
2) It's not my mom because she doesn't even know how to turn the computer on much less post a comment.
3) It's not Amanda because she can't even be bothered to e-mail me back much less comment on my blog. Besides, that kind of blog banter just isn't her thing.
4) It's not my dad because he's too annoyed with me and my letters to actually take the time to joke around with me.
5) It's not anyone in Tinos because the only one who even knows about my blog is Petros and his English is pretty limited. And Tally and Tassos don't even have access to a computer.
6) So basically, the only possibility left is Levi! And even though he can't really carry on a conversation in person, I'm willing to bet that like most people, he's better on paper (or in this case, on screen).

But before I make my next move (or, um, post), I have to think very carefully about how to proceed.

I mean, I could:

1) Continue as usual, blogging about all the usual, boring, mundane things I do here, acting as

though I have no idea that LEVI BONHAM IS READING MY BLOG. And then, each time he decides to leave a comment, I'll pretend like I think it's just about everyone BUT him, until he eventually gives up and reveals himself, then we can both enjoy a good laugh about it when he comes to visit me on his cruise!

2) I lie. Which basically means I start blogging about a life that's a whole lot better than the one I'm actually living. And then, when he comments, I pretend like I think he's just one of the many gorgeous, hot Greek guys that are lining up to go out with me. Though I have to be careful to not overdo it and keep it believable. I mean just because I'm far away doesn't mean anyone's gonna believe I suddenly turned into Amanda.

3) I act confident and forthright (which is pretty much the opposite of me) and the next time he comments, I write a reply like, "Hey Levi! Let me know when you're heading off on that cruise so I can TRY to meet up with you!" Though obviously I won't put the "try" part in all caps. But still, he'll get the gist.

And after reviewing all three choices, I think I'll go with #2. Basically because it's going to be way too hard for me to try to pull off #3, and I don't really want to take the

#1 approach and keep up my loser blog either, because actually, well, it's a little depressing. So obviously that leaves me with #2.

Besides, what could it hurt to make my life sound a little better than it is?

VERY RECENT UPDATE
(Technically July 10)

There's more!

OMG—get this! Right after dinner I went to my room, and I was barely in there two seconds when Tally knocked on my door and said, "Yannis is here."

And even though I had this immediate flash of his image in my mind, even though I knew exactly who she meant, I also thought it would be a good opportunity to try out my cool, new blog persona. So I narrowed my eyes and tried to look confused as I said, "Who?"

But I guess Tally's too smart for that, because she just shook her head and laughed and said, "Go on, he's waiting out front."

So I scooped Holly off my bed, peered into the mirror and ran my hands through my hair real quick, trying to fluff it up and make it look tousled and cute as opposed to flat and limp, then I went outside to where Yannis was sitting on his Vespa, looking just as cute (maybe even cuter!) as he did on the Fourth of July. And it was so amazing to see him sitting there like that, especially since I'd convinced myself I'd never see him again.

I hugged Holly tightly to my chest, watching as Yannis smiled in a way that showcased the dimples on either side of his cheeks, as his deep green eyes gazed into mine. Though I guess it was a little too close for Holly because he immediately started protesting, and squirming, and scratching at me to get away.

"So what's up?" I asked, setting Holly down and watching as he scrammed back inside the house, but not before leaving a burning red spot on my arm, where his claws nearly broke through my skin.

"I was wondering if you want to go for a ride?" Yannis asked, his gaze still on mine.

And it wasn't until I'd climbed on the back of his bike and wrapped my arms tightly around his waist, that I realized I'd forgotten to ask where.

But as it turned out, we ended up in town, at a club that seemed like it was filled with all of his family and friends.

"Have you been here before?" he asked, grabbing my hand and pulling me inside.

So of course, still trying to come off as cool, experienced, and worldly, I just shrugged and said, "Um, maybe. I really can't remember." And then I gazed down at my khaki shorts and black tank top and wished I'd at least taken the time to change before I agreed to go out with him.

But he just smiled, and said, "My cousin owns it." Then he proceeded to introduce me to like one hundred and thirty different people who all seemed to be somehow related.

"So is everyone on this island your cousin?" I asked,

no longer trying to keep all the names straight, and just nodding and smiling instead.

But he just laughed and said, "No, it only seems that way."

Then he pulled me out to the dance floor, where we stayed for most of the night. Only this time it was regular, modern dancing as opposed to that traditional, running-in-a-circle Greek dancing. Which also means I didn't have an excuse to hold his hand. But still, it was pretty cool just to hang out in a club, and enjoy a cocktail or two, and be treated like an adult for a change. Even though we didn't actually have any cocktails and just ordered two Cokes instead. But still, it's the KNOWING that you can have whatever you want that makes it so great.

Though I guess Yannis is probably pretty used to stuff like that since he grew up here and all. Well, both here and in Athens, since, as he told me, his family only comes here for the summers (which is why I saw him on the boat, he was coming back for the summer) and then he returns to Athens for school. Which actually seems like a pretty cool life. Except for the fact that he probably won't be here next summer because he's in his last year of high school and after that he has to go into the military for at least a year.

That's exactly what he said—HAS TO.

Like, no choice whatsoever.

Apparently the only choice he has in the matter is WHEN. Like, he can go right after high school, or right after college, or even put it off until he's in his forties. But in the end, he HAS to go. No exceptions. Which seems like it would really suck, but he didn't seem all that bothered by it.

So at one point, we were sitting in a booth, taking a break, when they started playing some traditional Greek song. And right out of nowhere (or at least it seemed that way to me) one of those girls from the Fourth of July party walked up, gave me a quick, sharp, not so nice once-over, then turned to Yannis and said something in Greek that, from what I could guess, was the equivalent of asking him to dance.

Seriously! Right in front of me! And even though it seemed really weird, I mean considering how we were obviously enjoying ourselves and not looking for any kind of distraction, it's not like I could do anything about it, since it's not like we're a couple.

I glanced back and forth between them, wondering what Yannis would do, my heart thumping hard in my chest as he smiled, shook his head, and stayed seated.

And then, just like in a movie, she narrowed her kohl-lined eyes on mine, tossed her long black hair over her shoulder, and marched across the room, all the way to the other side where her friend from the Fourth of July BBQ, the one with the botched dye job that left her hair an unfortunate shade of tangerine, stood glaring at me.

So then I looked at Yannis and went, "Um, who was that? Another cousin?" And then I laughed—though it was definitely more of a nervous laugh than a real laugh, but the moment was so awkward and tense I didn't really know what to do.

But he just shook his head and shrugged. Then he got

up to get us more Cokes, and by the time he came back, we moved on to something else, and I pretty much forgot all about it 'til now.

When the club was closing and it was time to leave, I climbed on the back of his bike, wrapped my arms around his waist, and buried my face in his neck, closing my eyes to the passing scenery, the full moon, the chilled air—losing myself in the warmth of his body and the way he managed to smell so good without the aid of cologne or aftershave or anything remotely artificial.

But by the time we made it back to my house, I suddenly felt so awkward, and funny, and nervous, and weird, I just hopped off the back and bolted for the door. And just when I realized I hadn't said thanks, much less good night, he called, "Hey, you forgot something."

I gazed down at myself, taking inventory of my shorts, my tank top, my flip-flops, seeing everything still present and accounted for, and wondering what he meant. But when I looked up again, he was waving at me to come closer, and I knew it was all just a ploy, some silly ruse so he could try and make a move.

But instead, he just reached inside his pocket and retrieved the silver Tiffany's bracelet I'd lost while we were dancing, the one I'd forgotten all about until it was dangling right before me.

So I offered my arm and held my breath, watching as his fingers brushed across the thin blue lines on my wrist, feeling the clasp snap shut, and becoming so dizzy and breathless I thought I might faint.

And when I looked at him again, I knew he was going to kiss me. And just as I was about to close my eyes and lean in, he smiled, mumbled something in Greek I couldn't even begin to understand, then started his bike and rode away.

The second he was gone, I ran for the door, repeating the phrase over and over, anxious for either Tally or Tassos to translate. But when I got inside, they were already asleep, and by the time I got to my room, and grabbed this journal, the words had disappeared.

July 10

Dear Tally and/or Tassos,

I MUST learn Greek! Immediately! And you can help me by ONLY communicating with me in Greek from now on.

I'm serious.

This means that even when you're talking to each other and I happen to walk in the room, it would really help if you could immediately switch your conversation to Greek.

This is what they call the Immersion Method.

This is how my Spanish teacher does it.

And this is why I got an A in Spanish III last semester.

Also, I need to ask you about these two girls that were here on the Fourth of July that I think you might know. One has long black hair, and the other has this kind of orangey colored hair (like she tried for blond but only made it halfway). Anyway, anything you can tell me about them would be greatly appreciated. Though I'm afraid this particular conversation will have to be in English, as I need to understand every word.

Okay, I'm heading into town to hang at the café for the rest of the day.

So—have fun at the beach!

Love,

Colby

July 11

Dear Dad,

Even though I just got off the phone with you, I realize there are still a few important things I didn't get a chance to say, so I will write them down here.

1) *I don't think it's at all fair for you to say that there are things that happen between adults that I cannot possibly understand. Because I DO understand, Dad—more than you can possibly know. It's YOU who never tries to understand ME.*
2) *If Mom and I have to move to ARIZONA then when will I get to see you? Did you ever think of that? Because it's a whole other state, which means joint custody and alternate weekends are pretty much out of the question.*
3) *The last time I spoke to Mom, she informed me that you have a new girlfriend. And even though I waited through our entire phone call for you to mention her, you never once did. And just as I was about to take the plunge and ask you myself, it seemed like you somehow sensed it and that's why you claimed you had a call on another line. So don't go thinking I was fooled, because I wasn't.*

Anyway, I'd really appreciate it if you could write me back at your earliest convenience, as I'm obviously in need of some answers.

Or if you're too busy to write, then maybe you can just send me a plane ticket so I can fly home and we can hash it out in person.

Seriously, Dad, this is no laughing matter.

Love,

Colby

July 11

Dear Mom,

Yes, I talked to Dad on the phone, and no, I didn't learn anything about his new girlfriend because he faked another call and hung up before I got a chance to ask. Though to be honest, I'm really not so sure I want to talk about it anyway. I mean, it's really kind of inappropriate, not to mention creepy.

Because the truth is, if anyone in this family should be dating—it's ME!

I'M the teenager.

I'M the one who's supposed to be single.

And I really hate to break it to you, but you and Dad already had your chance, you already got your shot at being sweet sixteen, so it seems pretty unfair that you pick NOW to attempt to do it again.

You don't get to be a teenager twice, Mom. It's just not right.

And by the way things are going, I'm sure it's just a matter of time before YOU decide to hook up too, so I'd like to make it clear, right from the start, that I'm really not interested in hearing any of the gory details.

Because the truth is, I'm just not up for any of this.

Probably because I didn't ASK for any of this.

And excuse me for saying so, but in light of recent events, I just can't help but think that the only reason you guys sent me away to begin with is so you could be free to date, and party, and basically enjoy all of the things that I should be enjoying, only I'm NOT, because YOU sent me HERE!

Which is so completely wrong on so many levels.

Ask your shrink, I'm sure she'll agree.

Love,

The Completely Desperate and Absolutely Serious,

Colby

P.S. I'm enclosing a picture of this famous church here called the Panagia Evangelistria where the Virgin Mary is said to appear, or where they found an old famous icon of her, or something like that (okay, I don't really know the history, but that's not really the point). The point is that every year ~~hundreds~~ no, make that THOUSANDS of religious pilgrims crawl on their hands and knees all the way from the port to the church (which, trust me, is pretty dang far if you're crawling), just so they can pray. And even though I've yet to visit, I'm thinking I might go there today . . . because as you can see, I'm running out of options, and am desperately in need of a MIRACLE.

July 11

To: AmandaStar

From: ColbyCat

Re: Thx anyway

Hey Amanda,

Good 2 finally hear from U & no, I guess I really didn't stop 2 think about how your trunk would be so full of shopping bags there wouldn't B any room left 4 the 4 Sale sign.

Tho I'm glad 2 hear UR having fun. Those pics of U and Jenna and her cousin Penelope (I didn't no she had a cousin? I also didn't no U & Jenna were friends again? When did that happen? Bcuz last I heard you sed U H8D her) at Fashion Island were v cute.

Things R better here, I've made a ton of friends & I'm kinda c-ing someone. But if Levi still wants 2 come, I'm sure I can make room!☺

In fact, don't even mention it 2 him—K?

TTYL—

Colby

July 11
To: NatalieZee
From: ColbyCat
Re: You're moving?
Hey Nat—

While I'm not really sure why the FOR SALE sign is still on my lawn, at this point it's really between my mom and my dad, since, like I wrote in my last e-mail to you, I'm spending the summer in Greece and I'm far too busy having fun here to worry about anything that's going on back home.

And while I truly appreciate your concern, you really don't need to continue to update me.

Though if you do feel like directing your concerns to either one of my parents, or, better yet, stopping by my house and getting rid of the sign yourself—that would be fine.

Hope you're enjoying the summer.
Take care,
Colby

CIRCLE IN THE SAND (FORMERLY CRUEL SUMMER)

July 14

Since someone who goes by the name of ANONYMOUS recently accused me of hating Tinos because of the name of this blog, I've decided to change it. Which shouldn't be at all confusing since no one but ANONYMOUS is reading it anyway, and I'm assuming he/she/they have it bookmarked already.

Anyway, it's funny because this is also named after a song my friend's (well, former friend's) mom used to sing all the time—I guess she was really big on songs about summer.

So I hope, ANONYMOUS, whoever you are, that you'll happen to agree that this title is much more neutral, and far less negative, though probably still not quite as upbeat as you were hoping.

Though maybe I should've titled it CIRCLE IN THE DIRT, because as you've probably noticed in the photos I've posted, there is no shortage of dirt in this place. Also, I recently learned that the Cyclades (which is what they call the group of islands that Tinos is part of) is actually ancient Greek for the word "Circle," so that seems pretty appropriate too. Not to mention how circles are continuous and have no end, and that's pretty much how this summer is beginning to feel—like an eternal loop of continuous days with no end in sight.

Though I'm hoping you won't read too much into what I just wrote and take it all wrong, because I guess what I'm really trying to say is that while I don't exactly hate it here anymore, if I was given the choice, I'd still rather not be here at all.

Though things might just be looking up, since just a second ago, Petros actually smiled and brought me a Nescafé Frappe—

ON THE HOUSE!

Maybe it's because I finally got a tan.

Maybe it's because I haven't been around the last few days since I've been so busy going to clubs, the beach, and hanging out with all my friends here, which gave him plenty of time to ruminate on the fact of just how much he needs me, and misses me, since I am his very best customer. But whatever the reason—just know this—it's really not as bad here as I once thought. But that doesn't mean that it's paradise either. It just means that it's no longer the opposite of paradise.

And now, for your viewing pleasure:

1) This is a picture (uploaded from a Web site since I didn't have my camera at the time) from a club I went to the other night with a friend. And just so you know, there are no age limits here, no I.D.

checks, no bouncers, no velvet ropes, no rules, no nonsense. Just equal-opportunity good times for all ages! Viva Tinos!

2) This is a picture of the scratch Holly Golightly made on my arm that very same night, right before I went to the club. Though it's actually not nearly as bad as it looks, and it really wasn't his fault since I held him too tight and I should know by now just how much he hates that. But still, it hurt like you cannot believe.

3) This is a picture of my aunt Tally and her boyfriend, Tassos, eating some sea urchin he caught at the beach. Seriously, they just pulled them right out of the water, cracked them right open (they have this special tool made just for that specific purpose), then they each grabbed a seashell and used it like a spoon to scoop out the insides, and I watched (and photographed) while they ate it RAW! I admit, I tried a little teensy bit too, but only because they're always telling me how it's good to keep an open mind and try new things. But even though I wouldn't exactly say that I loved it (because I definitely did NOT), I also have to admit that it wasn't nearly as gross as you're probably thinking! Though it definitely was a little bit gross!

4) This is a picture of Agios Fokas, which is the beach I'm heading to now, for the sole purpose of working on my tan, so I can maybe get another free frappe tomorrow!

Have a good day!

Love,

Colby

July 15

To: NatalieZee

From: ColbyCat

Re: You're moving

Thank you for trying to get rid of that stupid FOR SALE sign.

I really do appreciate it.

Though I have no idea why they've already replaced it with another.

But still, thanks for trying.

Colby

COLBY'S JOURNAL FOR DESPERATE TIMES WHEN SHE JUST CAN'T UNDERSTAND ANYTHING ABOUT HER LIFE

July 16

This is how desperate I am—I actually flipped through one of Tally's New Age, self-empowerment, or whatever you call them books, searching for answers to my current predicament, and even THEY couldn't help.

Though that's probably because I wasn't exactly sure what to look for. I mean, it's not like there's a chapter titled:

WHAT TO DO WHEN YOUR ENTIRE LIFE HAS GONE TO HELL AND IT'S OBVIOUSLY ALL YOUR FAULT.

Though maybe there should be.

It's like, when my parents first decided to send me here they tried to convince me that it was MOSTLY so I could experience life in a foreign country and enjoy a relaxing summer, and only PARTLY so they could shield me from what is turning out to be the world's ugliest legal grudge match.

And while I obviously did not for one second believe the MOSTLY part of their story, and knew it was actually more about the PARTLY part, the weird thing is, that for a place that's supposed to be so simple and laid-back and relaxing, how is it possible that my life has become way more complicated here than it ever was before?

For example:

1) If I thought I was stressed about holding on to my position as Amanda's good friend when I was back home, well, that's nothing compared to how freaked I am now. Because, not only has she not read my blog after that first time (which I now recognize as either an accident or fluke or an accidental fluke), but the few times she's even bothered to respond to my e-mails, she's attached photos that, to be honest, kind of hurt my feelings. Like the one of Levi and Penelope at that party. I so did NOT need to see that! I mean, granted, I haven't exactly confided in her about what happened between me and Levi (mostly because I know

better than to trust her), BUT STILL, it's just common courtesy, heck, it's common sense! And then when she sent me that pic of her and Jenna and Penelope all loaded down with Bloomingdale's bags at Fashion Island, all of them happily indulging in all of the summer fun and frolic I'm totally missing—I mean, that was completely rude and inconsiderate. Not to mention that the last I heard she was no longer even talking to Jenna. Just like I was no longer talking to Nat. It's like we'd both traded them in so we could hang with each other. That was our deal. But from the looks of their little Saturday excursion, they're now just one big happy family again, and I'm the orphan who got left in the cold. Not to mention how I can't believe she's back with Jenna after all of the TRULY AWFUL things she told me about her. And I cannot believe she's hanging with Jenna's cousin, Penelope (a.k.a. Levi's summer fling). Not to mention how if she can take the time to do all of those things then she can also take a few minutes out of her precious day to send me an e-mail and tell me once and for all just what the HECK is going on with Levi and his supposed cruise. And why he hasn't bothered to e-mail me. And just what, if anything, he's said about me. Because I'm really starting to go into meltdown mode. But has she bothered to do any of those things? Um, that would be NO!

2) When I first found out that I was coming here, my worst fear was that my parents might try to kill each other while I was gone. Seriously, they were fighting so bad and so often it actually seemed like they were well on their way to dividing the house right down the center and barbequing the family pets (luckily we don't have any family pets). But still, it was really starting to mimic this old movie I once saw where the couple ended up doing exactly that, only to end up all tangled up and dead on top of their chandelier (I forget how they wound up on the chandelier, but then again that's not really the point). The point is, that now, even though none of that happened, it's somehow managed to get even worse! Because apparently my dad just got a new bachelor pad and a new girlfriend to go with it. And my mom is acting so insanely jealous that she's started calling me and confiding in me and telling me all kinds of creepy things I never wanted to know about my dad. Like she thinks she's my friend instead of my mom. And even though it's true that I'm currently experiencing a shortage of friends, it's not exactly a crisis, and I'm not exactly looking to her to fill the void.

3) And then there's the little matter of the FOR SALE sign, which my supposed good friend Amanda just couldn't be bothered to remove, but that my former friend Natalie handled right away. And all that does is make me feel that much worse for how our friendship ended, and how she accused me of dumping her and treating her like crap. Which is not even fair since it's not like it's ENTIRELY my fault in the first place. I mean, we were both growing apart and wanted different things anyway, which, when you stop and think about it, is really neither one of our faults, because people change and grow and move on and things like that just happen. It's just the way life is. (Okay, I just reread that last part and now I feel totally creeped out since it's pretty much the exact same speech my dad gave me about the divorce.) Anyway, all of these things just lead to the next item on my list:

4) Most of the time I feel like I don't even know who I am anymore. I'm not kidding. I feel like I'm just wandering around, trying to hang on to a home I'll probably never see again, hang on to a dad who's more interested in his new life than his old one, hang on to a friend who was probably never much of a friend to begin with, and hang on to a guy who probably doesn't even remember my name, much less the fact that he spent almost four hours kissing me and

trying to take off my dress, before using our last minute and a half together to take my virginity. And no, I really don't think he's ANONYMOUS anymore, because that kind of thinking is not only completely delusional and stark-raving mad, but also requires a certain amount of OPTIMISM and HOPE that I just can't muster. And to be honest, I haven't the slightest idea who ANONYMOUS is. But with the way things are going, I'm sure it'll turn out to be some creepy online stalker, someone who's wanted in all fifty states, including the northern and southern territories.

5) Oh yeah, and to top it all off, it's not like I've made much of an impact here. Because I really would've thought that Yannis would've stopped by and/or called by now, but, big surprise, he hasn't.

UPDATE!

Believe it or not, it just went from worse to EVEN WORSE!

Apparently, I've now become so pathetic that even my own rescued kitty doesn't want to be with me. Seriously, just as I finished writing the above, Holly took one look at me, sniffed my shorts and T-shirt, jumped right off my bed, and scrammed out of my room as fast as he could.

Like he has a sixth sense or something.

Like he KNOWS what I am, and doesn't want to be beholden to a loser.

Obviously, this is probably a good time to stop writing for the night.

CIRCLE IN THE SAND

Blog Comments:

Anonymous said:

I'm confused. From your pictures it looks like you are in paradise.

Sun, sand, sea, and a kitten . . . What more do you need?

Please explain at your earliest convenience.

ColbyCat said:

I don't really know how to explain, because the truth is, you're right, it is really pretty here. The beaches are nice (except for the rocky ones) and my kitten is adorable (as you can see). I guess, it's a little more barren and rugged than I usually like, but hey, you can't have everything, right?

Maybe it's just that paradise is more a state of mind than an actual place?

Anonymous said:

Interesting . . . I never thought of it like that.

Thanks for explaining.

July 18
To: AmandaStar
From: ColbyCat
Re: !!!!!!!!

OMG—R U serious? Levi's actually really coming here & U gave him my e-mail???

U-R-The-BEST!

!!!!!!!!!!

Thank U Thank U Thank U!

(U sure this is 4 real & UR not messing w/me, right?)

Colby

July 18
To:NatalieZee
From: ColbyCat
Re: You're moving?
Hey Nat,

Sorry, but I really can't explain why there was an open house at my home yesterday. Though I do thank you for taking the opportunity to put all the books and CDs you borrowed back on my shelves.

And to answer your question, yes, I'm having a total blast here. And just in case you're bored, or curious, or even if you just want to know all the juicy details, you can read all about it in my blog. It's called "Circle in the Sand." And NO, I didn't name it that because of you or your mom or any of those songs she always used to sing. I just needed a summer blog name and it's the only thing I could think of on such short notice.

Well, actually, it's the second name, but whatever, just check it out if you want.

K—L8R (sorry, I know how you hate that, but I couldn't resist!)

Colby

P.S. Levi will be here soon!!!!! I can't wait!

July 18

Dear Mom,

For your information I know all about the OPEN HOUSE, which means we seriously need to talk, because NO WAY am I moving.

I thought we'd been through this already?

This cannot continue.

You must stop.

Please contact me at your earliest convenience.

Love,

Colby

July 18

Dear Dad,

Mom had an OPEN HOUSE and I'm holding you responsible.

You have to do something to stop her because NO WAY am I moving!

I thought we'd been through this already?

This cannot continue.

This must stop.

Please contact me at your earliest convenience.
Love,
Colby

Colby's Journal for Desperate Times That Require Desperate Measures

July 20

I don't know what's wrong with me. Seriously, you'd think I'd be happy, partly because—LEVI'S COMING. That's according to Amanda, who's still hooked up with Casey who happens to be best friends with Levi who said something about not being able to go to someone's surprise party because he's going on a Mediterranean cruise instead.

And also, YANNIS IS COMING. Here. Tonight. For a BBQ. But those two friends of his, Maria (black hair) and Christina (orange hair), who just happen to be related to one of Tassos's best friends (Christina is his friend's daughter, Maria is her cousin), are NOT invited (I made sure of that). Anyway, apparently the only reason he didn't call or come by sooner is because he had to go to Athens for a few days, and NOT because he suddenly decided he didn't like me, or anything remotely like that.

Please note the lack of exclamation points even though I really am excited about both of these things.

Though I must admit, the neutral punctuation is probably due to the fact that all of my excitement is currently being overshadowed by my mom and dad's last phone call, where they both informed me, under no uncertain terms, that they retain the right to divorce, date, throw open houses, and basically make a string of not just bad, but extremely reckless decisions that will surely result in the complete unraveling of my life, and quite possibly my future.

Also, I was reminded, that as a minor, there's absolutely nothing I can do about any of this, since they are the ADULTS, while I am merely their CHILD. At which point they went on to assure me that I shouldn't take everything so PERSONALLY as none of it is meant that way.

They are simply dedicating themselves to doing "What is in the best interest of everyone."

And all I can say to THAT, is:

If that's so true, and they're so DEDICATED, then how come they've yet to stop and consider what might be in the best interest of ME?

How come they can't just grow up, stay put, and:

JUST LET ME GET THROUGH MY LAST YEAR OF HIGH SCHOOL MORE OR LESS UNSCATHED?

Seriously.

I mean, just one more year, that's all I ask. And after that, after I graduate high school and head off to college, they're free to self-destruct or do whatever the heck they want.

Just let me complete my childhood first.

I wonder if I can divorce them?

COLBY'S JOURNAL FOR DESPERATE TIMES WHEN SHE'S SO HAPPY SHE CAN HARDLY BREATHE!

July 27

Haven't been blogging. Haven't been e-mailing. Haven't been letter writing or postcard sending. Haven't been to the Internet café. Haven't even turned on my computer in what seems like forever but is probably just over a week. And all of this is happening because:

I'M CURRENTLY IMMERSED IN A VERY SERIOUS CASE OF WHAT APPEARS TO BE—MUTUAL LIKE!

Ever since the night of the BBQ, when Yannis rode up on his bike and smiled at me, my stomach started doing a series of somersaults and backflips, which, to be honest, haven't really slowed down since.

But it's not the same kind of nervous and anxious feeling I had with Levi. It's more like a tingly, CAN'T BELIEVE THIS IS ACTUALLY HAPPENING TO ME kind of feeling. And even though I kind of felt like that back when Levi first kissed me, for some reason it's even better with Yannis.

I guess because being with Yannis feels more real, less borrowed.

Anyway, he pretty much just parked his bike, sat down beside me, and didn't really go anywhere else for the rest of the night. And the whole time we were talking and laughing and getting to know each other better, it felt like only half my brain was actually focused on what we were saying and doing, because the other half couldn't stop thinking: *I wish he'd stop talking and kiss me!*

But since Tally, Tassos, and all of their friends really weren't allowing for much in the way of privacy, I pretty much resigned myself to yet another fun, yet passion-free night.

But then, after we ate and it started to get dark, Yannis leaned toward me and whispered, "Wanna go for a ride?"

And of course I said yes.

And even though I was fully expecting to end up at that club again, this time, after riding around for a while, we ended up at his favorite beach instead. Then we parked on the road, and ran down to the sand, where he laid out a towel for us to sit on as we gazed at the moon and the stars, trying to spot the different constellations, until he finally worked up the nerve to kiss me.

That's right—HE had to work up the nerve to kiss ME!

Which means, I was making him feel just as nervous and giddy as he makes me!

Which is also the exact opposite of Levi, who pretty much assumes that every girl in any given room is totally willing to make out with him on a moment's notice. (Though to be fair, that's probably only because it's so true.)

But even though it's probably true for Yannis too, he just doesn't have that same kind of ~~confidence~~ arrogance as Levi. He's just way more polite, more respectful, and would never try to push someone to do stuff they may not be ready for.

Anyway, one minute we were talking about the Big and Little Dippers, and the next thing I knew he was kissing me. And let me just say that it was TOTALLY AMAZING!

Not awkward at all. Not even in the very beginning of the kiss, which is normally a pretty tense moment since both parties are striving to choreograph a duet that neither of them has ever rehearsed (at least not together).

But with Yannis, it was like both our lips just knew EXACTLY what to do and EXACTLY where to go, and it felt like magic.

In fact, it was so amazing and magical that we stayed there for hours, just kissing and talking, but mostly just kissing. Until it eventually got too cold for the shorts and T-shirts we were both wearing and he decided to take me home.

And this time when he dropped me off, he kissed me again, and said, "See you tomorrow?"

To which I just nodded and smiled and ran inside the house, thinking I would write it all down in this journal.

But in the end I chose to just lie on my bed, close my eyes, and relive it over and over again in my head, until I eventually fell asleep, where I dreamt about him too!

And sure enough, the very next day he came by again. And he's pretty much been coming by every day since!

So after just skimming through all of my previous journal entries I can hardly believe what a big whiny baby I've been. And it's so embarrassing to read all of that, I'm thinking about ripping out all of those pages and burning them at Tally and Tassos's next BBQ.

I mean, what could I possibly have been thinking? This place is BEAUTIFUL! It really is like PARADISE, only I was too blind to see it.

Granted, it may not be all that exciting or hip and trendy and jet-set and glittery like Mykonos, but when you're in the right company you really don't need all that flash.

It's like I wrote in my blog—Paradise is a state of mind!

And Yannis is just so incredibly sweet and cute and awesome, and he's even teaching me Greek! These are some of the words I've learned so far:

Koukla Mou—(Obviously I'm not using the Greek alphabet since our lessons haven't quite progressed that far.) Which literally means something like "my darling." Which actually sounds kind of old fashioned and weird, which is also why it's better to avoid the temptation to directly translate everything, and just take the overall gist of the word or phrase instead. Which in this case would make it more like: *honey,* or maybe even, *babe.* (Okay, still kind of weird, but I know for a fact that he means it in the nicest way!)

Omorphos—means pretty! (He said this about my hair on a day when I really didn't think it was looking all that *omorphos!*)

Apothe—means tonight! (As in, we go out just about every *apothe!* Which also happens to be true!)

Efcharisto—means thank you. But when I could barely get the hang of pronouncing it, Yannis told me to think of it as a person named F. Harry Stowe. Which I have to admit is so much easier!

And *Yannis*—means John. (But I still call him Yannis because it sounds way more exotic.)

Though *Colby* doesn't mean anything, it's just plain Colby. Which is what he calls me when he's not calling me *Koukla Mou.*

And, oh yah, *S'agapo* means I love you. Not that he said it or anything. Though I did ask Tassos how to say it just in case Yannis does decide to say it, then I'll know what it means. But I really hope he doesn't decide to say it because that'll just wreck everything. I mean, it's way better to keep things casual and not get all serious and over involved—just try to stay focused on having fun, and not make a bunch of false declarations and promises we'll never be able to keep.

Anyway, we actually see each other so often we've worked out a little schedule. Like, in the mornings he almost always goes to work, helping with the construction of the hotel his family is building, but in the afternoons he usually meets me and Tally and Tassos at the beach for siesta, or sometimes we just go on our own, and he always thinks it's so funny how I refuse to take off my top. But since I've yet to take it off when we're alone, I'm certainly not going to do it for the first time in front of a whole crowd of people. I mean, I actually managed to lose my virginity without once taking off my top, so why start now?

Anyway, at night we usually go into town and hang at

that club he first took me to, or we ride around on his Vespa, looking for some quiet place where we can be alone and make out.

And I have to admit that even though it's fun to hang out with all of his friends and cousins and stuff, my favorite times are always when it's just the two of us, all alone, gazing at the stars, kissing, or sometimes even just talking. And it's weird how I feel so relaxed around him, since I'm usually pretty nervous around guys (especially really cute ones like Yannis!) since it's not like I've had lots of experience with boyfriends or anything. But with Yannis, everything feels so natural and easy and comfortable.

Which, again, is pretty much the exact opposite of how I felt with Levi.

Though of course, wouldn't you know it, just as I'd given up, just as I decided to move on and forget about him completely, Levi decides to e-mail me about his upcoming cruise, and now I don't know what I'm supposed to do. I mean, luckily he's not coming HERE, because that would be really awkward now that I'm hanging out with Yannis so much. But still, he is going to MYKONOS, which is just a short boat ride away.

If I choose to make the journey, that is.

I mean, I've been DYING to go to Mykonos this whole entire time, or at least since my plane landed there and the guy I sat next to told me it was the only island worth visiting. Only now that I have an actual excuse to get on the ferry and go, I'm no longer sure that I want to.

Though luckily I have a little over a week to decide.

Okay, I can hear Yannis's bike in the drive, but let me write one more thing that's kind of been bothering me in the midst of all this incredible happiness:

I'm not sure why, but I haven't exactly been truthful with him about my life back home. I mean, I guess it's because it's just such a relief to be hanging out and having fun and not thinking about any of my problems that it kind of makes me reluctant to bring it up.

Though if I'm really going to be honest, then I also have to admit that the other reason is that I don't want him to think of me as sad, or pathetic, or worse. Because even though I've only met his cousins and his little brother, Christos, and I haven't met his parents or anything, when he talks about them, he always says such nice things that it makes me feel kind of weird to talk about mine. Especially since I'm not thinking so well of them at the moment. I mean, truth be told, I'm so upset, angry, and disgusted with them, I don't even think I could fake it if I tried. And I just can't bear to have Yannis think I'm a loser, or that my home life is one big disaster.

Even though it is.

Because right now he sees me as this happy-go-lucky, free-spirited, California girl. (Okay, one who won't take her top off, but still.) And that's the way I'm determined to keep it.

Okay, he's knocking on my bedroom door—so—gotta run!

Colby's Journal for Desperate Times When She's Desperately, Deliriously, Seriously Liking Someone

August 1

So last night Yannis took me to dinner. And even though it wasn't exactly the first time we'd eaten a meal together, it was the first time we'd eaten a meal without being chaperoned by Tally, Tassos, his little brother, or any one of his hundreds of cousins and friends. We even went to a restaurant that was a non-cousin-owned establishment. And I know, because I checked.

Anyway, it was awesome.

And dreamy.

And magical!

But all that magic actually started when he came to the house to get me, and I opened the door and felt my heart skip a beat—seriously! I mean, even though we see each other every single day, something about seeing him standing in the doorway, all dressed up, with flowers in hand (Yes! He even brought me flowers!), smiling like he really was happy to see me, well, it made it seem like the very first time all over again.

Maybe it was the cool jeans he was wearing, or the nicely pressed shirt, or the way his deep green eyes gazed into mine. Maybe it was the way he smiled, so genuine and warm and inviting. Or maybe it was the way his arm felt so right when he slipped it around my waist.

Whatever it was, I felt like pinching myself, since I

could hardly believe that this wonderful, cute, sweet, amazing guy had shown up just for me!

Anyway, when we got to the restaurant, they led us to a table in this tiny but beautiful courtyard that was all lit up by candles and moonlight. There was music playing in the background, and everything about it was just so perfect and romantic and amazing—the kind of night you always dream about, or see in movies, but doubt you'll ever experience for yourself.

So after this great dinner that included all kinds of food I can't pronounce, much less spell, we walked around town for a while before stopping by our favorite club to say hi to some friends and hang for a little while, before getting back on the bike and heading over to our favorite beach.

And I don't know if it was the caffeine (I had two and a half Cokes at dinner), or the moon (it was round and full and amazingly bright), or just that wonderful, expansive feeling of being so far from home and so free, but before I could even stop to think about what I was doing, I stripped off my dress and ran straight into the sea.

So of course, Yannis stripped off his shirt and pants and followed.

And then we swam, and splashed, and chased each other through the surf, going under, popping back up, until he eventually caught up with me. And when he turned me to face him, he kissed me in a way that reminded me of that very first night—back when we were new and hesitant and full of wonder.

And when I opened my eyes I saw his green ones gazing into mine, and his dark, wet curls curving against the sides of his face, and the clusters of water droplets shining silver in the moonlight as they clung to his tan, bare skin.

And he was so beautiful, and so tempting, and so alluring, and so immediately THERE, that I yanked free of his arms and ran right back to shore, struggling to get back in my dress before something happened to change my mind—unwilling to make the same mistake twice.

Then we lay on the sand and held hands, both of us enveloped in silence and darkness, as I closed my eyes and tried to capture the moment, willing it to never end.

August 3
To: Levi501
From: ColbyCat
Re: UR cruise
Hey Levi,

I jus got UR msg & 2 answer UR ? I'm not in Mykonos, I'm in Tinos. Tho I can C Mykonos bcuz it's pretty close by. So I'll def try 2 meet up w/U. Jus lemme no the xact day & time, K?

Ciao—
Colby

CIRCLE IN THE SAND

Blog Comments:

Anonymous said:

Where are you?

Please don't tell me you've given up on your blog?

ColbyCat said:

I'm back, it was merely a brief vacation, I assure you!

CIRCLE IN THE SAND

August 3

I'm back! And no, ANONYMOUS, I have not given up on my blog. Though I have discovered a little something I like to call GETTING A LIFE. And now that I've got one, I find it's taking up most of my time. Though apparently you're not the only one who missed me, because Petros actually gave me A HUG when I walked through the door! He said he was sure I'd gone back to America without even saying good-bye (which I would never, ever do!). But even though he claimed to be relieved and happy to see me, he still made me pay for my frappe. (Though according to his son, Stavros, the fact that I even got one free drink out of him is a bona fide miracle!)

So without further delay, here are some pictures for you to enjoy—

1) That is a picture of me attempting to windsurf. Can you believe it? My friend Yannis is actually really good at it, and he was determined to teach me, so I could be good at it too. But please don't be too impressed by what you see here, because the truth is, that photo was taken during the two and a half seconds I actually managed to stay up! Because, trust me, just one second later, I fell ack-basswards into the water!
2) That is a picture of Mr. Holly Golightly—notice how much bigger (and cuter!) he's gotten! Though he still gets all pissy whenever I try to cuddle him too much.
3) That is a picture of Tassos's studio, where he makes the most beautiful marble sculptures (Tinos has a very famous marble sculpting school where Tassos sometimes teaches) and pottery and stuff, don't you agree? Though don't be fooled by the simplicity of it, because it is way, WAY harder than it looks. Seriously. When he sat me down at the potter's wheel and tried to teach me how to do it, I failed. BIG-TIME. And what was supposed to be my vase totally collapsed and became nothing more than a big, runny lump of clay.
4) See that big, runny lump of clay? That's my vase. I so wasn't kidding.

5) That's a picture of Yannis petting Holly. Notice how he has no scratches on his arms. I have a terrible suspicion that Holly actually likes him better than me even though I'm the one who saved him from starvation. Apparently cats have short memories. Which means my next pet will be an elephant.
6) That's me and Yannis at the club, just hanging with some friends. See that guy standing behind me? That's Yannis's cousin. And the guy standing next to him? Also his cousin. And the girl in the far right corner? Yup, you guessed it, another cousin. And that guy next to me? That's his little brother, Christos. Ha! You thought it was another cousin, didn't you?
7) That's me and Yannis at the beach. Notice how it appears to be just us? But don't be fooled, one of his cousins was actually taking the picture.
8) Me and Yannis at one of Tally and Tassos's Saturday BBQs, where he's teaching me the actual steps to that Greek dance I thought I knew, because contrary to what I originally thought, you're not really supposed to just run in a circle, there are very specific steps, and it's much more intricate than I ever would've/could've imagined.
9) That's me and Yannis drinking frappes with some of his cousins at an outdoor café on the harbor. Frappe rocks. It's seriously growing on me. Especially that free one that Petros gave me that one time. That was definitely the best one yet!

Okay, that's it!

Hope this makes up for my little break—ANONYMOUS!

Love,

Colby

August 4

To: NatalieZee

From: ColbyCat

Re: Who's Yannis?

Hey Nat,

Yannis is a friend of mine.

A really good friend.

Actually, I guess he's kind of like my boyfriend. Though it's not like you need to tell anyone that or spread it around town, okay?

I mean, not that I think you would or anything, but still, I just feel like I should say it, since it could be kind of weird if word got out since Levi will be coming here soon.

Though maybe that still makes it more weird HERE than THERE?

See, I really haven't changed as much as you think. I'm still just as crazy and confused as ever!

Okay, well, thanks for reading my blog!

Hope your summer is going well—

Colby

August 4
To: AmandaStar
From: ColbyCat
Re: UR blog/Sandal Guy
Hey Amanda,

Thx 4 ckg out my blog. But no, Yannis is so NOT my boyfriend. He's just a friend. U no, someone 2 hang w/ every now & then so I don't die of xtreme boredom over here.

And 2 answer UR ? yes, believe it or not, most of the guyz around here wear sandals like that. But I guess IV just been stuck here 4 so long now I'm starting 2 get used 2 it. I mean, I hardly even notice them NEmore. At least not until U mentioned it.

Which is really pretty scary if U think about it!

So Levi will be in Mykonos in just 3 days, & I sooo can't wait!

I'll let you know how it goes ☺

K—C—YA—

Colby

CIRCLE IN THE SAND

Blog Comments:

Anonymous said:

Who is Yannis?

ColbyCat said:

A friend.

Anonymous said:

Tell me more about this friend.

ColbyCat said:

What do you want to know?

Anonymous said:

Is he your boyfriend?

ColbyCat said:

Define boyfriend.

Anonymous said:

The opposite of boy friend.

ColbyCat said:

Define boy friend.

Anonymous said:

You like to play games.

ColbyCat said:

You're the one who goes by ANONYMOUS!

Anonymous said:

True.

ColbyCat said:

Have you ever considered not being ANONYMOUS anymore?

Anonymous said:

Yes. I have considered it.

ColbyCat said:

And???

Anonymous said:

And I am still considering it.

ColbyCat said:

Okay, let me know what you decide.

Colby's Journal for Desperate Times When She's Gotten Herself into Such a Mess She Can't Find Her Way Out

August 7

Leave it to me to take a monumentally great thing and mess it up in such a hugely colossal way that there's just no fixing it. I mean, just when I was starting to be really happy, just when I was starting to think that my life was so great it was almost too good to be true—WHAM! I make sure that it isn't.

I mean, let's face it, I can barely handle one guy, much less two, so none of this should come as any kind of surprise to anyone, especially me. I guess I've just never been the kind of girl who can string 'em along and leave 'em begging for more, like Amanda, and practically everyone else in my cool new group (well, maybe I should've written FORMER cool new group instead, since, at the moment, I'm not exactly part of it anymore, and they haven't exactly given me any indication of missing me, much less remembering me).

Anyway, I guess I'm just too serious, too dorky, too nervous, too big of a geek, too honest—except when I lie. Because every time I try to lie about something, the lie somehow manages to get so out of control, expanding and growing so big it practically takes on a life of its own, a life that eventually sets out to destroy my very own.

I guess that's what Tally and Tassos refer to as *karma*.

Getting what you give.

So anyway, last night, when Yannis picked me up, he was acting all cute and sly and mysterious about where we were going. And even though I kept trying to guess, he just kept shaking his head, saying, "You'll see."

So when we finally ended up at what basically seemed to be a big construction site, I climbed off the back of his Vespa, took one look around and said, "Okay, I give up."

But he just laughed, grabbed my hand, and tried to lead me inside. And when I hesitated by the front door, he kissed me on the cheek and said, "Relax, it belongs to my family, I just want to show you around." Then he proceeded to give me a tour of the hotel he's been working on all summer, but that probably won't be completely finished until sometime this winter. And by the way he was smiling and pointing out all the little details, all of the things that were either his idea or that he'd personally worked on or built by himself, it was obvious he was really excited about showing it to me.

But no matter how proud he was, no matter how anxious he was for me to share in his excitement, I just couldn't match it.

I was too busy staring at his sandals.

Yup, the same exact sandals that I never even noticed until Amanda made that nasty comment about them in her e-mail.

But now that she had, all I could do was gaze at his feet and think—*What the heck are you doing, Colby?*

And even though I knew I was being SHALLOW.

SOOO INCREDIBLY SHALLOW.

I just couldn't help it.

Though I wish that were all, I wish I could say it stopped there, because unfortunately, it gets worse.

Because suddenly, the very same accent that, just yesterday, I found so adorable and sexy, started to grate on my nerves. And I found myself cringing every time he uttered something from his version of the cool American phrase book.

Stuff like:

Relax, it's no problem.

Or: *Slow down, it's no worries.*

Even his own language started to bug me, like when he, for the one millionth time, referred to me as: *Koukla Mou.*

It's like, practically overnight, with just one stupid, bitchy e-mail from Amanda, I started questioning everything about him, about US! Like I'd completely lost the ability to see anything as I once had. Like I literally went from thinking I might really, really, really like him, to not even responding when he told me he loved me.

That's right, he told me he loved me.

After we'd concluded the tour of the lobby, the reception, the kitchen, the bar, the gym, and a few of the other rooms and suites, he led me out to the pool area, that he just happened to have all set up with chairs and blankets and candles and music and food and drinks and flowers. And it should've been really romantic, because it WAS really romantic, except for the fact that the whole entire time all I could do was continue to stare at his shoes, cringe at his accent, and think:

What the heck are you doing, Colby? Summer will soon be over. August 31 is just around the corner. Levi will be here tomorrow. And now you have to make a choice.

You can either:

1) Stop being so shallow, and allow yourself to fall for this guy who up until yesterday you thought you really, really liked, and who happens to be really cute, nice, sweet, kind, and fun, and who, through no real fault of his own, just happens to overuse some weird phrases, in a weird accent, that you've just now decided gets on your nerves, and yes, who also happens to wear sandals that are so bizarre you can barely stand to look at his feet, even though you can't seem to stop staring at them. **OR:**

2) You can focus on your future, and get the heck out of here! Because even though Amanda is undisputedly shallow, to the point where it just might be contagious, the fact that she even bothered to write you back and read your blog in the first place proves you're still IN. Not to mention how Levi is coming all this way to see you. Or at least he plans to see you because he's coming all this way. At any rate, if you have half a brain left in your cloudy, foggy, overcast head, you will choose Levi and Amanda and prom and parties, which is the only SOCIAL SECURITY plan you currently have. BECAUSE GREECE IS NOT YOUR FUTURE, BUT CALIFORNIA IS!
3) Not to mention how YOU of all people should be very well versed in how LOVE NEVER LASTS! It's just another illusion that people like to fool themselves into believing. And even if, by some small chance, it did turn out to be valid, real, and mutual, it's still just a matter of time before it ends anyway, so really, what's the point of even going there? Just look at your parents, if you need further proof. Or half of Hollywood! Love is invisible, unreal! Besides, everything has a beginning, middle, and end and you're a complete sappy fool if you allow yourself to believe otherwise!

But what I also haven't mentioned until now, is that earlier in the day, when I was getting ready to leave the café, I saw Yannis standing by the harbor, right there in the fish market, talking to Maria. And even though they weren't doing anything other than just talking, seeing them together like that still managed to make my stomach go all queasy and weird, almost like someone had kicked it—really, really hard, right in the center of my gut.

And just after I thought: *Why is he in town, talking to Maria, when just last night he said he'd be working all day?*

I thought: *Why does it even matter? YOU don't live here. And this is nothing more than a fun, summer fling to keep you from dying of boredom! Soon you'll be going home and you'll never even see him again. And if Yannis wants to be with Maria—what's it to you? You just need to focus on yourself and get your priorities straight! You've had your fun, and now it's time to make a quick exit, get the heck out before you start believing you feel stuff that's not even real!*

But still, even though I knew all that to be true, it's not like it stopped the horrible pang in my gut, my shortness of breath, or the hectic beating of my heart, as I watched Maria lean in and kiss Yannis, once on each cheek.

So after Yannis lit all the candles and turned on the music, he pulled me into his arms, brushed his lips against my hair, and whispered, *"S'agapo,"* so softly I almost didn't hear it.

Except that I did hear it.

I just pretended I didn't.

And instead of responding, I just grabbed us each a Coke and started pouring them into some glasses. And for the rest of the night I just went through the motions, playing the part of a girl who was enjoying a fun, romantic, lighthearted date.

But all the while, deep down inside, I was thinking about which ferry I should catch ~~tomorrow~~ (now technically today), which would get me to Mykonos in time to see Levi.

And even though it may sound horrible, shallow, stupid, and disgusting,

In the end, I was only trying to be practical.

Because the fact is, Yannis doesn't go to Harbor High, but Levi does.

And I never should've let things go this far to begin with.

August 7
To: Levi501
From: ColbyCat
Re: Mykonos!
Hey Levi,

I'm going to catch the 1:00 ferry, so I'll meet U @ the dock when you get in.

C U soon—

Colby

CIRCLE IN THE SAND

August 7

Just stopping in for a quick hello because in just a few hours I'll be headed HERE!

Yup, that's a picture of MYKONOS!!!

And I can hardly wait to see it for myself, since I've been dying to go there this whole, entire time!

Anyway, a very good friend of mine from home is visiting there, so I'm planning to hop on the ferry and go visit. So hopefully I will have lots of photos to share with you tomorrow! (Or the next day—since I'm really not sure when I'll be getting back!)

So—

Kalo Takseethee to me!

(That's phonetic Greek for *Bon Voyage!*)

Colby

CIRCLE IN THE SAND

Blog Comments:

Anonymous said:

What's in Mykonos?

ColbyCat said:

Windmills, so they tell me.

Anonymous said:

What else?

ColbyCat said:

A world-famous pelican!

Anonymous said:

And?

ColbyCat said:

Wild nightlife?

Anonymous said:

Which are you most looking forward to? The windmills, the world-famous pelican, or the wild nightlife?

ColbyCat said:

Is this a test?

Anonymous said:

No, just a question.

ColbyCat said:

Then I'll tell you when I get back. Though mostly I'm going to visit my friend.

Anonymous said:

Which friend?

ColbyCat said:

Tell me who you are and I'll tell you who he is. Deal?

Anonymous said:

No deal.

ColbyCat said:

Your choice.

August 7

Dear Aunt Tally and Tassos,

I'm leaving this note on the fridge since you always head straight for it when you get back from the beach, so I figured you'd find it right away.

Anyway, I probably should have told you this before, but I'm taking the ferry to Mykonos. Though PLEASE don't rush down to the dock to come get me, because, the truth is, by the time you read this, I'll be gone.

Also, please don't worry, or stress, or anything like that because I'll be totally fine, and it's not like I'm mad at you, or trying to run away from home, or anything remotely like that. I just—well, let's just say that I'm meeting up with A Friend. Someone I know from school. And I'll probably be back late tonight, or maybe even tomorrow morning, since I forgot to find out how long my friend is staying. But if my friend stays overnight then I probably will too. Just to keep my friend company, since I don't know if my friend is traveling with other friends.

Okay, so I guess I'll see you either tonight or tomorrow, but please, don't come to Mykonos and try to look for me or anything, because:

1) I'll be totally fine. &

2) That would be totally embarrassing.

Okay, well, thanks for understanding. (I really hope you understand, but if not I'll explain it all to you when I get back either tonight or tomorrow, I promise.)

Love,

Colby

P.S. If Yannis comes over can you please just tell him that I'm sick, or not feeling well, or something like that? And if he still insists on trying to see me then can you please just inform him that I'm so sick and unwell that I'm not up to seeing anyone but that I will see him tomorrow, for sure?

P.P.S. Sorry about asking you to lie, because I know you think it's bad karma. But trust me, it's going toward a very good cause, which I will also explain later.

August 7

Dear Mom,

This postcard is not lying because the fact is, I really am in Mykonos. And from what I've seen so far, this is where you and Dad should've sent me in the first place. Because not only is it beautiful, but it's also cool and fun and way more exciting than Tinos. I mean, nothing against Aunt Tally, because she's really nice and NOT AT ALL CRAZY like you guys always said, and it's not like it's her fault that Tinos is totally boring compared to Mykonos.

And even though you're probably wondering why I'm here, I'm not going to tell you. I mean, it's not like you've been all that honest either, since I happen to know all about your new boyfriend even though you think that I don't. Though I guess we'll save that for an actual letter where there's more room to write.

Love,

Your disillusioned daughter,

Colby

August 7

Dear Dad,

The front of this postcard features a picture of some very famous windmills that are located in Mykonos, which is where I am now. Though I won't tell you why since even though you managed to tell me about Mom's new boyfriend, you failed to mention the fact of how you are now living with your girlfriend. Though I guess we'll just have to save that little conversation for one of those fun family conference calls you and Mom seem so fond of.

Thank you for curing me of my unbridled optimism.

Love,

Colby

August 7

Dear Nat,

I know you're probably pretty surprised to get a postcard from me, but I'm in Mykonos, sitting at the dock, waiting for Levi's boat to come in, and I'm kind of bored, and needed something to do, so I figured I'd send you a card.

Anyway, it's really pretty here, just like it looks in the picture, and, well, I think I see his boat so—

Take care,

Colby

August 7

Dear Amanda,

OMG—Levi's boat just got here, but I thought I'd say a quick HEY! since I haven't sent you any postcards since I got here. Anyway, obviously I haven't been to that beach yet—though maybe I'll go there with Levi—who knows?

Okay, he's here, so—

Later—

Colby

CIRCLE IN THE SAND

August 8

This post will be short and sweet because I'm TOTALLY EXHAUSTED! But that's probably only because I just got off the boat from Mykonos and came straight here to the café to download some of these photos, which probably wasn't the best idea since I've been up all night and I look pretty ratty, to the point where Petros is actually shaking his head and scowling at me from behind the counter. Not to mention how he refused to make me a frappe when I ordered one.

Instead he took one look at me and said, "No coffee for you! You look terrible! Like gypsy! Go home!"

Yup, you always know where you stand with Petros.

And since he seems pretty dang serious about sending me home, and is probably just seconds away from evicting me, I'll make it snappy!

1) Behold the famous Mykonian windmills. Pretty, huh?
2) The famous Mykonian pelican as seen from afar! And yes I know there are pelicans in Tinos too, but they're not exactly famous now are they?
3) The famous Mykonian wild nightlife! And just so you know, I took this picture especially for YOU, ANONYMOUS. But to be honest, out of all of these things, I have to admit that I liked #4 the best!
4) This is Little Venice, my favorite place of all! Probably because it was just so romantic, with the way the water laps right up against the buildings, just like the real Venice (even though I've never actually been, I've seen pictures). The funny thing is that this wasn't originally on my list of things to see. But my friend had a guidebook, and this place was definitely recommended. And even though this is not the best picture—I still think you can see why they'd suggest it.
5) This is a picture of Super Paradise beach, though we only stayed long enough for me to snap this

picture, because it was full of naked and/or nearly naked gay guys, which totally freaked out my friend.

6) Here's a picture of my friend and me at Paradise beach. It should be noted that this photo was graciously taken by an older, completely naked, German lady. And believe me, Levi's the one who asked her to take our picture, not me! Also notice how Levi and I are both fully clothed—trust me, we were the only ones!

7) Here is a club—I forget the name, but just know that it got even more crowded and wild than what you see in this picture. And yes, that guy dancing on top of the bar REALLY IS wearing nothing more than a black leather thong and motorcycle boots—your eyes are NOT deceiving you—though you probably wish they were!

8) Here's a picture of the motorbike that Levi crashed twice, even though he swears it wasn't his fault. The scratches are ours, though I solemnly swear that big dent on the side was already there when we got it! Scout's honor!

9) Here's a photo of me, lying on the beach, watching the sunrise.

10) Here's a photo of Levi waving good-bye as he boards his cruise ship.

11) Here's a photo of the ferry that took me back to Tinos.

12) Here's a photo of Petros scowling at me just seconds

after he told me to go home. See how his mustache is twitching to where it almost looks animated? That's how I know he's serious. Though, truth be told, he just might have a point. I am pretty sleepy so—

Later—
Colby

CIRCLE IN THE SAND

Blog Comments:

Anonymous said:

Looks like you had a nice trip. I am also going away. Though it's been nice knowing you.

ColbyCat said:

Where are you going?

Anonymous said:

Away.

ColbyCat said:

Okay . . . but are you coming back?

Anonymous said:

Not likely.

ColbyCat said:

So that's it? You're just going to disappear into blog oblivion without ever revealing yourself?

Anonymous said:

It seems so.

ColbyCat said:

That doesn't seem fair.

Anonymous said:

That's life.

Colby's Journal for Desperate Times When She's Messed Up Her Life So Bad She Has Nowhere Else to Go but Here

August 10

According to one of my aunt Tally's books, this is how karma works:

Action-Reaction

Reap-Sow

What goes around comes around.

What you give you get.

Though it's not like I need a book to explain it, because, believe me, right now I'm living it. And all I can think is that I must have put some seriously bad energy out there, because I'm definitely getting some serious payback now.

This is what I'm dealing with:

1) A not-so-happy, not-so-mellow, Aunt Tally and Tassos, who cannot get over the fact that I island hopped without their consent.
2) A boyfriend (?) who no longer comes over, no longer speaks to me, probably never really loved me, and I have no idea why. Though I did see him talking to Maria (again!) at the port, day before yesterday, when I'd just gotten back from Mykonos and was leaving the café, (and no, he didn't see me) so maybe I actually do know why.
3) An e-mail from Natalie telling me that the FOR SALE sign in front of my house has now been exchanged for one that says: SOLD.
4) A brief phone call from my mother who assures me she no longer wants to move to Arizona now that she's fallen for her (much younger) personal trainer, who, she informs me, is actually a REAL LIVE PERSON and NOT a cliché like I think.
5) A father who is too busy to call and/or send a note because he's apparently not just shacking up with, but is now engaged to his (also much younger, at least according to my mom) girlfriend, even though the divorce is not yet final, and may never be with the way they're battling over EVERYTHING.

6) An ANONYMOUS person who has gladly taken his or her place in the everexpanding line for "People Who Would Like to Register a Complaint About Just How Bad Colby Sucks," since he/she pretty much abandoned my blog in a big fat hurry with no explanation whatsoever.
7) A cat that apparently also thinks I suck since I recently discovered that when I left for Mykonos, I was in such a hurry to flee, I forgot to leave Holly's window open—and so far he's yet to return.

And all of that would be fine, had my clandestine field trip actually been worth it. But the truth is, it so wasn't. And all I've got to show for it now is:

_____(Nothing.)

Seriously, I'm just as empty as I was the day I first got here. Only now I get to return home to even less than what I started with.

So basically, Mykonos was a total bust, and this is why:

I admit, I couldn't have been more surprised when Levi got off the boat with his mom and dad and little sister and brother in tow. In fact, I was SHOCKED. I mean now, looking back, of course it seems pretty obvious that a seventeen-year-old guy isn't actually going to embark on a solo Mediterranean cruise. Yet for some reason, that's exactly what I'd convinced myself of. I was just so sure that Levi was traveling all this way, and only tolerating the stops in Capri and Crete, just so he could get to Mykonos and enjoy a long, leisurely, romantic evening with me.

Stupid, I know. But since that's only the first in a whole succession of stupid things I've done lately, we'll just refer to it as Stupid Exhibit #1.

Anyway, I can't say Levi's family was exactly what I expected either. Though, I guess they weren't exactly the opposite of what I expected, since I really wasn't expecting them in the first place. Nor had I given them any real thought before the moment they were standing right before me.

Though if I had, I hope I would've been generous, hopeful, and kind enough to imagine something better than how they actually were, because as it turned out, they were kind of embarrassing.

First of all, Levi's dad is REALLY LOUD. I mean, seriously loud. And now I know why foreigners always say Americans are loud—it's because a lot of us are. It's like somehow he got the idea that if he spoke in a really loud voice, to the point where he was practically screaming, the Greeks would better understand him. But even if that tactic did somehow manage to work, for the most part it seemed pretty unnecessary, since from what I could tell most of the Mykonians speak really good English, and don't exactly need to be yelled at.

And then his mom, well, I don't mean to be rude or

judgmental, and it's not like I think my mom's all that great at the moment either, but all she pretty much wanted to do was go on a guided tour of jewelry stores. As though the whole point to traveling abroad was so she could conduct an extensive study of minimalls, with ours always coming out on top. Seriously, when I mentioned going to Paraportiani, or the windmills, or the beaches, she'd just squint at Mr. Bonham and go, "How far away is that, Jim?"

Though I refuse to say anything bad about his little brother and sister. I mean, even though they were kind of spoiled and bratty and basically horrible, it's not like you couldn't see where they got it.

So anyway, getting back to the dock, the moment I saw them I did my best to just swallow my disappointment and shock, and not gawk at the size of his entourage. And then I waved both my arms in the air, going back and forth, forth and back, like scissor kicks, until Levi finally saw me. And after he mumbled something sounding like—*hey,* his dad marched right up and gave me this seriously firm handshake like we'd just closed a business deal, while his mom just stood there beside him, looking me up and down and squinting at me until she lowered her sunglasses and squinted some more.

Then his little brother laughed, and his little sister stared, as Levi leaned in to give me the world's most awkward supervised hug.

And then his dad lifted his arm to his forehead, and

just as I thought he was about to salute me, he made himself a little hand visor and surveyed the landscape. Then he dropped it just as quickly, and turned to me and said, "So, what are you going to show us first?"

And since I'd only been on Mykonos about twenty minutes longer than they had, I'd pretty much only seen the gift shop where I'd bought some postcards, and the dock where we were standing. So I just shrugged and did my best to explain how it was my first visit too. That I was actually living on that little island, just right over there, the one you can see if you look straight across the water, at an angle.

And after all five of them had craned their necks, they turned back to me, disappointment clearly stamped across every one of their faces, their dreams of a private Greek island tour suddenly dashed.

Then Mrs. Bonham handed Mr. Bonham the guidebook she carries in her purse, and after intense study of the section titled: WHERE TO SHOP & DINE, all five of us went clomping through town, wandering through streets so narrow and winding at times we were actually forced to walk single file. And every now and then, Mr. Bonham (our fearless leader) would look back at me and say, "Do all the buildings in Tinos look alike too? Because I can't tell one of these from the other. It all looks the same. Can't tell 'em apart!"

Or his mom would squint at me, purse her lips, and go, "Is Tinos this—*quaint* as well?" And the way she said *quaint,* it was pretty obvious that what she really meant was *small-time.*

But by the time they started asking me why the Greeks all—FILL IN THE STUPID QUESTIONS BLANK, I'd given up trying to entertain and inform them with my answers, and just started shrugging instead.

I mean, first of all, I'm certainly no authority on the Greeks, their islands, or why they do just about anything they do. Because the truth is, I'd spent the majority of the summer focused on one thing—trying to stay connected to home (which would be Item #2 on the Stupid Exhibit tour). And the one Greek I had allowed myself to get close to, I was currently betraying (that would be Item #3). So excuse me for being more than a little reluctant to speak on his, or his people's behalf.

So after a concentrated, quickie tour of every single gold store the town of Mykonos had to offer, after Mr. Bonham had successfully saved himself the equivalent of five U.S. dollars by bargaining down the price of an eighteen-karat gold Greek key design necklace in the loudest voice imaginable, all five Bonhams decided they were starved, and consulted the guidebook to see where they could get a hamburger.

That's right, A HAMBURGER. Just like the kind you can get back home, or, I don't know, maybe on their cruise ship, you know, the one that was docked in the harbor?

"Don't you want to maybe try a gyro?" I suggested. "They're really good, kind of like a Greek hamburger," I said, having grown quite fond of them in the short time I'd been in Tinos.

"Oh, I'd love to try one myself." Mrs. Bonham smiled in that tight, squinty way I'd come to know as her signature smirk. "But Salem and Duncan really prefer to keep it simple. They don't always do so well with these foreign foods," she whispered, motioning to the twelve- and thirteen-year-olds, blaming it all on them.

So, we headed to a taverna. One that was chock full of people they recognized from the boat. And while we were seated at the table, each of us hunched over our meals, chewing quietly and staring into space, I couldn't help but notice how different Levi was, how he suddenly seemed so opposite of the way he was at home, the way I'd remembered him.

I mean, at home he's like this uber-cool deity, the undisputed king who rules the school. But seeing him sitting across from me, dragging a fistful of fries through some ketchup as he admired his silver ring, I couldn't help but notice just how fake and phony and almost empty he seemed. Like he was so caught up in his clothes and his hair and his jewelry and his image, that there was no room left for anything else.

So then of course, the second after I thought that, I felt horrible, terrible, and guilty. I mean, so far, all I'd done was spend the entire afternoon judging them. Just like I'd spent all of the previous night judging Yannis. And it made me wonder if maybe I was the one who should be judged. Maybe the problem wasn't them at all.

Maybe the problem was ME. Maybe I was the one with no personality or identity. Maybe I was the one who was empty inside.

Because the truth is, when I gazed at all of them again, watching as they enjoyed their meal in silence, obviously feeling content with their lives and each other, I realized I was the exact opposite of content. That while these people knew exactly who they were, what they stood for, and seemed to be entirely at peace with it all, I myself was as lost and clueless as ever.

I had no idea what I was doing.

And lately, I didn't seem to stand for much of anything.

I mean, here I'd somehow convinced myself that I'd been humming along, making some major life progress, when all along I'd been slowly unraveling at the seams and was too dumb to notice.

For example—Stupid Exhibit #4 (obviously, none of these exhibits are in actual chronological order):

I'd been friends with Natalie Zippenhoffer for practically my whole entire life, and even though she's nice, and smart, and interesting, and real (and yes, a major geek), and even though we have tons of things in common (like the fact that I'm a major geek too, and we like the same books, songs, and movies—which are mostly all the books, songs, and movies that nobody even knows about, much less likes), I didn't even hesitate when it came time to throw her overboard. It's like the second I got a shot at being visible and cool via hanging with Amanda, into the water Natalie went.

I guess I just felt so flattered that someone who's as popular and important as Amanda would even want to speak to me, much less hang out with me. Not to mention how I hoped she'd be able to make me popular and important too. I just wanted to be known for something more than high test scores. So every time she wasn't so nice (which was pretty frequent), and every time she made fun of all the things I like (which was pretty much all the time), I either completely ignored it or pretended I no longer liked those things either. Then I did my frantic best to avoid Natalie when I passed her in the hall, so I could stay in good with Amanda.

So when I got my shot at Levi Bonham, I knew I hit the big time.

It was only after spending the day with his family, in a foreign place that's like a million miles away from everything that once made him so cool, that I could barely remember what the attraction was to begin with.

I mean, of course he was still gorgeous, anyone could see that, since it's not like distance and a new time zone could ever mess with his cool, movie star looks. Only now he seemed gorgeous in a way that was too intentional, too calculated, too premeditated, as though being cute had become a full-time endeavor, and something about that just really bugged me.

Anyway, after we finished our meals and his dad settled the check, his family decided they had "done" Mykonos and were eager to head back to the boat. Making it clear that Levi was free to stay and dance the night away with me.

So he did. I mean, we did. Though we didn't exactly start with dancing, since it was still early and really hot out. So I, thinking it might be fun to hit the beaches, managed to convince him to rent a Vespa together. But after we crashed it twice (not badly, but both times his fault) I insisted on taking over, since it was obvious he just couldn't get the hang of working the clutch since it's on the foot pedal, which, of course, I'd totally mastered thanks to Yannis's lesson in "Vespa Riding and Safety 101."

But even though we didn't crash again, it was pretty obvious that my sitting in front, taking charge of the driving, wasn't going over so well with him. It was like his whole alpha-male, he-man, jock persona just couldn't handle giving up control to a girl.

So when we finally made it to the beach with the very best name of them all—Super Paradise, he totally freaked when he saw it was full of mostly naked, mostly gay, guys. And I mean, FREAKED. Like he thought all that nudity and gayness was somehow contagious.

So then of course we had to get right back on the bike and head over to just plain old Paradise beach, which just happened to be filled with row after row of topless and/or nude girls. Which of course made him bug me about taking my top off, but only for a little while since there were plenty of other breasts for him to ogle. And believe me, did he ogle. I mean head swiveling, eye bugging, tongue hanging and dripping with drool kind of ogling. And he was so obvious about it I was actually kind of embarrassed to be sitting next to him. Because no matter how many times I've been to the beach with Yannis, I've never once seen him carry on like that. And even though that's probably because he's used to it, having grown up like that and all, I'm really not joking or exaggerating when I write that Levi was RIDICULOUS. Seriously, even after the sun went down and there were only a few people left, I practically had to drag him by the arms and legs just to get him out of there.

So then, because we were in Mykonos, and because that's what you're supposed to do when you're in Mykonos, we hit the clubs. I mean, we were still kind of sandy and messy from the beach and all, but after a cocktail or two at some pretty waterfront bar in Little Venice, it's not like we even noticed or cared.

In fact, I no longer cared about much of anything.

I no longer cared about my parents' divorce.

I no longer cared about moving.

I no longer cared about the fact that I was about to cheat on Yannis.

I no longer cared about the fact that I was about to cheat on Yannis with someone I no longer cared about.

Because suddenly, with my head all light, and cloudy,

and woozy, and with the music blaring so loud, and with Levi dancing so close—it was all good.

In fact, it was better than good it was—

Luminous!

And brilliant!

And shiny, and warm, and sexy, and glamorous, and exciting and fun!

And then suddenly my mouth was on Levi's, and his tongue was in mine, and his hands were sliding down my body, and my eyes were closed, and then the room started spinning, which was totally cool at first because I thought we were spinning together, like two people who are so madly in love they just spin across rooms. But then when I opened them again, I saw it was still Levi, and I tried to remind myself how much I once liked him, how popular he is, and how cute. How lucky I was to be there in his arms. How no other girl in our school, no other girl ANYWHERE had ever made out with him in a club in Mykonos. Not even that stupid Penelope chick. Not anyone. And then I remembered how I saw Yannis talking and laughing with Maria by the harbor, how he whispered *S'agapo* to me, and how I was leaving soon so it's not like it mattered. How there's no such thing as love. Just people who like to pretend they're in love. When the truth is it's false and invisible and doesn't really exist.

And I convinced myself so well of these things that I just kept kissing him back. Closing my eyes again, blocking everything out, letting the room grow calm and quiet until it settled around us, knowing that THIS was real. That fleeting moments like this were the best you could ever really hope for.

And so we kept kissing—between drinks, between songs, even after the club closed and we found ourselves a small, secluded beach where we kissed some more. We kissed as the sun came up. We kissed as he told me he had to head back to his boat. We kissed as he promised to e-mail. We kissed one last time before I headed off to my ferry, where I bought a ticket, climbed aboard, and watched as his boat sailed away from the dock—pressing my forehead against the smudgy, scratched glass, and wondering what the hell I'd just done.

CIRCLE IN THE SAND

0 Comments:

August 11
Dear Mom—

For your information, I KNOW you SOLD the house. I got it straight from my source. So I guess what's done is done, and there's nothing more I can do.

I'm sorry things didn't work out with your boyfriend (sorry, but I don't remember his name). But what I really need to know is if this means Arizona's back on?

Let me know—
Love,
Colby

August 11
Dear Dad,

I'm sorry I accused you of being engaged when you're not. I guess my source is not nearly as reliable as I thought.

See you in a few weeks.

(It feels weird to write that.)

Love,

Colby

August 11
To: NatalieZee
From: ColbyCat
Re: The sordid truth

It's true.

My mom sold the house. What can I say?

Though I want to thank you for all of your efforts in trying to sabotage it from the start. Seriously, for that alone I will be eternally grateful.

And, not like it probably matters much anyway, I mean, after everything that's happened and all, but I still want you to know that I'm actually really grateful for a lot of things that you've done. And I'm sorry that I acted like such a BIG FNB. (I know you hate abbreviations, but did you really want me to spell that out?) Or better yet—A BIG CONFORMING RETARD—like you once said.

And yeah, believe it or not the whole thing with Levi was totally real. But in the end it just wasn't as great as you'd think. Okay, maybe YOU never thought it would be even close to great, but we all know I did.

Well, if you want, I'm thinking maybe we can get together when I get back in town, before my mom makes me move to Arizona. (Yup, you read it right, though I'll explain it in another e-mail, on another day.)

Ya'Sou—

Colby

August 12

Dear Aunt Tally and Tassos,

I'm sorry that:

1) *I made you worry.*
2) *I didn't tell you I was going to Mykonos.*
3) *I asked you to lie to Yannis.*
4) *I broke the one and only house rule.*
5) *My parents forced me on you and made you take me in, thereby wrecking your calm, tranquil, peaceful life.*
6) *Etc. (I mean, I'm sure there's much more to be sorry for—but I'm hoping you'll accept a blanket apology for all of the infractions I may have missed.)*

Just know that I'm really, really sorry.

Love,

Colby

August 12

To: AmandaStar

From: ColbyCat

Re: summer lovin!
Hey Amanda,

Just responding to your e-mail, and thought I'd tell you that those pictures of you and Jenna and Penelope and Casey at the beach were really cute.

And to answer your questions:

—Yes, it was fun seeing Levi.

—And, yes those are real, live, alcoholic cocktails we're drinking in those pictures he sent you. There's no age limit here, so you can pretty much do whatever you want.

Anyway, I'll be home by the end of the month, but I'm not sure if I'll be going back to Harbor or not, since as you may or may not know, my mom sold the house, and I have no idea where I'll end up.

Okay, well, take care, and thanks for writing—

Colby

August 12
To: Levi501
From: ColbyCat
Re: party pics
Hey Levi,

Thanks for sending those pics. I forgot all about that one bar, though I definitely remember those blue drinks we both had! I think I might still be feeling it—just kidding! (Well, kind of.)

To answer your question, I'll be back on August 31, but

after that, I really don't know where I'll be since my mom sold the house, and I'm not sure where we'll be moving.

Anyway, it was good to see you too—

Enjoy the rest of the summer!

Colby

August 12

~~*Dear Yannis,*~~

~~*I know you don't want to talk to me, so I'll just keep this brief and say that I'm sorry.*~~

~~*I'm really, really sorry.*~~

~~*Though I have to admit that I'm not really sure what I'm apologizing for, and I just wish you'd talk to me long enough to tell me, so then maybe I could try to explain.*~~

~~*I'll be here until the end of the month, in case you change your mind about seeing me.*~~

~~*Colby*~~

~~*P.S. It would have been really nice if you had told me where you lived, or maybe even invited me over so I'd know where to send this stupid letter. I guess you didn't really* **S'AGAPO** *me like you said! And no way am I asking Tally and/or Tassos for your address!*~~

CRUEL SUMMER

August 13

That's right, CRUEL SUMMER is back, but only long enough to say good-bye. After a brief period of sunshine, the clouds have moved in and the forecast shows nothing but gloom and doom from here on, my friends.

Though maybe it's just another sign that the end of summer is near, that my time in Tinos is over, and that I'll soon be heading home—wherever that turns out to be . . .

So, thanks to those of you who took the time to stop by, read, and/or comment me.

I really do appreciate it.

Love,

Colby

Colby's Journal for Desperate Times When She's Feeling Really Desperate

August 14

So yesterday, just after I signed off from my stupid, depressing, loser blog I was on my way home, basically dragging my feet and alternating between hating myself and feeling sorry for myself, when I decided to quit acting like such a pathetic little baby, and just go to the hotel, find Yannis, and get to the bottom of things once and for all.

I mean, in just two and a half weeks I'll be going home anyway, most likely never to return, so what does it really matter if I make a fool of myself, say something stupid, and/or end up looking like the world's biggest dork? It's not like anyone at home will ever know, so it's not like I had anything to lose.

Besides, I just couldn't bear the idea of returning to

California and leaving things the way they were—messy, unfinished, just hanging. I mean, if Yannis had dumped me for Maria, then I really wanted to hear it from him. And if he dumped me for some other reason, then I needed to know that too.

It's like, the whole thing was just so sudden, and unexpected, I guess I needed to make sense of it. Because according to both Tally and Tassos, he never even came by the house that night.

Which means they never had to lie to him.

Which also means there's no way he could've known about me, Levi, and Mykonos.

Which means, whatever happened, happened because of HIM.

It also means that technically, I'd been dumped well before I even got on that boat.

I just didn't realize it at the time.

And once I had that all straight in my head, I gave myself full permission to stop beating myself up, to stop feeling so guilty about everything, since in the end, it really didn't matter anyway. Apparently I was free and single, I just didn't know it.

But even though shirking all of the blame did make me feel better, it was pretty short-lived. I guess because it also left me with the one, ugly, undisputable truth—

I'd been dumped for the Greek vixen otherwise known as Maria.

And even though the thought of that made me feel completely nauseous and sick, I still needed to have it confirmed. I needed to be able to face the truth so I could file it away and move on. I mean, since my summer already had a beginning and middle, I knew it was time to give it an end.

But if I'm going to be COMPLETELY honest, then I also have to admit the slightly embarrassing truth of how part of me just really needed to see him again—just one last time, before I went away and ended our story for good. I guess I just wanted to make sure that we really were truly and completely over. And to get myself some closure if it turned out we were.

So instead of going home, I grabbed a taxi and headed straight for his hotel, thinking it was early enough that he'd probably still be working, and hopefully not late enough that he'd be engaging in something horrible and heartbreaking like entertaining Maria by the pool, in the same way he'd done with me.

So after I paid the driver, I climbed out of the car and just stood there, squinting at this sprawling, dusty, chaotic construction site that seemed to just go on forever, since the hotel is built bungalow style as opposed to high-rise.

And not really knowing where to start, I just walked right up to a group of construction workers, cleared my throat, and said, *"Poo ee neh Yannis?"* Which to my understanding meant, "Where is Yannis?" But when I was greeted by a series of shrugs followed by elbow nudges and laughter, I started to get a little concerned that I might've gotten it confused with another Greek phrase.

But then this old guy came up, grabbed my elbow, and led me to the other side of the hotel, where he walked into a room and shouted, *"Ela! Yannis!"* Then he shook his head and laughed as he walked away.

At this point I would love to be able to write that Yannis turned, took one look at me, and pulled me into his arms, holding me tight, refusing to let go. But that's the stuff of romance novels and sappy late-night movies, not real life. Because the truth is, he took one long, lingering look, then turned back around and continued his work.

I stood there, taking in his tan, muscled back that was dripping with sweat, his strong defined arms, their muscles bulging and popping as he hammered a nail, the cutoff jeans that Amanda would totally make fun of (but that's only because Amanda's an idiot), and my throat was so hot and constricted, and my heart felt so heavy and sad, that I closed my eyes and willed him to look at me, having no idea what I'd say if he did.

I mean, what do you say to the guy you just might have loved if only you hadn't been so shallow, so unsure of yourself, so afraid of letting him know? How do you explain how having the approval of people who weren't really your friends, far outweighed anything you just might've felt? And how because of all that, you ran off to Mykonos to meet up with someone who turned out to be so completely and totally unworthy?

But then I reminded myself how I didn't actually need any of those words.

Because, it's not like he knew any of that.

Which meant there was no reason for me to confess, since it was now up to him to confess.

Because the fact is, he was hanging in the port with Maria, long before my ship even sailed.

He was the one laughing and talking and having a great old time.

He was the one who allowed her to touch his arm, as she leaned in to kiss his cheek.

Right there in broad daylight.

Right where I could see.

When just the night before he'd said he'd be working all through siesta, which was why he couldn't go to the beach with me.

Which was pretty much the ultimate final thing that made me decide to get on that boat in the first place.

So if anyone had any explaining to do, it was he.

I opened my eyes, cleared my throat, and said, "Hey, Yannis? Um, hello? Are you trying to ignore me?" (Talk about stating the obvious.) Then I continued to stand there, watching as he pounded the heck out of another nail, acting as though I didn't exist.

So then I cleared my throat again and went, "Hey, Yannis, listen, I know you're mad, but I also know you can hear me, so I'd really appreciate it if you could just stop hammering, turn around, and give me the courtesy of ten minutes of your time."

He kept pounding.

"Five minutes?" I said, knowing I was in no position to bargain since I was on his turf and would end up settling for whatever I could get.

More pounding.

"Fine. One minute and thirty seconds, final offer," I said, unaware I'd been holding my breath until he set down the hammer and I gulped some air.

And even though he still refused to look at me, I knew I had to take advantage of the moment while it lasted, and with no time to waste, I took another deep breath and dove in. "Why won't you talk to me?" I asked, my eyes searching the back of his head, willing him to turn around and acknowledge me once and for all. "Why'd you stop coming by and answering my calls? Are you mad at me? And if so, why? I mean, *WHAT HAPPENED?* Because I think I deserve an explanation. Because you can't just string someone along, whisper *I love you,* then act like they don't even exist," I said, immediately growing all red faced and shaky, my heart crashing against my chest, as my mind raced back to the I LOVE YOU part, which I tortured myself by playing over and over again.

And when he finally turned to look at me, my eyes went straight for his, hoping to find them soft, warm, and caring, the same way I'd left them last week. Only now they were different, changed, alien even. Their cold, hard detachment providing all the answer I needed.

And then he shrugged. And then he shook his head and said, "Listen, Colby, you're leaving in what? Two weeks?"

"Two and a half," I said, my stomach going all twisty and turvy and awful.

"Okay, so we had some fun, but now it's over. You go back to your life, I go back to mine." He shrugged. "Another summer is finished."

"So that's it?" I asked, my eyes stinging, not expecting to be brushed off and discarded so easily.

I mean, who was this guy? Did I ever even know him? Was I really so naïve to think I was anything more than just some stupid summer fling?

He shrugged.

"So that's why you decided to dump me?" I said, amazed that I could even speak with the way my throat felt so hot and constricted. "Because the summer's over? I mean, no long good-bye at the port? No postcards or e-mails? You just go cold turkey? Decide to get a head start and dump me two weeks early, without notice?" And then I tried to laugh, tried to make it sound as though I cared a lot less than it seemed. But in the end I didn't fool anyone, because it came out sounding really false and lame.

But even after all that, even after my whole tirade, all he could manage in response was a shrug.

Which turned out to be a really bad choice.

I narrowed my eyes, placed my hands on my hips, took a deep breath, and went full steam ahead. "Because I'm actually kind of wondering if it's maybe something else? I'm actually wondering if it might have something to do with the fact that I saw you at the port with Maria," I said, the sweat transferring from my palms to my shorts, not sure where I was headed, but unable (unwilling?) to stop. "I saw you guys together, by the harbor, at the fish market, the same day you couldn't be bothered to go to the beach with me because you said you had to work straight through siesta. And then the next thing I know, you stop coming over, won't take my calls, and pretty much ignore me."

And while I was waiting for a response, he did the strangest thing—he just shook his head and laughed.

LAUGHED!

And I was so surprised by his reaction it took me a moment or two to get that it wasn't the kind of laugh that was inviting me to join in. It was more the kind that was directed at US. How we were standing there together, in that room, sharing a moment that was so small it couldn't possibly be anything other than funny. As though the two of us together, was so unworthy, so insignificant, it became a big fat joke.

And when he finally stopped laughing, he said, "It does not really matter anymore, does it?"

I stood there, staring down at my suntanned feet, my eyes focused on my peach-colored polish, my silver toe ring, and the tiny star tattoo my mom still doesn't know about. Because even though I've always known we would end, I never imagined it would hurt like this.

So after biting my lip so hard I practically drew blood, after blinking my eyes so many times I finally chased away the tears, I brushed my hair off my face, tucked it behind my ears, and said, "You're right, none of it matters anymore. So . . ."

I wanted to finish with something light, and pithy, maybe even sarcastic. Something that would let him know I was right there with him, that I thought it was funny too, that I was perfectly okay, despite all outward appearances.

But in the end, I didn't say anything. Because my

throat was searing again, my vision was blurred, and since I couldn't afford to let him see me like that, I turned and ran straight out of that horrible, dusty room—and all the way home.

Or at least back to my summer home.

Tally and Tassos's home.

I guess I'm not really sure where home is anymore.

CRUEL SUMMER

August 17

Okay, I know that just a few days ago I swore the blog was history, over, kaput! But since there's still two weeks left of summer, I figured I may as well see it all the way through to the bitter end. Partly because it gives me something to do, but mostly because I'm turning over a new leaf, so to speak, which means I am newly committed to finishing the things that I start.

Also, I'm determined to hold my position as Petros's #1 customer. Which pretty much requires me to spend some serious time (and money!) right here in his café!

And even though I know it probably sounds crazy, especially since I spent the entire first month pretty much hating every single thing about this place (I mean, Tinos, not the café), now that it's almost time for me to leave, I'm actually kind of sad.

So with that in mind, I've been spending less time in my room, and more time at the beach and exploring the island, sometimes with Tally and Tassos, sometimes just out on my own, taking pictures of everything I experience—a few of which you can see here:

1) This is my still-missing kitten, Mr. Holly Golightly. He is a black male with blue eyes and a white streak across his forehead. He likes to be petted, but only a little, because mostly he likes to run free. So if you find him (and I hope that you do because he's been missing for more than a week—and I'm VERY worried about him) please pick him up gently (but don't hold him too tight, because he will fight like hell to get away), and bring him straight to Petros's Internet café, or my aunt Tally's gift shop (located at the very end of the same street).
2) This is the first vase I made that didn't collapse! It only took me about one hundred and eighty-five tries to get to this point—and trust me, that is only a SLIGHT exaggeration. And the only reason I even made it this far is because Tassos is like the world's most patient, kind, knowledgeable, and generous (did I say PATIENT?) teacher. And later today, he's going to teach me how to glaze it and fire it, and I can hardly wait to see how it turns out. (And if it's any good, I'll post a picture!)
3) This is a pair of earrings I made last night with Tally, while we sat outside on the terrace, eating this amazing rice pudding (with a name I can't pronounce much less spell but which has a direct

translation of "rice milk") as we watched the sunset, listened to the Beatles, and made jewelry. And even though I really like the way these turned out, I'm thinking I might give them to a friend of mine, because as Tally always says—"You should always give what you want for yourself." Whatever, I just hope my friend likes them too.

4) This is a picture of a place called Exobourgo, which is this amazing mountain that a friend of mine once took me to, and it's so pretty I decided to go back on my own. It only takes around fifteen or twenty minutes to hike all the way to the top, and once you're up there, the view is amazing! Seriously, you can see all of Tinos and some of the other Cyclades islands as well. It's really pretty magical, and if you don't believe me, then check out #5.

5) See? Is that not the most amazing view EVER? That was taken from the very top of Exobourgo, and I have to say I've never seen anything like it back home! Look how calm that turquoise water is, how the distant houses resemble shiny little sugar cubes, and how the surrounding islands look like glimmering brown jewels! It's so amazing I wish you could see for yourself, but for now, this will have to do!

6) Okay, since the rest are just pictures of landscapes, I'm not going to identify every single location shot. Besides, if you've been following this blog at all,

then you should be very familiar with dirt, rocks, and geraniums by now. I know I am!

Enjoy—
Colby

August 17
To: NatalieZee
From: ColbyCat
Re: Arizona?
Hey Nat,

I wish I could answer your question, but I can't. Because the truth is I have no idea whether I'll be going back to Harbor, moving to Arizona, or enrolling in Cyber School (and no, I have no idea what that is, but I heard my parents mention it once during one of their many fights, so I can't go ruling it out). Because as my mom recently explained, she had no idea the house would sell that quickly, and to quote her directly, she is now—"Doing my best, meeting with agents, frantically searching and putting the word out for a nice, affordable place for us to live, so DON'T go accusing me of not looking, or caring, or taking this seriously, Colby!"

She also assures me that she will let me know the moment she secures something, so I really need to "stop bugging her, stop second-guessing her, and just let her handle it."

Whatever.

Anyway, it's really nice of you and your mom to offer to let me use your address so I can stay at Harbor, but I really don't want to impose, or get you guys in trouble or anything, and besides, I still don't even know if I'll need it. But thanks anyway.

Also, to answer your question, NO. Amanda has not offered to let me use her address. So, feel free to draw your own conclusions.

Okay, Petros is closing up shop for siesta—so, gotta go!

Colby

Colby's Journal for Desperate Times

August 19

So yesterday started like any other day. I woke up, I ate breakfast, I showered, I checked all around the house, both inside and out, to see if Holly had come back (he hadn't) and then I headed out the door and down to the café, taking my usual route, and enjoying the nice, sunny, slightly windy day, but also thinking how it wasn't really so different from any other day I'd spent here. I mean, I actually remember thinking those very words.

But as it turns out, I couldn't have been more wrong.

Because by the time I'd made it to the café and was reaching for the door handle, I was no longer thinking about much of anything, no longer noticing my surroundings, because I was back on autopilot, expecting just to go inside, say hi to Petros, order my frappe, and sit at my usual table where I'd log on and start blogging away.

Which is why I was so surprised to find the door locked.

So surprised that I immediately tried to open it again. Only it was still locked. And even after I'd taken a step back and gazed at the sign in the window, clearly seeing how it read CLOSED and NOT OPEN, it was as though I still couldn't quite make my eyes believe it. So I cupped my hands around my face and peered inside. And even though I didn't see anyone in there, that didn't stop me from tapping hard on the window, and yelling for Petros to come out from the back room and unlock the door and let me in already.

And even after he still didn't answer, I just continued to stand there, gazing inside, wondering if it was some kind of holiday I wasn't aware of.

But after awhile, when my laptop bag started carving a nice, deep wedge into my shoulder as I gawked at the locked and empty room, I finally decided to just let it go and was turning to leave when I spotted Yannis, coming out of a shop, just a few doors away.

Well, my heart started racing, and my palms started to sweat, and I felt so suddenly panicked (not to mention suddenly ridiculous for feeling so suddenly panicked) that I looked all around, frantically searching for somewhere to hide, someplace I could duck into, where he wouldn't see me.

Only there was no place. Because I was trapped in plain sight, and he was heading straight for me. And left with no other option, I took a deep breath and ordered myself to just grow up, relax, and deal with it already. And just as I was doubting I could even do that, it occurred to me that he probably wasn't coming toward ME at all. He was probably just trying to get to the end of the street, a street through which no fault of his own, I happened to be on.

So then just as he got that much closer, I turned really quickly and started walking away, the soles of my sandals slapping the pavement as though I had somewhere to be.

And even after he started calling my name, going, "Colby! Hey! Please wait!" I just kept going. Even when I started to feel pretty winded, I pushed on. Because no way was I going to stop to see what he wanted. I mean, I'd barely gotten through our last little meeting, so I definitely wasn't up for a do-over.

But apparently, all that construction work has left Yannis in way better shape than me, because the next thing I knew, his hand was on my shoulder, and he was pretty much forcing me to stop, turn, and face him. And when I finally gave up and gave in, when I finally turned and looked, his face seemed so sad and so serious, my heart skipped a few beats.

Because in that exact moment I KNEW he was about to apologize. I was POSITIVE he was going to take it all back, everything he'd said, including the horrible way he'd laughed at me/us. I mean, it was so obvious, the proof was right there before me, all I had to do was look into his eyes and see it.

And the only thing left was for me to decide whether or not to accept.

But instead he said, "Colby, I'm so sorry, but Petros is dead."

I stared at him, for what felt like the longest time, but was probably only a few seconds, and then I said, "No he's not." Then I started back down the street.

Though I'd barely taken two steps before he was right on top of me again, and this time he put both hands on my shoulders, looked me right in the eye, and said, "Colby, Petros had a heart attack. He didn't make it."

But I just shook my head and pulled away. "You're wrong. I just saw him yesterday, and for your information he was totally fine," I said, trying to understand why he'd even attempt to do something so cruel. I mean, what did he hope to get out of it? Why was he trying so hard to hurt me?

But even though he was shaking his head, saying, "Colby, please listen, it's true. They were even going to airlift him to Athens but he did not make it. I'm very sorry to have to tell you this," I just turned back around and headed home.

And when I saw Tally and Tassos that night, they confirmed it was true. But even though they fussed all over me, asking if I was all right, insisting that it's perfectly okay to cry, I just couldn't. I mean, it's not like I knew Petros all that well. It's not like I'd let myself get all attached. He was just some guy who provided coffee and an Internet connection. That's it, nothing more.

Just like Yannis was a guy I once skinny-dipped with.

And Holly was just some cat I rescued until he was well enough to go off on his own.

And if at any time in the past, I was careless enough to

think that any of those things had any more value than that, well, I was over it now. Because the truth is, it's just a whole lot better to not let yourself get too involved with anyone, or anything.

Because in the end—everything comes to an end.

August 21

Dear Dad,

I don't know if I told you this but today they're having a funeral for ~~a friend of mine~~ this person I met here. But I'm going to the beach instead since it's not like I knew him all that well anyway, and since I only have a little over a week left, I figure I may as well spend it at the beach. I'm not sure why I even just wrote that, except maybe it's because summer's almost over, and I really don't have much else to say.

Okay, well, see you soon-ish.

Love,

Colby

P.S. Oh yeah, I meant to ask you if there's still enough room for me, for when I come visit you? I mean, now that your girlfriend is living with you. Let me know.

August 21

Dear Mom,

I would really appreciate it if the next time we talk on the phone you could stop telling me stuff about Dad, since I figure he can probably just tell me himself if he really wants me to know, and honestly, at this exact moment, the only news I really want to hear from you is where I'll be living when I get back. Really, that's it. I mean, I want to hear how you're doing as well, don't get me wrong, but I definitely don't want to hear about anything outside of those two things.

Sorry if that sounds a little harsh, but I just don't know how else to say it.

Love,

Colby

~~P.S. This guy I met here recently died and his funeral is today, but I think I'm going to go to the beach instead.~~ Sorry, ignore that! I don't even know why I wrote it.

August 21

Dear Nat,

I'm writing you this postcard because the guy who owned the Internet café (Petros) died of a heart attack and his funeral is today, which means the Internet café is closed. So I just thought I'd write instead. And then I guess I'll go to the beach, since I don't really see the point in going to the funeral of someone who I barely knew and wasn't actually like a true friend of mine or anything.

Still no word on where I'll be living—can you even believe it?

Okay, well, see you soon—

Colby

August 21

Dear Amanda,

I don't know if you've tried to e-mail me or not but I don't have Internet access right now since the guy who owned the café (Petros, you know the one whose mustache you made fun of?), well, he had a heart attack and died suddenly with no warning whatsoever. Which means his shop is closed—so no more blogging or e-mailing for a while, maybe even forever, I really don't know. Though it's definitely closed for today since it's his funeral, but I'm just going to spend the day at the beach instead.

Okay, well, I just thought I'd let you know why I'm not answering back in case you do/did try to message me.

C U soon—

Colby

August 21

Dear Tally and Tassos,

I'm going to the beach today, so I probably won't see you until later this evening. Have a good one.

Love,

Colby

Colby's Journal for Desperate Times When She Has No Idea Why She Feels So Desperate

August 21

Hard as it is to believe, today marks the first time I dragged my journal out of the house and down to the beach. But then again this is also one of the first times I've gone to the beach by myself. And I'm not even sure why I chose to do this today, except for the fact that I felt like being alone. Though I was sick of being alone in my room, since I've wasted far too much time in there already, so I figured I may as well go someplace warm, beautiful, and sunny, but also quiet.

And it's funny how sitting here on my towel writing this kind of makes me feel like I'm keeping up my routine, since I'm used to spending my mornings writing in my blog, and sending e-mails, and postcards and letters, even though it was always at the café, never here, and always while I was sipping frappe, and not from a water bottle. But still, somehow it makes me feel like everything's still normal, that my routine is still useful, and that nothing's really changed.

Even though I'm really not delusional enough to actually believe any of that.

Much Later:

Okay, just after I wrote that, I started feeling all choked up. Seriously, my throat started aching, and my eyes started stinging, only this time there was nothing I could do to stop it. And even though I tried to fight it, even though I tried to hold it all in, it wasn't long before the tears started pouring down my face. So I got up from my towel and ran into the sea, where I dove under the water and swam out as far as I could, my eyes shut tight against the stinging saltiness, blind to everything in front of me, but not even caring. And when I couldn't hold my breath any longer, I popped back up, gasping and taking huge gulps of air before ducking back under and continuing on, swimming as fast and far as I could, my arms and legs aching from the strain, until they became rubbery, weak, and useless. And when I finally stopped, I allowed myself to surrender to the sea, just float on my back with my eyes closed tightly against the sun, the heat drying my face, leaving grainy salt trails across my cheeks. Shutting down the thoughts in my head, refusing to tune into anything more than the gentle slap and sway of the water, until my fingers and toes were all pruney. Until the threat of emotions had passed.

Then later, as I made my way toward shore, my stomach dropped to my knees when I saw Tally sitting next to my towel. But I just took a deep breath and kept moving, putting one foot in front of the other until I was standing directly before her. Then acting as though everything was perfectly fine and okay, I smiled and said, "Hey, Tally, what's up?" Then I twisted my hair into a long spiral, squeezing it tightly between the palms of my hands, watching as seawater poured through the ends.

She smiled and shrugged, then mumbled something about it being a great day for the beach, and my stomach leapt from my knees to my throat when I saw how I'd left my journal lying right there on my towel, all propped open and ready for anyone interested enough to read.

And just as I started to grab it, frantic to think what she might've seen, I remembered that this was Tally, my peace-loving, privacy-allowing aunt who would never even consider peeking at someone else's diary.

Which pretty much makes her the exact opposite of her sister/my mom who would dive right in without a second thought.

So instead I just nudged it aside with my foot, as though it held no real significance or value, then I sat down beside her and admired my tan as I splayed my legs out before me (well, at least until I got to my toenails which were desperately in need of fresh paint). And since she was just sitting there beside me, not saying a word, I turned to her and said, "Where's Tassos?" Even though I figured he was probably busy working at his studio. But then I didn't really care about the answer—I just wanted to plug up the silence.

But she said, "At the house, getting ready."

And just as I was about to ask—*getting ready for what?* I REMEMBERED. So I shut my mouth and left it at that.

"I just thought I'd stop by and sit with you for a while. I hope that's okay?" she said, giving me a cautious look, which made me feel kind of bad, but still I just shrugged. "You're leaving soon, and I feel like we didn't get to spend enough time together." She laughed. "Crazy, huh? We've lived together nearly three months, but somehow it just flew by." She smiled.

I glanced at her and nodded, then I focused back on my toes, partly because I didn't trust the awful way my throat was starting to feel again, but mostly because I was wondering how she was going to segue this little conversation into that of Petros's funeral, mentioning how weird it was that neither of us were there. Especially me.

But instead she just sighed and said, "I hope it wasn't all bad, Colby, your time here, I mean. I know my lifestyle isn't quite what you had in mind for your summer vacation."

I just shrugged, because while the majority of it was indisputably bad, it's not like it was her fault.

"I have to admit, when your mom called to ask if I'd take you in for the summer I was more than a little surprised." She laughed. "But then she explained about the divorce, and I thought it would be a good break for you. Because believe me, I've been there."

I looked at her, wondering what the heck she was getting at. I mean, how could she have "been there" when the only reason Grandma was single was because Grandpa died? How could she know how horrible it is when your parents wake up one morning and mutually decide that from that moment on they'll totally hate each other?

"I was married." She smiled, answering the question I hadn't yet asked. "A long time ago, right before I moved here, it only lasted a year, and you were just a tiny baby, which is why you probably don't know."

"Was it horrible?" I asked, preparing to hear a really juicy, if not tragic, tale.

But she just shrugged. "Not really." And when she saw my expression she laughed and said, "Not all endings are bad, Colby. Just like not all endings are happy. Some endings—just—are." She shrugged. "But no matter what happens, you always come out okay."

And when I looked at her I thought:

More peace and love crap coming right up!

But then I felt immediately guilty for thinking that, so I just scooped up a handful of sand, cupped it in the center of my palm, and watched as it slipped through my fingers, landing right back where it started, settling into place as though it'd never been disturbed. And after it was quiet for so long I just couldn't take it anymore, I said, "Well, maybe that worked out all fine and well for you, but just so you know, my parents' divorce isn't even final yet, and my dad's already living with someone, and my mom sold the house and has no idea where we'll go because she's too busy obsessing over my dad's new girlfriend, and they just continue along like that, happily screwing up all of our lives, and there's nothing I can do about it! Not one damn thing I can do to change it! So yeah, I guess you're right, I just have to accept it because it is what it is, but that doesn't mean I'm going to be okay, I mean you can't PROVE that because there's just no guarantee—" But even though I was poised and ready to go on and on and on, in the end, I cut it off there, since I couldn't guarantee I wouldn't do something completely embarrassing like start crying right in front of her, or worse.

But Tally just shook her head and said, "You're right, Colby. You had no choice, and everything you're going through is out of your control. But what I really meant to say is that even though it's true that all of these things have happened to you, the fact is, you've lived through it, and you're still fine. And you'll continue to be fine. Your mom will find somewhere for you to live, and you'll be fine. And if you have to go to a new school, it won't be long before you learn your way around, make new friends, and you'll be fine again. You'll meet your dad's new girlfriend, and whether or not you like her really doesn't matter, because either way, you'll still be fine. Life brings nothing *but* change, Colby. Our job is to make the necessary adjustments, so we can continue to be fine."

But she'd barely gotten to the end of her speech before I was already shaking my head. "Um, excuse me for saying this, but how would you even know? I mean, it's not like your life embraces change," I said, thinking how she'd moved to a place that's so unbelievably stagnant and slow it seems like nothing's changed for over a century. "I mean, you buy your eggs off an old lady on a donkey, you buy your fish off a boat in the harbor, you don't even have a computer, much less a TV, not to mention how you and Tassos basically keep to the same routine, day in and day out, come rain, shine, or Meltemi wind. So, not to be rude or anything, but in light of all that, I really don't get how you can possibly claim to be such an authority on change. I mean, you're practically living in a time warp!"

But even though I was poised for a fight, Tally just laughed. "You're right," she said, her legs crossed, her hands folded in her lap, her face as serene as the Buddha statue she keeps in her garden. "And that's exactly why I moved here at first. I was searching for someplace stable, steady, and calm. And you know what I got? More change. Maybe not as intense as before, but still, it ebbs and flows here just like any other life. Sometimes the change is small, sometimes it's not, but in the end, you always come out better, wiser, or maybe just okay. And if you're lucky, you get all three."

And that's when I rolled my eyes.

I know I shouldn't have done it, but it's not like I could help it, because as much as I'd grown to like her, as much as I'd learned to tolerate our colossal differences, sometimes she was just so dang full of it.

I watched as she calmly got up, grabbed her keys, and then looked at me as she said, "The trick is to learn to see with your heart, not with your eyes, Colby."

And when I called after her, to ask where she was going, she just smiled and said, "I have a funeral to attend."

August 21
Dear Tally and Tassos,

The mailman just delivered your new COMPUTER!
I left the box in the kitchen, next to the table.
Is this for real?
Let me know if you need me to show you how to use it!
Colby

COLBY'S JOURNAL

August 22

The second I heard Tally's jeep drive away, I got up from my towel and ran after her, waving my arms and yelling into the cloud of dust she'd left behind, but it was too late, she'd already gone. So I ran back down to the beach, shoved everything in my bag, and headed back up the road and all the way home. Ignoring the searing pain in my side as I gasped for air and pushed on, concentrating on nothing more than changing out of my wet bathing suit, and into something appropriate enough to wear to Petros's funeral.

Because the second Tally was gone, I knew she was right. It was time for me to stop worrying about how everything APPEARS. To stop worrying about how it will all END. And learn to enjoy what I have—for as long as I have it.

And just as I was about to walk through the door, a delivery truck pulled into the drive, and some guy climbed out holding this big huge box in his hands that he asked me to sign for, and I nearly fell over when I saw it contained a computer.

But it's not like I had much time to really stop and gawk since I knew the funeral had probably already started, and I didn't want to be any more late than I already was, since the Greeks take their traditions very seriously.

So after taking a really quick shower, and twisting my clean, wet hair back into a bun, I threw on a black dress, slipped on some sandals, and flew out the door, running all the way down to the church where I really, really hoped it was being held, since in this case, being wrong meant I had 699 others to choose from. And when I slipped inside, the room was so dim and cloudy with incense it took awhile for my eyes to adjust, and even though I immediately spotted Tally and Tassos somewhere in the middle, I decided to just hang in the back and try not to attract any more attention than I already had.

I leaned against the back wall, listening as the priests in

their long, ornate robes chanted an endless string of words that sounded completely unfamiliar, as my eyes searched the crowd of mourners, seeing Petros's son, Stavros, struggling to remain stoic even though he was clearly overcome with grief, his arm wrapped around a small, pale, trembling woman I figured to be his mother. And after seeing the guy who works at the bank, nodding at the guy who runs the gyros stand, and acknowledging and recognizing a whole host of others, I realized that as much as I'd tried to fight it, I'd somehow become a part of this community.

Then I froze, I mean seriously I could not blink, breathe, or move when I saw Yannis standing next to Maria. But it only lasted a second. Because even though seeing them together made my stomach pang with this deep terrible ache, in the end I forced my eyes to look away, reminding myself that I was there to honor Petros, not to revisit my long list of regrets.

After the ceremony, everyone filed out of the church and headed for the cemetery, and I was standing by the door, waiting for Tally and Tassos to catch up, when Yannis came right up beside me and whispered, "Walk with me." Not like a question, though not quite an order either, I guess it was more like a suggestion.

So I did. I headed out the door and walked alongside him, neither one of us saying a word, just following the flow of the crowd, until he grabbed my hand, pulled me against the wall, and let everyone pass, until only we remained.

Then he looked at me and said, "Are you okay?"

His eyes were on mine, and his face showed such warmth and concern and care, that I just couldn't help it, I burst out laughing.

Not that I thought it was funny or anything, since obviously it was a completely normal question under the circumstances (unlike my response, which was anything but normal). But after listening to that little speech of Tally's at the beach, somehow it all just seemed kind of funny. Because the fact was, until he'd asked, I didn't even realize that I was okay. That, come to think of it, I'd been okay all along. That even though I was still really sad about Petros, and still really worried about my future, and still beyond annoyed with my parents, and still quite possibly choosing the wrong friends over the right ones, I, Colby Catherine Cavendish, was still okay. And there was a pretty good chance I'd remain that way, no matter what.

That with a little effort, most of the stupid mistakes I'd made could be fixed. And as for the rest? Well, I'd just learn to deal. And for some stupid reason, that I can't really explain, all of that made me feel like laughing, even though it was obviously NOT the response he was after (nor was it appropriate conduct from someone who just came from a funeral). But I guess it also felt good to laugh again. It'd been far too long since the last time.

And like always with laughing, it wasn't long before Yannis joined in too, though it was pretty obvious it was more of a hesitant, confused laugh, like he wasn't exactly sure why he was participating, but figured, well, what the hell?

So when I finally calmed down, I looked him right in the eyes and said, "Oh my God, you're anonymous aren't you?" Even though I hadn't realized I knew until exactly that moment.

He nodded.

So I said, "And that's why you dumped me, because you read about my trip to Mykonos." And as I watched him nod again, I couldn't believe how it'd taken me so long to figure it out. Though I still had no idea how he even knew about my blog in the first place, since it's not like I ever told him about it. But I also knew it didn't matter. What did matter was the way I'd hurt him. So I looked at him and said, "I'm sorry." Which seemed a little inadequate, so I added, "But it's not what you think because nothing happened, I swear. I mean, I'm not going to lie, we kissed—" I glanced at him briefly, then quickly looked away, the pain in his eyes being too much to bear. "But that's it. *Really*—"

I lowered my gaze and focused on my feet, wishing I could go back and change things, yet knowing I could only move forward. So I took a deep breath and said, "I guess I was just so afraid of what I might lose, of what I might be missing out on, that I forgot to enjoy what I have. And I somehow believed that by pushing you away and rejecting everything here, I could reclaim my old life, the one I left behind. Only it didn't work. It just left me feeling sad and awful and empty inside."

When I looked up again his eyes were on mine, and it took everything I had not to look away.

"Is he your boyfriend?" he asked, his eyes narrowed.

I shook my head. "I don't even like him."

"And nothing happened?"

I gazed at him and swallowed hard, hating the words but knowing I had to say them. "We kissed, but that's all."

My hands were shaking, my palms were sweating, and my lips were pressed so tight it hurt, and when I glimpsed his expression, just seconds before he shook his head and looked away, I knew it was useless, I knew it was over.

But then he shrugged and said, "I'm sorry too."

I froze, wondering if he had his own confession to make, something about Maria. And not really sure if I wanted the details, but knowing he deserved equal time, I asked, "What are you sorry for?"

He shook his head. "It was a stupid game, pretending to be anonymous. I should have told you. I just wanted to know you better. You always seem like you are keeping something back. You could have told me about your parents, and your friend coming to visit. Why did you keep it a secret?"

And even though it was a good, reasonable, valid question, that doesn't mean I had an answer. So I just shrugged and said, "Well, now you know. But how did you know, about the blog? I mean, is Petros another cousin?"

Yannis laughed. "He is a cousin of my cousin, but not a direct relation. I stopped by his café one day when you were in there, and I recognized you from the boat, but you didn't see me since you were too busy typing. And when I asked Petros about you, he told me about your blog, and I started reading it so that I could learn more about you. The only reason I showed up at the Fourth of July BBQ was so that I could meet you." He shrugged.

"So you were stalking me?" I asked, realizing that for someone who thought she knew all the answers, I really didn't know much of anything.

But he just laughed.

"And Maria?" I asked, still feeling that pang in my gut, despite everything he'd just told me.

But he just shook his head and slid along the wall, moving so close I could feel the warmth of his body, his breath on my cheek, as he looked at me and said, "The only reason I was in the port that day is because I was buying the flowers and food for our date. I'm not interested in Maria." His eyes searched my face. "Unfortunately, I'm still interested in you."

"Unfortunately?" I murmured, barely able to breathe as he brought his hand to my face, his fingers traveling along my temple, my cheekbone, stopping just long enough to tuck a loose strand of hair behind my ear, before returning to the curve of my chin.

"You're leaving." He shrugged, his eyes gazing right into mine, his fingers tilting my face toward his. "It's unfortunate."

"So what happens now?" I whispered, as he kissed the side of my neck, halfway between my ear and my necklace.

"We make the most of it," he said, his lips meeting mine.

We kissed. Right there, next to the whitewashed wall, smack in the middle of town, where anyone could see. Just clinging to each other, lost in our own little world, oblivious to everything around us, until an old woman walked by and *tsk'd*.

Actually, she muttered something under her breath as well. But even though I asked Yannis to translate, he just shook his head, and said I was better off not knowing. Then he grabbed my hand and led me to where another old woman was selling flowers from a basket hanging off the side of her donkey.

So of course I said, "Oh, you don't have to buy me flowers." Even though I was secretly thrilled that he was.

But he just laughed and said, "They're not for you, they're for Petros. Come on, it's a tradition."

By the time we made it to the cemetery, the ceremony was over, and everyone had moved on, so Yannis and I walked right up to the grave site, and I watched while he placed a single white rose on the grave and said a few words in Greek. Then I placed a pink rose beside his and said, "Thanks for being my friend. And thanks for giving me good advice and telling me to turn off my computer, go outside, and get a life. And thanks for pulling no punches and letting me know when you thought I was up to no good." I peeked at Yannis right after I said that, wondering if Petros had told him about the day I came back from Mykonos and how awful I looked and how I reeked of alcohol and sweat, but he was still gazing at the grave, so I took a deep breath and went on, "And thanks for that free frappe. I'll miss you."

And even though I thought I'd probably start crying the second that was out, I didn't. But not because I was embarrassed, or wanted to appear strong or cool in front of Yannis—I guess just knowing it was okay to show emotion made it no longer necessary to hide it.

And after saying good-bye to Petros, Yannis grabbed my hand and we headed into town, anxious to make up for all that lost time.

CIRCLE IN THE SAND

August 25

I'm back! Thanks to Tally and Tassos who are now totally hooked into the new millennium and have finally gone wireless! Yipee! Which means I can now blog from the comfort of my room, the kitchen table, the couch, the terrace, wherever! And it's all because they said they wanted to keep in touch with me! And even though I don't doubt that to be true, I also happen to know that they're thinking of selling all the art and stuff they make in their own online store, which means they pretty much needed a computer to do that.

Anyway, you were probably a little confused when you saw the blog name, right? I know, I know, I just can't seem to stick with a title. I guess I tend to be a little fickle, somewhat flighty, and perhaps even just a tad bit impulsive (but those are only a few of my many, many quirks, I assure you). Though let me also assure you that "Circle in the Sand" is officially back and will hold at least until I leave on August 31, which unfortunately, is now just a few days away.

Yup, you read that right, I said UNFORTUNATELY. Because even though I spent the better part of the summer longing to be just about anywhere but here, wouldn't you know it, now that it's nearly time for me to leave, this has pretty much become the only place I want to be.

Still, the fact remains that my days here are few, and since I'm determined not to waste any more than I already have, I will keep it short and sweet and show you what I've been up to:

1) This is a picture of me and Yannis out on his cousin's boat. I thought I was teaching them how to wakeboard, until I discovered that they already knew how to wakeboard—way, WAY better than me.
2) That's me and Yannis lying on the beach, that very same day, after the wakeboarding instruction. Notice how wrecked and exhausted I look. That's what wiping out on the wakeboard, over and over again, will do to a person.
3) That's me and Yannis's cousin Nikos eating a sea

urchin that I caught! Seriously! I mean, I pricked my finger pretty badly when I picked it up, but still, it was awesome. That's right, believe it or not I've really learned to love them and I have no idea what I'm going to do when I go back home and I won't be able to eat them all the time anymore. But I guess, there's always frozen yogurt—which is something they don't have here!

4) That's us, at the club, dancing. Blah, blah, blah, I know you've seen those same kind of shots like a thousand times already. So, moving on . . .

5) Oops! Okay, again, another club picture of us drinking (non-alcoholic, I swear!) and hanging out in our usual booth. I like to think of it as the VIP booth, even though it's not.

6) This is a photo of our (Yannis and my) favorite beach. Though the reason you can't see it very well is because it was taken at night, after the club, so it's pretty much just dark sand, darker water, and really dark sky.

7) This is another picture of my cat, Mr. Holly Golightly, who has been missing for several weeks now. If you should find him, please, please pick him up gently (because he does NOT like to be cuddled or held for very long—and trust me, you do NOT want to get scratched!) and deliver him to Tally's Gift Shop located in the harbor front. I promise there will be a reward.

That's all for now!
Ciao!
Colby

August 26
To: AmandaStar
From: ColbyCat
Re: Wazup W/U & sandal guy?
Hey Amanda,

I got your e-mail, and just thought I'd let you know that SANDAL GUY has a name—it's YANNIS.

And just so you know, he also happens to be MY BOYFRIEND.

And the only reason I didn't tell you this before is because I knew you'd make fun of both him and me. But now I no longer care about things like that, so there it is.

Feel free to forward this e-mail to the entire Harbor High School student body if that'll make you happy, since the truth is, I no longer care about stuff like that either.

Sincerely,
Colby

CIRCLE IN THE SAND

Blog Comments:

Anonymous said:

It's so good to have you back!

ColbyCat said:

It's AMAZINGLY good to be back!

August 26

Dear Mom and Dad,

Just so you know, I'm sending each of you a copy of this exact same letter so you don't have to freak out and arrange another conference call. I mean, if you want to call, then of course that's fine, but I just want you to know that you're both getting the exact same information at more or less the exact same time, since I plan to express mail both of these as soon as I'm finished writing them.

Anyway, the purpose of this letter is that I have a proposal to make. And even though you'll probably not take it very seriously, or think I'm joking (at least when you first start reading), it shouldn't take long for you to realize just how serious I am.

And while I realize this may be hard for you to believe, especially in light of my past behavior, not to mention all of the complaining and manipulating I previously engaged in, I am now forced to humbly admit that you guys were completely right in sending me here.

Yup, you read that right! I sincerely believe that just by being here and experiencing everything I have, not only have I learned, not only have I grown, but I now truly believe I am not stretching the truth when I say (write) that I'm a much better person than I was when I left.

So with that in mind, I would really appreciate it if you would please hear me out, before you go thinking this is just another attempt by me to sway your vote in my favor.

So here goes:

Right before I left, I heard you guys arguing, and one of you (I don't remember who) mentioned something about Cyber School. And while I'm still not exactly filled in on all of the details, I have to say that over the last few days I've conducted a fair amount of online research, and have found what seems to be a multitude of Virtual Academies to choose from.

And even though I've yet to run it by Tally and Tassos (mostly because I wanted to approach you and gain your consent first, which also means that I hope you won't mention it to them before we've had a chance to discuss things), in the end, I think we'll find them to be in full agreement with my plan.

So—believe it or not, I've really grown to like it here.

I mean, I REALLY like it here.

And so I'm wondering if I might be allowed to stay and finish my education by enrolling in Cyber School, since my Greek's not good enough (yet!) to attend the local school.

And before you roll your eyes, shake your head, and say NO, please just consider this—if you agree with my plan to let me stay and attend an online school, then:

1) *Mom—You will be able to move wherever you want. You can even get a one-bedroom apartment, thereby SAVING A TON OF MONEY since you won't have to worry about me, or be forced to stay within my current (high-rent) school district.*
2) *Dad—ALL of these online schools are totally ACCREDITED and LEGITIMATE, so my dreams of college will not in any way be compromised and/or hindered.*

3) *Also, by staying here, I will become bilingual! A plus on any college and/or job application.*
4) *I will still be able to fly home to visit with both of you on Christmas and New Year's, and you can come visit me for Easter—which happens to be a very big holiday here, and it would be so fun to celebrate it with you! Or even just one of you. Whatever you can arrange.*
5) *And even though online school is not exactly free, I think once you both take the time to sit down and do the math, you will find it to be VERY COST EFFECTIVE.*
6) *Also, just for the record, because I think it needs to be said, Tally and Tassos are NOT CRAZY. They are nice, kind, generous, smart, wonderful people who have become VERY GOOD ROLE MODELS for me (not that you aren't as well).*
7) *Besides, it would only be for the next year. Which, when you think about it, is really just twelve months. Which as you well know, will just fly by before any of us even realizes it's over!*
8) *Not to mention how if I CAN'T return to Harbor High, then I'd really rather just stay here.*
9) *And even if I CAN return to Harbor High, then I'd still rather just stay here.*
10) *And just so you know, this plan practically GUARANTEES both my current and future HAPPINESS. And we all know how important it is to be happy in life.*

So now that you've taken the time to read my letter, I hope you'll also take the necessary amount of time in which to fully consider my proposal.

Though it would also be helpful if you could get back to me as soon as you can, since time is clearly running out.

Love,

Colby

P.S. Dad, I've also decided to send this via e-mail as well as fax it to your office in hopes that you will alert Mom the MOMENT you receive it, because even though I'm springing for express, one-day airmail, as you can see, time is of the essence.

August 26
To: NatalieZee
From: ColbyCat
Re: Thanks for the earrings
Hey Nat,

You're not going to believe this, but I'm totally campaigning to get my parents to let me stay in Tinos! I have no idea if they'll actually go for it or not, but I just sent them a very detailed letter making the best case I possibly could, so now I'm just crossing my fingers and hoping for the best.

I mean, it probably sounds weird and all, especially since I started out really hating it here, but even though I'm not sure exactly when or how it happened, I've somehow really grown to like it. And it's NOT just because Yannis and I are back together (though I'm not even sure you knew we were apart, I guess we have a lot to catch up on!), because in just a few weeks he'll be going back to Athens to finish up his last year of high school anyway, which means we'll only be able to see each other on the occasional weekend. But the truth is, I really like this simple, uncluttered, island life. And even though I've made a mess of so many things since I got here (I promise to fill you in on all of that too), somehow my life feels a lot less complicated HERE than it does THERE. No yelling, no fighting, no domestic upheaval, everything's just tranquil, quiet, and peaceful—three things I didn't appreciate until I came here. Not to mention how there's really not much for me to return to, so I guess I just don't see the point in returning at all.

I mean, of course there's still YOU—that is, if we're back to being friends???

But other than that, there's really not much for me to miss, since I'm pretty much over that whole Amanda and Levi scene, so allow me to take a moment to say—You were right! You were right! You were so very right!

Not to mention how I don't even miss any of my "stuff" as much as I originally thought I would—which is pretty weird, since I really, really thought I would.

So anyway, if they let me stay here, then I'll be enrolling in some kind of Cyber School, not sure which one, since there's plenty to choose from. But if not, then it's anyone's guess where I'll end up.

Okay, well, I'm meeting Yannis soon—so, e-mail me back when you can!

Colby

P.S. Oh yeah, I'm so glad you liked the earrings! I made them myself! Though I probably already told you that!

August 27

Dear Tally/Tassos,

You'll be happy to know that the computer DID NOT CRASH!

It just ran out of battery, which means you have to plug it in and let it recharge for a while, that's all.

If either of my parents (or both!) happen to call—please tell them I'll call them back as soon as I return.

But please DO NOT ask them why they are calling, since I already know the reason, and it's kind of private, and not really all that important.

Thanks!

Love,

Colby

COLBY'S JOURNAL FOR DESPERATE TIMES WHEN SHE'S DESPERATELY IN LOVE AND DOESN'T CARE WHO KNOWS

August 29

So yesterday, when I went to the beach with Yannis, I finally worked up the nerve to take off my top! But only because neither Tally nor Tassos nor any of his three hundred cousins were there, which meant we were completely alone (well, other than the other tourists and beachgoers), but even then, I only had it off for like ten seconds, before I put it right back on.

And the second after I did it, Yannis rolled onto his back, squinted at me, and said, "Did you just flash me?"

But I just laughed as my fingers worked at retying my

straps. And once everything was secured, covered, and stowed away safely again, I leaned in and kissed him and said, "Baby steps. You know, one small baby step at a time. That's how you do it. That's how all great change begins."

And as he pulled me down on top of him and started kissing me back, my mind went straight to the pack of condoms I had stashed in my beach bag. And I wondered if we'd end up using them.

Ever since we got back together, it was like I'd become obsessed with the idea of sleeping with Yannis. I mean, not that I hadn't thought about it like a million, gazillion times before, because I had, probably even more than that. But now that we were definitely back together, now that I just might be forced into going home, the whole idea seemed to take on a life of its own, filled with this overwhelming urgency (well, to me anyway, since it's not like he was even aware of it).

Besides, I really, really like him. And even though I used to think I really, really liked Levi, now I realize I was wrong. Because my liking Levi had everything to do with Levi the Image and nothing to do with Levi the Person. I mean, I barely even knew him as a person, and what little I did know, well, I really wasn't all that crazy about. But with Yannis everything is different. We have things in common, we laugh at the same jokes, and we can carry on a conversation just as easily as we can make out.

I guess what I'm trying to say is that Yannis is also like my good friend. And in light of all that, buying a pack of condoms just seemed like the right thing to do.

So the day after Petros's funeral, I got up early, went into town, and purchased a three-pack at the local pharmacy. And I have to admit that the whole entire time my heart was racing, my face was burning, and it was almost as embarrassing as the time I had to buy tampons from this kid in my ninth-grade biology class who was working the register at CVS. But then I reminded myself how I'm not exactly from here, which also meant that the anonymous woman with the furry upper lip who was ringing up my three-pack probably assumed I was just another slutty tourist who she wouldn't think twice about after I left. And even though she did glance from the box to me while raising her eyebrows, I just rolled my eyes and brushed it off, positive I had nothing to worry about.

And the second I walked out of that store, with the small brown bag clutched tightly in my fist, the contraband condoms secured in my possession, the specifics of just HOW and WHEN I would actually go about using them became pretty much all I could think about.

Seriously, it's like every morning I wake up, I can't help but think:

Will today be the day I sleep with Yannis?

And since time is seriously running out, I was starting to think that today was probably as good a day as any.

Though it's not like I'd planned to do it right there on the beach.

Yet, wouldn't you know it, just as I was really getting

into kissing him back, I accidentally kicked my bag with my foot, which made the whole thing tip over, which made all the contents spill across the sand. And it's not like I even would've stopped kissing him long enough to notice, except that when Yannis came up for air, he also started to clean up the mess.

And when he came to the small, silver packet, he looked at me, and said, "So you really did buy condoms. I thought they were making a joke."

"What?" I gasped, sitting up so fast an entire constellation of stars swirled before my eyes, watching, in complete mortification, as the little packet, my most embarrassing purchase ever, dangled from the tips of his fingers.

"Christos told me," he said, the condoms swinging back and forth in a rush of silver, as though I was being hypnotized. "But I think it was Georgos who told him. But actually, it all started with Katerina, Maria's aunt. She's the one who owns the pharmacy."

"Your LITTLE BROTHER told you I bought condoms?" I asked, going straight to the most horrifying on the LIST OF PEOPLE WHO KNOW I BOUGHT CONDOMS, as I frantically tried to wrap my mind around how this could possibly ever have happened. I mean, wasn't there some kind of law against this? Wasn't there some kind of INTERNATIONAL PROPHYLACTIC PURCHASING PRIVACY ACT? And if not, WHY not? "And who's Georgos? Do you mean YOUR COUSIN Georgos? And is that the Maria I'm thinking of?" My eyes were bulging, my palms sweating, my heart racing, my mind spinning, watching as Yannis just nodded, clearly amused.

"You mean the WHOLE TOWN, no, scratch that, you mean the WHOLE ISLAND, knows I bought condoms?" I yelped, clearly on the verge of hysteria.

He nodded again. "And now the entire beach too," he added, laughing and glancing around at all the surrounding gawkers.

"Oh my God, this is NOT HAPPENING! It's too horrible!" I buried my face in my hands, unable to look at him, unable to look at anyone, possibly ever again.

But he just laughed. "That's Tinos," he said. "You sure you still want to live here?"

"What's that supposed to mean?" I asked, lifting my head and peering at him, my eyes searching his face, wondering where this was leading. Did he not want me to stay? Had he changed his mind—about me, about us? And if so, was it because I'm the kind of girl who buys condoms?

"Colby," he said, dropping the stupid, silver package and cupping my face in his hands. "Things are different here. It's not like what you're used to back home. The island is small, everyone knows each other, and people like to talk."

"I'll say." I rolled my eyes, wondering how I'd ever face those nasty gossips again, not to mention his brother and cousin, and so on.

"Think of it like high school. Or at least the way you described American high school to me. Only here, high school is not so—contained to one place. High school is where you live, all of the time, and there's no escaping it. Ask your aunt Tally, she'll tell you."

"Tally knows I bought condoms too?" I said, thinking how it just seemed to get worse and worse, wondering if the list would ever end.

But he just laughed. "Probably. But what I meant to say was, she knows just how small this place can be. Why don't you ask her about it sometime? You two never really talk, do you?"

And the moment he said it, I felt kind of angry. I mean, who was he to act like he knew something about Tally that I didn't? I'm the one who just spent nearly three months living with her. But just as I was about to defend myself, and let him know how we happen to talk all the time, I realized he was right. We didn't talk much at all. And when I really stopped and thought about it, I actually knew very little about her. Of course, I knew her likes and dislikes, was fully indoctrinated in all of her wacky beliefs, but I guess I didn't really know all that much about her personal history. I didn't really know much about HER. So in the end, I just looked at him and shrugged. But little did I know it was about to get worse.

Because then he looked at me and said, "And Colby, I want you to know that you don't have to do this."

"Do what?" I asked, my head spinning with so many things, I was no longer sure what he might mean.

Then he gazed down at the condoms and back at me, and it didn't take a mind reader to know what he was getting at.

"You mean—you don't want to?" I asked, unable to hide my shock. I mean, the whole entire time I'd been obsessing over it, I was sure the final decision would be mine and mine alone. I never even considered he might have a say.

But he just shrugged. And the moment I saw it, the second I witnessed that casual rise and fall of his shoulders, my face burned with shame, my heart filled with humiliation, and I reached for that stupid package with fingers so shaky and hectic I was sure I would drop it. But then I picked it right up and tossed it back in my bag, making a big show of hurling my sunscreen, books, and magazines right on top, ensuring it stayed out of sight, buried, forgotten underneath.

Then just as I reached for my T-shirt, thinking it was as good a time as any to leave, he placed his hand on my arm and said, "*Koukla Mou,* please don't go."

And I caved. Completely folded, cried uncle, and tossed my T-shirt aside. Basically because ever since we got back together, I cannot resist when he calls me that. But that doesn't mean I wasn't annoyed.

Then he looked at me and said, "What I meant was, you don't have to do this for me. Or because you think I want to do it. Or because you think you might be leaving soon, and that you'll never see me again, and so you have to do it. Or because you think that if you don't do it, then I might forget you. Because even though I want to do it, Colby, more than you will ever know, none of these reasons are very good for you. And I don't want you to do something that you might someday regret."

"Why would I regret it?" I said, feeling totally, inexplicably annoyed. I mean, it wasn't natural, wasn't normal. What guy turns down the opportunity to have sex? Who in their right mind does that?

But he just laughed. "Well, you can be a little impulsive, in case you haven't noticed."

I rolled my eyes. Because even though that may well be the case, what was it to him? I mean, what did he care if I lived to regret it? Chances were we'd never see each other again anyway, so what then? I mean, I definitely regretted the first time, but somehow I managed to get through that. So what's the big deal if the second time turns out to be an even bigger mistake? But no sooner had I thought it, than I realized that was pretty much what he was getting at to begin with. That it was completely and entirely possible to avoid future regret, if you stopped long enough to really think things through.

So then I looked at him and said, "Well, maybe you're right. But then again, since the whole town thinks we're already doing it, don't you think we should maybe just go ahead and do it?" And then I laughed, but not a real laugh, just my stupid nervous laugh, the one he was probably very familiar with by now.

But he just smiled, and leaned in to kiss me. "We have three more nights together," he whispered, his lips moving against mine. "Take some time to think about it, and then let me know. Really, it's no worries."

I looked at him for a moment, then I shook my head, pulled away, and lay back on my towel. "You're a really weird guy, you know that?" I said, turning my head to peer at him.

But he just smiled. "So you tell me."

August 29
To: CarlCavendish
From: ColbyCat
Re: Is that your final answer?
Dad:

I just got home and read Tally's note saying you will see me at the airport on the thirty first of August and I'm taking that to mean either:

1) You haven't received my prior e-mail, fax, and/or letter and therefore are unaware of the other, very reasonable and valid options I have presented. **OR:**
2) You are familiar with all of the other options, but for some reason that is not only unclear to me but that I cannot possibly begin to fathom, have chosen to reject them.

Please advise me of your position at your earliest convenience.

And in the event that you have chosen to reject my proposal, then I need to know if this was a decision made jointly (between you and Mom) or if it's one you have taken the liberty to decide on your own, unbeknownst to Mom.

Love,

Your daughter who is in desperate need of clarification,

Colby

P.S. I am attaching a list of relevant Web sites for your perusal. Please take the time to view them.

August 29
To: CarlCavendish
From: ColbyCat
Re: Is that your final answer?
Dad,

I assure you that I am not "horsing around." I am completely serious, and was hoping you would take me seriously too. Cyber School, Online Education, Virtual Academy, call it what you will, it is definitely NOT a joke. It is a valid, legitimate education option, as all of the schools are ACCREDITED. Which, I might add, if you'd actually taken the time to look over those Web sites I forwarded to you, then you would know that by now.

And furthermore, I don't see how you can possibly be in a position to make any kind of decision for my future when you are so clearly closed off to all of the options but one. And while I'm sorry to say it, I think you should know that I'm very disappointed, not to mention shocked by the unjust unfairness of it all. I am also both saddened and upset to see the way you are handling my life in such a cavalier and random manner.

So I ask you again, would you PLEASE just do me the favor of taking TEN MINUTES out of your very busy day, and click on the links that I sent you in the last e-mail and that I am attaching again in this e-mail. And then pick up the phone and CALL MOM, so that the two of you, TOGETHER, can take a calm, rational, logical, inclusive approach to the one and only thing I need to secure a happy and successful future.

That's ALL I ask.

Love,

Colby

August 29
To: CarlCavendish
From: ColbyCat
Re: Is that your final answer?
Dad,

Fine.

See you on the thirty-first.

Colby

August 30
To: AmandaStar
From: ColbyCat
Re: Yo, Bitch!
Hey Amanda,

I know. You are so totally right. NOBODY gets away with talking/writing to you the way I did.

Though maybe you should let them, because you just might learn something.

But no worries, since it's not like we'll be talking all that much in the future anyway. Partly because I'm back to being best friends with Nat, but mostly because there's just not much point in us talking to each other anyway.

So—all the best to you—see you around Harbor. (That's right, I'll be back!)

Colby

August 30
To: NatalieZee
From: ColbyCat
Re: Home sweet home
Hey Nat,

I'll keep this short and sweet since I've only got one day left here in Tinos and I don't want to waste it on the computer since I've wasted way too many days like that already. So here's the short list of things you need to know:

1) Cyber School is out. Apparently my parents are even more close-minded than I ever could've imagined. Oh well, at least I tried.
2) Harbor is in! That's right, read it and weep! My mom found an apartment for us, and we're moving in next month!
3) I may or may not sleep with Yannis. Which means tonight could turn out to be a VERY BIG NIGHT—or not. It re-

mains to be seen. . . . Either way, I'll give you all the details when I see you! There's so much to tell!

4) I just want to take the time to say that I'm really glad we're still friends, and that next year is totally gonna rock! Even if Amanda does totally hate me and will probably do her best to sabotage me and/or take me down every chance she gets. (Like #3, I'll explain when I see you.).

See you soon!
Colby

Colby's Journal for Desperate Times When She'll Soon Have to Start a New Journal

August 31

It's funny to think how at the beginning of this summer, back when I was still in California, and my mom gave me this journal, I was sure I wouldn't even crack it open, much less start writing in it. But now that the summer's almost over, and I'm about to head home, I've managed to fill up nearly every page.

I guess I was just so mad about being sent here I'd convinced myself that I couldn't possibly experience anything worth writing about.

And now I'm just glad I was wrong.

So today (well I guess it's technically yesterday, but whatever), anyway, so in light of it being my last day and all, Tally and Tassos planned to throw a big going-away BBQ for me. But I guess I should backtrack and say that first, way before the party, we decided to spend the day at the beach. But just Tally and me since Tassos was busy working on a big sculpture that some guy in France commissioned, and Yannis had to work at the hotel. And even though I felt kind of bad that I'd been too wrapped up in myself to do it before, I figured it was better late than never, so I dove right in and asked Tally about her life.

And as it turns out, I learned a lot. Stuff I never knew, stuff I never could've imagined.

Like:

1) She met Tassos the very first day she arrived in Tinos. And just like Yannis and me the first time they saw each other was on the boat. But unlike Yannis and me they actually spoke on the boat. Because when Tally accidentally knocked over her coffee, Tassos was sitting beside her and offered to help clean it up. But even though she said she thought he was cute, it wasn't until two years later that they actually got together. Partly because she said she was reluctant to date anyone so soon after her divorce, and partly because Tassos was totally grieving over his daughter's suicide.
2) That's right, Tassos was also married before, and he had a seventeen-year-old daughter who died of an overdose. Only it wasn't an

accident, and they happen to know this because she left a note. Though I have no idea what the note said, and believe me, it's not like I asked. Anyway, I have to admit that hearing that really freaked me out. I mean, his daughter was the same age when she died as I am right now, and even though at one point I thought my life was just about as bad as it gets, I guess it was never really all that bad after all.

3) So apparently, not long after the overdose, Tassos and his wife split. Tally said they were both really sad, and angry, and sort of lashed out and blamed each other. And right after they got divorced, his wife moved back to Sweden (where she's from) and Tassos quit his job in Athens (apparently he was an airline executive—which trust me, I NEVER would've imagined, because he is so NOT the buttoned-up, super serious, suit-wearing, type A, type!) and moved back to Tinos, where he's originally from, and enrolled in the famous marble sculpting school they have here, determined to follow his passion, try to be happy again, and live a life that mattered, or something like that.

4) But when he came back to Tinos, he was surprised at how everyone was gossiping about him and saying some not-so-nice things about him, his wife, and his daughter, until

he eventually became so depressed and distraught, he became like a total recluse, barely leaving his house.

5) Then one day Tally and Tassos ran into each other at the agricultural co-op and it wasn't long after that when they started living together, which made people talk even more, because shacking up is pretty much frowned upon here. But they both agreed to live their lives like they want and not to care about what anyone else thinks.

And then, I guess because we were kind of on a sharing binge, she told me how she knew all about the condoms I'd bought.

And I felt myself turn every shade of red, even though I'm actually really, really tan, which means she probably couldn't even tell that I was blushing. But still, I felt so embarrassed I could hardly even look at her (and believe me, this time it had nothing to do with the fact that she was, once again, topless).

And then she asked me if we needed to, as she put it, "Have a little talk."

So I said, "Well, apparently not, since *I'm* the one who was smart enough to buy the condoms."

And then we both laughed.

And when she asked me whether or not I was planning to use the condoms, I looked her right in the eye and told her the truth. "I have no idea," I said. "I guess we'll just see how it goes."

And even though I hadn't planned on sharing anything more than that, even though I really thought I'd gotten over it already, before I even realized what I was doing, I started telling her all about that night with Levi, and how ashamed and stupid I felt after, and how lately I was thinking that maybe sleeping with Yannis could somehow erase it, or at the very least, correct it.

And then I just kept going, telling her all about how I dumped Natalie so I could hang with Amanda, about everything that happened (and didn't happen) in Mykonos, and how lately I'd been feeling so confused, like I had one foot in Tinos and the other in California, and I just wasn't sure where I fit anymore. How when I was in Mykonos, all I did was judge Levi and his family for their predictable American ways, and how the night before that I'd judged Yannis for being so quintessentially Greek. But how really, deep down inside, I knew the real problem was me.

But she just looked at me and smiled when she said, "Colby, there's no right way or wrong way, there's just your way. And you'll be a whole lot happier when you figure out what that is."

"But that's the thing," I said, feeling immediately frustrated by her usual obscure statements.

But she just shrugged and said, "You can never go wrong when you act from love."

Well, shortly after that I got up from my towel and waded deep into the sea, going so far out I was forced to stand on the very tips of my toes in order to breathe. Then I tilted my head back, closed my eyes, and let the water support me, thinking how there were few greater feelings than that—of being so light and free you were hardly even aware of yourself.

I stayed like that for a long time, partly because it felt far too good to stop, but mostly because I was reluctant to head back to shore, back to the gravity of my body, my life, my choices.

But as I allowed myself to float some more I thought: *Maybe I'm still overthinking everything. Maybe I'm still trying to control stuff that's out of my control. Maybe I should act the same way on land as I do in the sea, learn to let go, to aim for what I want without trying to force it so much. Just see where the current leads me, since it's not like I'm not a good swimmer, it's not like I can't find my way back to shore.*

And when I climbed out of the water and headed for my towel, I told Tally I was ready to head back home and prepare for my going away.

By the time we got back, Tassos was already there, marinating the meats, chopping vegetables, peeling potatoes, and basically handling all of the party prep duties. So after taking a quick shower and changing into a new dress I bought in town a few days before (a day which will forever be known as CONDOM DAY), I headed outside to help.

And while I was setting the tables and rearranging the chairs, I happened to mention how sorry I was about his daughter.

At first, with the way he looked at me, his eyes so startled and wide, I immediately regretted bringing it up. But then he nodded slowly and said, "Tally told you?"

I nodded. "But please don't be mad, because—"

But he just shook his head. "I'm not mad, Colby."

And as I started lighting the candles, he put on a Jackson Browne CD, and then I turned to him again and said, "Do you blame yourself?"

And even though he just shrugged, it was obvious he did.

I held the match, watching as the flame crept near my fingers, inching dangerously close before I shook it out and said, "Well, you shouldn't."

He looked at me and smiled. "I know."

And even though I should've just let it end there, I had something more to say, so I looked at him and added, "I just want you to know that you and Tally have really helped me this summer."

Then his eyes grew wet and mine started to sting, so I started slicing potatoes as he turned to prepare the salad.

It wasn't long after that when all the guests started arriving, and even though it still surprises me to write this (never mind having lived it), I'm proud to say that this time I made sure both Maria and Christina were invited. I guess I just didn't see the point in trying to keep them away. And even though we didn't exactly hang out together, and even though they were probably pretty happy that it was my GOING-AWAY party, it just didn't matter anymore.

So after way too much food, a good amount of dancing, a little bit of drinking, and an endless amount of laughing, I hugged every single person good-bye (yes, including Maria and Christina), and after they'd gone, Tally and Tassos hugged me and Yannis good night, then Tally looked at me and said, "Stay up as long as you want. But just remember you have a ferry to catch in the morning."

Then they both went to bed, and Yannis and I remained on the terrace, both of us acting so weird and nervous that any casual observer would swear we'd just met.

"Well, that was a fun party," he said, smiling at me in this polite, formal way.

"Yes it was," I answered, feeling inexplicably awkward, then adding, "a really fun party." Which made me roll my eyes, shake my head, and cringe.

"Should we go for a ride?" he finally asked, his voice sounding thick and uncertain, suspended in silence.

I nodded, my stomach feeling all jumpy and weird as he reached for my hand, my eyes searching his face when I asked, "To our beach?"

But he just smiled and helped me climb onto the back of his Vespa.

This time when we ended up at the hotel, I can't say I was all that surprised, but when he led me up to the pool, I was surprised to see it filled.

"Want to go for a swim?" he asked, busying himself with lighting the large, oversize lanterns that were scattered all around.

"I forgot my suit," I said, kneeling down near the edge, dipping my fingers into the water, surprised to find it cool, but inviting.

"That didn't stop you before." He smiled, blowing out the match now that the candles were all lit.

And even though I still hadn't made up my mind about exactly how the night would end, I also knew I should stop thinking about it, and just see where it led.

So I pulled off my dress and dove right in. And not five seconds later, Yannis had joined me.

We swam, and played, and kissed, and swam some more, and by the time we'd climbed out and were wrapped in large towels, he took one look at me and said, "You look just like you did the day I first saw you, only happier."

And when I rubbed my towel over my face and saw how it came away all streaked with mascara, I couldn't help but laugh.

Then he grabbed my hand and led me through the lobby, and up a narrow stairway to a large second-floor suite. And when he opened the door and motioned me inside, I saw there were more candles, a CD player, and a fully made bed.

"I didn't realize you'd finished all the rooms," I said, going over to part the dark blue drapes, gazing out at what should've been the view if the night hadn't been so dark.

"They're not finished," he said, coming up behind me and nuzzling the back of my neck. "Only this one."

"But what about your parents? Won't they get mad?" I asked, knowing how traditional the Greeks could be, trying not to think about getting caught.

But he just shrugged. "It's different for boys. If I was a girl, then yes, it would be a problem."

"Is that why I haven't met your parents?" I asked, thinking it was a weird time to be having this conversation, but still, I was nervous, unsure, and it was something I'd been wondering anyway. "Because they wouldn't approve of me?" I continued, wondering if he'd answer honestly, or just try to hedge and stall and beat around the bush.

But he just laughed. "You have met my parents. Well, you've met my father, you just didn't know it."

I turned to look at him, my mind racing, trying to recall when that could've been.

"The day you came to the hotel to yell at me." He smiled.

"Which one was your father?" I asked, remembering the group of workers, how they'd laughed and elbowed each other when I'd asked where he was, all of them too young to be his dad. Well, all except for one.

"He brought you to me."

"Oh, great." I closed my eyes and turned away. "That's just great. No wonder you never bothered to introduce me to your mother." I shook my head, wondering if his dad had eavesdropped by the door, listening to every stupid thing I'd said. "So, go ahead, lay it on me, what did he say? What was the verdict? Does he think I'm a freak?" I held my breath and waited.

"Does it matter?" Yannis asked, whispering the words in my ear.

I just shrugged, even though I was beginning to think that it did.

He sighed. "Well, if you really must know, he told me that I should be careful with you. That I should have fun, but be careful."

"Careful of what?" I asked, turning to look at him again.

"He said you might try to get pregnant and wreck my life."

I rolled my eyes. "Please, did you tell him that *I'm* the one who bought the condoms? Oh wait, never mind, I'm sure he already knows, heck, all of Tinos knows."

Yannis shrugged. "I told you things are different here, relationships aren't so—casual as where you live. Here, when two people date, everyone starts talking about marriage. It's better not to bring anyone home until things are serious."

I looked away, torn between worrying that we were just a casual summer fling, one that he'd soon forget, and wondering if I really wanted it to be anything more.

Then I looked at him and asked, "Are we casual?"

But he just smiled and pulled me toward the bed, his lips moving softly against my ear as he whispered, "Come with me, *koukla mou*."

August 31

Dear Mom and Dad,

You may notice that this letter is written on a coffee-stained Ellas Ferry Lines napkin (not unlike a previous note I sent several months ago). Well, that's because I'm on the ferry to Mykonos. So that I can then fly to Athens, so that I can then fly to Frankfurt, so that I can then fly to New York, so that I can then land in L.A., so that you can then pick me up and drive me home.

But unlike my last napkin letter, this one is not angry.

In fact, it's not even close.

Because believe it or not, I'm actually looking forward to seeing you (an event that will happen long before you receive this, but I'm mailing it anyway), so that I can thank you for packing me up and shipping me off to spend the summer with my CRAZY AUNT TALLY in Tinos.

It was an amazing experience.

Love,

Colby

P.S. Mom, just so you know, the ONLY reason I'm sending this to Dad's address and not to yours is because I know we'll be moving soon and I'm not sure if you've started forwarding the mail yet, and since I don't want this to get lost . . . Anyway, that is the one and only reason, and I just wanted you to know that so you won't think I'm playing favorites. Hope this part of the note doesn't upset you, I just wanted to make myself clear. ☺

Colby's Journal for Desperate Times When She's Stuck at 37,000 Feet and There Is No Internet Access and She's Almost Out of Paper

August 31

I tried, I really, really tried. But somehow I still ended up on this airplane, in seats 24G and H (got two to myself! Yipee!), far enough away from the bathroom that I don't have to suffer that pervasive God-awful smell, but still next to the window so that I can lift my shade and look out at—

EVERYTHING!

Because even though each passing second takes me farther and farther from where I'd really rather be, there's just something so cool about looking out at the sun and the moon and the endless blue sky and thinking—

That's the same sky Yannis sees!

That's the same sun that warms both our skin!

And every night when we go outside, we can both look up and gaze at the exact same moon! (Granted, ten hours apart.)

All of which means we're not as far apart as it seems. That no matter where I end up, no matter where I go from here, in some vast, eternal way, we'll always be connected.

And even though I'd give just about anything to be with him now, I'm also determined to be perfectly okay with my choices—even the ones that are made for me.

Like last night, when Yannis and I slept together. In the end, we didn't ACTUALLY sleep together.

And it's not like I didn't want to, and it's not like I wasn't ready, because I was. In fact, I really, REALLY wanted to, and I really did feel ready. And without being too graphic, I think I can say that he was ready too.

And even though I'd made up my mind to go through with it, even though I'd convinced myself that the time was perfectly right, at this one point, when we were lying on our sides, facing each other, he brought his hand to my cheek, tucked my hair behind my ear, looked straight into my eyes and said, "*S'agapo,* Colby."

And unlike the last time when I wasn't at all ready to hear it, much less feel it or share it, I gazed right back at him, and said, "I love you too, Yannis."

And somehow, just allowing myself to not only hear the words, but also to accept them, and say them right back, felt so huge, so monumental, and so overwhelmingly good—that I just wanted to hold on to it. I wanted to keep it, and savor it, and enjoy it for what it was.

And I didn't want it to compete with anything else.

And even though it probably sounded pretty weird and stupid when I tried to explain that to him, he just pulled me into his arms, pressed his lips to my forehead, and assured me it was plenty enough for him too.

Then we slept, all wrapped up in each other's arms, and I felt so good, and so safe, and so complete, that I didn't wake up until it was way, way late.

"Oh my God! Oh crap!" I yelled, jumping out of bed and frantically pulling on my dress. Not realizing I was wearing it backward 'til I started shoving my feet in my shoes.

"Yannis! Get up!" I cried, shaking his shoulder, before searching the room for my purse. "You have to take me to the port! No! Wait! You have to take me home so Tally and Tassos can take me to the port! Only, you're coming too, right?" I stopped long enough to look at him, hoping that my mascara-streaked face, backward dress, and fright-wig hair would not be his very last impression of me.

But Yannis was already dressed, his keys in one hand, funky, weird sandals in the other, as he opened the door, smiled, and said, "Relax, it's no worries."

And I broke out laughing. Bent over, side-clutching laughing. I mean, I could hardly believe how dumb I'd been to almost miss out on LOVE all because of some awkward-sounding slang and an odd pair of sandals. And even though I tried to stop, I just couldn't. So he grabbed me by the arm and pulled me out the door and over to his bike, muttering, "Crazy California girl," as he got me safely settled onto the back.

And by the time we got to Tally's, I completely panicked again when I saw that Tally and Tassos were not even there! But as it turns out, they were out looking for me. Starting at our secret make-out beach (which apparently was not such a secret, but hey, that's small ~~town~~ island living for ya) and ending at the port, where they confirmed my boat was ready and waiting, although I was not yet on it. And by the time they got back to the house, I was sitting in the drive, bags packed and ready, allowing them five more minutes to show before I'd leave without them.

So I climbed in the back of the jeep, as Yannis followed behind on his bike, and we all caravanned down to the port. And even though I fully admit that the whole entire time I was hoping for some sort of nautical malfunction, or horrendous, catastrophic summer storm—something to keep my boat from sailing so I'd have no choice but to stay put—in the end, I was greeted with a perfectly clear, Meltemi-free day. Which I pretty much took as a sign that, like it or not, I was destined to leave.

And by the time we parked and made our way down to the dock my boat was already well into loading mode, which didn't really leave much time for good-bye. But then again, that's probably also a good thing since I've never been much good at final moments anyway.

So after hugging Tassos, and basically thanking him for EVERYTHING, I leaned in to hug Tally, and burst out crying so fast and hard, I could hardly even believe it. But she just let me cling to her, as she ran her hand over my hair, whispering, "It's okay, it's all going to be okay."

And when I finally pulled away, I wiped my eyes, and smiled, and said, "I know."

And then we promised to stay in touch and e-mail each other as often as we could, and then I made some dumb joke about how if they needed any help in figuring out the e-mail then they could just e-mail me and let me know. And even though it was totally lame, and obviously not at all funny, it really helped ease all of the tension and sadness, so we all laughed anyway.

After hugging them again, I walked the rest of the way with Yannis, holding hands as we made our way toward the gangway, but then Yannis suddenly stopped and said, "Colby, isn't that—?"

I gazed in the direction he was pointing, not sure if he was right until I saw the beaded collar, then I knew for sure. He'd grown, since I'd last seen him, A LOT. But still, between the collar, the shiny black coat, and the cute little white streak, I knew I was looking at Holly.

"Where are you going?" I asked, watching as Yannis charged toward the little dark-haired girl in the bright yellow sundress, the one who was cradling Holly, singing in his ear as she stroked his shiny dark fur.

"What do you mean? That's YOUR cat, Colby, I'm going to get him back!" he said, walking that much faster.

I grabbed his arm, making him stop long enough to face me. "No, Yannis, please. Just leave him," I said, not knowing if I really meant it until the moment it was out.

But Yannis just shook his head and started off again, saying, "No worries, she's the daughter of my cousin, I can get her another one."

But again, I grabbed his arm, forcing him to look at me as I said, "No, Yannis, I'm serious."

His eyes searched my face, his expression showing just how crazy he thought I was. "But why? I don't understand. I thought you said you missed him? I thought you wanted him back?"

"I did miss him, and I did want him back." I nodded. "Until now."

Yannis narrowed his eyes, gazing at me.

"Just look," I said. "*Really* look."

So he did. And then he turned to me and shrugged. "I don't get it. It is Holly, right?"

"Yes, and look at the way that little girl is holding him, how he's pressed up so tight against her chest, and how her arms are wrapped so snugly around him. Look at how he lets her do that. He never did that with me. Not once. With me he always scratched and struggled to be free."

"He's older now," Yannis said, shaking his head and squinting.

But I just shook my head and smiled. "No Yannis, he's home."

By the time we got to the gangway, we kissed so long the boat nearly sailed without me. But in the end, I'm glad we managed to keep it honest and real, that we managed to say good-bye, and say "I love you," without forcing a bunch of false promises on each other, ones we might not be able to keep.

Because the only thing that was certain was that we loved each other, that we had each other's e-mail address, and that we'd see where it led.

Because if there's one thing I now know for sure, it's that nothing is ever sure.

CIRCLE IN THE SAND

September 7

Well, I guess this blog title was more appropriate than I realized way back when I chose it, since I really have come full circle, and now I'm right back where I started. Even though almost everything is different from the way I left it. But since circles have no end, I guess it's really just the beginning of another cycle, and who knows where that'll lead?

But in order to keep you up to date, let me just say that by the time I made it to LAX I was completely, and totally, exhausted. But even though I was so tired I could barely keep my eyes open it was still pretty great to see both my parents, standing side by side, no legal counsel in sight, and with no obvious grievances (at least none that I could see), both of them looking relaxed and happy to see me—just as I was happy to see them.

And since I know better than to hug one of them before the other, I just walked right up, with my arms spread wide, pretty much forcing them into a big group hug. And even though they resisted at first, after a moment or two, they finally let go, and gave in. And the second I pulled away, I couldn't help but think of Tally, since she's the one who taught me how to deal with resistance.

And even after explaining how I'd spent the last twenty-some hours snacking on candy bars, potato chips, and just about anything else that could be shrink-wrapped and sold in an airport gift shop, they still insisted on taking me to dinner. Which meant it was time for me to stop resisting and give in to them.

And although there's like a ton of things to write, I'm just too busy with unpacking all of my boxes and decorating my new room—not to mention how school's starting up in less than a week—so in light of all that, I thought I'd leave you with these photos, provide a little commentary, and let you draw your own conclusions.

1) That's a picture of my old room. Though of course it wasn't empty like that when I occupied it! I guess I just didn't really think to take a picture until I'd already packed everything up for the big move. But it's weird how seeing it looking so bare and abandoned like that makes me realize how in the end, it was never anything more than just four walls, a door, a closet, and a window. Which makes me feel kind of dumb for allowing myself to get so attached to it. And if you need any further explanation on just what exactly I mean, then please feel free to check out photo #2.
2) So what we have here, ladies and gentlemen, is basically four walls, a door, a closet, and a window. Which also happens to be all of the elements that make up my new room. Which means it's not all that different from my old room. And even though the carpet's a little plain for my taste, my aunt Tally promised to send me one of those cool, Greek flokati rugs like I had in my room at her place, you know, just to jazz it up a little (and remind me of my other home!). Which just goes to show that HOME, like PARADISE, is really just a state of mind.

3) That's my best friend, Nat, who was kind and generous enough to dedicate her one and only day off (well, this week anyway) from her job at the *You've Been Framed!* art supply shop to help me unpack most, though not all, of my boxes (but only because there turned out to be far more than either of us bargained for, which, I have to admit, has made me reconsider my aunt Tally's philosophy toward accumulation and mass consumerism, as I can't help but wonder if she just might be on to something!). Nat also helped me organize my closet and drawers, which is so incredibly nice of her and lucky for me since she's really good at "spatial relations" (her words, not mine). Notice the uber-cool earrings she's wearing? I made those ones too!
4) That's a picture of my dad, his girlfriend, Melanie, and me having dinner at the condo he just bought. And even though it wasn't really necessary, since it's not that far from the apartment, I still ended up staying the night because they were sweet enough to go to the trouble to decorate my room, and they were anxious for me to try it out.
5) This is a picture of my room at my dad's place. Notice the boy band picture on the wall? Well, just so you know, it's no longer there. Because Melanie and I took it down, then snuck it into my dad's office and hung it up behind his desk when he was in a

meeting, since both of us are convinced that he's the one who secretly likes boy band music!

6) This is a picture of Mr. Holly Golightly that Yannis sent me all the way from Tinos. Just so you know, Holly is now living with his cousin's little eight-year-old daughter, Tatiana, and he seems to be quite happy and very well fed from what I can see. And Yannis continues to visit every now and then just so he can whisper in Holly's ear and make sure he never forgets me.

7) This is a picture of Harbor High School, that was taken the day Nat and I stopped by because she was so excited about the new art lab she just couldn't wait until school started. I don't know if I mentioned this before, but Nat is REALLY into art. She likes to paint, no, actually, she LIVES to paint, and she's really good at it too. She's also good friends with the art teacher (yup, she's the kind of girl who makes friends with her teachers, what can I say?), and by the time we left I'd decided to switch one of my electives to an art class too. They have this pottery class I didn't even know about, but now that I do, I'm really hoping they'll let me switch.

8) This is a picture of Amanda, Jenna, Levi, and Casey, who we just happened to run into that very same day, since the guys were there for football practice and the girls were there to watch them. And even though I'm not positive, I kind of think

Amanda and Levi might be together now, since she seemed a little disturbed when he came over to talk to me. But I am totally sure that Jenna and Casey are together, mostly because they were hanging all over each other. Though you know how these things go, and by the time you read this they could have totally switched back, or moved on to someone else entirely. And while I have to admit that it felt really awkward to run into them at first, in the end, we pretty much just said hey, shared some news, and went our separate ways.

And that's it!

So if anyone is actually out there and reading this—then don't forget to comment!

Love,

Colby

CIRCLE IN THE SAND

Blog Comments:

Tinian Arts said:

We mailed the rug today, so expect to receive it in a few weeks!

We both really miss you—the house is so quiet without you!

Love,

Tally & Tassos

Natalie Zee said:

Yup, I'm a big art-fart dork who makes friends with her teachers, and now the whole world knows! Are we still on for tonight? My art show starts at eight—I'm so nervous!

ColbyCat said:

I'm just about to upload one of your paintings so "the whole world" can see how awesome they are! See you at eight! Don't sweat it—you'll be great!

Anonymous said:

I'm still here, still reading your blog, still missing you.

ColbyCat said:

And still ANONYMOUS?

Anonymous said:

Hopefully not to you.

ColbyCat said:

DEFINITELY not to me.

Anonymous said:

By the way, our moon is half full tonight.

ColbyCat said:

I'm heading out now.

Anonymous said:

Kalinichta!

ColbyCat said:

Kalinichta!

Don't miss a single alyson noël novel

Cruel Summer
Kiss & Blog
Laguna Cove
Art Geeks and Prom Queens

Available wherever books are sold

www.alysonnoel.com

ST. MARTIN'S GRIFFIN

Can't get enough of The Immortals ?

Then check out the new series all about Ever's little sister, Riley!

Riley has crossed the bridge into the afterlife—a place called Here, where time is always Now. She has picked up life where she left off when she was alive—but she soon learns that the afterlife isn't just an eternity of leisure. . . .

The *Radiance* story continues as Riley takes us back in time to a place where she is the only one who can set things right.

For free downloads, hidden surprises, and glimpses into the future visit WWW.IMMORTALSSERIES.COM.

SQUARE FISH

Enter the world of **the immortals**

BOOK 4

BOOK 5

BOOK 2

BOOK 1

BOOK 3

"Addictive. I couldn't put it down. I dreamt about this book. And when I was finished, I couldn't get it out of my head. Simply breathtaking." —*Teens Read Too* on *Evermore*

For free downloads, hidden surprises, and glimpses into the future

Visit www.ImmortalsSeries.com.